NATIL DREAMED . . .

The starlight was far from her, but for now she was not worried. For in a time without starlight, what mattered was *rebirth*. There would be a land far across the ocean. She herself had trodden its length and breadth decades ago, searching fruitlessly for elevenkind. Far in the future, though, after a long winter of the world, the eleven blood would reawaken. How might it begin? she wondered. But perhaps she had seen exactly how it might begin. With the openness of the dreamer, she saw that it might begin with one man driving west, following the setting sun, following the season of rebirth. But there was one thing she didn't see in that distant future. Natil did not see herself. . . .

SHROUD
OF
SHADOW

by

Gael Baudino

A ROC BOOK

ROC
Published by the Penguin Group
Penguin Books USA Inc., 375 Hudson Street,
New York, New York 10014, U.S.A.
Penguin Books Ltd, 27 Wrights Lane,
London W8 5TZ, England
Penguin Books Australia Ltd, Ringwood,
Victoria, Australia
Penguin Books Canada Ltd, 10 Alcorn Avenue,
Toronto, Ontario, Canada M4V 3B2
Penguin Books (N.Z.) Ltd, 182-190 Wairau Road,
Auckland 10, New Zealand

Penguin Books Ltd, Registered Offices:
Harmondsworth, Middlesex, England

First published by Roc,
an imprint of New American Library
a division of Penguin Books USA Inc.

First Printing, November, 1993
10 9 8 7 6 5 4 3 2 1

This book is dedicated to the memory of

Jeanne C. Arguello
Anne D. Needham
Regina Kobak
Mary Sanchez
Margo Green
Nancy Cunningham
Amanda Young
Jan Coleman
Francesca Torrez
Pamela Blandon

and to all the other women of Colorado
who, in the course of the writing of this book,
were murdered by their husbands and boyfriends.

It's worse further on up.

—a soldier of the Great War

CHAPTER 1

Ante diem festum Paschae, sciens Jesus quia venit hora ejus, ut transeat ex hoc mundo ad Patrem . . .

Easter was late that year. So was spring. Out in the Bay of Maris, the water was cold and gray, the breakers washing whitely the feet of the steep headlands that guarded the harbor. Gray water, gray sky, gray rock. The foam was the color of milk . . . or of death.

And Omelda was washing the floor of the Betancourt mansion.

. . . cum dilexisset suos, qui erant in mundo, in finem dilexit eos.

The water in her bucket was gray, and it foamed whitely as she sluiced it across the gray stone floor of the kitchen. Spill, slosh, scrub. Omelda's knees were sore, and her back was sore, too. Her hands were dry and cracked from weeks of scrubbing and laundering and cleaning, and her hair hung in sweaty tendrils despite the cold that whispered winter's parting words at the windows and the chimney and the doors.

. . . sciens quia omnia dedit ei Pater in manus, et quia a Deo exivit et ad Deum vadit: surgit a coena, et ponit vestimenta sua: et cum accepisset linteum, praecinxit se.

Holy Week. Maundy Thursday. Vespers. The house was silent, with no stump of the polished, mercantile boots of Nicholas Betancourt himself, no patter of the steps of his prim and pretty little wife, no unctuous tread of his servants. Everyone was at church in the great cathedral. There, and in a hundred smaller churches and private chapels in the city, the mysteries of the Passion and Death were being commemorated even now: choirs singing the gospel and antiphons, men—sad-eyed men, avaricious men, men whose hands knew the slick feel of gold and the chill of silver, men who had been born into sheets of linen and silk—baring their feet as their priest, whether mitered bishop or humbly tonsured friar in orders, knelt to wash them in memory of another washing, now fifteen hundred years past.

And Omelda washed the floor. Alone.

Mandatum novum do vobis: ut diligatis invicem . . .

More water—on the feet, on the floor, against the cliffs.

Beati immaculati invia . . .

The cathedral and the churches were distant, but Omelda knew exactly what the cantors intoned and the choir sang in reply as the water trickled over bare feet. She knew because she heard it. She was a mile away from the nearest service, but the words and the melodies, made a part of her by over twenty years of cloistered monasticism, rang in her mind, shouldered her own thoughts aside, blurred her washing of the kitchen floor into the washing of the feet.

Postquam surrexit Dominus . . .

It was always this way. The music had long ago become an inescapable part of her nature, and whether she was an obedient nun—a prisoner of custom, enclosure, and church law—or a contumacious and apostate scullion, *de facto* excommunicate for her absence and her lack of repentance, the music was still there, an incessant, intrusive, violating presence.

She had fled the nunnery to escape the melodic possession. But though she could climb walls, and though she could elude the beadles and sheriffs and searchers, she could not so escape from her own mind. For two years, she had run, hidden, prayed for relief. To no avail.

Every night, she would awaken to a ghostly choir of memory and habit singing matins and lauds, and she would lie sleepless until they were finished. With the sunrise would come prime, and then mass . . . all in her mind. And whether, during the eight periods of monastic prayer and worship that occurred each day—the Hours of the Holy Office—she ran errands, washed dishes, cooked food, or, as now, scrubbed the floor, she did so to the inner accompaniment of plainchant. In her mind, the psalms ran their full course each week, the feasts and holy days came and went, and the special antiphons that the Benedictine order zealously kept separate from the body of the Church sounded quietly and austerely.

Dominus Jesus . . .

Her inner cantor intoned the first words, and then as the waves of the North Sea rose up to batter the cliffs about the harbor, so the choir's response, plexed, multi-voiced, rose in a wave of song and flung itself against the private thoughts and conscience of Omelda the nun, Omelda the apostate, Omelda the damned—

. . . postquam coenavit cum discipulis suis . . .

—and she had at last reached the conclusion that it would never end. No amount of labor, physical privation, mental discipline, or distance from her cloister would ever banish that invisible choir, would ever give her the inner silence that she craved. Two years now, and nothing had changed about the endless violations save her will to endure them.

. . . lavit pedes eorum, et ait illis . . .

She dropped the brush she was holding and put her soapy hands to her ears. But the voices were within her, and they continued, unperturbed:

Scitis quid fecerim vobis . . .

"Stop," she murmured.

. . . ego Dominus et Magister?

"Please . . ." Aching with the defeat and the utter futility, she bent her head. Cold water trickled down her cheeks, mingled with her hot tears.

Exemplum dedi vobis, ut et vos ita faciatis.

"Dammit! Stop!"

Her words echoed off the roof, fell into silence amid the rustle of embers in the hearth. The wind answered her, the wind and the voices in her mind:

Credidi, propter quod locutus sum . . .

She wept, but she did not scream again. It was dangerous to scream, for the fact that she was not at church, that she kept instead behind closed doors and windows and labored alone into the evening could not but engender questions. What kind of heretic was she? A Lollard? A Waldensian? A Hussite? And if she were none of these, then why was she not in church like a good Christian?

No one would understand her tale of the creeping madness of melody that was stalking her, that forced her to absent herself from services of any kind lest, so encouraged, its tyranny become absolute. No one, indeed, would sympathize with an apostate nun whose presence,

if discovered, would bring the whole city under episcopal
interdict. And certainly no one would heed her protests
against being returned to her cloister, there to face an
interior horror that would make any discipline ordained
by the abbess seem paltry and trivial both.

No, it was very dangerous to scream, for screams
would bring the beadles and perhaps even the Inquisition
. . . and the voices in her mind never listened to her
screams anyway. But dangerous and futile though they
were, the screams bubbled within her, now and then rising to her lips only to be choked off in a spasmodic
whimper. And thus she washed the kitchen floor.

Standing at last, shaking, her frustration turning her
heedless, she opened the shutters and let the cold April
air smack into her face. Evening had fallen, and the grays
of the city were shading into black. Silence: only the
bloodless sound of the wind and the intrusive plainchant
in her mind.

Dead to the world, they had told her. Dead to everything. No man, no children, no family. Dead. And she
had fled it. But whether she considered her mind, shack-
led by the ritual that rang unceasingly in its depths, or
her body, numb and unresponsive, she was still dead.

And here, on this Thursday of Holy Week, with the
spring late and the wind cold and the evening gray as a
stone, she could no longer think of a reason for continuing with this parody of existence.

The house was a tomb. The city was a tomb. She was,
she reflected, damned already: would suicide make that
much difference? At least she could ordain her own physical death.

Ubi caritas et amor, Deus ibi est.

She put her arms on the sill, cradled her head. "Love
me, God," she said. "Just love me. I'm going to do it
tonight. Please love me anyway."

And still the choir sang on: *Et ex corde diligamus nos
sincero.*

Maundy Thursday. Feet were being washed throughout
Europe.

The central mystery of Christianity was but three days
away, but the body had to die before it could rise again,
the exalted had to be humbled . . . and so feet were be-

ing washed. Touched. Handled. Water trickling over toes
and insteps, tinkling into basins all agleam with the light
of a hundred candles.

Fifty leagues to the southwest of a window out of which
a young woman stared into the night and contemplated
suicide, in a shabby little church in a shabby little city,
Siegfried of Magdeburg, a friar of the order of Dominic,
took into his hand the foot of a man named Paul Drego.
An acolyte held a pewter basin ready as another handed
Siegfried a pitcher of water, but Siegfried's eyes were not
on basin or pitcher or foot: they were on Paul's face. He
was wondering what he saw in Paul's face.

As the water trickled over Paul's foot, as Siegfried's
hand mechanically registered the fleshly fact of bones,
sinew, skin, and hair, the friar wondered. There were so
many layers to a human being, so many levels of deception and self-deception, so many lies and masks that made
up a mortal life. And as Siegfried was Inquisitor of Furze,
it was his constant business to look beyond those layers
and levels and deceptions and masks, to examine every
flicker of every emotion over every face with which he
was confronted, to spy out—vigilantly, indefatigably—
what lay beneath, what lurked in the dark recesses of
conscience and private thought.

Washing feet on a Maundy Thursday, holding a pitcher
of water, staring into the face of a man who made hats
for a living . . . he was yet the Inquisitor. And so he
paused with his hand cupping Paul's heel, weighing his
bare foot, considering, for a moment, what methods
might be required to lay bare the hatmaker's inner world.
Here, for example, just below the ankle, was a place in
which to put a needle. Not quickly, mind you, but slowly.
There were certain boots in certain rooms of the House
of God (it was just down the street, one would reach it
in the space of time it took to say a *Confiteor*) made just
for that purpose, with straps to hold the foot steady and
a screw thread on the needle so that it could be inserted
hair's breadth by hair's breadth.

Or the toenails. Or this tendon. Or here . . . or here
. . . or here . . .

Siegfried knew that strangers had taken shelter in Paul's
house, had stayed a few days, and then had departed.
Peddlers? Beggars to whom the hatmaker had, in Chris-

tian charity, offered the hospitality of his home? Representatives of the Aldernacht firm who had come down from Ypris to further the plans that Paul and his friends had formulated, plans to bring gold to Furze and revitalize the moribund economy?

Perhaps. It could be. Or perhaps it could be . . . something else.

What lay behind Paul's wide eyes? What lay behind the lies that made up his life? A little fear, maybe? A little guilt? Those strangers, Paul. What about those strangers? *Barbes* uprooted by Cattaneo's valor in the Alpine valleys? Some Fraticelli come out of the Apennine fastness? A Lollard or two with a Bible in the vulgar tongue and a collection of pious aphorisms? Something else?

Layers. Masks. It was all layers and masks. Siegfried himself was at one with his thoughts, and his personal lack of inner duplicity, he knew, added to the fear that his office evoked in those who had enmeshed themselves in a web of heresy. They knew him for what he was, and he—a joining of the cornerstones of will and spirit so perfect that a scrap of gold leaf could not slide between them—would inevitably find out what they were.

Up near the altar, Bishop Albrecht cleared his throat, a gentle, supposedly unobtrusive prompt for Siegfried to proceed with the rite. And Albrecht, too, had his masks and layers: dazzled and deluded by his fruitless dreams of new cathedrals in old cities and his belief in a naive piety that would triumph over the pernicious evils of the world, the bishop had essentially ignored Siegfried's twenty years of constant, exhausting work against heresy in Furze.

Lies. Lies to oneself, lies to others. Again, Albrecht cleared his throat. Siegfried sighed, frustrated, but he reminded himself that the work went on, that Albrecht's dreams had not, could not, interfere with the Inquisition; and therefore, his eyes still on Paul's face, he dried the hatmaker's foot, gave him a thin smile and a quick squeeze of the ankle, and moved on to the next man.

The wind came in from the sea like a black knife, and it stuck its cold point through the threadbare places in Omelda's cloak as she made her way toward the wharves.

It was night, the services were over, the Betancourt family was abed, and the streets of Maris were empty save for this runaway nun who was taking the road to the sea and to death.

Her goal was not the wharves or the shore. That kind of ending would be too slow, and her body, losing courage, might drag her back to life. No, she needed something quick. If she could actually get out of the city, there were cliffs to the north. A steeling of the nerves, a quick plunge, and that would be the end of it. God could judge her then.

With the ending of formal services in the cathedrals and churches and monasteries, her inner plainchant had subsided. It would, to be sure, begin again in the predawn hours with matins and lauds, but for now she leaned against the wall of a salt-stained warehouse and peered out towards the water and the sea with a silent mind. She could wade out, pass the chains that locked up the harbor at night, and gain the outer shore, thereby avoiding the city wall with its gates and its guards. From there, she could climb to the cliffs. She would have silence until just past midnight. And, if she actually reached the cliffs, she might have silence forever.

She pushed on, and she had almost reached the water when a large hand seized her cloak and pulled her back into a pair of muscular arms.

''Well, what have we here? A li'l barnacle, looking for som'ting t'fix on?''

The man laughed, and his companion—yes, there were two—joined him. Omelda was square and stocky, but she might have been as slender as Nicholas Betancourt's pretty wife as she was whirled about like a willow wand and sized up by the two watchmen.

''What're you doing here?'' said the second.

Omelda glanced out at the waves, at the distant cliffs that she could more sense than see. ''I'm taking a walk.''

The men laughed. ''You're up t'no good, girlie,'' said the one who held her. He scratched the stubble of a black beard on his shoulder. ''What sha' we do with you?''

''You can let me go,'' she said. Here she was, standing and gabbling at these men, wasting precious minutes of mental silence. But she had no choice. Thirsty though she was, fate had snatched her water away.

The second man folded his arms and eyed her up and down. A crafty look had crept into his face, one that she had seen often, and she was not surprised at all by his next words. "What'll you give us to let you go?"

The look, the tone of his voice: she knew precisely what she could give them. In any case, they would take it whether she offered it or not: that they were willing to bargain at all was an unexpected stroke of luck. "Whatever you want, sir," she said, and though she felt the dull numbness already creeping through her groin, she was grateful that she could do something that would, in the end, make them leave her alone.

They took her to a dirty lean-to, laid her down on a pile of sacks, and took turns pumping her full of sperm. But though Omelda's body was occupied, her mind was relishing the silence in which the men left her while they grunted and strained and satisfied themselves: the silence within her, the silence they could not touch.

When they were done, they let her go, and she waded out into the sea. The water—rank, stinking with sewage, clotted with the pitch that the aging Hansa boats persisted in throwing off like shit from diarrheic cows—weighted her garments, and she half-staggered, half-swam out to the pilings that held the harbor chains. Low tide. She was still in luck.

In another two hours, she had reached the shore outside the walls of the city and climbed the rocky path out to the cliffs. The viscous sperm dribbled out of her in clammy rivulets, and the wind turned her damp garments into a shroud of cold, but the chants were still, for the moment, silent; and now the ruins of the old fishing village that marked the tip of the precipitous headlands was in sight, shimmering in the bright gleam of a moon just past full.

Spring was indeed late: not even a handful of grass or wildflowers softened the hard earth and clumped boulders of the cliffs. A hundred feet below, the North Sea raged and flung itself at the base of the rocks as though determined to have them down, but Omelda, worn out as much by the men's use of her body as by her long trek, sat down at the edge of the drop and, wrapping her sodden cloak more tightly about her shoulders, bent her head.

The world hung at midnight, passed, and, in the dim corners of her mind, she heard a whisper, like a child's voice starting up out of a tomb:

Astiterunt reges terrae, et principes convenerunt . . .

She could not thrust it away. In her old convent, in all convents and all monasteries, those consecrated to God had begun the first office for Good Friday. And Omelda, if she allowed herself to live, would hear it all. Antiphons. Psalms. The Lamentations of Jeremiah. The Mass of the Presanctified. Chanted, hymned, and intoned, the Hours would progress through matins, lauds, prime, terce, sext, nones, vespers, and compline, and Omelda would be, as she had been since her father had deeded her body to the Church when she was three, an unwilling participant.

And she had so wanted to die with her own mind.

She put her hands to her face, felt the grit of salt and sand. Her vulva was burning: the men had been rough enough to make her bleed. It should not matter. It really should not matter. A brief pitch forward into the wind, and it would all be over.

Quare fremuerunt Gentes, et populi meditati sunt inania.

Would that be Hell? Would that be the particular flavor of eternal punishment—divinely fitted with excruciating exactitude to her crime—to which she would be condemned? Never to hear silence? Never to experience anything save an endless round of chants and psalms and hymns and adorations and processions that would go on and on until her soul, plunged into a dementia from which there was no escape—

A lull in the wind. She heard a harp.

Only a note, two notes, and then the sound was drowned once again in the rush of air. But before that soft chime of bronze strings, the voices of her inner choir had faltered, and for a moment, Omelda stared stiffly out at the roiling, moon-gleaming ocean, not knowing whether to be startled, frightened, or grateful.

She turned around to the heaped ruins of the fishing village. There was a light there, very dim—Omelda did not wonder that she had not seen it before—and, in another lull, the harpstrings rang again, and again they scattered the chanting voices that had come creeping back into her consciousness.

She rose and followed the sound and the light; and as she approached, she heard the harp more clearly. Now the sound of plucked wire, soft and dulcet though it was, was cutting through the howl of the wind and the crash of the breakers . . . and it was cutting through Omelda's heart and the voices in her head, too.

She had never heard such music before. Upheld firmly by a counterpoint of open fifths, its notes constantly changing durations and inflections, it flowed like speech, or like a river. The notes rang, wove in and out, cascaded in sparkling arpeggios, all the while speaking with un-alloyed clarity of sunlight and good weather, of azure sky and blue water.

And the voices in Omelda's head wilted before them.

She followed the light and the sound to a tumbled-down house that still possessed an intact chimney and a single room. There she peered in through a window that had long ago lost its shutters and saw a woman sitting before a fire. A small harp was in her lap, and her fingers were on the strings. Her long dark hair, shot with much silver, was uncovered and unbound save for a single, small braid in which was tied what looked like an eagle feather, and her clothing was such a patchwork of out-landish and foreign garments that Omelda could not but wonder whether this were one of those fabled women who had forsaken their homes and their families to run off with the gypsies.

But it was no exotic gypsy strain that the harper played. The music—at once shining and humane, comforting and sympathetic—was like a warm hand; and Omelda, lean-ing against the weathered sill with blood and sperm run-ning down her thighs, wept. Whoever this harper was, whatever she was doing, she had the power to still the voices.

But after a time, the harper stopped, bowed her head, sighed. Her hands fell to her lap.

"Please," said Omelda. "Please play some more."

The harper gasped, turned. Startled blue eyes fixed themselves on Omelda. "Dear Lady . . . I had no idea."

Omelda clutched her cold cloak about her cold shoulders. "I'm not a lady. I'm just a woman. Please . . . please play."

The harper was silent for a moment, and then she nodded slowly. "Of course, beloved. Of course I will play for you. Come in and share my fire. You must be frozen." There was no suspicion or caution in her voice: the offer of a fire and of music was wholehearted, without reservation. "But what are you doing out in this weather?"

Omelda pushed in through the rickety door, swung it to behind her. The voices were bubbling up again, and she plunked herself down by the fire without answering. "Please . . ." she said, "just play. It's been so dreadful, and . . . you're the first to . . . to . . ." She shook her hands gropingly. There were no words for that long, awful running.

The harper regarded her calmly. "What is your name, child?"

"Omelda. Please play."

The harper nodded slowly. "My name is Natil," she said. And then she played, and the music rose up like a wave, swept away Omelda's inner choir, and left behind only a quiet, dark silence.

CHAPTER 2

Natil was dreaming.

She should not have been dreaming: Elves did not dream, nor, for that matter, did they sleep. But though Natil did both now, she did not begrudge herself the failing, for dreams—dreams of the past, of faces long vanished, wishful dreams—were all she had.

Once, the world had been all ashimmer to her eyes, the patterns of the Dance, of the plexed causality and interrelation that made up the universe, obvious, immediate, immanent. Then, Natil had lived the Dance with perfect knowledge, had harped it in her music. She had spoken with the Lady who was at once her Creatrix and her identity not wordlessly and from a distance as the Christians communed with a God veiled beneath outward manifestations of bread and wine, but, rather, directly, face to face.

So it had been once with all her people. Once. But no more. The Elves had faded, and as the race had dwindled from thousands, to bare hundreds, to tens, to an isolated few and then, finally, to this last—a harper maid returned now to Adria after a century of wandering—so the knowledge and the vision of *Elthia Calasiuove* had dwindled, too. Natil saw no more than a human, the stars had faded from her consciousness, and her bronze-strung harp rang only with memories.

And so now, like any human being, she slept. And now she dreamed, the images shifting and fluttering in a mind that had once known only the illimitable and constant light of the stars. Sunlight. A sliver of a crescent moon. Trees—pines and aspens—and mountains (she was sure they were not the Aleser) rising up, craggy and majestic, their summits white against a deep blue sky. A hawk floating in a high thermal.

Even for one so new to dreaming, these were old visions, for they had come to her each night for a long time. The same sky, the same mountains, the same trees. But it was a pretty scene, and she relished it despite its familiarity, for it was as much of the Lady as she expected she would ever see again.

But tonight, she saw something else, too. Something that flew higher than the hawk, much higher. Something that left a streak of white against the blue sky, that sparkled as though it were made of glass and . . .

. . . and metal.

Natil's eyes opened, the heavy human sleep evaporating into a dingy, refuse-choked room, a low burning fire that flickered in the draft from the shutterless window, a stocky, dark-haired woman who lay with her head on Natil's shoulder.

She eased out from beneath Omelda and lowered the young woman's head down to the wadded bundle that was serving as a pillow. Omelda did not stir. She had seemed exhausted when she had first appeared, and fatigue had taken her quickly. Natil had actually found it necessary to break off in the midst of her playing and catch her as she toppled toward the fire.

But as she bent to wrap Omelda's threadbare cloak about her, she was startled by the sight of the dark blood that had soaked through it at several points. Menstruating? Natil sensed not. Sickness? Wounds? But Omelda had been unconcerned about anything save music.

Gently, Natil lifted Omelda's skirts, examined her bloody thighs, frowned. Rape. Or . . . something like rape. The man or men had not been gentle. She remembered another young woman who, years ago, had been abused by a renegade nobleman, who had come to herself raging with an anger that had, in the end, transformed worlds. Omelda, though, had not raged. She had, instead, pleaded. *Play,* she had said.

Natil shook her head. Once, she would have been able to look into the patterns of the Dance, the interweaving strands of starlight, and see exactly what so tormented this woman. Once, with her music and her mind, she could have woven her own pattern, infusing Omelda's torn flesh with healing and health. Now, though, she would have to be satisfied that the bleeding had apparently stopped of itself. As for the genesis of Omelda's pleas, Natil would simply have to wait . . . and ask her when she awakened.

She wrapped Omelda in her cloak, added her own for warmth, then rose and went to the window. The wind had died, the stars were bright. The moon was swinging low. Close to dawn.

And Natil thought of her dream.

Sun, moon, trees, mountains, sky. All these she knew. But that thing in the sky was nothing that she had ever seen before. Glass . . . and metal. It had to be the work of humans. But what humans could do such a thing? Not even Leonardo had known the secrets of natural law that would put something like that into the air.

It flew. It was flying. And that meant . . .

She did not know what it meant.

The wind stirred, rustled the eagle feather that hung from the braid in her hair. She touched it, smiled softly in spite of her sorrow. Her journey had been long, but she had found kindness in many places. Even now, as human as she had become, she still had friends in the world. But the time of the Elves was over, and Natil had come home to Adria and to Malvern Forest in order to follow her kind into oblivion.

Oblivion. It was an attractive thought after so long, after so much loss and disappointment. But the dream intruded. A flying thing of glass and metal. What had she seen?

Omelda stirred.

Putting the puzzle aside, Natil went to her, knelt. With the return of consciousness, Omelda's broad forehead had knotted, and her dark eyes, half closed, had turned faraway and pained. "It's prime."

Natil glanced involuntarily at the window. True: the sky was just beginning to lighten on this Good Friday morning.

"Oh, God . . . ." Omelda's hands went to her head.

"Are you in pain?"

"It doesn't hurt."

"I find that hard to believe, beloved."

"It never . . . hurts. Not that way."

Natil tried again. "Did they not hurt you?"

Omelda's eyes, still glassy, flicked fully open. "They? Who?"

"The . . ." Natil indicated the bloodstains on her cloak and skirt. ". . . the men."

Omelda peered fuzzily at Natil, then at the stains. "Oh . . . that . . ." She shrugged. "I guess they did. I'll heal."

Natil found herself at a loss. "You're not . . ." She was suddenly groping for words.

"Not what?"

"Ah . . . upset . . ."

Even through the fuzziness, Omelda finally understood. She glanced at the blood again. "Why should I be? My body's dung."

Natil's incredulity grew. "Who . . . who told you that?"

Again, a shrug. "Saint Benedict."

Natil puzzled over the woman's words, but Omelda heaved herself to her feet and groped her way to the window. "Prime."

"That . . . that is so."

Omelda seemed to come to a sudden recollection, turned to Natil. Her dark eyes were vague, but her voice was urgent. "Can you play something? For me?"

Play for her? Of course Natil would play for her. She might sleep, she might see nothing but darkness behind her closed eyes, but she could at least play, could at least offer what shreds of elven comfort were still hers to give. "What . . . what do you wish to hear?"

Omelda again put her hands to her head, grimaced as though in futility, dropped them. "Anything. Just . . . just play."

She had said much the same thing the night before, and there was a creeping desperation in her tone that made Natil put her questions aside and take up her harp. The instrument—old and well seasoned—had held its tuning throughout the night, and the first chord of an old *lauda*, a human song she had learned in Tuscany, rippled out from the strings.

Omelda leaned against the wall and allowed herself to slide to the ground. Her eyes had closed as though in expectation, but, suddenly, they reopened. "Not that. That's too much like . . . like . . ." Her brow furrowed, knotted anew. "Play . . . what you were playing last night. Can you play that, please?"

Natil blinked. What she had been playing last night was her homage to the Lady she could no longer see. "I . . ."

"That . . . please . . ."

Natil hesitated. One did not simply play worship. It was not a song to be reeled off like wool from a ball of yarn. The notes started out with thought, grew into spirit, fleshed themselves in music. It was not simply playing: it was incarnation. "Beloved . . . I . . ."

But her own words stilled her protests, put her harp back on her lap. *Beloved.* The Elves had always addressed humans so. Like younger siblings, or like sons and daughters, they had been dear to Natil's people, and in spite of the persecutions, genocide, and hatred that had been directed at the Elves, the word remained, the feelings endured. *Beloved.* And one of these fragile creatures who knew at most only eighty or ninety years of life had asked for help, had asked to be freed from the pain of a moment.

It was, perhaps, the whole reason for Elves, and, having become so human, Natil clung to it. In a minute, with only a hint of an inner tear for all that she had lost, for all the innumerable swords that had pierced the elven heart, she was offering homage and love to the Lady, calling up a faint shadow of the music that had sustained her from the Beginning.

Omelda's face went slack, and then the fuzziness left her, to be replaced by such intensity and focus that Natil wondered whether this young woman might be one of the many who carried some small trace of elven blood, a genetic remembrance of a time long ago when mortal and immortal had loved . . . and had consummated that love. It was likely. After so long, after so many generations, most humans had a little of the blood . . .

Natil played the last note, and as the strings of her harp rang into metallic silence, she fought down the discouragement that had become her constant companion.

. . . as though it would ever do them any good.

A brief flash of embers from the low fire. Natil stared at it. Metal. Flying. A sparkle of glass like a star in the blue vault. What . . . ?

She bent her head, dropped her hands. Wishful think-

ing, more than likely. A human dream: that was all. But
Omelda, intense and awake, was rubbing her face, and,
after a moment, her eyes fell on her cloak. She lifted it,
examined the blood spots. Brusquely, she pulled up her
skirts, prodded experimentally at her smeared thighs and
her vulva, winced only a little. "You probably think I'm
crazy."

Natil shook her head slowly. "I do not."

"Then you're the only one."

"I daresay."

Omelda hardly noticed her words. She dropped her
hem carelessly. "Well . . . it'll heal."

Natil discovered that her patience had run out much
sooner than she had ever thought possible. "Woman, are
you so indifferent towards your own body?"

Focused, black eyes returned her stare. "I told you.
It's dung. I wanted them to leave me alone. They wanted
sex. I gave it to them. If they're interested in dung, that's
their business. At least they left me alone."

It happened. It happened everywhere in Europe. It
was, in fact, worse in other places. Natil, nonetheless,
felt a little dizzy, passed a hand over her face. *I have
been alone too long. I have wandered too long. It has
become a terrible world: I shall be glad to fade.*

Omelda, without noticing Natil's distress, had stumped
over to the window. She leaned out and looked to the
right to watch the sunrise. "I'm glad they left me alone,"
she said over her shoulder. "It gave me time to think. It
gave me time to reach the cliffs. I . . ." She turned back
into the room, hands crammed into the pockets of her
apron and the spots of her blood brown against the coarse
cloth of her skirts. "I found you."

Found her she had. Natil nodded, wondering what it
meant.

Omelda's mouth worked for the better part of a minute. Then: "What do you do?"

"I am a harper."

"No, not that." Omelda stared at her, intent, stubborn: a plowhorse with its eye fixed on the end of the
furrow. "What do you do with that music you play? It's
the only thing that's ever . . ." She suddenly grimaced,
turned back to the window. "There it is again."

Natil stared, speechless. Omelda might well have been mad.

Eyes glazed, Omelda murmured softly, the syllables clumping along with metronomic regularity: *"Pueri Hebraeorum, portantes ramos olivarum, obviaverunt Domino, clamantes, et dicentes: Hosanna in excelsis. Per omnia saec—"* She broke off, clutched at her face, slid her hands back to cover her ears. "There it is again. I can't . . . help it."

Natil lifted her hands to her harp, struck a chord. The effect was instantaneous: Omelda shuddered, gasped, let go of her ears. Intensity and focus returned. Black as they were, her eyes burned.

"Can you . . . can you teach me to do that?" she said.

"To play the harp?"

"To make the voices go away."

"Voices?" Natil found herself bewildered—and dismayed by that bewilderment.

"The voices in my head. I . . ." Omelda seemed to struggle with words. "You'll think I'm crazy . . . but . . ." A hysterical laugh rose up out of her like a bubble from a mud hole. "But why should I care? You already know I'm crazy."

Omelda was in pain, and Natil's being was crying out in response, yearning to heal, to help. The Elves were gone, faded and fading, but their yearnings remained.

Omelda plunged on. "I hear the chants of the Office. All of them. Eight times a day. I can't get rid of them." She suddenly glanced at the window and the door almost fearfully, as though listeners might be there, and her voice dropped to a whisper. "I ran away . . . from my convent . . . because of that. The voices. They were driving me crazy. Every time I'd hear them, it would get worse. So I left, and I hid. I'm still hiding. But I stay away from churches . . . because the voices get worse every time I hear the chants."

Natil was beginning to understand, but understanding did no more than deepen her discouragement. She could not heal Omelda's body; she could not heal her mind. Only a century ago, the magic had still been there, but now . . . nothing. Now, Natil was but a harper. That the strings she plucked had any effect at all was witness only to the depth and beauty of what was fading, guttering into darkness and shadow.

Four and a half billion years of starlight. And now this. It would be good to fade. She wanted to fade.

Omelda's eyes swung back to Natil, and the harper almost winced at the touch of that hot, demanding glance. "I heard your harp, and the voices went away. And when they started to come back, you played, and they went away again. Can you teach me how to do that so . . . so I can stay sane? So I can have my own mind? So I can think? Can you? Would you?"

"Can I teach you?" Natil sighed, set her harp aside, felt the impossibility of what Omelda had asked, knew that her question demanded an honest reply. "I could, given time, teach you to play the harp," she said. "But I am not sure what else. What I play and what you might someday play might well be two entirely different things." Different? Of course they would be different. The magic was gone. Only shreds and patches remained. "And, in any case, it would take time. And I will not be in Maris much past Sunday." And, she considered, she might not be in the world much past that.

"You're leaving Maris after Easter?"

"I will harp in the square on Sunday, for I need money for food. I will leave afterward." Natil hung her head, discouraged. Omelda was asking for something that was dead. The magic was gone, the healing was gone, the Elves were gone. The days of miracle and wonder were long past. She could, in fact, hardly remember them.

Omelda pressed. "Where are you going?"

"South. Towards Furze."

"I'm coming with you." Despite Omelda's forthright declaration, though, there was a hint of anxiety in her tone. Apostate nuns, Natil recalled, were hunted rather mercilessly by both Church and State.

She regarded the runaway for a moment. "Your convent is near Furze, is it not?"

Omelda's manner abruptly turned hunted. "How . . . how did you know? Are you with the Church?"

Natil did not laugh: she was afraid to allow herself to be so bitter. "Ever since the Council of Ephesus, the Church could not be more against me." Omelda blinked at her words, but Natil was not worried: the world neither believed in Elves, nor, in fact, had much of a reason to believe. Doubtless, Omelda would think her sense of humor rather quirky, that was all. "But be at peace," Natil continued. "I am not with the Church. I simply know that there is a Benedictine monastery down that way, and that the abbot is a pious man who models himself after Blessed Wenceslas. That monastery fathered a nunnery, also good."

"Dame Agnes is a holy woman." Omelda's words were toneless, regretful. "She's very fair. I rather liked her. I wouldn't have left except . . . except . . ."

Her words trailed off, and Natil sensed that the Office was again growing on her. Rising, she put a hand on the young woman's shoulder, felt the strong muscles that the life of a char had given her. "Omelda, beloved . . ."

"Play something, please."

"I cannot be with you always. You must learn to do this yourself." And had not Terrill once said much the same to a fledgling Elf struggling to accept herself and her new identity? Terrill, though, had at least given Mirya the tools she had needed to help herself. Natil had nothing so lasting to offer.

Omelda's eyes were glazed. "Play something," she said. "You've got . . . to stay with me."

"I cannot. I must go south."

"Then I'm coming with you."

"Dear child, where I am going, you cannot—"

But Omelda would not be put off, and she took hold of Natil's tunic, not weeping, but dry-eyed and with that terrible intensity. "I don't know who you are, Natil," she said, "but I don't care. I've been living with these voices for twenty years, and you're the only person who's ever made them go away. Now, I came up to these cliffs last night to throw myself off—I mean, I'm damned anyway, aren't I?—but I didn't. I found you."

It was so, Natil thought. In all these times of fading, in all this globe over which she had walked these last hundred years, she had been found in a derelict fishing village above Maris . . . by someone who needed her. There was meaning in that, just as there was meaning— there *had* to be meaning—in that brief, incomprehensible vision of a flying thing of metal and glass.

Nothing happened at random. Not even now. The

Dance went on whether Natil was cognizant of it or not, and therefore, everything—*everything*—had meaning. Even a dream. Even this young woman who was so tormented with inner voices. Even Natil and her discouragement and her absurd, incessant, elven desire to help.

Yes, Omelda had found her. And after eons of helping and healing, Natil could not easily forsake what was left of her ancient soul. "Where do you live?" she asked. "Are you wandering?"

Omelda shrugged impatiently, groped fuzzily through the interior voices. "I wandered . . . for a while after I first ran away . . ." She laughed with bitterness. "Right now, I keep house for a merchant in Maris. I scrub floors, clean pots . . ." She lifted her hands, waggled the chapped and split fingers with as much disdain as she had regarded her torn womanhood. "What do you . . . think, Natil? If you won't play for me, can you teach me to play for myself?"

Natil tried to examine her dispassionately, but the old elven dispassion—at once loving and objective—was gone along with everything else. She might as well have been one human woman examining another, a mother regarding an abused daughter. "I think not," she said slowly. "But you can sing, I daresay, and that might be enough."

Omelda winced, shook her head violently. "I . . . I don't want . . . to sing. I don't want to sing ever again." She waved her hands vaguely, trapped by the inner voices. "These words . . . these damned words. Can't you . . . play something?"

Natil weighed the choices. Ahead, to the south, lay Malvern . . . and hoped-for oblivion. But here, now, was Omelda. And she had asked for help. And nothing happened by chance.

Abruptly, she bent, picked up her harp, struck a chord. Another followed, and another. One-handed, her teeth clenched, she played a fragment of the Dance that she remembered, throwing the weight of a past universe and a brighter world at Omelda's infirmity. Omelda shook with the sudden cleansing, but her eyes cleared, and she sat down on the floor like a felled tree, put her face in her hands. "Thanks."

The sky was lightening. Away to the east, the sun was rising. Natil ran a hand back through her hair, felt the brush of the eagle feather. "I will teach you what I can," she said slowly. "You come with me, and as . . ." She hesitated. ". . . as long as I am in this world, I will teach you."

Omelda looked up. Her eyes were wide. "I won't be a problem. I'll do anything you want me to. Just don't ask me to sing."

Just don't ask me to breathe, she might as well have said; but Natil nodded, feeling the weight of the burden she had again assumed: the world, prolongation. The Elves had known them both. And now, Elf or not, with spiritual sustenance or without, she would continue to know them.

"I might ask," she said. "I might not. I do not know." She offered her hand, and Omelda took it. "But we will find a way. Together."

CHAPTER 3

"In the name of God and profit."

The sunlight trickled in through the cracks in the shutters of the dark bedroom, dribbled down the wall, pooled on the floor. It was a cold morning, but Jacob Aldernacht, seventy years old and growing older with each new drop of the brimming day, had seen colder. Back when that crazy French girl was routing the English at Orleans, when Jacob was just drawing his first breath in what was then a tiny cottage on the outskirts of town, it had snowed. No, this morning was not too bad at all. And it was Easter to boot.

"In the name of God . . . and profit."

Jacob's cracked lips moved again, whispering into the semi-dark. He had come to despise those words, but he uttered them nonetheless, for the Aldernacht fortune was built upon them. The motto appeared at the top of every ledger book, was chiseled into fine Carerra marble over the door to Gold Hall, appeared in cryptic monogram on the plate and silver off which the family—sons and grandsons and no wife (odd how he thought of Marjorie now only as an absence, a piece of property misplaced or stolen)—ate every day. In the name of God and profit.

The house was astir. Footsteps in the hall: old Eudes, the chief steward, treading toward Jacob's door with the customary morning sop. No . . . no, this was Easter. Communion. No morning sop, just a knock on the door . . .

The knock came: respectful, polite.

. . . and a good morning . . .

"Good morning, Mister Jacob," came the steward's dry voice. An old voice, old as Jacob's own. Jacob could not recall when Eudes had come to serve the family. In truth, he seemed a part of the furniture, like the wardrobe in the corner of the room or the rosewood desk in

Gold Hall. Eudes was here. Eudes was always here. Furniture. It was Marjorie who had left, not Eudes.

. . . and a lifting of the latch.

The latch lifted, and Eudes, dry and dusty, entered Jacob's bedroom and opened the shutters. The sunlight was like cold water. The sky was clear . . . like blue crystal, or that sapphire the Aldernacht ships had been smuggling out of Arabia right under the nose of the Venetian monopoly.

"Did you have a pleasant . . . night, Mister Jacob?"

"Pleasant enough." In the spill of cool air, Jacob wondered idly whether a village girl—or two: he was wealthy enough to buy two, old enough to fantasize about it, wise enough to leave it at that—might keep him just as warm as the pile of down comforters that locked him in a nightly vapor bath. He felt his wrinkled face crease up into a wry grin. Girls. After all these years, he could still think about girls. Well, maybe there were still a few squirts left in the old prick. If they didn't kill him on the way out.

The house was indeed astir. More footsteps, sounding clearly from the open door. Servants' chatter. Bustling preparations for mass. In the distance, Francis was intoning "A blessed and holy Easter to you" to someone, making sure, as he always did, that he intoned it loud enough for everyone in the house to hear him whether they wanted to or not. Through the unshuttered window came a few unskillful plucks of an out-of-tune lute: Josef was still working on that Italian song. It was still so wretched as to be unrecognizable, but, well, that was Josef.

Jacob sighed. Two sons. Three if he still wanted to count Karl, or if Karl wanted to count him. Obviously, whether it killed on the way out or not, sperm, like Spanish oranges, lost its freshness after a time.

After modestly closing the door, Eudes came over to the bed, hoisted the comforters away, and held up fresh linens for Jacob. "A most blessed . . . Easter, sir."

Jacob stood, cackling. "You didn't say it half loud enough, Eudes. You have to shout it, you know, like Francis does, so that everyone will know how virtuous you are."

And, yes, there was Francis's voice again, plainly audible even through the closed door: "A blessed Easter! God bless you!"

Eudes—loyal old wardrobe!—lifted an eyebrow, said nothing, laced up Jacob's linens . . . performing his morning task, Jacob suspected, as everything in the family was performed, as everything (he was certain) in the world was now performed: in the name of God and profit.

It had not always been like that. Once—and Jacob privately admitted that he was more than likely indulging in an old man's senile reminiscences about times that never had been—the world had occasionally taken notice of something besides money. Nobles and wealthy men had, now and again, thrown it all up and gone off to serve God, whether on a crusade or in a monastery. Cathedrals had been raised. Pilgrimages had consisted of more than sightseeing and souvenir collecting. To be sure . . .

"A blessed, blessed Easter!"

. . . money had been at the bottom of much of it, but there was at least a faint hint of an alternative. People had at least *thought* occasionally of God without fear of sin or fear of Inquisition to prod them; and they had not linked Him so indissolubly to profit.

And would Jacob ever throw it all up and settle for something else? Begging his daily bread, maybe, in the streets of the town he more or less owned?

He snorted.

"Sir?" Eudes was dusty, dry, polite.

"Get me dressed, Eudes," said Jacob. "We'll have prayers instead of breakfast, and then we'll all go to mass." He snorted again. "In the name of God and profit."

The Chapel of Our Lady of the Angels was a dumpy, Romanesque pile, round shouldered as a slattern. Four centuries ago, the baron of Furze, Harold delMari, had caused it to be raised by the simple expedient of funneling half of a year's income from his prosperous estate into the fabric fund. The chapel, built to atone for some unnamed and unknown sin that had tormented Harold's conscience, had risen from foundation to dome to cross in five years. Harold had seen it dedicated . . . and had died on his way down the steps.

This morning, the chapel, dumpy as it was, was bright

with candles and silks. White candles. White silks. It was Easter Sunday. Jesus had risen from the dead for the redemption of all humankind, just as the chapel had risen from a patch of bare earth for reasons that were, doubtless, considerably more sordid and mundane; and Albrecht, bishop of Furze and celebrant for this high mass, vested and attended by deacon—inevitably (dear God!), it *had* to be Siegfried—and sub-deacon, and accompanied by the almost-tuneful jubilation of the choir that Brother Pierre had managed to scrape together, processed to the foot of the altar, careful that his right knee, which was none too steady, did not fail him.

But when he turned around to bless his congregation—a gesture which, though not specified by the ceremony, he, as bishop, decided to add—he found that, despite strict instructions to his eyes, he was looking not at the people, but out beyond them.

Through the open doors of the chapel, straight across the town square, he could see something that was not dumpy and round shouldered but rather tall, high, and gothic. At least, what there was of it was tall, high, and gothic. In truth, the cathedral of Furze that so drew Albrecht's eyes was not even a quarter finished, and Albrecht doubted that it would ever be more than a quarter finished. Despite his dreams of reconstructing it, he was enough of a practical man (at least, he hoped he was) to know that an impoverished, economic wasteland like Furze could never hope to accomplish such a herculean—and expensive—task.

The unfinished cathedral, therefore, rose up amid the houses and hovels of Furze like the back half of a skull. The stonework of the choir and the apse was complete up to the level of the vaulting, but there was no vaulting. There was no glass in the clerestory. There was no roof, either, and rough wooden planks and straw thatch had to serve where concrete, stone, massive timbers, and lead would (as Albrecht devoutly hoped and prayed) someday rise. The nave and transepts were no more than a few columns and a series of holes partly filled with foundation stones.

Jesus had preached poverty, and Albrecht often thought that Furze had been a zealous convert. One hundred years ago, the city had been all but razed by the same robber companies that had taken and sacked Shrinerock, and the town had thereafter slipped in and out of municipal consciousness for several decades. The economy, founded squarely and symbiotically on the rich dairylands surrounding Belroi, had broken down completely, and when Albrecht had been given the city as his bishopric—a move that he always suspected had its origins in a desire of old Innocent and his cardinals to be rid of the silly old fellow with the gimpy leg and the delusions of piety—he had arrived to find a pauper town, pauper merchants, pauper artisans, pauper churches . . . and paupers themselves who were so crushed by their lot that any one of them, he suspected, would have gladly thrown everything up for the comparatively more remunerative life of a galley slave.

Fresh out of Rome and heartily tired of intrigues and politicking, Albrecht had welcomed the simplicity that came with poverty. Though he did not like the attendant strictures any more than anyone else, he had taken Furze in order to beat Rome much as a man might take wormwood in order to beat the plague. To be sure, the imbiber of the wormwood was looking forward to a time when he would not have to drink the bitter draft anymore, and, likewise, Albrecht was looking forward to a different Furze. A prosperous Furze. A wealthy Furze that would have plenty of money for clothes on its back, food on its table, help for its poor, and, incidentally, money for the fabric fund of the cathedral.

Surrounded by candles—and by the frumpy chapel—Albrecht blessed his people, giving an especially generous smile to the knot of shabby merchants who, with their families, stood together with Paul Drego and his matter-of-fact wife. The wool cooperative was trying to revitalize Furze, to shift its shattered dairy economy over to sheep and cloth, and Albrecht suspected that, with the help of Aldernacht gold, they just might succeed. Paul and his fellows had drunk their share of wormwood in Furze, but their eyes were firmly set upon the future.

Another smile—a fitting expression for Easter, Albrecht thought—and the bishop turned back to the altar. As he did so, though, he noticed that Siegfried was also looking at Paul and his small knot of foresighted merchants. The Inquisitor, though, was not smiling.

Albrecht held out his hand for the aspergillum. Siegfried, staring at Paul, did not seem to notice. Quietly, Albrecht cleared his throat, and the Inquisitor came to himself suddenly and handed him the implement. Albrecht nodded, but, with a sense of discomfort that he could not exactly place, did not give Siegfried an opportunity to kiss his hand.

He sang the old chant:

"Asperges me, Domine, hyssopo, et mundabor; lavabis me et super nivem dealbabor."

But as Albrecht sang, trying hard to be mindful only of the great mystery that he was about to celebrate, he was, unwillingly, aware of other things. Siegfried's thoughts, he was sure, were on the mass no more than his own. The wool cooperative was keeping its own counsel. Another few weeks, and Jacob Aldernacht himself would be coming to make the final arrangements for the loan that might lead to the transformation of Furze.

Albrecht appreciated poverty, but he also dreamed of a cathedral. Siegfried dreamed, he supposed, of heresy . . . and for some reason did not appreciate the cooperative at all. Paul Drego and his fellows dreamed of wool. Jacob Aldernacht . . . well, his dreams were his own business.

Had it always been like this? Albrecht had seen the bad business in Rome, and he had heard about its occurrence in other places as well. Lorenzo de' Medici had been openly attacked during a solemn mass just like this one, and poor Fra Girolamo had been hung and burned just two years ago for preaching publicly what most layfolk agreed upon privately. But although Albrecht supposed that there had been abuse and veniality since Peter had passed the shepherd's crook to Linus—not that the bishop ever suspected anything of those holy men themselves!—he also desperately hoped that at times it had been otherwise.

There had been miracles in the past. The Virgin herself had ofttimes taken a hand in the affairs of her children, and the old cathedrals had gone up across the continent in a mixture of legend and sanctity. But though those qualities had apparently been completely replaced by unabashed commerce—Alexander had declared a Jubillee Year, after all!—Albrecht desperately wanted to bring them back.

He knelt, but behind Siegfried's dark presence, beyond the faces of the merchants and the others, through the open door of the nave, across the open square, he sensed the beginnings of a cathedral. The last cathedral of Europe. It could be wonderful. It could bring back the legend and the sanctity. Maybe it could even bring back the Virgin and her gentle, lovingly meddling hands.

"Introibo ad altare Dei."

Yes, yes: but would he ever go to the altar of the cathedral of Furze? Probably not: he was getting old.

But would anybody?

Whispers.

Whispers in Adria. Whispers throughout all of Europe. Whispers in a dark tavern. Whispers in the sitting room of a common house. Whispers in an alley.

Siegfried heard whispers in Furze, but in reality (just as he, the Church, the Inquisition, and all suspected) the whispers were everywhere. Even Natil, who by nature stood so far outside the mores and customs and beliefs of human beings that she expected her existence to terminate not in death but in fading, heard them. Whispers.

"God can go into the host, and He can come out, too."

"There is more God in a barrel of malt than there is in a church."

"A priest in mortal sin has no sacramental power."

"I will not worship stocks and stones."

"I will confess to God alone."

But there was no room for whispers in the Church: its foundations were built upon an orthodoxy that, like the monodic chant that had once characterized its monastic practice, provided for no departure or improvisation. But the chant itself had long ago broken into octaves, and then fifths, and then had come full polyphony. Omelda's convent was one of the few that still limited the Office to a single line of melody; elsewhere, whispers of another kind had sent up shoots, leaves, flowers, and fruit that, though shaken to earth and stamped into pulp by reforms and papal bulls, had only rotted into compost and nurtured new sprouts. Now there was Josquin in the cathedrals, and even the complex and carefully wrought organum of Perotin and Leonin was looked upon as primitive, dated, not at all to the general taste for melody and harmony as ornate as the new tower at Chartres.

Nonetheless, throughout it all, the Church had continued to adhere to its single stem of doctrine, patiently and sometimes brutally lopping off heterodox branches. But a single stem could only grow so long. Change had to happen. The ancient and fertile enthusiasm of the Apostles and the Fathers could only sustain itself in rote practice for so long before, like a tree, it had to cleave, fork, become something else.

Had the Elves, Natil wondered, been just like that? Since the Beginning, since the primitive Earth had cooled into a jagged landscape of tortured basalt and seething pools of magma, they had been as a single stalk, one that, lengthening through years, centuries, millennia, had but grown thinner. They had fostered life, had healed and helped where they could, had taken on the appearance of one age after another, but they had remained Elves. They had not changed. They had never branched. And they had therefore dwindled.

Harp in hand, Natil stood at the edge of a dark abyss of non-existence just as she stood at the edge of the cathedral parvis this morning in Maris. She could not cross into the parvis—there was too much pain there—and she could not cross the abyss.

But once, years ago, an Elf named Varden had looked into that same darkness, and though he had been unable to cross, and though he himself had eventually faded (vanishing on a night of snow after a last meeting with a half-human son who wanted nothing more than to deny him), he had at the time looked beyond the abyss, sorting through the strands of starlight, the interlocking probabilities, following the potentials of existence to the other side of the deep, deep shadow—and he had seen . . . something: something that had given him a small glimmer of hope, as small and yet as bright as that glitter in the sky that Natil had seen—once again last night—in her dreams.

Elves and humans are two, the Lady had said to Varden, her eyes mirroring both the starlight of the Elves and the moonlight of the witches, *but both are my children. Not one of my children shall be separate from Me.*

The sunlight, though cold, was bright, and the colors of early spring, just now beginning to show, had the depth of oceans to Natil's eyes. Here were flowers—lilies and crocuses and daffodils—unfolding as they did every spring after a long sleep in the darkness of the earth.

Not one. And Natil suddenly thought of the elven blood, sleeping in humanity like a sower's pouchful of seeds new planted, waiting for spring, waiting for the future.

Varden had seen. And now Natil, too, had seen . . . something.

"Are you going to play here?" Omelda was tugging on Natil's cloak, an exotic patchwork of fabrics from a hundred different lands, feathers from the far side of the Atlantic, stones and beads from the East Indies and the southern tip of Africa. Just the thing for an itinerant harper. She might well have been a gypsy, a professional wanderer. Perhaps she was. "This makes me nervous." Omelda glanced around. "There are . . . there might be . . ."

Natil turned, looked into her intense eyes. Sleeping. But seeds had to be planted before they could grow. Surely she had learned that much in forty million centuries!

She felt herself smile. "Not here," she said. "We will go to the town square. The priests would not like secular music so near to their sanctuary."

Omelda clutched at her ragged cloak. There was a cold wind, and she shivered. "I thought you told me that you didn't play secular music."

"I do not. But the priests would not see it that way." Natil took Omelda's hand, and they set off through the holiday crowds. They had made a point to stay out of the city until well after mass, and, indeed, Natil would have preferred to stay out of the city entirely; but she needed money for food: with the encroachment of farms and settlements on the forests, she had become as much a prisoner of economics as any human.

As they walked, though, Omelda's eyes clouded. Natil glanced at the sun, realized that it was sext. The services for the people were over, but the Divine Office was beginning once again.

"I can't stop it." Omelda was groping suddenly in the bright afternoon. "I can't. I want to . . . scream. Play something."

Natil held fast to her hand. "I told you before: I cannot always be with you. You will have to learn to do this yourself."

"I don't even have a harp."

"You do not need a harp. What is being sung right now?"

"Beata immaculati."

"Sing it for me."

Omelda blinked at the betrayal. "I'll . . . go . . . go mad!"

Natil continued on her way, drawing Omelda towards the square, struggling to hold fast to the way of the Elves in the face of an abyss that wrapped the future in a deepening shroud of shadow as it wrapped her present in a deepening humanity. "Sing, please," she said. "Come now, Omelda: you have a voice, and you have a body—"

"It's . . . dung!"

Natil gave her arm a gentle shake. "It is *not* dung, O woman. Sing."

Trembling, still fuzzy from her inner possession, Omelda quavered out the notes as though each one were red hot:

"Utinam dirigantur viae meae, ad custodiendas justificationes tuas!"

The syllables thumping out with monotonous regularity, Omelda plodded through the chant as she and Natil threaded their way through the streets of Maris. The afternoon was clear, the weather was warming, and the city, like the Church, had thrown off the dark sobriety of winter and Passion Week. In the square, jugglers worked the crowds. Acrobats tumbled. A musician, after a comradely nod at Natil, started up a song. There were smiling faces and new clothes; people were talking, laughing, wenching. Even the stern face of the baronial fortress seemed gentled by the general consensus that it was time for winter to become spring.

Omelda labored on through the hated and obsessive

Office. "Stop for a moment," said Natil suddenly. "Think: what are you singing?"

Omelda blinked. "The Office."

Natil found a vacant spot on the steps that led up to the Hansa factory and sat down. The eagle feather in her hair glinted in the sunlight. "What were the words you just sang? Say them."

Omelda grimaced: even a hint of the Office was more than sufficient to pain her, but: *"Concupivit anima mea disiderare justificationes tuas, in omni tempore,"* she said dutifully.

"You did not say them as you sang them, did you?"

"I just . . . said them, that's all."

"Ah," said Natil, "but you said them with expression and with feeling, as though the words actually meant something. Dame Agnes did not neglect your knowledge of Latin, did she?"

Omelda shook her head, put her hands to her ears. "No, she didn't. I can speak Latin. But can't you just play something, Natil?"

Natil smiled, pulled Omelda's hands down. "I shall. But listen to what I play, for I am going to play what you just sang . . . but I will play it as you said it."

"Is that supposed to help?"

Natil checked the tuning of her harp, glanced up. She was already attracting a cluster of listeners. She was used to that. An outlandishly dressed woman who did not cover her head and who carried such a strange-looking harp almost always caught the attention—and usually the sympathy—of everyone within sight . . . even before she played a single note. There would probably be a few gold coins today. "Helping is what I do, Omelda. It is what I have always done. Now listen . . ."

The strings of her harp sparkled into music, and she could not help but recall again the thing that had glittered so brightly against the profoundly blue sky of her dreams. Was it just a dream? Or was it perhaps a vision that allowed her, like Varden, to pierce a dark and abyssal shroud of shadow?

CHAPTER 4

The sunlight glittered on the windows of the 747, the white contrails of the jet even whiter for the very blue Colorado sky. It was April. The Rocky Mountains were still stippled with snow, but below, in Denver, elms had leafed, apple trees had budded, and cottonwoods were hung heavy with catkins.

There was something in the air that came inevitably with spring: a stirring that had nothing to do with temperature or weather, but which arrived every year, returning unfailingly even after the deepest, most frost-bitten and pipes-bursting-like-popcorn cold, an echo of all past winters, a promise of the newness of all future springs. And so the westbound 747 glittered in the sky, seeming itself to be a premature blossom of spring, as though 747s have been hanging whitely in the blue and April air since the beginning of time, promising connection, promising newness.

George Morrison drove west along Highway 6, feeling old. Denver felt old. The apartment he had left behind felt more than old: it smacked of ruin and of rot, of Kleenex that had been used, wadded up, and thrown away.

In the space of a day, he had lost his job, lost his lover, lost any feeling of roots or of belonging in the city in which he had been born. At the security firm, they had told him that his performance had not improved sufficiently. Tina had told him much the same thing.

"I'm tired of beating my head against the wall. I'm tired of scrounging. I'm tired of watching you sitting in front of the TV while I try to figure out where the rent's gonna come from. I'm tired of everything."

"But . . . ."

"I can do better by myself."

It had been coming for a long time. George knew that.

The fights, the sulks, her crying jags and his temper . . .
The signs had been obvious. But he had, in a most human
fashion, lied to himself as much about the inevitability
of the split with Tina as about his inadequacies and fum-
bles on the job.

He had sunk his final check and most of his savings
into a diamond engagement ring, but when he had come
home in the middle of the day, Tina had been loading
her belongings into her tiny car. Another man might have
pleaded with her, might have gone so far as to grab her
arm, show her the ring, force her to stay in the shabby
little living room with delusions of making up and happy
sex in the back of his mind. Another man might have
become enraged at the affront to male pride and prerog-
ative. He might have slapped her around a bit, or he
might have killed her. It was, after all, 1980. Things like
that happened.

But George had instead stood in the middle of the asphalt parking lot as Tina had driven away. He had not
even told her about the engagement ring. He had waved
good-bye, that was all, but he had known that she was
not looking back. Tina was not one to look back.

Afterwards, in the backwash of silence left by the
countless arguments now forever ended, the apartment
had turned stale, the sounds of radios and stereos and
televisions drifting in from other units altogether too
loud, too oppressive. George had endured it for three
days, and then he, too, had left . . . and he had not
looked back.

He did not know where he was going. He knew only
that he was heading west, into the mountains, following
the 747 that hung in the top half of his grimy windshield
like a promise of something better, a promise of spring
for the world. He was, perhaps, looking for the spring.
He was looking for the promise. Denver went on, pollution, politics, traffic and all, as ancient and weathered
as a half-rotted Burma Shave sign; but George, following
instinct—or, rather (though he did not know it), following
something like instinct, something that was appearing in the
world for the first time in half a thousand years—was looking
for the New Season.

Highway 6 took him out through Golden where the
Coors factory sent plumes of steam slanting westward

into the air: even the breeze and the weather seemed to have decided to go in the direction of the seasons and the sun. Beyond Golden, the highway shrunk to two lanes and wound along beside Clear Creek, but George kept driving, still wondering where he was going, but looking at—and, in a way, beginning to dimly appreciate—the trees and the sky and the sharp road cuts, veined with a hundred minerals and colors, that stood up before and then fell away behind his rattling van.

And perhaps because he had so thoroughly lost himself in the trees and the thoughts of the 747 and the vague and inexpressible visions of newness that were swimming unaccountably up from depths in his mind that he did not know he had (that, at another time, might have terrified him), he found himself suddenly veering off the highway and onto a dirt road.

He was heading up a steep slope before he realized it, the engine laboring in low gear, the sleeping bag and box of food he had tossed onto the bare metal cargo deck sliding aft with a rush and a clatter. There were no signs telling him not to trespass, nothing to indicate what lay ahead.

Up, down, around, gravel skittering from beneath four bald tires and branches scraping against the windows. Sunlight filtering and flickering through new leaves. Aspen now: gray green trunks, a few pastel buds. The pines here were tall, straight, and, surprisingly, the land appeared unspoiled by the refuse that normally characterized a wilderness so close to the city. This place seemed bent upon putting on a good face, opening itself to George as though an old friend had met him at the porch of a mansion, thrown the doors wide, and beckoned him in with a smile.

And as he crested a ridge and started down a slope, George suddenly felt it. It was spring. New, reborn, spring had come to this hidden valley, had cupped it in a strong hand, was reaching out now to George and drawing him into its mansion like a friend, coaxing him to gun the engine a little more, to take the curves a little faster.

Come on. Come on in. Get your ass in here, boy.

George came, got his ass in there. Looking for a real spring, suddenly and inexplicably receptive to the potentials of openness—there was nothing behind him, after all, and as he had only a vague supposition that there was anything ahead, he would accept whatever came—he had suddenly found it, found its beginnings, found the first few syllables of its language. He was seeing the spring, hearing it; and he was starting to believe that, maybe . . .

The van crunched to a stop where the road ended in a puddle of gravel and rock that seemed to have been poured into the middle of a forest clearing like a ladle of pancake batter. George shut off the engine and let a different kind of silence backwash into the van, into his heart. Birdsong. The sigh of pines. A flicker boinged somewhere nearby, flashed red wings at him. A sparrow hawk appeared with a flutter and perched on a branch a few feet away.

Private property, I guess, George thought. *It always is.* But it was not private property. Or rather, it was the most private property of all, for it could not be owned, could not be touched or even be seen save by those few who were open enough, who listened, who had come to believe—desperately or not, despairingly or not—in spring.

Haec dies, quam fecit dominus: exsultemus . . .
Omelda struggled up out of sleep as she struggled through everything: plodding heavily along, surrounded by the voices of nuns. They had escorted her into sleep with compline, befuddled her dreams with matins and lauds. Now, with prime, they were lifting her up to greet the new day.
Deus, qui hodierna die . . .
She opened her eyes. Dawn. But something was wrong: there was no roof above her, only gray sky. Her father had committed her to the cloister with the understanding that she would be entombed alive as a bride of Christ, and since then, whether it was of wood, or plaster, or figured with intricate vaulting, a roof had always been over her head, and walls—stone or stained glass—had always surrounded her.

But here there was no roof, there were no walls, and she cringed at the terrible openness, fearful that the heavens might suddenly swing open like vast shutters to reveal the face of God leaning down towards her—white brow, hooked nose, gray beard, eyes piercing as stars—transfixing her in the field like a bug on a carpet.

Domine Deus omnipotens, qui ad principium . . .

A murmur from close by. Omelda gasped, turned her head. A few feet away, Natil was curled up in her fantastic cloak of patchwork and feathers. The harper was asleep, and she must surely have been dreaming, for her brow was furrowed, and her delicate face wore an expression of deep concentration.

Then—slowly, laboriously, plodding through the voices that continued to intone the chant in her mind—Omelda remembered. She was not in the convent, she was not in Maris, she was not in any of the hundred towns and cities through which she had passed in the course of two years. She was sleeping in the open, with Natil, and Natil was . . .

. . . Natil could . . .

Omelda prodded herself to her hands and knees, crawled to the harper's side. "Natil!"

. . . *Jesum Christum Filium tuum* . . .

No response. But the idea that her head could suddenly be silent spurred Omelda into actually shaking her companion, picking up her carefully wrapped harp, thrusting it into her limp hands.

"Natil!"

"What . . . ?" Natil opened her eyes, blinked at the graying sky. "What is it, child?"

"Can you play . . . something, please?"

Natil regarded her silently for a moment, then sighed. "Good morning," she said politely.

Omelda suddenly felt ashamed. "I'm acting . . . badly," she said. She sat down hard on the grassy ground, hung her head. "I'm surprised that you want to . . . keep me around."

Natil lay, eyes unclosed, looking up at the sky. They were a few miles south of Maris, near the shore of the Bergren River. New as the morning was, a boat was nonetheless already passing downstream, the steersman alternately yawning, blowing on his hands, and grumbling a snatch of song. Closer was a stand of trees, half leafed. Birds were building nests. Singing, too.

Benedicamus Domino.

Omelda writhed in guilt. "Really, Natil: I'm sorry. Go back to sleep. I won't bother you again."

Natil's gaze flicked back to her. "Good morning."

Omelda looked up. There was kindness in the harper's eyes. "Good . . . good morning, Natil."

The harper nodded her approval. "And blessings upon you. The voices again?"

Omelda dropped her head back down. In the convent, the deserved rebuke would have come quickly, but Natil seemed to have no rebukes in her save in response to comments that equated flesh and dung. Omelda, nonetheless, could not shake the feeling that she had transgressed. "Yes," she nodded, "it's the voices."

Natil pushed herself up, sat, stretched in the manner of one who was not used to stretching: one arm at a time, as though inwardly remarking how strange a thing was morning stiffness.

Mors Sanctorum ejus.

The chant hemmed Omelda in, made her ask in spite of her guilt: "Can you . . . can you play now?"

Natil shook her head. "The strings of my harp are cold and will take much tuning. What are you hearing?"

With a shrug, Omelda started up the chant, her outward voice blending with her inner, obsessive choir. *"Si consurrexistis cum Christo—"*

"Stop," said the harper. "That is not the way I taught you to sing yesterday."

The chant thudded within Omelda's mind like a chronic headache. She wrinkled her nose. "There's not much to it. It's just a tonus with . . . a flex and a metrum. It's not really a melody."

"It is *all* melody," said Natil. "Even the spoken word is melody. Sing properly."

Painfully, Omelda backed up to the beginning of the Short Lesson and began again, stressing the syllables in accordance with the cadence of speech, uttering the Latin not in monotonous, plodding rhythm, but lightly, conversationally.

But when she reached the end, the chant went on within her, plodding along with severe cadence:

Adjutorium nostrum in nomine Domini . . .

Omelda hung her head. "It's no . . . good, Natil."

Natil was almost dispassionate. "It is a start. Does the chant in your head sound any different now?"

"No."

Natil's dispassion crumbled, and she passed a hand over her face. "Dear Lady," she murmured.

Natil's invocation was a homely reminder of convent life. *By Our Lady* had been Dame Agnes's favorite exclamation in time of joy or trouble. In spite of the chant, Omelda smiled at the memory. "You like her, too?"

Natil had apparently lost herself in thought. She looked up, almost startled. "Like? Who?"

"Mary. The Virgin." Omelda laughed as much as she could with that terrible vault of blue growing over her head and the chant ringing in her mind. "I used to talk to her. I always had the . . . feeling that she actually listened."

Unaccountably, Natil's eyes had misted. "She always listens. Always. Even . . ." The harper bent her head quickly, as though to hide tears. "Even now."

Omelda shrugged, feeling strange that someone like Natil had been so affected by a few words. "Oh, Natil," she said, "Mary's supposed to hear everyone, all the time. Even someone . . ." She laughed again, heard the sob behind the sound. ". . . even someone like me. There's even a story about a nun who left her convent and ran away . . . just like me. When she finally came back, no one had missed her because Mary had taken her place. Mary does things like that."

Amen.

The voices trailed off. Prime was done. In Shrinerock Abbey, Omelda's sisters in Christ were filing out into the cloister, preparing for the *mixtum*. Relief flooded into her, and she put her hands to her face, rubbed, blinked as though only now had she really awakened.

On the river, the boat was still passing, moving off into the distance, fading out of sight like the convent and the convent life and all the predictability and surety Omelda had ever known. She suddenly missed the four thick walls, the gardens, the constant reassurance of unutterable sameness. Only her knowledge that the voices—incessant, battering—would return at terce kept the longing from turning abruptly into heartbreak. "At least, they say she does."

Natil was watching her.

"But . . ." It was a painful admission, but Omelda said it. "But I don't think that would happen if I went back," she said. "I don't think things like that happen anymore. Besides . . ." She shrugged heavily, indicated her head.

Natil's eyes were damp. "I understand." She looked off at the sunrise. "Perhaps they might happen again. Someday."

Omelda felt herself grow hopeful. "Do you believe that?"

The harper's face was solemn. "I want to believe that. I want very much to believe that. I think that I have . . . dreams . . . of that. I want very much to believe those dreams."

The conversation had taken an odd turn, and Omelda felt the sudden chill and queasiness that came from a close encounter with a prophet . . . or a madwoman. "Some say that dreams come from the devil," she said cautiously. "Dame Agnes said that they come from impure thoughts, and that we should ignore them."

Natil was still staring off at the sunrise. "Do you think that is what they are? Simply impure thoughts? Is hope an impure thought?"

These were genuine questions. Natil really appeared to have no idea what to think about dreams. "I . . . I don't know," said Omelda. "God says we should hope. It's a virtue, after all."

Natil nodded slowly. "Do you dream?"

"Yes . . ."

"Do you ever dream dreams . . . that come true?"

"I don't know." Omelda writhed. "I . . ."

Natil became aware of Omelda's distress. "I am sorry, beloved. I did not mean to pry."

The harper said nothing more about dreams. Instead, she made food, and the two women ate eggs and bread from Maris and three fish that the harper coaxed from the water. Omelda, hungry, and trying to shake her sudden homesickness, crammed her mouth full as she muttered an inward grace. Natil, however, bent her head over her meal and remained so for the better part of a minute.

Omelda flushed. Here was a musician more devout than a nun. Hastily, she put down the bread in her hands and

crossed herself, trying hard to make her second thanks-
giving more sincere and deliberate than her last.

Natil lifted her head, smiled. "Everything worth doing, Omelda, is worth doing consciously, attentively.
Eating, harping, saying grace . . . even chanting."

Omelda shrugged heavily. Natil's words seemed obvious: how else did one plod through a life? But, still feeling guilty about the rudeness with which she had awakened the harper, she did not pursue the subject until after
they had both finished breakfast. Then: "What can I do
. . . about the chant in my head?"

"What can you do?" Natil wiped her hands, un-
wrapped her harp, tried the strings. The morning had
warmed, and the instrument with it: the chord rang true.
"I fear you might not like what I have to tell you."

Like? Did she like the chant? "Tell me anyway."

Natil spoke simply. "I believe you will have to live
it."

"I'm . . ." Omelda had hoped for more. She had
hoped for hope. "I'm already living it, Natil."

Natil shook her head, plucked a few strings. "You will
have to live it consciously, attentively, and with knowledge."

They spent a few minutes with music, then. Natil drew
melodies from her harp and politely requested that
Omelda sing them. At first, she tried popular songs—
bawdy and sentimental both—but when Omelda proved
to know very few of them, she turned to chant. Omelda
balked at the task, for chant in any form awakened too
many echoes of her inner voices; but Natil, insistent,
made her sing the same chant over and over again with
the inflections and cadences and stresses of ordinary
speech until the old, monotonous plodding was beginning to fade in Omelda's mind and she could think of the
chant in question only as a plastic, organic, living thing
with all the taut springiness of a freshly clipped lawn.

"But what good is it?" Omelda finally asked. "I can
learn this chant this way, but there are all the others . . ."
She lifted her large hands, let them fall into her lap. One
chant? There were thousands in the Church liturgy. An
entire shelf of the abbey library was given over to chant
books—the Antiphonary, the Graduale, the Hymnarius—
and a dozen others. What was one chant among so many?

And Omelda could not even see the use of the alterations upon which Natil had so insisted.

Natil took up a soft cloth, wiped the strings of her harp, wrapped the instrument. "It is a start," she said. "I do not know where it will lead you."

Omelda opened her mouth, but Natil looked at her with bright blue eyes and she shut it again.

"I did not know where I would be led when I came into life," said the harper. "I did not know where I would be led when I looked up from my harp and saw you standing in the window. I do not know what next week might bring, or even . . ." A flash of pain and loss in those blue eyes. ". . . or even tomorrow. But you asked me to teach you my music, and so I am trying to do that."

Chastened, feeling again a sense of transgression, Omelda rose silently and gathered the remainder of the food. Woman's work: cleaning up, plodding from one task to another. There was always something to do, whether in the Divine Office or in housekeeping.

"I'm sorry, Natil," she said suddenly.

Natil looked up. "Sorry, beloved?"

"For complaining. I'm always complaining." Omelda almost smiled: her sisters would be in chapter right about now, confessing to one another, asking God's forgiveness for personal faults and failings. Turn and twist and run as she would, she could not escape the life to which she had been committed. "Forgive me."

Natil nodded as she rose. "I forgave you the moment you uttered the words, Omelda. Forgive yourself."

Omelda stared, speechless. In chapter, faults would be confessed and punishments and disciplines meted out by Dame Agnes. But Natil—oh, what a difference was this!

Natil bowed. "It is a hard thing to forgive yourself deeply and sincerely, is it not? But it is an important thing to learn rightly."

Omelda found her voice. "Only God can truly forgive. God and the priests."

Natil straightened, fixed Omelda with her blue eyes for a moment, then bent and picked up her harp. "So say the priests, beloved." But Omelda sensed that the harper—prophet or madwoman, she did not know—did not believe a word of what the priests said.

CHAPTER 5

Darkness. Absolute darkness. The darkness of the grave. The darkness of the crypt. The darkness of death.

Siegfried of Magdeburg, Inquisitor of Furze, stood silently in the deepest corridor of the House of God. A soul newly flown from its body, he imagined, saw and felt this profundity of darkness. With full knowledge that, about it, but now forever beyond its grasp, the world of mundane concerns went on just as the world of Furze and poverty and wool cooperative plots went on outside the walls of the House of God, the individual soul, like the prisoner in the room ahead, like Siegfried himself, waited alone and in darkness.

And so Siegfried stood, silently meditating on the task ahead of him. But, as always, troubling thoughts arose. Fredrick, the prisoner, would see Siegfried and would know his fate, and the soul, waiting in darkness and silence, would eventually find itself confronted with its Supreme Judge. Siegfried, though . . .

Adoro te devote, latens deitas, the Angelic Doctor had written. But Fra Thomas had been a mighty soldier of God, with more than enough faith to see beyond the simple appearances of bread and wine, defy the pronouncements of touch and taste and sight, and look straight into the heart of the divine mystery that the Sacrament concealed. Siegfried, however, found himself ever open to doubt and unfulfillment. The dead saw. Even the heretical prisoner saw. What did Siegfried of Magdeburg see?

Adoro te devote, latens deitas. And Siegfried did indeed adore that hidden God. But always he hoped and wished that, after waiting in such darkness, he might someday open the metal door at the end of the passage and find there not a chamber full of torches and implements, men unwashed for a month, and the reek of urine squeezed out of panicked bladders; but rather a vision of divinity, a vision of God. No bread, no wine, no hidings and layers and tests of faith: just an honest acknowledgment of the Creator to His created, a pat on the shoulder perhaps, perhaps even a *Well done, Siegfried*.

Was death the only way to know, to see? Oh, there had been some petty heresy years ago—even Bernard Gui had not taken it seriously, and only a fool like Cranby would have pursued it—about seeing God face to face. Pernicious enough to be sure, but certainly nothing like the ravings of the Fraticelli and the Cathars and the Waldensians. Just a little isolated dream. They had insisted that they could see God. Any time they wanted.

To see God . . .

Siegfried bestirred himself and went down the corridor to a metal door that he had, in the course of twenty years, learned to find in the darkness as effortlessly as he could find his nose. He had been expected, and, beyond the door, the room fell silent save for breathing, the crackle and sputter of torches, the drip of something onto a dirt floor grown soggy with bodily fluids: *plat*.

Eyes turned to Siegfried. *Plat*. The notary assigned the arduous task of recording every question, every answer, every (*plat*) perversion of true faith, every scream—sat with his pen poised above his tablet. *Plat*. Fra Giovanni, Siegfried's assistant, was dragging the sleeve of his habit across his brow. It came away sopping: it was hot in the room. *Plat*. The men in charge of the instruments dropped their hands to their sides, waiting for orders. *Plat*.

"Well?" said Siegfried.

The men shuffled their feet. Giovanni shook his head. The notary made an entry.

Siegfried looked at the man in the center of the room, who, in truth, looked more like a strange insect, or a crustacean dredged up from the bottom of a lake. Here was a steel carapace about him to hold him fast. Here was a skeleton helmet of steel bars, with spines that thrust in so as to bring pressure upon his head. Here were iron boots and iron gloves to grip his feet and hands. And here also were two eyes that, from within the helmet and the spines, rolled whitely up at Siegfried, looking, seeing.

. . . latens deitas.

Giovanni bowed his head, chagrined, dejected. "Brother Siegfried, I've . . . I've sinned."

Siegfried nodded understandingly. *Ecclesia abhorret a sanguine,* but in the heat of a battle for such a precious thing as a soul, excesses invariably happened. Long ago, though, Pope Urban had foreseen such frailty and had allowed for it: Inquisitors forgave one another regularly for having become *irregularis.*

Siegfried lifted his hand. *"Ego te absolvo, Giovanni."*

Giovanni bowed.

Plat.

Once again, Siegfried examined the prisoner. Fredrick's fingers—what was left of them—protruded from the ends of the metal gloves. Giovanni had perhaps seen to his fingernails himself. Or maybe to his feet: the screws that held the needles ready at the anklebones had been turned down all the way. Perhaps Giovanni had been guilty of that, too.

But Fredrick had only himself to blame for his torment. He had been given opportunity after opportunity to confess and recant these last three years, and he had stubbornly refused. And he had at last come to this.

"Fredrick, my son," said Siegfried. "Are you ready to admit your errors?" He kept his voice patient, consoling. The duty of an Inquisitor was to win souls, and even at the extreme to which Fredrick had brought himself, souls were most readily won by kind words.

Silence. *Plat.*

Contumacious. Hardened and contumacious. When first ordered to appear before the tribunal, Fredrick had actually attempted to flee, but while he himself had been unsuccessful, his wife and children had, in fact, escaped to Hypprux.

Well, the woman and the whelps could go. Their heresy would be their downfall eventually, even in Hypprux; and by the powers granted the Inquisition to confiscate the possessions of heretics, Siegfried had Fredrick's lands and his house now, properties that were already, by revenue and sale, providing for more spies to report heresy, more tribunals to determine the truth of it, more Inquisitors to exterminate it at its roots. Fredrick, whether he confessed or not, whether he liked it or not, had done his part for Holy Church.

Plat.

Fredrick's tongue, dragged forward out of his mouth by a pair of cast iron pincers, seared with a hot iron, and held in place with a spiked clamp, stirred, fluttered. A faint whine came from his throat.

Siegfried bent low to peer between the bars of the skeleton helmet. The white eyes followed him. Seeing. *Adoro te devote.* And when would Siegfried himself see? "Will you confess, now, my son?" he said. "All you have to do is tell the truth."

Plat.

Fredrick did not even blink, but his tongue fluttered again.

"We know you are a heretic, Fredrick," said Siegfried. "We know beyond any doubt. You would not have been accused had you not been a heretic. You would not have run away had you not been a heretic. You would not have been brought before the tribunal had you not been a heretic. You would not be here now if you had not made statements of belief contrary to the teachings of the Church. Do you realize the seriousness of your crime?"

Plat.

Fredrick made no further movement, no further sound. His eyes, though, watched as Siegfried turned to the others present. "Leave me alone with him," said the Inquisitor. "I will question him in private."

The torturers, the notary, and Fra Giovanni all bowed. Siegfried often asked to be left alone with a prisoner. This was nothing unusual. Frequently, confessions followed such private interviews, and confessions were the entire reason for the Inquisition: the important thing was the salvation of the soul.

And so the other men filed out and the metal door swung to. Siegfried was alone with Fredrick, alone with the blistered and seared tongue, the fingers without nails, the feet with needles in the ankles, the broken thumbs and the mouth gag and the scourged and lacerated body fastened within the imprisoning armor and the steel bars.

Plat.

Siegfried dragged a stool up beside Fredrick and sat

down. He put his face close to the skeleton helmet, as close as he could without bumping into the handles of the screw spikes, but Fredrick was no longer looking at him.

Plat.

Siegfried examined Fredrick for a long time. Silence.

Plat.

"God must love you very much, Fredrick," said Siegfried at last.

Fredrick did not move.

Plat.

"Do you know how I know that He loves you?"

No reply.

Siegfried watched the eyes, waiting for a sign. A flicker. A glance. Something. But, no: nothing. Did he see? Was he seeing now? *Latens deitas*. Hidden God. *Hidden*! Siegfried bent a little closer, until the handle of a screw spike rested against his cheekbone. "I know that he loves you, Fredrick," he whispered, "because He has given you a chance."

A flicker. Of the tongue or of the eyes, Siegfried could not be sure, so fleeting it was, but it was a flicker.

Plat.

"You think that we hate you, do you not?"

Another flicker.

"Because we hurt you . . ."

Yes, there it was again. Fredrick was listening!

"But we hurt you because, like God, we love you. We love you greatly, Fredrick."

The flickers abruptly stopped. Siegfried reached up, gave a sudden turn to the screw that bore down on the top of Fredrick's head.

A whimper, then . . . silence.

Plat.

Siegfried rose, stood before the chained, bound, manacled man, leaned toward the helmet. Inches from his face, the blistered tongue was a skewered bit of red and white meat, oozing pus and lymph and blood, but flickering again, flickering.

Siegfried took a breath. "You think that these torments are excruciating, Fredrick, do you not? And yet, these are . . ." As always, he let the word hang on the edge of speech for a moment. ". . . nothing."

Plat.

"For if you die a heretic—and you surely are a heretic—you will suffer pains beyond anything you have ever known here or will ever know here."

Plat.

"The pains of hell, Fredrick."

Plat.

Siegfried spoke earnestly. This was not a bauble or a toy or a gold florin he was attempting to win, but an immortal soul. Fredrick's body was forfeit—his crimes were too great to be pardoned—but if the Inquisition could send him from the stake straight into the arms of God, then all the pain and suffering and entreaty and questioning would be proven worthwhile. "Think of it, Fredrick, my dear son. Hell is not for a moment, or for an hour, or for a day or a month or a year. It is . . . forever."

Plat.

Fredrick's eyes were closed, clenched as tightly as his hands would have been, Siegfried was sure, had they not been rendered a mass of pulp by the thumbscrews and the lever forceps. But Fredrick, contumacious and persistent heretic though he was, could not clench his ears. That was fitting: even the unrighteous could not block out the word of God.

"Forever," Siegfried persisted. "Endless. Eternity. And as you burn and writhe and scream—yes, scream, Fredrick, for the Scriptures tell us that those who are in hell cry out continually—you will know that there is no escape from God's justice, and that you will burn and writhe and scream . . ." Another pause. ". . . forever."

Plat.

Siegfried peered into the helmet. He had to win Fredrick. For the sake of God. For the sake of the Church. For the sake of Furze. "And so God has given you a chance. A chance for repentance."

Plat.

"And all you have to do . . . is tell the truth."

A murmur from within the helmet, a spasmodic shaking. Fingers, broken beyond writhing, beyond clenching, writhed and clenched nonetheless. A burned and mangled tongue wrestled futilely with the spikes and clamps that held it. Moisture that was not blood or pus or lymph dribbled from tight-shut eyes.

Fredrick was weeping.

Siegfried had seen it before: the rush of grief that brought tears even to the most hardened of heretical faces when confronted with the absolute, incontrovertible, inescapable love of the Most High. It was, as always, a moving sight, and Siegfried's own eyes were moist as he put his hands up and cradled the skeleton helmet as though he held the head of an infant. "Will you tell me the truth, my son Fredrick?"

Another murmur. Tears ran down the scabbed, gaunt, imprisoned face.

"Will you confess your heresy?" Fredrick's heresy, though, was undoubted: the man simply would not have been so tortured and broken had he not been the most flagrant of heretics. Siegfried knew what the answer would be here—he had after all, seen the tears of grief and repentance—but he did not know what answers Fredrick would give to other questions, questions much more far reaching and important.

Another murmur, gratifying in its quickness, its eagerness.

"Will you tell me about your associates?"

Fredrick wept and murmured.

"Will you tell me about the wool cooperative? About the money they intend to receive from Jacob Aldernacht?" Siegfried's fingers gripped the bars of the helmet. The wealthy Alpine Waldensians had held out even against Cattaneo's concerted crusade, had even the audacity to turn the force of civil law against their persecutors! Money for them had been a shield and a bulwark behind which they could practice their pernicious vice, and Siegfried knew that with an influx of gold into Furze, another shield would take form, one that, considering the Aldernacht millions, could hide anything, protect anything. His course was therefore clear: prosecute now, destroy now. The tares had to be uprooted immediately, for if left in the field they would themselves uproot the corn.

But there was no murmur in reply to his impassioned questions. Fredrick's tears ceased abruptly.

Siegfried pressed on, shaking the helmet softly in cadence with his whispered words. "About Paul Drego? About Simon the Jew. About James the furrier. About all the rest?"

Plat.

"So that God can show them how much He loves them, too?"

Fredrick's eyes opened wide, stared through the metal bars. In contrast to their white terror a few minutes ago, now they were almost luminous. They met Siegfried's gaze, and, for a moment, the Dominican thought that surely Fredrick—his soul dangling as it was over an abyss of pain and certain death—was seeing beyond the walls of stone and earth, beyond the world, into what lay beyond; that he was seeing, face to face . . .

A whimper from Fredrick, another quiver of the tongue, a sudden frantic straining against unyielding bonds. Siegfried understood, and with practiced hands, he removed the spikes, spun the clamps loose, unfastened the catches that held the helmet shut and threw it back on its brazen hinges. In a moment, Fredrick's head—seamed, lined, emaciated—was free.

Fredrick's tongue moved, licked his parched lips, left a trail of pus and slime behind.

"You see how much we love you," said Siegfried.

His eyes filled with the luminous glow of revelation, Fredrick opened his mouth. "I . . ." His voice was dusty, weak.

Siegfried leaned closer.

"I . . ."

Latens deitas. "Yes, my son?"

"I . . ." Another lick. Fredrick's eyes grew wider. "I . . . hate you."

Siegfried pulled back, blinked.

Fredrick found his voice at last. "I . . . hate you. I hate your religion. I hate your Church." His voice, raw and dusty, grew in strength, his thick tongue no impediment to the emotion and despair that rushed out of his mouth. "If this is God's love, then I hate God, too!" His voice edged into hysteria, edged into a scream. "Damn you! *Damn you all, you filthy bastards! I'll go to hell before I'll share heaven with you!*"

And, with what strength was left to him, Fredrick gathered a mouthful of spittle and blood and lymph and pus and belched it into Siegfried's face.

"*Damn you!*" he shrieked. "*Damn you! Damn you! Damn you!*"

The door was flung open: Giovanni and the others had heard Fredrick's blasphemous shouts. Crowding into the room, they stopped short at the sight of the mutilated, mangled figure that continued to spew abuse and blood both.

"Damn you! Damn you all! D—"

Fredrick fell silent, sagged in his bonds and chains. Shaking, Siegfried wiped blood from his eyes and peered at him. The prisoner's face was slack, his eyes glassy. Pink drool wound down his cheek, joined the fluids that had pooled on the sodden floor at the base of the chair.

Plat.

Plat. Plat.

Siegfried wiped his face. "He is dead."

Giovanni crossed himself. "He didn't confess, did he?"

"No," said Siegfried. "But he said enough to perhaps gain him a little mercy from a greater tribunal than ours." He hung his head, discouraged. "Take Fredrick's body out and burn it. God will have to make the final judgment, for I cannot. But he implicated Paul Drego before he returned to his heretical ways, and therefore I want Paul watched. I want his comings and goings made known to me. I want records of what he says, of his visitors and his guests."

Fredrick's glassy eyes saw nothing . . . or perhaps everything. Siegfried looked carefully into his face. Perhaps, just at the moment of death, Fredrick had seen . . . . something. Something that might have left some faint mark of hope or terror in his visage. But no, nothing.

Plat.

Plat.

Plat.

What was he seeing now? God? The devil? Anything? What did heretics see? What had they been seeing when, years ago, they had naively claimed that a living man or woman could look into the stars and see the face of the Creator?

Siegfried mopped his face again, turned away. *Adoro te devote.*

Natil dreamed.

The starlight was far fled from her, but for now she was not worried about the starlight, for at a time when starlight was unthinkable, starlight was valueless. In a time without starlight, what mattered was rebirth.

There would be a land, a land far away across the ocean. She herself had trodden its length and breadth decades ago, searching fruitlessly for elvenkind. Far in the future, though, after a long winter of the world, a long slumber beneath a shroud of shadow so dark that it seemed absolute negation, it was there that the sleeping, elven blood would reawaken.

How might it begin? she wondered. But perhaps she had seen exactly how it might begin. Amid sights and sounds that, with the openness of the dreamer, she accepted and called by their proper names—automobile, jet, radio—she saw that it might begin with a man named George Morrison, who, after standing in a fold of the Rocky Mountains, rapt by the coming of spring and by the undeniable response he felt in his blood and bone and fiber and sinew (no airy spiritualism here, but a stirring as visceral as an orgasm), was again driving west, following the setting sun, following the season of rebirth.

The mountains stayed with him, somehow, as though they had found a small vacancy in his heart: a bare room with a bare bulb hanging from the middle of the ceiling, a mattress on the floor, perhaps a rickety table in the corner. Not quite flophouse accommodations, but certainly spartan and mean. But the meanness could be gotten rid of later, was, in fact, going away already, and George was satisfied that the mountains had decided to move in, to plunk a ratty old toothbrush into the unwashed plastic glass on the back of the toilet, to give him a wave and a cheerful *Hi, roomie!*

But he knew that he was not supposed to remain in the mountains. He would return, but he could not stay. Not now. He had other things to do. And so, following that inner surge of life that echoed the rising sap in the pines and the aspens, his face stubbly and his shirt beginning to smell after an entire day of staring at mountains and trees as though he had never seen such outlandish things before—mountains, trees: what did that mean, anyway?—he had climbed back into the van and continued west, picking up I-70 after a few minutes, rumbling up to the Continental Divide in second gear, passing through the Eisenhower Tunnel (the van rolling smoothly now, like a bullet through a rifle barrel) and down the Western Slope.

He drove throughout the night with the moonlit mountains rising about him like cupped hands. April. Spring. But it was not just April or spring—he sensed dimly that it was much bigger than that. He had heard about the Age of Aquarius foolishness that was bandied about by people who wore headbands and spoke a little too quickly, but it was, yes, bigger than that, too.

George found that he was thinking of it as a matter of breath. Somehow, as he had stood entranced in the little valley just off Highway 6, the earth—the whole planet, perhaps the whole universe—had *breathed*. A long exhalation had ended, to be abruptly replaced with a sucking in, a filling, much as a man might awaken from a long sleep, rub his face, belch, gape, and smile broadly as he pulled in a big, jowly gulp of air from a world that could not possibly deal in loaded dice or stacked decks . . . because it would not fucking *dare*.

And so George was feeling good as he crossed into Utah, and he still felt good even when he realized that he had driven all night beneath a moon as big as a beach ball and as bright as a teen-age girl's smile, driven and been even further entranced. But even the bespelled had to eat, pee, and wash their faces, and so, with the dawn coming up over the Rockies as though the stars had all melted together and run down into the east, George pulled off the highway and onto the small streets of a small town named Cisco. A diner was open. Breakfast, it said.

And maybe because he was already thinking of a girl's smile, or because the mountains were with him, or because of something else, something indefinite, something that had caused him to come to this very diner at this very moment in this very mood of hope and strangeness that had so intermingled in his reborn soul that he was now ready to move beyond mountains and trees so as to see—really see—people, he walked into the diner, pushing through the door that rattled as badly as the van and was losing paint even worse, and looked up to see a young woman wiping the Formica counter.

She looked up to see him, too. Her eyes were the color of cornflowers, and she was slender and rather pretty; but what struck George was that he was absolutely certain that she was someone else who was feeling more than April, more than just the spring.

Hope? Fancy? Reality? Natil did not know. But she watched George walk across the worn linoleum floor and order breakfast and a cup of coffee, saw him smile at the young woman in a way that she had never before seen a human being smile, saw that same smile returned.

It might happen. It could *happen.*

And then she was being prodded awake, and she opened her eyes to the morning. Beside her, Omelda sat back and shrugged apologetically. Her eyes were cloudy. "Play something, Natil," she said. "Please. It's prime."

CHAPTER 6

Hypprux, to Natil's eyes, had not changed much in the
last hundred years. To be sure, the city had grown, and
there were new buildings, new faces, a city council with
a charter from the baron, and a bishop who was more
interested in hunting than in heresy; but Hypprux was
still a city, its streets were still unyielding and hostile to
an elven foot, and, within it, men were still hitting
women and women were still scolding men. There was
shouting, and human sorrow—beggars crouching in the
thin sunlight and thieves staying well out of it.

Natil and Omelda paid the toll at the north gate and
entered the city along the Street Gran Pont. Natil walked
with uncovered head, carrying her harp, ignoring the
stares drawn by her demeanor and clothing. Omelda shuffled along, head down, furrow-browed because it was
terce: the Divine Office went on.

"We will go to the square," said Natil. "I will play
there, and you can sit next to me and listen."

They made their way up the crowded street towards
the bridge that spanned the River Tordion. Here were
hawkers, vendors with pies, young boys selling circlets
of dried flowers. A man, standing on a box, was an-
nouncing that the Platonic Academy of Hypprux, under
the generous patronage of Damal a'Verne, baron of the
city, was sponsoring a series of lectures about the new
Italian humanism. A few onlookers seemed interested,
but a few others snorted and shouted that Italy was a den
of vice. Unperturbed, the man on the box replied that
Italy was also the seat of Rome and the papacy.

"See?" said one of the scoffers. "It just goes to
show."

The man on the box flushed. "You're talking about the

Holy Father!'' he said. "What are you, some kind of heretic?''

"You pig!'' said the scoffer. "You watch what you go calling people! I'll show you heresy! You're teaching humanism right under God's own nose!''

"Humanism belongs under God's nose!''

"Who's a heretic now?''

And Natil, a little pale because of the speed with which tempers had ignited, dragged Omelda away from the ensuing brawl. No, Hypprux had not changed in the least.

"What was that?'' said Omelda, blinking as though she had been asleep. Under the influence of the chant, she had at times only a vague idea of what was going on about her.

"One man called another a heretic,'' Natil sighed. "A serious charge, and a foolish one to make in public, even in a city without an Inquisition.''

"How did . . . how . . .'' Omelda batted ineffectually at her ears. "How did he know the . . . man was a heretic?''

"In truth, beloved, the man probably was not. He simply said the wrong thing. Just as is the case with most supposed heretics.''

The harper's statement appeared to cut through Omelda's mental fog. "Are you saying . . . there aren't any . . . heretics?''

Natil wished fervently that the subject of heresy had not come up, for the mere mention of the word tended to attract too much attention of exactly the wrong kind. "There are people who were never taught the religion they are expected to practice,'' she said, "and who are therefore condemned for not knowing what they were never told. There are people who think, who are condemned because they demand some privacy for their thoughts.'' She eyed Omelda. "Just as there are those who demand some silence. I myself will not call anyone heretical, because I myself do not know what heresy is.''

Omelda nodded, slipping back into vagueness. Natil had continued to demand that she learn to fight her own inner battles against the intrusive chant, but Omelda had continued to be uncooperative, absolutely refusing to sing unless Natil pressured her mercilessly, thereby making an already difficult task essentially impossible: she simply had no tools with which to work, and little hope of acquiring any.

But it was not all her fault, nor did Natil blame her. The harper could talk about consciousness and knowledge, but these were but words, and words alone could not communicate to Omelda the intentional and willing union with music, the flow of melody in one's own body, the release of art, like breath, into the world. And, in any case, words were not what Omelda needed. Omelda needed to do it. She needed to be it.

Now, Omelda rubbed at her ears again as Natil tossed two pennies into the toll basket at the bridge, but she sighed and dropped her head as she followed the harper over the river. "You're . . . right, Natil."

The water flowed beneath them, as polluted as it had ever been. "Right?"

"You can't keep . . . doing everything for me." Omelda shrugged, discouraged. "God can't help me. Why should I expect you to?"

To Natil, Omelda's words were a near-physical pain. She hugged her harp close as a cart loaded with bolts of linen rumbled by and nearly knocked her down, but her eyes were unseeing for a moment. "It is true, Omelda," she said. "I cannot do everything for you all the time. But does your God not reward those who work diligently toward a goal?"

Omelda blinked at her strange choice of words. *Your* God? But: "Yes . . . I think so," she said after a moment.

"Then you must work. And sometimes work is unpleasant." Natil remembered the words she had spoken, long ago, to another young woman who had been dealing with an internal and deeply personal torment. "It takes time. There is time."

Omelda nodded, but slowly, doubtfully. Natil read in her face that she did not believe in time any more than Miriam had.

But as they walked into the city square that was bounded by the cathedral and the chateau, pushed past the money changers who worked in defiance of the sabbath and the indulgence sellers who did a sparkling business because of it, Natil could not but wonder whether she herself still believed in time. She had promised to help Omelda, but promises, like everything else, took time to make good, and there did not seem to be much time left.

Her brow suddenly tight, she drew Omelda to a seat on the coping that surrounded a planter. The small trees within were in leaf, and on the branches were buds that promised blossoms.

The trees said it perfectly: Hypprux, like Adria, like all of Europe, was opening out to a warming spring, a spring that was as much of the human spirit as of the seasons. Regardless of any prudish objections or accusations of heresy, the Platonic Academy would give its lectures right under God's nose, or orthodoxy's nose, or, for that matter, the Inquisition's nose, and new translations and interpretations of Aristotle and others—printed on presses—were already taking their places beside handwritten copies of Averroës. Books, ideas: a burst of intellectualism like meadowflowers opening in the warming weather.

But there was no room for Elves on the bookshelf or in the meadow, for this was a human spring and a human summer, circumscribed by mortal concerns and limitations as much as these trees were confined by pavement and marble. And, still, it was all just words in the end, for Hypprux could have altered its shape to that of a Rome perfected, with the very best of Vitruvius's art dictating the placement of every house, the design of every wall, the flow of every fountain—and there would still be men striking women, women scolding men, and, in the hostile and unyielding streets, beggars in the sunlight and thieves out of it.

Natil's eyes were drawn to a woman across the way. She flickered in and out of sight among the people who took the air and showed off their fine clothes in the square this morning. With her ragged cloak wrapped about her two emaciated children, she hugged the base of a sunlit statue, searching for warmth.

Beggars. Her husband was dead, or perhaps he was in prison for saying the wrong thing at the wrong time. What mattered, though, what made Natil weep inwardly not only out of pity but because of her own loss of ability to intervene, were the stark facts, the facts that never changed: women and children, ragged clothes, and hungry mouths. This was the world she would leave, the world that had simply grown too big and too diseased for the Elves to heal.

"Natil?"

The harper came out of her thoughts. Omelda was watching her curiously, almost concerned; and a group of people were standing nearby, eyeing her harp, waiting expectantly.

With a forced smile and another look at the woman, Natil put her harp on her lap and played, letting the echoes of elven melody mingle with human tunes. A lifetime dedicated to music and harping—a lifetime beyond all human conception of a lifetime—allowed her to make music when she felt none, and Omelda, who had begun to show an odd talent for busking, worked the crowd as the harpstrings flensed her mind of plainchant.

Natil played for an hour, bought food for herself and Omelda, played again. But the oppression of the city burdened her more than usual this morning. This was no place for an Immortal: Elves needed open countryside and mountains, places that did not reek so much of humans and money and the slow eroding of mortal flesh. At times, she had to fight the urge to rise, throw her hood over her face, and make her way out of the city. Direction would not matter, destination would not matter: just out.

But she was not alone now, and so she stayed, for food for two took more coins than food for one. Omelda's cloak, too, was a disgrace, and a new one would take more coins still. And therefore, as the money clinked on the tables of the changers and in the coffers of the indulgence sellers, it clinked also into the cap that Omelda proffered to the burghers of Hypprux.

"Not bad," Omelda said at the end of the day. Shadows from the Chateau and the cathedral were lengthening, crowds were dwindling, and Natil's endurance was ebbing. "I did pretty well." She forced a tentative giggle. "And the Benedictines aren't even a mendicant order!"

Natil permitted herself a small laugh. But she saw that across the way, the woman and her children were wrapping their thin cloaks about themselves, preparing to look for shelter after a day of fruitless begging: they had neither Natil's music nor Omelda's talent to help them.

Natil watched. There was nothing the Elves could do anymore, and soon, very soon, there would be no Elves left to try. Perhaps there were none left already. But, her spirit unexpectedly growing defiant, she fished into the cap and pulled out, from among all the silver, the single gold coin she had earned that day: Baron Damal himself had given it to her. "You say that the Benedictines are not a mendicant order, Omelda?"

Omelda was almost offended. "Of course not. We're contemplatives. We work and we study and we pray." Abruptly, though, she looked at herself, at her cracked hands and her rough frock still stained with her blood. Natil could see memories of labor and flight and rape and exploitation flicker across her face. "At least we are when we're where we're supposed to be."

Natil handed her the coin. "Everything that happens," she said, "happens exactly as it should, when it should." She struggled to believe her own words. "We are here in Hypprux today because we are needed here." She nodded toward the woman and her children. "Give that woman this coin: she needs it more than we." Omelda stared at her for a moment, plainly puzzled, then shrugged and turned to perform the errand; but Natil caught her arm and held her for a moment more. "And look into her face when you do, beloved, for that is music also."

Another stare, and then Omelda left with the coin. Natil's eyes turned moist of a sudden, and she looked up at the late afternoon sky, wishing again that she might see a 747 crossing it.

"Well, you know, Father, it's daft."

Jacob Aldernacht blinked, shoved his spectacles up to the bridge of his nose, squinted at his son across the expanse of rosewood desk that dominated the main room of Gold Hall. It was after hours, and the clerks and accountants and money counters and secretaries had all gone home: he was alone with Francis. "Oho . . . we're saying that the old man is daft, are we?"

"That's not it at all." Even though he spoke only to Jacob, Francis uttered his words as though he were addressing multitudes. But he always spoke like that. Jacob occasionally surmised that his eldest son practiced in the marble-walled privy, where the acoustics—echoing and sonorous—could not but lend him the desired air of godhood. "Not at all."

"What, then?"

Francis sighed with great patience. "Furze is a cauldron . . ." He examined the metaphor as another man might savor a wine, nodded approvingly. ". . . yes, a cauldron of Inquisition. Paul Drego told us about it himself. Siegfried of Magdeburg has that city in the palm . . ." He clapped his hands together for emphasis. ". . . of his hand."

Jacob was used to Francis's theatrics, wondered sometimes whether there was anything to his son *besides* theatrics, but kept his expression noncommittal. "So?"

Francis folded his hands like a prelate addressing his flock. "The laws of confiscation, Father. Everything the heretic owns goes to the Inquisition and the Church, and any contracts he might have made are declared null and void." Francis leaned forward across the desk, his voice deepening with gravity. "Well, you know, it's completely non-acceptable, just non-acceptable, but they do it anyway." A nod like the keystone of an arch thudding into place. "It's put a damper on business all over Europe—it only takes one suspicious Inquisitor to bring down an entire firm." He sat back, snorted as loudly as his narrow face would allow.

If Jacob was unsettled at all, it was not because of his son's words, but rather because of his face. Marjorie's face. Francis had a little of Marjorie's face, but—poor Francis! poor Jacob!—he had too much of his father's heart.

"I wouldn't be at all surprised if that was the reason the Medici fell," Francis finished.

It was Jacob's turn to sigh. "I've told you over and over: Lorenzo's family went down because Piero was an idiot. He let the silver exchange rate get out of hand. I warned him, but he over extended himself. Just like that idiot Genoese fellow. Did you hear? They brought him back from his last voyage in chains. He over extended himself. But that doesn't make him a heretic, even to Ferdinand and Isabella." He leaned forward, stabbed at the air with a finger: his own theatrics. "And Paul Drego isn't a heretic either."

"He doesn't have to be. I . . ." Francis broke off, looked about the room. There was no one there, but he nonetheless leaned forward and dropped his voice. "I really think, Father, that half the heretics they sentence aren't really heretics."

"Half?" Jacob chuckled dryly. "A good nine-tenths, if you ask me." He poked at the elegant but unfigured candle holder on the desk. Another family with the wealth of the Aldernachts would have bought themselves a patent of nobility by now, would have had their crest engraved on everything that did not move. But Jacob was a businessman. He had nurtured his investments and his fortune with his own sweat—indeed, in the beginning he had carried much of it on his own back! He was proud of that, he was proud of his plain candleholders: he could hold his head up higher than those asslicking Fuggers!

But he could see Francis's point. Furze was a risky business indeed. If even one member of the wool cooperative was found to be heretical, the Inquisition could take everything. Jacob knew that, knew that it was perhaps unwise to link the fortunes of a family whose motto was *In the name of God and profit* with the uncertainties of a struggling town.

But there were two parts to that motto, and though Francis knew profit, he inevitably overlooked God. Jacob would never have admitted to his son that God had anything whatsoever to do with his negotiations with the wool cooperative, and, in fact, he was not sure that he would have admitted it to himself, either. He would, however, go so far as to confess that a man who, after driving his wife away, had subsequently raised one bloodless profiteer, one mercenary, and one nitwit, could do much worse than lend a little money to a group of men willing to work hard and pull their city out of an economic swamp.

Confiscation was a possibility, but Jacob doubted that any confiscation ordered by the Inquisition could affect the Aldernacht business save in the most trivial ways. Perhaps the loan to the tobacco growers in Spain would fall through. A few investors might be frightened off. But little else.

No, it was much more likely that Jacob's eldest son—who was absolutely sure that 1) upon his father's death, he was going to exercise absolute control over the family business, and 2) said death would be (dammit, *had* to be) coming soon—did not want even a single florin squandered on ridiculous ventures. Save, perhaps, tobacco growers in Spain.

Jacob steepled his fingers, peered at Francis through his spectacles. Beneath his feet was the skin of a large lion, a fitting rug for the desk of the Aldernachts, and on an impulse, Jacob kicked off his shoes and burrowed his toes into the warm fur, smiling in a manner guaranteed to disturb Francis. *I'm not dead yet, you young whelp. My heart isn't what it used to be, and my pecker might kill me yet, but I'm no corpse. You'll just have to wait.*

But, inwardly, he was shaking his head. Francis: so much like him, so little like Marjorie. But then, he had driven Marjorie away: she had had no influence in the growth of her children. Fitting, then, that Jacob be at last confronted by his own reflection, a reflection determined to devour him.

"We'll go to Furze next week, Francis," he said slowly, surprised to find a catch in his voice. Marjorie had been gone for almost thirty years: odd that her absence should still affect him so. But though he could not clear his mind of the past, he could clear his throat of tightness, and he swallowed and settled his spectacles. "You'll be able to see for yourself."

From Hypprux, Natil and Omelda made their way south across the vast flax fields that surrounded the town and made it wealthy. The road was a narrow ribbon of dirt, the close-sown flax crowding up against it. Above them, the sky pressed down like a burnished plate, squeezing the travelers between heaven and earth.

This was the way Natil traveled, the way she had traveled for the last century: slowly, on foot, in the open. But while she herself had no complaints about such a life, she knew that the terrible openness of the plains and the nights spent far from any shelter save trees and perhaps a ditch were a constant torment for her companion. Sleeping beneath the sky, playing and busking in roofless plazas and squares: what little security Omelda had once possessed was now gone, and Natil could give her noth-

ing with which to replace it save the wanderings and uncertainties of a harper's life.

They stopped to eat in the meager shade of some neglected trees. What had once been a stream wandered
nearby, a muddy ditch whose water had probably been
diverted for irrigation. Omelda took her food silently, but
though the dullness in her eyes told Natil that it was sext
more surely than any distant tolling of cathedral bells,
the young woman did not ask for aid. She seemed resigned, discouraged, depressed. She could not learn what
Natil presumed to teach.

Presumed to teach. The harper winced. How could she
presume to teach anything when her own encroaching
humanity made her less than sure of it herself?

She glanced at the sky, a gesture that had become for
her as habitual as Omelda's sweeps at her ears . . . and
just as fruitless: she was looking for something that would
not exist for five hundred years. She was looking for a
glitter. She was looking for a 747. She was looking for
hope.

Omelda spoke. "Where are we . . . really going, Natil?"

Natil felt herself squirm inwardly. What had she hoped
to do? Had she really thought that there was sufficient
time left to her to do anything? It was not a matter of
technique: it was a matter of living. What had made her
think that, fading as she was, she could teach Omelda
how to live?

"I . . . have business in Malvern Forest," she said.

Omelda nodded. "Does . . . it include me?"

Natil kept her eyes averted.

Omelda nodded, sighed. "I can't learn what . . . you
want me to learn. I know that now."

The harper found herself unwilling to admit defeat.
"You could learn, given time."

Omelda fixed her with dark, clouded, disbelieving
eyes. "But there isn't time, is there?"

Natil was fighting with herself. She wanted to say that
Omelda was right. She wanted to give up, to fade, to
stop this endless fool's errand of trying to help a world
that was far too damaged for any kind of mending.

But a few feet away, a girl with demons in her head
was sitting beneath a scrubby tree, and five hundred years

ahead and two thousand leagues to the west, George Morrison and a woman as yet unnamed were standing in a run-down diner. Natil was seeing the present, the dying, but she—perhaps, maybe, it could be so—was also seeing the future . . . and the living.

She was not seeing the past and the pain and the despair: she was seeing the present and the future. She was seeing faces.

And she caught her breath. Because she was suddenly unwilling to fade.

For a long time, she sat silently, examining Omelda. Finally: "Do you want to go back to your convent?"

Omelda's eyes had closed, and she had slumped back against the tree. There was nothing above her but a few bare branches and the endless sky. There was nothing ahead of her save . . .

"It was safe there," she whispered, "but I'd go mad if I went back. I don't want to go mad."

Natil nodded. "Then we must go elsewhere." She rose, picked up her harp and her bundle.

Omelda opened her eyes. "Where?"

Natil pointed to the east. No 747 confirmed her course, but she knew it nonetheless. "Ypris is in this direction. It is a young town, recently rebuilt. There is wealth there. We will find you a position."

Omelda dropped her head. "Natil . . ."

Natil took her hand, pulled her to her feet. "I said that I would teach you. It will take time, and you will have to learn to endure your voices for a while, but I promise you . . ." She felt an inner tremor, pressed on in defiance of it. "I promise you that I will be with you until you are well. I might have to travel, for I must earn my bread; and I might have to leave you at times, but I promise that I will always be back . . . until . . ." She squeezed Omelda's hand. ". . . until your voices are stilled."

She led Omelda to a crossroads. They turned east, towards Ypris.

CHAPTER 7

Albrecht had seen Rome. They could have Rome.

They, in this case, were the cardinals and the Curia, the sycophants and hangers-on and assorted parasitical little (try as he might, Albrecht found his generosity failing him here) human beings who presently governed Holy Church. Michelangelo might carve stone until his strong Florentine arms dropped off, and Raphael could paint until the colors blinded him without altering in the slightest the fact that Rome was a smelly city full of people so concerned with gold and glory and worldly matters that they had done much to shatter the faith of an entire continent.

And Bishop Albrecht, riding the trail that switch-backed up the slopes of Shrinerock Mountain, crossed himself, because his thoughts really were getting rather out of hand. He stopped his horse, gave the thoughts and the memories a good shove off the edge of the cliff, and listened, satisfied, as they were dashed to bits on the rocks far below.

Mattias, his chief clerk, reined in also, motioned for the other clerks and notaries to go on ahead. "A fine day, Excellency." His voice was cheerful amid the passing clop of hooves and swish of tails.

"A godly day, Mattias," said Albrecht. And it was, too. The grasslands, though rank and overgrown—all that was left of formerly rich pastures—swept out towards the north, green with the arrival of spring. Even Furze looked promising from this altitude. The cathedral *could* have been progressing, the economy *might* have been improving. From a distance, anything was possible, and it was such a warm, pleasant day that Albrecht was willing to believe the best. "A godly day," he repeated.

With a nod to Mattias, he tugged at the reins, and his

horse took him up the road toward Shrinerock Abbey.
The landscape below grew greener with distance, Furze
grew smaller, and, oddly enough, Saint Adrian's Spring,
though it bubbled out of a cave near the base of the
mountain, grew louder and louder, until its sound at-
tained the strength and constant presence of a guardian
spirit.

Albrecht, as was customary, had given the abbey formal notice of this annual visitation and examination several weeks ago. Dame Agnes, the abbess, ran such an
exemplary convent that Albrecht had never yet had cause
to register anything about Shrinerock save *omnia bene,*
but one of the duties of a bishop was to visit the women's
religious houses within his diocese; and certainly Shrinerock, well run and placid, was an exceedingly pleasant
duty in a cure beset by financial ruin and an arrogant
Inquisition.

Dame Agnes was pious, efficient, and thrifty; and she
and her ladies invariably approached visitation—which,
in other houses, was frequently a rather frightful ordeal—
with cheerful equanimity. But when the wooden gates did
not swing open at the approach of the bishop and his
party, when Dame Agnes herself did not step out of her
abbey, crosier in hand, all ready to escort him to the
chapel; when, instead, the elderly porter assigned to the
gate stared at him from the loophole with an expression
of consternation and bewilderment on his gnarled face,
and he heard a woman's voice shouting:

*"O my God! It's Bishop Albrecht! Someone run and
call Dame Agnes!"*

. . . Albrecht realized that something was wrong.

This was most strange: along with the other papers he
had brought, Albrecht had a receipt from Dame Agnes
herself, written in her own hand, in the very best Latin,
and sealed with the abbey signet, acknowledging his notice to her of today's visitation. He had assumed that all
would be ready for his arrival. Such had always been the
case.

Until now.

Still bewildered, though apparently concluding that it
would not do to leave the Bishop of Furze waiting in
front of a closed gate, the porter opened the heavy
wooden doors, giving Albrecht and his men entrance into

a clean, simple courtyard with neat herb gardens. Nothing amiss here, certainly, and from what Albrecht could see as he waited, still astride his horse, the entire abbey exhibited the same care and attention and good housekeeping as the gardens.

Odd. Very odd.

Dame Agnes—plainly out of breath—arrived in a few minutes. A novice—arriving from an opposite door—brought the crosier and thrust it into her hands. The nuns—exchanging many a look of something close to terror—assembled hurriedly. The abbey church was hastily prepared for the customary high mass, and the chaplain knelt at the door to kiss the episcopal ring.

Albrecht did his best to act as though nothing were amiss, and he managed to celebrate mass with dignity and attention. But his thoughts were running slightly ahead of him, and he unrobed afterward with the fervent hope that the upcoming meeting in the big hall of the castle that served as a chapter house would explain matters.

But, no: worse and worse. Dame Agnes had apparently prepared no formal receipt of the summons to visitation, and evidently had to send her prioress and subprioress to rummage through chests and files for the documents relating to her election and installation, the *status domus,* and the charter granted to the abbey by Baron Martin delMari when he turned the ruined castle over to the Benedictines.

The parchments arrived. Albrecht took them from the prioress and subprioress and nodded his thanks, disliking intensely the fact that Agnes was crimson with embarrassment and her nuns, from the obedientiaries down to the novices, were obviously frightened. Siegfried, he thought, might appreciate such reactions, likewise the members of the Curia, but not Albrecht of Hamburg.

Troubled, therefore, Albrecht laid the requested documents aside and said that he was sorry that he had inconvenienced the abbey in such a manner, and that he would defer the personal examination of the nuns until the next day.

"Dame Agnes," he finished. "Would you dismiss the good sisters?"

Agnes nodded. She signed to the nuns that they could leave.

Albrecht cleared his throat. "And please remain behind after they have left, Dame Agnes. We obviously have to talk." With a glance at Mattias. "Alone."

The nuns filed out of the hall. Mattias, with a knowing air, herded the clerks and notaries after them. Agnes stood silently in her place, hands clenched within her sleeves, and the door of the hall closed with a sound not dissimilar to the shutting of a tomb.

Albrecht passed a hand over his face. This was not at all the impression he wanted to create. But, "My dear Dame Agnes," he said, "I think you need to explain some things."

Dame Agnes, though, was so mortified that she knelt before him and repeated the *Confiteor* in fright. Albrecht, just as mortified, raised her to her feet, led her to a chair, and made her sit down.

He hobbled over to another seat as Agnes produced a small handkerchief and dabbed at her temples. "Forgive us, Excellency," she said. "This is so . . . unusual. This is just so utterly . . . unusual."

Albrecht, who could think of nothing particularly unusual about anything save the nuns' reactions, nodded slowly. "I was under the impression that you'd be expecting me."

"Well, yes," said Agnes. "But—by Our Lady!—not so soon after, you see."

"After?"

Dame Agnes dropped her handkerchief to her lap. "After Brother Siegfried."

Siegfried? Albrecht flushed a little, cleared his throat. "Dame Agnes, I beg you: start from the beginning."

A long pause. Agnes stared at Albrecht as though she stood accused of some crime she knew nothing about save that she had obviously committed it because she would not otherwise be accused of it. "Siegfried arrived last week. We'd already received your notice of visitation, and Siegfried had sent a messenger the day before, so we welcomed him . . ." She paused again. Albrecht was staring carefully at his thumbs, trying very hard not to form any opinion in particular. "I hope that was all right," she said quickly.

It certainly was not, but, "Of course it was all right," Albrecht said just as quickly. "Pray, continue."

Agnes put the handkerchief away, having collected what scraps of her composure she could find. "He celebrated mass," she said, "and then we went into chapter. One of his assistants—I think it was Giovanni—preached a sermon, and then Siegfried asked for the usual documents. He was Your Excellency's deputy . . ."

Deputy! Albrecht fought to keep his eyebrows from lifting towards his gray hair.

". . . and so we brought them. We had them ready, of course, since we expected him." Agnes blushed. "I mean, you." She blushed harder. "I mean, Your Excellency."

Albrecht nodded. "Of course," he said faintly.

Dame Agnes went on to explain that, after inspecting the documents, Siegfried had examined the nuns one by one. The usual form: *detecta, comperta,* a battery of clerks taking everything down on the fly, and a final summoning of the convent to the chapter house for injunctions.

As Albrecht knew already, there really had not been much to find out or to make judgments upon. *Omnia bene,* as usual. But although the bishop felt a certain satisfaction that the virtuous nuns had, by simply being themselves, thwarted Siegfried's plans—whatever they were—he was nonetheless dizzy with the thought that the Inquisitor of Furze had so blatantly pre-empted episcopal authority, and had, bald faced, gone ahead with a visitation and examination to which he had no right, official or unofficial.

But had not that sort of thing been going on for a long time? Furze was a poor city, and Albrecht, not so much interested in money as in hearts and souls, had insisted upon taking care of his cure on a personal level—talking with housewives, looking into shops, pressing an occasional coin even into the hands of the professional beggars who nightly shed their infirmities in the Miracle Quarter—running the business of the local curia simply, with a gentle hand and the good advice of Mattias. Siegfried's Inquisition, however, large enough to begin with, had grown substantially in the course of each of the twenty years of its existence, assuming more and more power and authority. It was a huge bureaucracy now, almost a shadow bishopric, with more clerks and notaries and secretaries and minor officials and informers and judges and beadles than Albrecht could ever imagine the use of.

A shadow bishopric. The thought was a chilling one. And now Siegfried, independent as he was of any control, sacred or secular, was even making his own visitations, as though he were Furze's bishop as well as its virtual master.

Albrecht decided not to discomfit Agnes any more. "Well," he said when the abbess was finished with her tale, "this is fine. You know, Siegfried has not had time to give me his report. Why don't you just tell me what he found?"

"Well, Excellency, he didn't really find much. Or so we thought . . . before Your Excellency showed up. Then . . ." Agnes shifted in her chair. "Then—by Our Lady!— we could only surmise that he must have found something terrible."

"My dear Dame Agnes! What could he possibly have found?"

Agnes's old eyes were stricken. There was, after all, a hideous potential inherent in any visit of an Inquisitor. "Heresy?"

Albrecht was angry. Heresy? In Shrinerock? The nerve of that Dominican! *Domini canes,* indeed! But the conversation had suddenly taken on a darker tone, almost black, and he put on his best look of surprise so as to disarm the abbess' fears. "Oh, dear, not to my knowledge. I'm sure he didn't find anything. I came up myself to . . . to . . ."

Nothing came to mind. Agnes was looking at him, waiting, still frightened. The accusation of heresy was a terrible one, made worse by the fact that it could arise seemingly out of nothing: a chance remark, a wrong word, an incautious expression of a thought . . .

Albrecht was suddenly wondering about Siegfried and the Inquisition. The Dominican had intruded into episcopal business, and that was bad enough; but now he was casting his inquisitorial nets much wider than was right. There was about as much chance of Shrinerock Abbey harboring heresy as there was of it taking in stray prostitutes.

Agnes was still waiting, and every moment that Albrecht hesitated obviously added to her fear. *I'm a very poor liar,* he thought. *No wonder I didn't fit in Rome.*

". . . to share a glass of wine with the most virtuous women of Adria," he said finally.

Agnes stared, then laughed. The darkness evaporated. "By Our Lady, Your Excellency is teasing us!"

"Not at all." No, it was Albrecht who had been teased. By Siegfried, and in earnest. What was going on? Could he even ask about it? He was a bishop after all: surely that counted for something, even in the poorest diocese of Europe.

Oh, yes, he reminded himself, he could ask anything he wanted, but he would receive an answer only when the Inquisition felt like giving him one.

Albrecht forced a smile. "Tell me, though: did anything come up when Siegfried was here?"

"By Our Lady," said Agnes, "there's not much that happens up here. We all have our little routines, and by God's grace life just goes on. The only scandal in the last twenty years was that one girl running off two summers ago."

"That was . . ." Albrecht remembered the incident. He had sent out the sheriffs, sent out the beadles, made inquiries, but the girl had disappeared. "That was . . . Omelda, was it not?"

"You have a good memory, Your Excellency."

Albrecht shrugged modestly. "It makes up for my bad leg." He thumped the recalcitrant limb, chuckled. "Did she ever turn up?"

"No." Agnes shook her head. "And we all still miss her. Such a sweet woman. A little too placid at times, but a good heart. What got into her, we just don't know. She just turned . . . restless." And Agnes sang softly, her old, tranquil nun's voice belying her words:

"Heu misella!
Nichil est deterius tali vita
Cum enim sim petulans et lasciva."

Albrecht blinked. Where on earth had someone like Agnes heard such a thing? But he reminded himself that Agnes was a woman as well as a nun. Doubtless, she had experienced her own temptation and doubt, and her understanding of both had brought compassion.

"It's just a guess," she said. "We don't really know.

Omelda was an oblate—her father brought her to us when she was three—and sometimes it's so hard to blame them for trying to run away. Even grown women mistakenly choose the veil . . . and spend the rest of their lives regretting a choice that can't be unmade. How can one even think to decide for someone else . . . and a child at that?''

Albrecht nodded. The abuse, though, was widespread. "She arrived well before you became abbess, though.''

"Indeed,'' said Agnes. "We haven't taken oblates since before I was elected. Omelda was the last.'' She shook her head sadly. "Her father was noble, and he had connections. He offered us money . . . though I daresay it was considerably less money than he would have spent on Omelda's dowry, which I think was the reason she wound up here. In any case, we needed what he offered. The roof had fallen in just then, the chapel and storehouse both needed repair, and poor Sister Thomasine didn't even have a kirtle to call her own! And so we took her.''

Albrecht's curiosity had been aroused. "Who was her father?''

Agnes colored again. "I . . . ah . . . can't really say, Your Excellency. Secrecy was one of the terms of Omelda's being given over, a term to which I'm bound. But he was a . . .'' She glanced at the window meaningfully. ". . . a local baron.''

Albrecht followed her eyes. After a moment, he rose, tottered for a moment because his knee decided to be difficult, but managed to reach the sill without mishap. Below, across a deep gulf of clear air, was Furze: tiny, distant, sparkling. Even from this far away Albrecht could see the fine city house of Baron David a'Freux. David had inherited it—along with the title and the city—from his father, and had been taxing the townsfolk as much as he could in order to add to it and furnish it in what he considered to be an adequately opulent manner.

"Oh," he said. "Well, I won't pry then. And as for Siegfried: I'm sure he won't . . . ah . . . pry either.''

"She was such a sweet thing,'' said Agnes. "A good singer. She might have taken charge of the choir, had she stayed.'' She fidgeted with her sleeves like a grandmother. "Oh, Your Excellency, apostasy is a terrible thing, but—by Our Lady!—I'd take Omelda back in a heartbeat. No penance, no humiliation . . . no kneeling before the convent gate for that one. I'd just take her back—we'd all take her back—and we'd go on from there.''

Albrecht was smiling into the open air. Yes, they could have Rome. ''You are a holy woman, Dame Agnes.''

''Oh! Your Excellency!''

''And a merciful one.''

''Jesus was merciful,'' said Agnes, as though the point were obvious. ''How can any of us be otherwise?''

Albrecht nodded. ''Indeed. I wonder.'' He was still looking down at Furze, and his face turned somber of a sudden, for his gaze had fastened upon the House of God.

Her name was Sally. Sally Hennock. She worked the graveyard shift at the diner, and though it was early for most people—too early for anyone save the bespelled and the visionary to be interested in breakfast—it was late for Sally. But that was all right, because it was late for George, too.

At first they talked awkwardly about commonplaces. Who they were. Where they were from. Where they were going. George ate, listening more than he spoke, appreciating for the first time that listening, simply listening, could be a pleasure, that even the stupid and clumsy words of strangers could flow like music when they shared simple human concerns and sympathies. Sally, though, spoke as though no one had listened to her before. At first she attempted the illusion of work by filling salt and pepper shakers and wiping things that did not need wiping, but after a few minutes, her need overcame her, and she just leaned on the counter with slender arms, her small hands splayed out against the green Formica while she talked.

And so they told their stories in their own ways: through silence, through words. George was from Denver, was going . . . somewhere. Sally was from Montana, was going nowhere. Her ex-boyfriend had been a welder, a boomer who had brought her to this part of Utah because of the rising interest in oil shale. But the projects had died early on, the jobs and the money had never materialized, and Sally's lover had grown discouraged and restless. And then she had returned one evening to their small apartment . . .

George spoke for the first time in twenty minutes. "He'd taken everything, right?"

Sally nodded. "The cash, the checks, cleaned out the accounts . . . what there was in them." She smiled clumsily, almost apologetically. "At least he left my stuff."

"So you had to stay."

That smile again, the one that bordered on nerdy, but which held also an echo of what had brought George to the mountains . . . and then through them. "No money and no car." She straightened up, pushed back her dark hair with both hands. "I still don't have a car. Can't afford one." Again, the smile. "I'm stuck."

The world this morning (yes, there was the dawn light now, as pink and gold as a christening) was almost too new, almost too wonderful. George had driven all night by starlight and by moonlight, had stood enraptured by the mountains, had, bending to touch the earth, felt more than the earth. All of a sudden, veils had been torn away from existence, and he was seeing miracle and wonder in everything: mountains, dawn, desert . . . even in the spoon with which he stirred his coffee.

He looked up at Sally's soft face and saw the morning written there as clearly as in the sky. It was a spell. It was abnormal. It was strange, weird, fantastic . . . and George was going under quickly, because he wanted to go under. "You know," was all he found to say, "you're absolutely beautiful."

From another man the compliment would have been a come-on, an opening salvo in the battle to get her pants off and her lithe little body between the sheets. But bed was far from George's mind: he had said that Sally was beautiful because it was true. He could also have said with equal truth and sincerity that the drive that night had been beautiful, that the mountains had been beautiful, or that (Christ!) even the goddam fucking Oneida stainless steel teaspoon was beautiful. And Sally appeared to understand that, for she nodded after a moment. "Thanks," she said. "So are you."

"Have you . . ." A quick look around. But no, the diner was empty. No one would hear his madness. "Have you got any idea . . ." He dropped his voice, almost lost his nerve, but he said it. "Have you got any idea what's happening?"

There was a sudden flare of hope in her face, like sunrise, like spring.

"I mean, to us."

Slowly, softly, her human clumsiness faltering suddenly and dropping like the rest of the veils, she shook her head. "No," she said. "But I want more of it."

She looked out the window. The desert was shimmering in the sunrise, and George saw in that shimmer a sense of light that was building—he could think of no other way of putting it—from *within*, from within him, as though a subtle radiance were percolating through the unused corners of his mind.

"I remember days like this in Montana," Sally was saying. "I'd get up in the morning, and everything would seem just right. And then Mom would drive me to school, and we'd pass the wheat fields." She glanced at him. Was this some city boy who thought wheat was something one bought at the health food store? But George heard her thought—he did not realize until later how distinctly he had heard it—and he laughed, and so she went on. "Winter wheat. It'd just be coming up, just speckles of green. And that seemed just right, too. Like it was always right there, like you could . . ." She blushed. "Aw . . ."

"No. No, go on."

She giggled, embarrassed and happy both. "This is crazy."

George felt the same way. "I don't care. I like it. I want more of it." He wrapped his hands about his coffee cup. "Tell me about the wheat."

"It was . . ." She straightened, looked off as though she could see the wheat there, growing and growing and going on across the Montana plains, continuing even up past the Canadian border. "It was like if you got scared or worried, you could . . . like . . . wrap it around yourself like a shawl. Put it on like a coat. And then you'd be safe. Because the wheat was always there, and it always would be." She was blushing furiously by now, but she was smiling, too. "Sometimes . . . sometimes I wanted to *be* the wheat. And just be there like that." She shrugged, looked at the damp rag in her hand, gave the counter a swipe. "Then I got into school, and then high school, and I got crazy like a stupid kid." Her face turned tragic, poignant. "I forgot about the wheat."

"The wheat's still there."

"Yeah . . ." She was suddenly wistful. "It's still there." She glanced at the empty diner. "And I'm here."

"I . . ." George's turn. "I stared at the mountains most of yesterday. I was up there, alone, and it just seemed right. And, you know, I . . . I took them with me when I left, because they're inside me now. Wherever I go. And it still seems right. Is that crazy or what?"

Sally shrugged. "No crazier than anything else."

"Well, you've still got your wheat with you. Wherever you go."

Struck by his words, she stood straight, her face as full of wonder as if she had been staring after a handsome man. "Yeah . . . I do."

George smiled, sheepish of a sudden. "Be the wheat."

Her lips moved silently: *Be the wheat.* "I never thought of it that way."

"Crazy, huh?"

"Yeah," she said. "Bats."

"But good bats."

She nodded, still staring. "Good bats."

She turned to him then, and all the scars of abandonment and disappointment fell away from her for a moment; and in that interstice of unabashed vulnerability, George understood—and knew that she understood also—that this meeting of two who were seeing, feeling, and touching an ineffable but immanent knowledge with tips of wonder was important, important above all else. Critical. Essential.

Shaking, Sally licked her lips, fought for words. "I'm . . . off in another five minutes," she whispered. "What are you doing after breakfast?"

George shrugged. It seemed silly that, on a morning fraught with such consequence, he could think of nothing that he actually had to do. But perhaps, he thought, that was the point.

He laughed a little, shrugged, peered once again at the coffee spoon as though it held everything . . . and found that it did. "Anything . . . anything you want," he said.

CHAPTER 8

The business of Ypris was wool.

Even from far away, one could tell that. There was wool in the air, wool on the ground, wool in the earth. The dyers' vats were fragrant, and the slap and whiffle of the tenters' fields could be heard a mile away, as could the rhythmic tramp of the fulling hammers. The flocks of sheep themselves—fluffy and creamy white as pastry filling, their fleece uncut this early in the season—were spread widely across pastures that stretched all the way from the Bergren River to Malvern Forest.

Wool. Hypprux had its linen, but Ypris had its wool, and, sturdy burghers that they were, its citizens seemed bent upon biting their collective thumb at their northern rival. Linen might be used here for shrouds and sheets and shifts, but everything else was wool. Wool cloaks. Wool stockings. Wool shirts. Wool caps. Wool jackets and hats and slippers. Wool dressing gowns. Fine wool veils for the ladies. Thick wool doublets for the men. Wool carpets and hangings and tapestries of every kind.

A hundred years before, Ypris had been razed, but within fifty years, the people had returned in trickles and in streams, had rebuilt their city upon foundations of wool, and, in the end, had not only bought, outright, a charter and independence from the Baron of Hypprux in exchange for a cash payment rumored to be close to what it had cost Charles VIII to finance the Italian Wars, but had also ensured that their coffers would be speedily replenished, for Ypris had become synonymous with wool for most of Adria—indeed, for much of Europe.

And the Aldernacht family had become synonymous with Ypris.

The spire of Gold Hall, rising, appropriately, straight up from the center of town, completely overshadowed the

church tower; and as Natil and Omelda entered the north
gate, they could see that its pinnacle glittered with the
brightness of solid gold. Everything was new in Ypris,
and the two women blinked at the clean stone walls, the
street cobbles round and even as eggs, the tiled roofs of
many colors. The Yprisians—and the Aldernachts—had
deliberately set out to best Hypprux, and they had succeeded, for the latter, though untouched by robber band
or political conquest for five hundred years, seemed bent
beneath its age, while Ypris, in contrast, was bright,
shiny, young: its most ancient buildings had seen but two
generations, and the great majority had gone up in the
last ten years.

But if Hypprux was old, then what was Natil? For a
moment, despite her determined promise to Omelda, despite her new-found unwillingness to fade, all the sorrow
and despair came back to the harper. Men and women
were young and growing. The Elves were old and fading,
had already faded. Natil wanted desperately to join them.

But she dashed the thoughts from her as she dashed the
sudden mist from her eyes. Humanity was young, but there
was elven blood—minute and sleeping—even among this
welter of mortal flesh, and someday that blood might take
fire from the youth and the growth that had sustained it,
ignite with alchemical fervor, and, perhaps, awaken.

Someday. Perhaps. Natil had come to be convinced
that she was beginning to see that someday, that perhaps.

"What do you usually do to find a position, Omelda?"
she said.

Omelda was still more than a little dubious of Natil's
plans. "I knock on doors." She shrugged. "Nearly everybody needs someone for something. But . . ." She
looked depressed. Here in a city that hummed along like
a well-regulated loom, unemployment or idleness seemed
out of place, job hunting a fool's errand. "Can't I just
stay with you?"

Natil shook her head. "You cannot live in the open,
and therefore you must have a roof. I do not need a roof,
nor do I want one, but I will make sure that I stay near
you . . . and teach you."

Simple words, complex task. She still wondered how
she would accomplish it.

Omelda looked at the sky, winced involuntarily at the bigness of the blue vault. "I'd make a bad shepherdess."

Natil touched her shoulder. "Peace, beloved. We will find you something in a house."

As usual, they headed for the square. Even if Omelda found work, Natil would still need money; and if Omelda failed, Natil would need money all the more.

It was a market day, and the square was crowded with shops and stalls, each profession and craft grouped together as was the custom. Over at one edge were the horse sellers. At the other, the bakers' fires sent up a haze of smoke. In the center, dominating all, the weavers and the fullers presided, while, about them, the butchers carved, the leather workers squinted at their labor, the carpenters and the furniture builders and the instrument makers eyed one another suspiciously.

One of the latter, though, was also eyeing Natil, or rather, her harp. He was a thin, stoop-shouldered man whose gray hair and gray beard and weathered expression made his years seem much greater than she sensed they actually were; and his stall seemed rather an aggregation of the products of all the trades immediately about him, for hung on the walls and suspended from the ceiling and standing on the floor was an assortment of lutes, harps, chairs, cabinets, recorders, hardwood chests, tables, and even a number of traveler's staves. Unfortunately, to Natil's eye, most everything displayed seemed to resemble more or less the thick-walled, iron-bound strongbox that sat in the middle of the shop like a square toad. Instinctively, she clutched her slender harp to her side.

"You want to play while I look?" Omelda was listless.

Natil pulled her gaze away from the man in the shop. "I think that would be best." She looked up at Gold Hall, which bounded one entire side of the market square. Its spire rose up above everything, was visible anywhere one went in the city or the surrounding countryside. "It must be very hard to become lost in Ypris. You will be able to find me easily enough."

Omelda, listless and resigned, nodded. "I'll be back," she said, and she turned away.

Natil looked after her for a moment. "I know you will, beloved," she said softly. "And I will be here for you."

Her words, hearkening back as they did to the old ways,

the ways of help and healing, made her feel light, elven, and for a moment, she wondered whether she had caught a glimpse of starlight out of the corner of her inner eye. But starlight lay not in the present, but in the future—with George, and with Sally who wanted to be the wheat.

Another hopeful thought. She lingered over it, smiling faintly, and then she found a place to sit, set out her cap, and began to play the wheat, weaving into her bronze strings a sense of green shoots climbing out of the ground, of yellow fields ripe and ready for the scythe, of (her human dreams bespelling her now as much as reality was bespelling George and Sally) blue Colorado sky and pines and aspens. Her fingers moved on their own, her mind guiding them only with the thought of the desired evocation, and the melody grew with the wheat and arched as widely as the sky.

She was deep into the web and texture of the music when a voice—derisive, almost accusing—spoke up beside her:

"Are you using that shit?"

As though she had been backhanded, Natil started and almost dropped her harp. The world of Ypris and commerce came back, the market square came back, the cap, now dotted with appreciative coins, came back . . . and so did the strange man who appeared to be a combination of carpenter, furniture builder, and instrument maker. He was standing at her elbow, and his pale eyes were peering at her harp as though he wanted nothing more than to snatch it out of her hands and take it apart.

"Well?" he said. "Are you?"

Shaking, Natil swallowed, struggled to regain her composure and courtesy. "I am afraid I do not under—"

"Those strings of yours." The pale eyes glared at her for a moment, turned again to her harp. "They're bronze."

"Ah . . . indeed . . ."

The man shook his head. "Brass. Got to be brass. Haven't you looked at real Irish harps? They use brass. Brass all the way: top to bottom. Their tone is supposed to be . . ." He spread his arms, flapping them out like wings. ". . . melting. Melting." He nodded, glared again at her instrument. "That's not a real Irish harp you've got there."

"That . . . is true," said Natil. She plucked a chord, letting its sound ripple out like the chiming of bells.

"That's just it," said the man. "You have to study these things. Trial and error is all well and good, but for building real instruments, you just can't beat a background in boxes. Now, if you'd talked to me before you built that thing, you'd have known that you should have strung it with brass. You should have made the forepillar shorter. You should have made the soundbox bigger." He nodded toward his shop. "Now, over there is a real Irish harp."

Natil noted again the similarity between his strongbox and his harps . . . none of which, strongbox included, looked particularly Irish. "As you wish, sir."

"I could have built you a better one," he said. "*I* don't work by trial and error." His pale eyes swooped down on Natil's harp again. "I've got . . ." He peered at the strings, shook his head disdainfully. ". . . equations."

Natil was still shaking from the brutality with which she had been torn from her music. "Equations."

"Yup." He nodded vigorously. "I can build anything. And I can build it right the first time. Equations. It's all equations."

"All right, Jahn," said someone else. For the first time, Natil noticed that the strange instrument maker had a companion. "That's enough," he was saying. "I want to hear her play some more."

"I can't see why, Mister Josef. She's playing it all wrong."

Mister Josef was a flaxen-haired man who seemed both a little too young for his face and a little too old for his clothes, for although he was obviously in his mid-thirties, he was dressed foppishly in the Italian style, and his hair was elaborately curled. In one hand he carried one of the strongbox lutes, from his belt hung a little leather book with a silver clasp, and the feather in his scarlet cap waved back and forth as he smiled and nodded at Natil. "Jahn is probably right," he said. "He's always right about things like that. He's studied all about how real harpers play. But . . ." His hand flew to his heart. ". . . you certainly play well enough. Divine. Absolutely divine. I've never heard anything like that before."

"I am . . ." Natil wanted nothing more than to resume her harping. "I am sure that you have not."

Josef nodded, nodded again. "They must play that way in Italy. Is that where you learned to play that way? Everything that's divine comes out of Italy. I mean, have you *heard* some of those songs they sing? Oh!" Again, his hand went to his heart.

"They . . . do play very beautifully indeed." Natil glanced about. In the course of her playing, she had managed to attract a substantial number of listeners, but though for now they were waiting eagerly for her to continue playing, she knew that their patience would not last.

"Have you been in Italy?" Josef pressed.

"Ah . . . I . . . ah . . . have."

"Urbino! Say it! You must have been in Urbino." Josef would have clapped his hands had he not been holding a lute in one of them. "Ah! Guidobaldo da Montefeltro! Baldassare Castiglione! The gentlemen! The gentlewomen! Ah, all the light of Europe in one place!" He leaned down, and his watery eyes peered at Natil as though she were a fish in a bowl. "Surely you were there."

In fact, Natil had indeed been there for a few days, and, at this moment, with a plainly hostile maker of strongboxes with musical pretensions on one side and a wealthy fop on the other, she wished that she were back in that sun-warmed courtyard beneath a clear Italian sky, the women and men of that peaceful fellowship listening to the sound of an elven harp—bronze strings and all—and an elven harper.

They had not known who she was or where she was from, but they had known beauty, and though Natil did not now want to admit her presence there, she must have looked wistful, for Josef forgot himself to the extent that he did indeed clap his hands together (wincing as he found the neck of the lute between them). "I knew it! I knew it!" Immediately, he offered his hand. "I must remember my manners in the presence of one who was welcomed—and rightly welcomed—at that august court. I am Josef Aldernacht. This . . ." He indicated the maker of strongboxes. ". . . is Jahn Witczen, of Prague. He builds all my instruments."

Natil took Josef's hand gingerly. "All?"

"Oh, I have lots. I play them all, you see. It's the mark of a humanist."

"I . . . see . . ."

To demonstrate, Josef swung the lute up, and strummed—very badly—a number of chords. The lute was out of tune. He did not seem to notice. "Do you know any Tuscan songs?" he said suddenly. "You must."

"A few." Natil by now wanted desperately to escape.

"Do you know the one that goes . . . that goes . . . ah . . ." Josef fumbled with the lute, plunked out a few half muffled notes, then looked up at her expectantly. "You know: that one."

As near as Natil could tell, the song Josef was attempting was German, not Tuscan. "I think so," she said, and, putting her hands on her harp, she played while Josef, muttering to himself and tunelessly singing words that were unlike any Italian that Natil had ever heard, strummed along with her. He was playing in a different key than Natil, singing in yet another. He did not seem to notice.

It went on like that for almost an hour: Natil, habitually polite, playing tune after tune, Josef Aldernacht accompanying her on the Jahn Witczen strongbox while Jahn Witczen himself muttered about Irish harps and brass strings. Bystanders smirked, an occasional coin mercifully appeared, but by the end of the affair, Natil was exhausted and wanted nothing more than to flee into the nearest stand of trees, throw her arms about a gnarled trunk, and shake. She kept wishing that Omelda might return soon and thereby afford some excuse for a quick departure.

Suddenly, though, Josef put down the lute. "Are you looking for a position? You could play for my father. He hates music, but I'm sure he'd like you. And we've got a big house: we have parties and banquets, but we just dismissed our last master of entertainment, and we need someone to arrange music and things. It's nothing like Urbino, but it's quite nice. You'd have a roof over your head, and good clothes, and lots of money . . ." A roof, clothes, and lots of money held not the slightest attraction for Natil, but the feather in Josef's cap was bobbing excitedly. ". . . and you'd be in the pay of Jacob Aldernacht himself!''

Natil could only stare at him blankly. There was no Lady, no starlight . . . nothing to sustain her. She simply wanted to run. But her promise to Omelda held her.

Josef suddenly looked up. "Oh, there's my brother!" On tiptoe then: "Francis! Come listen to this harper! I want her for the house!"

The crowd parted and an older man appeared. He was as somber as Josef was gay, and, pausing only briefly to present a beggar with a gold coin while surreptitiously glancing around to make sure that his charity was noticed by all, he came straight up to Josef with the weary expression of a parent humoring an overindulged child. He took no particular notice of Natil.

"What is it, Josef?" he said.

Josef gestured at Natil with a flourish. "Francis, allow me to present . . . ah . . ." He looked at the harper quickly. "Your name, mistress?"

"Natil of Malvern," she said, resigned.

"Allow me to present Natil of Malvern. She's a harper, and she's played . . ." Josef seemed ready to go up on tiptoe again. ". . . at Urbino! She can take care of the music for the house."

Francis still looked weary. "Yes, yes, Josef: whatever you want. Take her up to the house and have Charles draw up the documents." Almost as an afterthought, he looked at Natil. His eyes widened, and he turned immediately back to his brother. "Are you sure, Josef?"

Josef's hand went to his heart. "She's wonderful!"

"Yes . . . of course. Well . . ." Another dubious look. ". . . go ahead, then."

Natil made herself smile politely. "Honored gentlemen, I am not looking for a position."

Josef stared. Francis appeared not to have heard.

"I have a friend who is looking for work, though," the harper continued. "Her name is Omelda. She would serve you well in your kitchen or your chambers."

No reply. The idea that anyone would actually turn down a position in the Aldernacht household seemed unimaginable to Josef, and Francis appeared not to hear anything said by anyone beneath his social status.

"I . . . ah . . ." Josef looked uncertain, faltered a

response at last. "I'm sure we can find her something, too."

Francis glared at his brother. "Josef, what are you saying? Are you going to let this . . ." He stared at Natil. Natil regarded him more calmly than she felt. ". . . this whatever dictate terms to us?"

"I heard Eudes this morning," Josef said in a tone at once defiant and appeasing. "He was telling Charles that Martha needed some help in the kitchen. One of the girls was . . . ah . . . I mean . . . she wound up . . ." He looked at the bystanders, abruptly decided to retreat from any direct statement. "She left. Unexpectedly."

"Left? Without permission? Father *allowed* that? Didn't he call the men to bring her back?"

"I believe it had something to do with . . . ah . . . Edvard and Norman."

Francis flared. "Leave my boys out of it. You've always hated them."

Josef became angry in turn. "I don't hate them: they're just that way. And I'm simply telling you what Eudes said."

"Then I'll have Eudes dismissed!"

"Oh, I'd like to see that."

"I can do it if I want."

"Over Father's dead body!"

Both men seemed rather appalled by what Josef had said. Tremulously, as though attempting to clear the suddenly tense air, Josef turned to Natil. "Will you take the position, Mistress Natil?"

It would not be the first time that Natil had been a musician in a human household, but given Francis's pomposity, Josef's enthusiasm, and Jahn Witczen's arrogance, she was unwilling to accept the offer. But she was not alone now: she had Omelda to think about, and just then the runaway nun appeared at the far side of the square, head down, frowning. Natil judged that she had been unsuccessful.

"Will you . . ." Unwilling to say yes, she was also unwilling to say no. "Will you employ my friend also?" she said quickly, before her conflicting emotions tied her tongue.

"Of course," said Josef.

"Don't be silly," said Francis.

The two men glanced at one another. Josef pouted. Francis looked suddenly resigned. "Oh, all right," he said. "Have it your way." He turned and walked away. "Nitwit."

Josef flushed with anger, but, upon examining his prize, was once again rapturous. "Oh, this is wonderful. I'll take you up to the house immediately, and Charles can draw up the papers, and then you'll be one of us. You simply have to tell me all about Urbino, and we'll play duets together. Did you know I write music as well as play it? Poetry and essays, too. I do them in Latin, and I'm learning Greek." He patted the book that hung from his belt. "Petrarch is my absolute idol. Only the best, you know. I'll write some duets. It'll be wonderful."

Omelda approached, her face crestfallen, her steps so despondent that the last few were but a shuffle. She glanced, puzzled, at Josef and Jahn, shrugged, and turned to Natil. "I didn't find anything," she said.

Natil, feeling trapped by considerations that were uncomfortably human, shrugged. "That is quite all right," she said softly. "I did."

Eudes, the Aldernachts' chief steward, was as old and dry as an antique wardrobe that had been left in the attic for half a century; and when Josef presented his finds to him later that day, he looked at Omelda dubiously, but he examined Natil with open suspicion. "You realize," he said, "that once you have taken a position with the Aldernacht family, you are bound to it until you are formally . . . released."

Eudes's doubt did not equal even a small fraction of Natil's. Upon their arrival at Gold Hall, she and Omelda had been confronted with the articles of indenture that they were required to sign, and she was now wondering whether she should simply decline the position and drag Omelda off to some other city where the people were perhaps saner.

But she also doubted that there was any real sanity left anywhere. The Free Towns had fallen into petty squabbles and then into collapse, and the hereditary mayor of Saint Blaise was now as much an overlord as any baron. Saint Brigid was deserted, Castle Aurverelle had been blown to bits with artillery twenty years ago, and Shrine-rock was a convent. There was nothing elven left in Adria save tales and legends.

And with a chill, she realized that there was every chance that the statement was precisely true.

Omelda was staring unabashedly at the splendid room. This was Gold Hall, and even this small office demonstrated the wealth of the Aldernachts: rosewood desk, gilt hangings, gold and silver pens and candlesticks, rows of fine leather ledgers and record books. The indentures were written upon parchment embossed at the top with the Aldernacht monogram and motto, and Charles, the Aldernacht lawyer, wore the bored but crafty expression of a man who had many other things to do, important things, things that involved money and power.

Omelda at last looked at Natil. "It's . . . wonderful."

To Natil, it looked like a trap, but so eager was the expression on Omelda's face—eagerness being something that Natil had not often seen there—that the Elf nodded to Eudes. "I understand, sir."

Eudes was unwilling to let the matter drop. "There was a young woman much like yourself who left the family without leave a few years . . . ago. Mister Aldernacht himself gave orders that she be pursued. She was. We eventually had two thousand mercenaries besieging . . . Kirtel." He examined Natil dustily. "We are a very determined family, mistress Harper."

Natil smiled. "It is a gift, I am sure."

Eudes attempted to stare her down, failed, turned loftily to the window. "It is a virtue. It has made the Aldernachts what they are."

Charles was growing impatient. "Well?"

Natil shrugged. Indentures were meaningless. All that was left was her word—her word to Omelda, her word to the Aldernachts—and she would keep that so long as it remained in her power to do so.

Omelda grabbed the pen and signed, then looked at Natil, waiting. After a moment, Natil sighed, dipped the pen. Her signature, pinned down in black half-uncials on white parchment, looked vulnerable, brittle, human.

Eudes witnessed the documents with a quick, practiced initial. Charles rolled them up and thrust them into a leather case. "Good then," he said in a voice that

indicated that he cared little whether it was good or not.
"All agreed. Congratulations to you both."

The door opened, and Josef thrust his head into the
room. The feather in his cap waved back and forth like
a flag. "Finished? Wonderful!"

Eudes sniffed. "I'll see to it that they are attired more
. . . appropriately."

Josef was indignant. "Not at all, Eudes. Omelda needs
clothes, but I want Natil just the way she is. I think she
looks wonderful. She's played in Urbino, did you know?"

Eudes cleared his throat. "I think, Master Josef, that
they do not dress that way in . . . Urbino."

"I want her just as she is!"

Charles leaned back in his chair, slowly winding a
scarlet cord about the leather document case. "I have
orders from Mister Jacob," he said. Josef and Eudes fell
silent immediately. "Mister Jacob is leaving for Furze
tomorrow morning. He is taking Francis, a number of
servants and guards, and . . ." Charles looked at Natil.
". . . a few musicians. Mistress Natil will be in charge
of the latter."

Omelda was stricken. "Tomorrow morning? What
about me?"

"You have work to do in the house," said Charles. He
looked at Natil again. "You'll need Aldernacht livery.
The chambermaids will see that you're supplied with it."
His lips pursed disapprovingly. "And get rid of that
feather in your hair, will you?"

CHAPTER 9

Jacob Aldernacht was a wiry little ape of a man with a bald head, a square jaw, and a pair of spectacles that perched on the bridge of his sharp nose like a chip on the shoulder of a belligerent boy; and when Natil, appropriately attired in blue gown and white wrap, presented herself to him the next morning, his mouth pursed up as though he were confronted with a batch of highly dubious wool.

He was silent for the better part of a minute. About them, the courtyard of the Aldernacht house was filled with shuffling Aldernacht horses and mules, Aldernacht servants lashing Aldernacht baggage to Aldernacht saddles, Aldernacht soldiers rubbing their eyes and laughing at one another's jokes in steamy puffs, and three or four Aldernacht musicians—Natil's charges—standing off together and examining their mistress just as suspiciously as Jacob Aldernacht himself.

At last the master spoke. "This was Josef's idea, wasn't it, Francis?"

Francis Aldernacht, pulling on a pair of gloves with an air of purposeful importance, looked up from wriggling a thumb into place. "Well, you know, I tried to convince him otherwise," he said, "but he wouldn't hear of it. He took this one; and to get her, he took the other girl, too."

The morning was cool, the sun not quite up yet, the alleys and streets of Ypris still shadowed, but Natil felt herself begin to grow warm. And since there was no starlight left with which to fight down her anger, she had to think of something else. Of music. Of a gold coin passing from the hand of an apostate nun into the hand of a beggar woman with two cold and hungry children. Of 747s and highways stretching westward into what she hoped was elven rebirth.

The flush receded even as Francis continued: "He herded them straight up to the Hall and signed them on. This one will do for a chief musician, I guess."

Jacob glanced impatiently at his son. "Will do? Of course she'll do. Josef might be a nitwit about everything else, but he knows music." He squinted at Natil. "Even if he can't play a note to save his life." He laughed, squinted a little harder. "What's that in your hair?"

Natil offered a curtsy. "It is an eagle feather, Mister Jacob."

"Where the hell did you get that?"

"Friends in a far land gave it to me."

"China?"

Natil shook her head softly. "Farther away than that. Much farther."

"Hmmph. You've done some traveling, I see."

"I have."

Jacob squinted again at the feather. "How come you don't cover your head like a proper woman?"

Awry: it was all going awry. In order to keep her word to Omelda, she had given her word to Jacob Aldernacht; and now, because of the second obligation, she could no longer fulfill the first. But she made herself answer politely. "Because, sir, I am not a proper woman. I am . . ." An Elf. She could have said it. An Immortal. One of the Firstborn, the People of the Stars, who had seen life arise from a pit of slime and grow into something like this Jacob Aldernacht who was asking her about head coverings and proper womanhood. But she refrained. ". . . a harper."

Jacob's eyes narrowed, and Natil thought that she detected a trace of a smile at the corners of his hard mouth. "Right out front," he said. "I like that. Well, be a hussy if you want. And keep your feather. Maybe it'll bring us luck."

"It is meant to bring luck, Mister Jacob."

Jacob laughed: a hard, brittle sound. "Well, we'll need it in Furze!" He looked at Francis. "Let's get going."

Francis examined the harper once more, shook his head, turned for his mount.

Jacob swung back to Natil. "You get your ass up on your horse, girl. And I daresay you'll learn to cover your head in Furze!"

Natil blinked. "Why is that, Mister Jacob?"

"Siegfried of Magdeburg is reason enough for anything," said Jacob. "He wants women to be obedient, properly cowed, and respectful. Just like he wants everybody. Just like *I* want everybody." He motioned for a servant to bring the harper's horse, stared Natil in the face with narrow, parsimonious eyes. "So I'll let you in on a little secret, girl," he said in a confidential whisper. "Siegfried hasn't met up with Jacob Aldernacht yet. He's got a lot to learn about some things."

They started off then. Jacob and Francis rode in the lead, escorted by picked members of their private army. Following them were the servants and the musicians and the luggage and more soldiers. It was a businessman's entourage: here was finery, to be sure, but only of the solemn, straight-to-the-point variety, the kind as equally suited to audiences with kings and barons as it was to contracts and bargains and screaming at the son of a bitch on the other side of the table that he was an idiot and a fool for not seeing it the right way, the only way, the Aldernacht Way.

And as one of the other musicians told Natil after she introduced herself and took her place among them, this trip would perhaps partake of a little of all of the above, for any dealings with Furze would involve, by necessity, *four* parties.

"There's Mister Jacob, of course," said Harold as the horses and mules clopped across the morning-damp cobbles of the deserted streets, "and there's the wool cooperative. That's two." He grinned at her, the pouty underlip of a shawm player evident even in the proximity of so many white teeth. "But then we have David a'Freux, the local baron, to deal with, as well as . . ." He waggled his eyebrows roguishly. ". . . Siegfried of Magdeburg."

"The Inquisitor." Natil looked down at her horse's mane, sighed.

Again the white teeth. "You've heard of him, then."

Natil mustered a thin smile. The Inquisition had not been kind to the Elves. "Who in Adria has not heard of him?" she said.

Harold feigned a pout, his shawm-lip turning suddenly comical with exaggeration. "And here I thought I was telling you something wonderful and new. But . . .'' A flicker of a grin. ''. . . here I am flirting with my superior.''

In spite of her concerns about Omelda—who was, this prime, on her own—and about her own present situation, Natil laughed outright, and even the men of the Aldernacht guard looked up, startled by the sudden brightness of her voice. ''I will not give you permission to flirt with me, youngster,'' she said.

''Youngster!''

''Youngster.'' She knew how incredulous he was: Harold was in his twenties, but she herself looked little more than eighteen. ''But I will not insist upon formalities, either.'' She turned to the other musicians. Grown men, all of them, given over to a young woman's charge as though they were a troop of little boys. ''I am a harper,'' she said. ''We are all musicians. I ask that we treat one another in accordance with the holiness of our calling.''

Dumbfounded stares. Holiness?

Natil cleared her throat. ''Holiness, gentlemen.'' Turning back to Harold, she smiled politely. Always polite these Elves: all that they held sacred might be torn apart, their world might be at an end, their loved ones might be murdered before their eyes . . . and yet they would be polite.

A painful thought. No. Not always. Something had happened long ago . . . something that had ended with Natil laying her harp on the pyre of a friend. She shook off the memory, though. Mirya was gone now—gone for good, gone beyond all returning—and so were all the rest. Everything elven was in the past. The far past. There was but one Elf left now, and she was beginning to doubt her claim to that title.

She glanced up at the morning sky. No 747. She felt disappointed.

''What about David and Siegfried?'' she said to Harold. Her voice was soft.

But before the pouty shawm player could reply: ''Mistress Natil,'' came the shout from the front of the columns, ''Mister Jacob wants you.''

Harold abruptly looked wise. ''Ah, the old man has a taste for young women. He'd best watch his heart.'' A waggle of the eyebrows. ''In more ways than one.''

"I do not understand."

Harold blew a spit bubble from between his half-open lips, let it pop. "Paper thin, mistress. Paper thin."

Natil did not comprehend, but the summons was repeated, and she lifted an arm to wave her acknowledgment. The town gate was narrow, but once she had passed through, she trotted her horse up alongside the road to Jacob's side.

It was still early, and much of the landscape was clad in mist. To the south, though, Natil could make out a dark line of trees: Malvern Forest. There, she had hoped to find an end, but Omelda had come, and then the Aldernacht family. And so: "You called me, master," she said.

"My father would like—" began Francis.

"I'll do my own talking," said Jacob. He glared at his son. "Always sticking up that nose of yours. God knows, you didn't get that from your mother."

Francis's jaw clenched. "No, I didn't get it from Mother. I got it from you."

A flicker in Jacob's eye? A sudden faltering in his glare? But: "I'm glad you remember where you came from."

Francis kept his eyes fixed on the horizon. "I remember. I think even Josef remembers."

"Then shut up and drool over your memories." Jacob turned to Natil. "What kind of claptrap has Harold been giving you?"

"Hardly claptrap, master. We discussed the state of affairs in Furze, and then he offered the common homage tendered by any man to any woman."

Jacob's glare turned stony. Natil realized that she had said the wrong thing, and at decidedly the wrong time. No stars, no futures, no sense of probabilities here: Natil lived in the present, made mistakes, shoved her foot into her mouth now with as much alacrity as the silliest mortal.

"He *what*?" said Jacob.

"I am sorry, sir," Natil said quickly. "I think of common gallantry as such."

"I know gallantry," said Jacob. He eyed Natil. "It's all rat shit and bird farts."

Perhaps I will be lucky, thought Natil. *Perhaps they*

will simply relieve me of my obligations here and let me go.

But she had no more luck than Omelda, it seemed, and an outright dismissal was not forthcoming. Jacob's expression abruptly turned cunning. "What did Harold say about Furze?"

Natil looked at Francis. Francis was doing his best to look elsewhere.

"No," said Jacob. "Don't pay any attention to Francis. Pay attention to me. I pay you, I own you. I'm your master as long as I live." He leered at Francis. "Any particular plans, Francis?"

Francis blinked. "Well, you know, I'm sure I haven't any idea what you're talking about, Father."

Jacob thumped his chest, feigned a hacking cough. "Oh, dear," he said in a wheezing voice, "the lad doesn't know what his dying father is talking about. And what will become of the company? All that money just left lying around idle because the son doesn't understand. Ugh! Ugh!"

Paper thin. Natil suddenly understood Harold's words. Paper thin . . . in many ways.

Francis did not look at his father, but a muscle up near the corner of his jaw had begun to twitch. Natil, who had positioned her horse directly between the two men, wished fervently that she was somewhere else.

"I'll tell you about Furze, Mistress Natil," Jacob continued in a normal voice. "There are some bright young lads down there who are sick of living like beggars. They've decided to bring industry back to their city. My industry." He eyed the harper. "Ever been to Furze?"

"I have." She discovered that she was smiling wistfully. All she had now were memories . . . and a few hopes. "But that was . . . a long time ago."

"Well, they used to be dairy down there, everything was dairy. Milk, cheese, butter. But when the city went down, Belroi picked up all the business, and now there isn't much left for anyone. You've heard the saying: even the rats don't like Furze. But Paul Drego and his boys are sticking it out, and they're going to try wool. And I'm going to help them." Jacob looked at Francis. "Despite my son's counsel."

"It's a bad idea, Father," said Francis. "It's just non-acceptable. The Inquisition could take everything."

"They'll not get a penny."

Francis frowned. Natil, still in the middle, was again wishing that she was not.

"I'll tell you something, Francis," said Jacob. "I think you're jealous of Paul and his boys."

"Jealous!"

The old man jabbed a finger at his son. "They've got spunk. They've got drive. They've got ambition. They're not waiting around for their father to die off so they can inherit the family fortune. There isn't any family fortune, so they're rolling up their sleeves and making one of their own. I like that. I admire people who work with their hands." He glanced sidelong at Natil, and the intimation was clear: though the harper might—just might—be included among those who worked with their hands, Francis certainly was not.

"Ah . . ." said Natil into the tense silence. "Harold mentioned . . . ah . . . David a'Freux and Siegfried—"

"Siegfried of Magdeburg," said Jacob. "Well, we have to take David into account because he's still the baron down there. His family took over after old Martin the Faggot . . ."

Natil's hand tightened on the forepillar of her harp. But Jacob's epithet for Martin delMari was as offhand as a remark about the weather.

". . . couldn't get an heir on a woman to save his life. Things might have been different if men could whelp through their assholes!" Jacob laughed. Francis laughed with him, but Jacob silenced him with a glare that made Natil flinch. "But David is of two minds about the whole affair, which is easy enough for him, because he doesn't have much of a mind to begin with. Typical a'Freux: he wants the money to come to Furze because that will give him more taxes; but he doesn't want the money to come to Furze because that will mean that he has to deal with townsfolk who are a little better off than serfs." He cackled. "So he winds up working for both sides at once . . . and accomplishing nothing. Of course, the man he's really working for is Siegfried of Magdeburg."

"The Inquisitor?" Jacob, Natil realized, was a man who knew many things and enjoyed demonstrating it.

Since he obviously expected admiration, she, like a proper woman, nodded in agreement and asked questions to which she already knew the answers. Men like Jacob Aldernacht did not normally converse so casually with their employees, but she was, in fact, not an employee: she was a possession. Jacob might as well have been talking to a wall, to a dog, or to himself.

"David carries out Siegfried's sentences," said Jacob. "He's the secular power in Furze, and so he has to. Inquisitors can make people do anything." He rode silently for a moment. "That is, people who care anything about their immortal souls." Again, he glanced sidelong at Natil, this time as though to defy her to propose that Jacob Aldernacht cared anything about an item that could not be weighed, spun, fulled, or woven . . . and sold. "Although I'm sure David doesn't fuss about the arrangements as long as he gets his share of the confiscated property."

Francis squirmed.

"And . . . and how does Siegfried feel about the wool cooperative?" asked Natil with an uneasy glance at the son.

Jacob turned crafty again. "A real question, eh? What a sharp little girl I've got for my harper. The answer is: I don't know. Siegfried is a mystery. I don't understand him at all." Again, a silence. Natil felt Francis's tension.

"I had a man down there a few years back," Jacob said at last. "Name of Fredrick. He was supposed to find out a few things for me. About the wool cooperative. About Siegfried." He glanced at Natil. "He was a spy," he said patiently.

Natil nodded, wide-eyed and dutiful.

"Failed completely. Disappeared, in fact."

"It was the Inquisition," said Francis.

"Maybe," said Jacob.

Francis finally burst out. "He'll take everything, Father! Inquisitors can do that, too! Contracts are null and void! Money and property are forfeit! Is that what you want?"

Jacob examined his son coolly. "I want to make money," he said at last.

"There's none to be made in Furze!"

"Then I want to lose money. *My* money." Jacob was

not looking at Francis, but Natil noticed his smirk. "I'm an old man, Francis. I have to worry about my soul. Everybody else seems to be buying their way into Paradise these days: why should I be any different? Maybe I'll give my money to Siegfried. He's doing God's work after all. Then again, poor old Albrecht is trying to get a cathedral up down there: maybe I'll give everything to him." Jacob smiled, but Natil caught a whiff of fear and utterly impotent rage from Francis. The combination, she knew, could be a deadly one.

But: "Play something for us, harper," said Jacob. "I want to hear a song."

Natil nodded, set her harp upright. It was a little difficult to play when riding, but she had been harping for a long time, and so her hands were steady as she put them to the strings. "Do you . . . do you like music, Mister Jacob?" she said courteously.

"Hate it," he said. "Bunch of garbage. Bird farts. But I'm paying you, so I suppose I ought to get my money's worth."

He seemed to enjoy Natil's discomfiture. Natil glanced at the sun. Two hours to terce. She thought of Omelda.

George awoke in Sally's bedroom, opened his eyes to a darkened ceiling. *I must have fallen asleep,* he thought.

They had left the diner with the dawn, and what Sally had wanted was to go home, to eat a breakfast that was, for her, dinner, to talk. And so they had gone to her little apartment, and she had eaten, and they had talked . . . and all the while, the spell had grown on them. Toward mid-afternoon, Sally had arisen to brew coffee, and George had stared, stricken dumb at the sight of the aura, as of silver, that had flickered across her bare arms and throat and face, adding an opalescent sheen to features that had already turned unutterably beautiful to his eyes.

And she, in turn, had come back to the tiny living room of her apartment only to stand in the doorway with the liquid in the two cups trembling in the afternoon light . . . because her hands had been shaking . . . because she had been seeing the same thing in George.

It was mad. It was crazy. Things like this did not happen, and those who insisted otherwise were best confined, kept off the streets. But it *was* happening, and as

George lay awake in the darkness of the bedroom with Sally a bare, sleeping presence at his side, he found himself torn between all the normalcy he had ever wanted—the normalcy he had left behind—and all the wonder of what lay ahead . . . if he would but accept it.

Perhaps he and Sally had both been searching for a little of that normalcy when they had made love, but the wonder had been there, too, inescapable, and it had abruptly taken them both beyond the common love of man and woman—love tainted with the questions of dominance and vulnerability so intrinsic to any mortal endeavor—into something that was a melding of spirit and soul, and then beyond even that into realms that had nothing to do with man or woman or even with anything human: a widening of the heart that had extended their expression of erotic esteem first to the land, then to the world, and then, sweeping them out to the edges of all that they could imagine, to the universe, until they had drifted in a profound silence, weeping at what had become of them . . . because it was so terrible, because it was so wonderful.

And afterward, as George, still trembling, had stared into Sally's very blue eyes, he had seen that they had been touched with a light like that of the stars, and it had occurred to him then—incongruously but appropriately—as it again occurred to him now, that *Sally* was a poor name for someone who had such light in her eyes, such breadth to her heart, who had seen the wheat as he had seen the mountains, who had taken those tossing golden fields into her soul.

"Wheat," he said softly.

Beside him, she stirred. "Huh?"

"Wheat." It seemed so obvious. "That's who you are. Wheat. That's your name."

A low, sleepy laugh. The laugh of a woman who knew the truth when she heard it. "And what am I supposed to call you? Mountain?" Another laugh.

He lifted a hand, saw a flicker about it, realized suddenly that the dark ceiling was no longer quite so dark to him, that he was seeing it in soft shades of lavender and blue.

He caught his breath. His heart was suddenly throwing itself against the inside of his chest as though struggling back toward a former life. But that life was far away now. Even last night, when, stubble-faced and ripe with the odors of a man, he had driven through the mountains . . . even last night was far away.

"Mountain man," she laughed. And then she choked. "Dear God. What's happening to us?"

When she lifted her head, he noticed that she looked younger. Her face had altered subtly, too: something about the cheekbones. This was Sally and yet not Sally. And then he realized that this was not Sally at all. Sally was gone. This was Wheat.

He was afraid. Afraid of what was coming. Afraid that he could not stop it. Afraid that he *could* stop it. Afraid to try either way.

But Wheat was staring at him in the darkness of the room that he knew was no darker to her eyes than to his. And he could guess a little of what she was seeing. "You've . . . changed . . ." she said.

"Yeah . . ." he said. "I guess so."

Again, he lifted a hand. The shimmer about it was clear: a shadowed silver. Some of the roughness was gone from the fingers, some of the squareness from the palm. And when he closed his eyes to sigh softly with the air of a man confronted with the incomprehensible, he saw another shimmer, one that bordered on the familiar. Eyes closed, he stared at it for a moment, puzzling over yet another puzzle, then gave up.

Wheat sat up, looked at her hands, her arms. Slowly, she traced a finger along her softly luminous skin, felt her face. Another laugh, but nervous now. "I . . . I imagine we'll wake up tomorrow morning . . . and this will all be ri—" She touched her face again. Familiar, and yet not. "—diculous."

"You sure?"

"No."

George nodded.

She was peering at him again. "What do you want me to call you?"

"Huh?"

She shrugged as though she had been caught playing a silly children's game, as though she did not give a damn that she had been caught. "I'm Wheat now. Who are you?"

He shrugged. "Who should I be?"

"Not George. Not anymore. Do you have a nick-name?"

"In high school, they called me Lumpy."

Her laughter was as a sound of bright bells, and she covered her face. "We'll have to try something else. What's your middle name?"

"Hadden."

She lifted her face from her hands. "Oh . . . how lovely."

Her language, he noticed, was changing. So was his. There was a lilt in their speech. But, yes, it was a lovely name. "It was my grandmother's maiden name."

"It's you."

He nodded. He knew that.

"OK, Hadden," she said. "By the way: you're glow-ing."

He took a deep breath. "I know."

"Are you scared?"

"Shitless."

Wheat passed a hand through her dark hair. Even the individual strands seemed to glisten now. "You know," she said, "I have a feeling that if we really rejected this, if we really didn't want it, we could make it go away."

A long silence. A truck passed, westbound, on distant I-70. In the kitchen, the refrigerator came on.

"Is that what you want?" Hadden said at last.

Another silence. Then: "No."

"Same here."

Arms about one another, then, they lay back down, kissed, and drifted back off into sleep with the certain knowledge that when they awoke, the last shreds of George and Sally would be gone, purged away by the light and the wonder. Frightening though that was, Had-den was looking forward to it, looking forward to a morning that could not but be glorious when suffused with so much and such inner radiance.

CHAPTER 10

Natil dreamed. Albrecht fretted.

There was only a little moonlight to break the deep darkness of midnight, and in it the columns of the unfinished and roofless cathedral stood like the fingers of pale hands that stretched up toward heaven, begging to be made complete. From the apse triforium—the only part of the gallery that existed—the bishop could see them glimmering, beseeching . . . incomplete. Terribly incomplete.

The apse and the choir, the columns, and no more than that. There was no glass for the few window apertures, no floor in the nave save earth, no west wall, not even a plan for a rose, not a trace of a tower.

For a time, Albrecht considered what he saw—and what he did not see—and then, with a sigh that told of sleeplessness and nocturnal melancholy, he sat down on the edge of the gallery (careful that his undependable knee did not suddenly pitch him headlong into empty air) and let his feet dangle. One hundred and twenty feet below him lay as much of the marble floor as had ever been laid, the legacy of Blessed Wenceslas, who, almost a century ago, had confronted the devastation left by the free companies and met it with the foundations of a cathedral.

But the money had not been there, and the beginnings had remained beginnings: the foundations, a few walls, some columns. Albrecht had added to them, had managed to push the apse and choir walls a little higher and top them with a gallery, but it was still only a beginning.

And so it would remain, it seemed, because . . . because Siegfried . . .

Albrecht could not be certain—indeed, given the secrecy of the Inquisition, he could be certain of absolutely nothing—but he was beginning to suspect that Siegfried's unauthorized visitation at Shrinerock Abbey had been but the shilling in the armpit that indicated a great and deeply entrenched ill; and the ache that had begun gnawing at his stomach made him think that perhaps a shilling in the armpit might have been more reassuring. At least one did not have to live with plague for very long.

Unwilling as yet to confront the Inquisitor directly, Albrecht had asked questions where he could, and had rapidly discovered that no answers would be forthcoming. Casual visits with Siegfried's ministers and subordinates resulted only in casual conversations. Formal interviews yielded polite but firm reminders of the privacy and autonomy of the Inquisition and its immunity from local (local!) interference. Albrecht had even attempted to enter the House of God, but had not been admitted. Siegfried's orders, it seemed.

Convinced, as he had always been, that his work lay invariably with souls, and that bureaucracy and politics were, just as invariably, impediments to that work, Albrecht had, he now realized, allowed the episcopal power in Furze to slip away from him. Away from him . . . and toward Siegfried. Even the cathedral chapter—the chapter to whom it was but a mere technicality that no cathedral actually existed—seemed much more concerned about the Inquisitor's opinions and plans than about Albrecht's. And, worse, the treasurer of the fabric fund had been unwilling even to discuss the moneys that, penny by trickling penny, had been building up since construction on the cathedral had tottered to a halt five years before.

Albrecht put his face in his hands, stared down between his fingers. The marble floor was a pale blankness twenty fathoms below.

Something was wrong. Terribly wrong. Albrecht did not normally consider matters of money save as they involved the worship of God or the bare essentials of his office, but he had suddenly begun to wonder how Siegfried was managing to pay all the ministers, officers, beadles, secretaries, notaries, and (the bishop mentally crossed himself) torturers he employed. The money and property confiscated from heretics counted for something, to be sure, but Furze was a poor town: even the heretics were poor. Siegfried's expenses were great. The fabric fund had grown by mites into something that might raise the west wall someday, but the treasurer did not want to talk about it.

And that meant . . .

Albrecht did not want to think about it.

. . . that meant that . . .

The bishop was struggling in vain with his suspicions when the sound of footsteps came from the stairway up to the arcade. It was very dark, and not until the visitor spoke did Albrecht know him.

"A fine evening, Excellency."

"Oh! Hello, Mattias. What are you doing up here?"

The clerk's smile was evident in his voice. "Watching over my superior, Excellency. I heard you go out, and when you did not return, I thought I might find you here."

"Well," said Albrecht, "you were right. Come, Mattias: sit. I can use the company. Let's talk about . . . about . . ."

"Cathedrals?" said Mattias, coming closer.

"No," said Albrecht quickly. "About . . . say . . . Furze. Jacob Aldernacht will be arriving in the city shortly. What news is there?"

Mattias settled himself cross-legged on the floor . . . a good ten feet from the edge over which Albrecht was still dangling his feet. "Well," he said, "there certainly has been discussion in the cooperative. Paul and James were in favor of a splendid display upon Jacob's arrival. But our good Simon, with characteristic Hebrew wisdom, counseled that such diversions would convince our guest that his services—and his money—might not be as desperately needed as he thought."

Albrecht laughed. "What will it be, then?"

"The wisdom of the Jew, and the welcome of peasants," said Mattias. "Good food made by wifely hands, and backslaps all around."

"Jacob Aldernacht will like that," said Albrecht. "He prides himself on being a businessman. A peasant. I've heard that he just turned down a patent of nobility from the king of France."

"Ummm . . ." said Mattias. "That might well have been pride. Or pure economics. The king wanted to borrow money for the Italian Wars and offered the grant as full payment.''

Money. There it was again. But was that not the way it was these days? Money, money, and more money. Albrecht covered his face again. Mattias was suddenly solicitous. ''Would Your Excellency like to be helped back to bed?''

''It would be a waste of time,'' said Albrecht. He was tempted to add *and of money,* but he did not.

Mattias said nothing, but Albrecht thought he detected a nod of understanding from the shadow that was the clerk.

''You've seen the world, Mattias,'' he said after a time. ''What do . . .'' But, no, he did not want to hear what Mattias might say about the fabric fund. His chief clerk had a sophisticated and unprovincial mind: he might speak the truth . . . and Albrecht did not want to hear the truth. So, instead: ''What do you think of Siegfried of Magdeburg?''

The bishop felt Mattias's glance as though the clerk had tapped him on the shoulder. ''I believe he is a very ambitious man.''

Not at all what Albrecht wanted to hear. ''Ambitious?'' he said, still trying to deny his own suspicions. ''Why do you say ambitious, Mattias? Siegfried is a holy man.''

Again, there was a smile behind Mattias's words. ''Ah, Excellency, there are all kinds of ambition, even among holy men. In the years before Saint Benedict gave his rule to the monastic life, hermits often vied with one another in the severity of their practice. They would mortify their flesh in ever-harsher ways, attempting to demonstrate their holiness to one another. In that, they were ambitious. I think that Siegfried, though he may not know it, is ambitious in much the same way.''

''He serves God.'' Albrecht noticed that his protest sounded as uncertain as his bad knee.

''But he serves God to . . . hmmm . . .'' Mattias mused. ''How shall I say this? He serves God to show others, perhaps to show himself, just how much he serves God.''

''That doesn't . . .'' It did. ''. . . make sense, Mattias.''

Mattias laughed. "Oh, Excellency: we are human beings! God absolved us from making any sense after the tremendous farce in Eden!"

Albrecht blinked. "Be careful that Siegfried doesn't hear you talking that way, Mattias. I'd miss my chief clerk greatly."

Mattias's tone abruptly turned somber. "My point exactly, Excellency. He is ambitious. His practice is as rigorous as that of the old hermits."

Something about his clerk's choice of words made Albrecht uneasy. He thought again of the House of God. They . . . tortured people in there. True, the crime of a heretic was heinous enough to warrant torture, even death, but still . . .

Mattias continued. "But I have thought it wise always to remember that ambition can take one in either direction."

"Heaven or hell?"

"Well . . . up or down. There have been many with ambition who have suddenly found themselves and all they have worked for ground into dust. By their own ambition. Or blown up by it as a town might be blown up with gunpowder." Mattias shrugged: a rustle in the night. "Boom!"

"Boom," said Albrecht, suddenly wrestling with his own conscience. Ambitious. Was he ambitious? How much pride did he take in his office and his title? Was the cathedral he so desired a tribute to God or to himself? He was suddenly uneasy. "Boom . . ."

"Exactly. Boom. The Wheel of Fortune takes one up, and it also casts one down. The highest Tower can be struck by lightning and laid low." Another shrug, another rustle. "Boom."

"You've been looking at heathenish pictures, Mattias."

"All the better to serve God as best I can," said the clerk. "If, because of what I know and what I think, Siegfried wants to call me heretical and kill me, then he will call me heretical and kill me. There is nothing, absolutely nothing, that I can say or not say that will change his mind."

Albrecht was once again disturbed. "I thought you said that Siegfried is a man of God."

"I said also that he is ambitious," said Mattias as though that explained everything. And, after a minute's consideration, Albrecht admitted that it did.

Natil awoke, picked sleep from the corners of her eyes with a long fingernail, tasted the musty palate of morning mouth. Still drifting half in and half out of a dream in which Hadden and Wheat floated in visions of starlight, she stared blearily at the walls of the tiny room that contained her tiny bed.

She could appreciate the symmetry: as the man and the woman became more elven, so she herself became ever more human. Only a week ago, she had slipped in and out of her slumbers as she might pass through a door. Now, though, her limbs were heavy, her mind clouded, her breath rank. An Elf? Still? Was she sure?

She stumbled naked to the basin and pitcher that stood on a table near the window, poured out, splashed her face. The smack of cold water brought her wits back. An inn. Belroi. The Aldernachts had made good time, and Francis, ever obsessed by propriety, had insisted that Natil (the only woman in the party) be given a room to herself.

The harper rubbed her eyes, stretched, yawned. Well, not exactly a room. More like a fair-sized cupboard. But at least she had been able to sleep without having to worry about groping hands, or about accidentally uncovering her ears when she braided her hair for the night or tossed and turned with her dreams.

Wrinkling her nose, she freed the braid from its clasp and unplaited it. As if anybody would think that the shape of her ears meant anything save deformity.

But she was remembering her dreams now, remembering Hadden and Wheat and what she knew to be the starlight that was steadily growing within them. Reality or fantasy? She did not know. She had seen George and Sally become Hadden and Wheat, had noted not only the beginnings of physical changes that, continuing, could not but lead to an elven appearance, but also had heard evidence of mental alterations to match. But dreams were as pliant as music, and as Natil could effortlessly shift a grief-stricken aeolian melody into a more bittersweet dorian, or even into a comparatively optimistic mixolydian, so her sleeping mind could just as easily have taken her hopes and her wishes and transformed them into visions that told her no more than what she desired to be told.

"Dear Lady," she murmured. "I do not know. Is it from myself or from You that these visions come?"

And then she realized it: there was something missing from the tale of Hadden and Wheat. The Lady was missing. Hadden had seen the mountains, and Wheat had been transformed by an almost Eleusinian vision of Montana grain, but in none of it was any sense of the presence of *Elthia Calasiuove*.

But She was there. She had to be there. She *was* the mountains, She *was* the wheat. She was, in fact, the very being and substance of Hadden and Wheat themselves. But no . . . nothing. Nothing direct. In her dreams, Natil might well have been witnessing the awakening of the elven blood, but if that were so, then she was also seeing it awaken without a glimpse of its Creatrix; and from what she had deduced about the ethos and mindset of the future, Hadden and Wheat probably did not even suspect that She existed.

Dream? Or reality? Her face still stinging from the cold water, Natil stood shocked at the utter humanness of her quandary. If her dreams were indeed no more than manifestations of her own wishes, then surely they could not but include the face of the Woman who was everything. That she saw nothing of the Lady argued most tellingly for the veracity of her visions. But that meant . . .

She covered her face.

. . . that Hadden and Wheat did not see. Might not ever see. Might not recognize even if they did see.

"O dear Lady . . . what has happened to us?"

Elthia might come later, she reminded herself. That vision of immanence and of unconditional love might, heralded by other visions, other realizations, manifest eventually. It was not too late.

But then it all might still be a dream.

A tapping at the door. Natil realized that she had clenched her long hair in her fists. "Who . . . who is there?" she said, forcing calm into her voice.

"Just me, mistress," came Harold's voice. "Come to wake you. We've a shorter ride for Furze than we did for Belroi, but Mister Jacob wants an early start."

"Ah . . . certainly . . ."

"I've brought . . . breakfast."

Perhaps it was her confusion, and perhaps it was that the starlight had been so long fled: regardless, she did not hear the catch in the shawm player's voice. Throwing a light shift on over her head, therefore, she went to the door, unfastened it . . .

. . . and Harold was suddenly pushing into the room, kicking the door closed behind him, clasping her about the waist. He drew her to him, held her fast, planted his lips firmly on hers. One of his hands was attempting to slide the gown from her shoulders.

Natil broke free of the kiss. "Let go of me."

But the old, inhuman steel had been shaken out of her voice. Harold, doubtless, heard nothing more than the protest of an impatient woman. "Come now, Natil," he said as he groped for her crotch, "you've been wanting this ever since we left Ypris. I could tell."

He had gotten one of her shoulders bare, and now he applied his lips to its soft curve, bit delicately at her pale skin.

"I can tell," he mumbled. "You're a woman just like any other. I know."

And perhaps he did. Natil was suddenly struck with the fact that she was now included under the simple designation *woman*. No Elf-maid, no immortal, nothing non-human here. Just a woman. A woman whose fleshly desires, Harold had assumed, matched his own.

But if Natil had lost her heritage, and if that heritage had, in turn, lost the world, she could at least possess her own body. She grabbed the pouty shawm player by the hair and lifted, and Harold's eyes widened at the strength of her hand and arm.

"Perhaps, O man, you know women," she said. "But you do not know me."

He gave her a smarmy grin. "Awww. . . ."

Angered, she flung him against the closed door. He hit with a solid thud and, eyes glazed, slid to the floor. "Natil . . ." he mumbled, persevering. "I . . . don't have time for games."

Her foot met the side of his head, and he went sprawling. Natil grimaced more at her anger than at the impact. The stars were gone, the Lady was gone: perhaps, as had been the case once with Mirya, anger—stupid, human anger—was now all she had left.

Bending, she heaved Harold up off the floor and dropped him into a chair, then dashed the basin of cold water into his face. Wet, humiliated, faced with a woman he now knew could best him in any kind of an even fight, he simply stared at her. "Where . . . did you learn to do that?" he managed.

"An Elf taught me," she said, and though she tried to remain angry, the emotion trickled out of her, leaving her numb, empty, hollow. Human anger, human sleep. What had become of the Elves? What had become of Natil?

"Oh . . . sure . . ."

"Is there . . ." She wanted to kick him again to ensure that there would be no repetitions of this incident. But she did not kick him. She simply stood in her shift, dripping with water from the backsplash, her fists balled and her damp hair falling lankly. She might have been any housewife in any city. Dear Lady!

"Is there any breakfast to be had in this . . ." She lifted a foot experimentally. He flinched away. ". . . brothel?"

"I'm sorry, Natil . . ."

"I am talking about breakfast. Is there? Master Jacob will not want to wait. I am pledged to the Aldernachts. I will keep my word."

"Downstairs," he mumbled, his face bright red where it was not bruised.

"Then get out and let me get dressed."

He got to his feet shakily. "I really am sorry."

She had turned away to find her clothes, but at his words she turned back. "You are sorry," she said flatly, "because you did not succeed. Would you be so sorry if you were between my thighs at present?"

He was offended, shocked. "Certainly not!"

And so she did indeed kick him again. And to Harold's obvious astonishment, she cried afterward, because it had been such a human thing to do.

The Aldernacht house was a combination of the solidly burgher and the undeniably erratic. The former showed itself in plain furniture, businesslike windows, simple rugs, and unobtrusive stonework. The latter, though, manifested in the structure of the house itself, for the mansion sprawled involutedly across nearly an acre of ground (not counting the gardens, courts, stables, outbuildings, lawns, gazebos, ponds, and landscaping that lay behind the main structure), its separate and manifold compartments connected by a labyrinth of corridors and passages that Omelda found incomprehensible. Sent on errands, she would inevitably become lost within minutes, and after perhaps an hour of desperate searching, would at last find herself in an entirely different part of the house than that for which she had originally set out.

Old Eudes, dry as a dusty wardrobe, only nodded understandingly when he found her wandering in the fifth parlor (or was it the fourth?), a tiny tray of dragées in her hand and her eyes clouded not only with the chants of sext but with a more immediate bewilderment. "It happens," he intoned, arching one of his moldings and curling up a drawer pull in what passed for a smile. "It always happens. You'd best take yourself back down to the kitchen and tell Martha to keep you there." A flicker of a hinge. "You can learn the rest of the house . . . later."

Nunc sancte nobis spiritus was filling Omelda's head, but she fought to keep Eudes in mental focus. "You mean, this can . . . be learned?"

"Oh, it is a little . . . confusing," said the steward. "Mister Francis has added a great deal to the old house, and he has . . . an intricate way about him. Most of us learned it as it was built; but give yourself a few years: you'll come to know it as well as . . . any."

"A few . . . years?"

Eudes examined her as though she were a chair for which he had to find an appropriate place, at which time she would be glued, screwed, and nailed to the floor. Forever. "Mistress Omelda, your tenure here will be lengthy, I assure you. The Aldernachts take on only the best, and they do not let the best go . . . willingly."

Omelda recalled the story of the runaway servant girl, and for the first time, she realized how tightly she had held to a small hope that, someday, healed of her affliction, the intrusive chant banished from her mind, she might be able to return to Shrinerock Abbey. Natil's promise to her had revitalized and fostered that hope. But Natil was gone, the chant . . .

Surrexit, ac Paraclito . . .

. . . was very close, and now Eudes was, in effect, telling her that a return to Shrinerock was out of the question. Forever.

She suddenly wanted to tear off the Aldernacht livery, to run for the nearest door and blunder through the house like a sun-dazzled moth until she found an escape.

"Mistress Omelda?"

She passed a hand over her face. There was no escape, either from the chant or from the Aldernachts. "I'm sorry, sir. I'm . . . I'm just . . . giddy."

Eudes nodded wisely, still examining the new chair for proper placement. Permanent placement. "I'll take you to the kitchen . . . myself."

And as she followed him, her eyes cloudy with plain-chant, Omelda felt a rising sense of panic. She had wanted a roof over her head, and she had gotten one: the roof of a cage, the roof of a tomb. She nodded at Eudes's explanations of the layout of the house, but the rooms, corridors, and passages all blurred with her whirl of fright.

They reached the kitchen. Martha was there, as usual, but there was present also a short, stout woman who stood on the scoured flagstones as though a heavy desk had been shoved out into the middle of the room. Her hair was tucked up severely beneath a cap in a style fifty years out of date, but what escaped to curl limply over her high forehead was as gray as the steel hairpins that attempted to push it back. This, Eudes explained in a whisper, was Madam Claire, Francis's wife.

Claire was apparently conducting an impromptu inventory of the kitchen supplies, for her eyes were continually flicking back and forth from Martha (who was scurrying from drawer to cupboard to sack to barrel), to the drawers and cupboards and sacks and barrels themselves (which Martha opened and unlatched and held up and lifted so as to display their contents), to the wax tablet she held (which was covered with minute entries denoting what she had ascertained to be in the drawers and cupboards and sacks and barrels as a result of Martha's opening and unlatching and holding up and lifting).

''How much?'' Claire's voice was flat, heavy, like a damaged trumpet.

''Fifty pounds, ma'am.''

''Fifty? Are you sure? Let me see.'' Claire's eyes abruptly ceased their flicking and screwed themselves into a tight focus as though to seize Martha by the neck and wring the truth from her like water from a sheet. ''Looks to me like forty-nine,'' she said at last. She made the entry on her tablet, and her eyes resumed flicking. ''And that: how much?''

And Martha, who was not a young woman, climbed up on stools and ladders, and went down on hands and knees, and stretched herself on tiptoe in order to fulfill the rain of demands made by Claire and her tablet.

After a minute, though, Claire suddenly became aware of Eudes and his charge. ''What's this?'' she said, turning as though to examine yet another drawer, cupboard, sack, or barrel. ''Why, this must be the new girl!''

Martha, panting, leaned against a counter and wiped her streaming face with her apron. She mustered a weak nod and a weaker smile at Omelda.

''Oh, isn't she the cutest little thing!'' Claire was saying, her damaged trumpet of a voice apparently containing an equally damaged dove. ''Such a fresh-faced little doll!''

''Madam Claire,'' said Eudes, ''may I present Omelda. The . . . new girl.''

Claire nodded and cooed for a moment more, and then she stooped suddenly and jutted her fuzzy jaw at Omelda's face. ''You may kiss me, Omelda.''

Omelda stared, frightened. Eudes nudged her. She offered a tentative peck to Claire's cheek.

''Oh, how sweet,'' said Claire, straightening. ''A true child of God. Sweet and innocent, just as she should be.''

''I thought it best that she be kept in the kitchen,'' said Eudes, ''until she learns a little more about the . . . house.''

''Quite right, dear Eudes,'' said Claire. ''Such a sweet thing you are, too! Another child of God. How wonderful! I'll just finish up with Martha here, and then Martha (oh, Martha: up straight-away!) will give Omelda her duties.'' She smiled. Omelda was suddenly and violently afraid that Claire would demand another kiss.

But Claire swung abruptly away, cleared her throat, and pointed to a large barrel in the corner. Martha was already running for it.

''Pickles! How much?''

Omelda watched, listened, added her own mental voice to the slow singing of the convent choir. But she herself was not singing: she was screaming. Screaming for Natil.

CHAPTER 11

Listen. This is how it happens.

It had been a long day. Days in Furze were usually long, for there had come to be a sense of the interminable in a continuing penury that dictated that coins be inevitably and endlessly counted, hoarded, picked out of a snarl of threads at the lint-filled bottom of an old purse; that dickering in the marketplace be lengthy and desperate (a single penny spelling the difference between a full belly and an ache in the stomach that said that supper had not been quite enough); that there be never enough of anything to go around, and little hope of a change.

And then there was the Inquisition, and that made everything that much longer, for in all the counting and the hoarding and the dickering, every word had to be weighed, uttered carefully, considered judiciously. A stray doubt, an angry retort . . . and one's fate could well be one with that of Fredrick, whose body had been burned in the town square a few days ago, the Church's vengeance pursuing the unabjured heretic even beyond death.

But at the end of this particular long day, although it was not his custom to enter taverns and ask for alcohol, Paul Drego was having a drink before dinner. His day had been longer than usual, much longer, and this was, perhaps, fitting, for as it had been Paul who had originally come up with the idea of converting the Furze economy from subsistence dairy to profitable wool, and as it had been Paul who had first written to the Aldernacht firm a year and a half ago to audaciously propose that a substantial loan might turn out to be a profitable venture, and as it had been Paul who had wheedled, begged, and cajoled his fellow merchants of Furze, dragged them into meetings, preached to them his gospel of economics, forced them to proclaim that this gospel included both the Christians and the Jews of the city, and convinced them to form the wool cooperative, so, now that Jacob Aldernacht himself had arrived that morning with son, guards, servants, and even a few musicians, it was Paul who was personally representing the entire city to a man upon whose good will—and, possibly, whim— rested the future of Furze.

Standing at the head of his motley little band of poor merchants and even poorer artisans and minor tradesmen, Paul had shaken hands with the rich man, had smiled and bowed and made his welcome and hoped that it was a good enough start for the business. And now it was late afternoon, and now the wives of the cooperative members were readying a good burgher feast in the rickety town hall, and now Paul was tired. Deeply tired. He was also—terribly—doubtful. Doubtful of the enterprise. Doubtful whether he could hold it together long enough to make it work. Doubtful whether, even if he did indeed hold it together, there would be any opportunity for any growth to take place in a town so overshadowed by Siegfried of Magdeburg and the fearful silence of the Inquisition.

"Evening, Paul."

Paul looked up from his beer, recognized his friend, James, the furrier. With a deep sigh and the cock-eyed smile of a man determined to make the best of a ridiculously bad situation, Paul offered a hand. James took it and settled down on the other side of the table.

"So," he said. "Ha' do you think it went?"

"So far, so good," said Paul. He rested an elbow on the table, put his face in his hand. "Dear God, I'm terrified."

"It all cams down to this one week, dan't it?" James called for a small—a very small—beer of the third quality, paid for it with a penny, received a halfpenny in change.

Of all the members of the cooperative, James was, perhaps, the poorest. Furs and fur garments did not sell well in a town with little enough money to spend upon food. But, with his eye on a better future, James had worked hard for the wool cooperative, and at the same time had managed to scrape up a slim living for himself and his sweetheart by repairing the few old and well-worn fur garments that existed in the town. The occasional meager commissions he received from David a'Freux also had helped, though James freely admitted that they had likely been offered more for David's amusement than because of any real desire to help the local trade.

James tasted his beer and made a face. It was truly wretched stuff, but if was affordable. "It all cams down to tomorrow," he said, refining his first estimate.

Paul shook his head, drank his own bad beer. "It all cams down to tonight."

James smiled optimistically. "I've just cam from the church. I prayed to Saint Jude."

Paul laughed. "Lost causes!"

"I'm just covering my wagers. Yesterday, I lit candles before the Virgin and offered to make a pilgrimage to Chartres if we succeed . . ."

Paul lifted an eyebrow. "Bargaining wi' the Queen of Heaven?"

"Joseph was a poor carpenter," said James. "I imagine it took a good businesswoman in the kitchen to keep clothes on the Baby Jesus."

Paul nodded. Votive candles and promised pilgrimages were not exactly his idea of business, but he was a practical man: whatever it took. "I imagine so."

"And the day before last, I gave money to the poor in memory of Saint Francis."

"Very good. Very good indeed. You know, I've a'ways been partial to Francis. Though, like old John XXII, I ha' some disagreement with his poverty."

They both laughed.

Now, please, look over here in the corner, where someone else is having a drink: a laboring man, whose clothes are just as shabby and just as worn as those of any other of his station in Furze. At first glance, indeed, there is nothing remarkable about him. But how does someone so obviously poor afford to drink beer by the full measure? And, now that one oddity has surfaced, here is another: he speaks with no one, but seems, rather, to listen to everything that is said, even if it is said on the far side of a relatively crowded room, even—or perhaps especially—if it is said between Paul and James.

"So," said James, "I feel good about tonight. I'd be willing to *swear* that Jacob is going to give us the help we need."

Paul shook his head slowly. "I'm na willing to swear to anything. I think that only God can tell what's going to happen tonight." He finished his beer. "I'm na overly interested in being rich: if we can get just enough out of this to live decently, I'll be very satisfied."

"Well," said James, laughing, "I'll take your share, then. *I'm* interested in being rich." He laughed again. "And, since I've gone to mass and . . ." He winked. ". . . bribed the necessary Friends in High Places . . ." Another wink. ". . . very high . . ." Wink, wink. "I ha' no doubts."

Paul smiled. James's laughter was welcome, but it did nothing to dismiss even a single particle of the fatigue he felt. "All right," he said quietly.

James's laughter and winks stopped. He leaned toward Paul. "You do?"

"What?"

"Have doubts."

Paul considered having his cup refilled, shrugged and did not. A half penny was a half penny, and he had a family. "I doubt e'erything these days, James."

"E'erything?"

Paul heard the unspoken query. "E'erything."

James looked plainly hurt. "What about God?"

Paul shrugged, thinking of a man named Fredrick he had known once, thinking of many others. "I think—"

James shook his head suddenly, put a hand on Paul's arm. "Dan say it."

"All right. I wan."

"It's too frightful. Paul . . . I din't realize . . ."

Paul shrugged. "We just do the best we can, James."

James was genuinely concerned. "Have you talked to anyone about this?"

"Talk? Do you think I'm mad?"

"I mean, to a priest. In confession. They're there to help."

"And to burn and torture?"

James looked plainly uncomfortable. "I . . . I know." He squirmed a little. "My faith is important to me, Paul. I think it's important to everyone. Dan doubt God just because of a few . . ." He was plainly aware that he had backed himself into a verbal corner. ". . . well, you know."

Paul chuckled tiredly. "Yes. I know."

"The Inquisition is doing the work of God." James sounded more certain, Paul was sure, the more uncertain he became. "There are souls in heaven right now because of the Inquisition. Are you saying that's na saintly?"

Paul opened his mouth, considered, shut it again. After a time: "I dan really know what I'm saying." The church bells began to chime. Vespers. "Cam on. It's time for dinner. Let's just leave it at that."

Leaving it at that, though, appears to be quite enough; for the laboring man, the one with the full measure of beer, the one who listens, rises as they rise. But where Paul and James, arm in arm, make their way towards the town hall, the listener goes another way, his feet carrying him rapidly toward the House of God.

And that is how it happens.

Jacob Aldernacht did not need a speck of his son Josef's mania for music to know that Natil certainly could play the harp. Although the woman had only met her fellow musicians two days before—and in the case of the pick-up group that Furze had gotten together for this banquet, that very afternoon—she joined effortlessly into the ensemble. She obviously knew her instrument, and she obviously knew her tunes; and though Jacob understood nothing about music—nor did he care to—he smiled as the shawm went *blat* and the vielle went *squeak-squeak* and the harp went *ding-dong* and the cornetto went *honk* in time to the nattering drums, congratulating himself on yet another fine addition to his hoard.

But it was the hoard, he knew, that was the problem, for the faces about him at the table—smiling faces, cordial faces—were smiling and cordial only because he was Jacob Aldernacht, a potential source of gold and silver. Had he been a poor friar, or a leper, or simply a run-of-the-mill beggar, he doubted that the faces would have been so smiling, so cordial . . . or so much in evidence. Oh, to be sure, he might still have received food and even a few coins from the Furzers, since the poverty of the town had made its folk very conscious of the plight of those more unfortunate than they; but the town hall would never have been thrown open, the food would never have been so plentiful, and certainly he would never have been offered so many hands and toasts.

"To Mister Jacob Aldernacht: our friend!"

A little premature, perhaps, but Jacob drank their wretched wine. It was all part of the little game they were playing, a game not unlike Francis's sham charity or the feigned and ironic filial devotion of Edvard and Norman that did nothing to disguise their contempt for their father.

"To Mister Jacob Aldernacht: the greatest man in Adria!"

This was a little better, though *in Europe* might have been more appropriate. Still, Jacob considered, Furze was poor: perhaps their imaginations had been stunted along with their purses.

"To Mister Jacob Aldernacht: a prince, a true prince!"

No, this would not do at all, and therefore, before the applause could rise, Jacob stood up. The room fell silent. Those at the table paused with their hands up and about to clap, or with cups half raised.

Jacob was silent. He let them worry. This was the way it was done.

"I'm no prince," he said at last. "I'm a businessman. I buy and sell. I buy and sell wool. I buy and sell jewels. I buy and sell spices. I buy and sell . . . people like you." He scowled. Paul Drego, his eyes hollow with what must have been a sleepless night—or a sleepless week—wore the face of a man who was watching his house burn down. James, the furrier, still had pasted on his face that same damned silly grin he always seemed to wear, though right now it had a bewildered edge to it. The others were much the same. Only Simon the Jew remained inscrutable. Lending money, collecting interest, being burned alive in their houses . . . Jews, Jacob had found, seemed to be like that.

But, beside him, Francis—whose face, until now, had been anything but smiling and cordial—had suddenly begun to look hopeful.

Jacob regarded his son with the sneer reserved by the unsubtle for the outright transparent. Yes, it all came down to money. It always came down to money. Popes, kings, merchants, beggars: it was money. Money he had. Money they wanted. And Francis and his entire family were no different.

Jacob fingered his wine cup. No, Francis himself was a little different. The second generation of wealthy Aldernachts numbered three: one nitwit who squandered his allowance on musical instruments and books of poetry . . . and waited for his father to die; one mercenary who spent his days breaching Italian fortifications and his nights breaching Italian maidenheads . . . and waited for his father to die; and this one here, a gutless viper . . . who was probably unwilling to wait.

No such luck, Francis. You'll take your turn just like all the rest. If your mother were alive . . .

His thoughts brought him up short. He did not know for certain that Marjorie was dead. She might be alive. Somewhere. Suddenly, amid so many expressions of so many emotions, he missed her. But he had driven her away.

And the faces about him—Francis's included—were still waiting.

"I'm no prince," he said again, wanting to tell them all to go to hell. "You'd all better understand that. If I've got money, it's because I earned it. With my hands. With my sweat. I didn't lah-di-dah it around and get it from my father."

The faces about him had turned pale. Even James had lost his grin.

"You want to know who my father was? He was a weaver, just like me. We wove wool."

Natil, who had silenced the musicians with a glance when she had seen her master rise, was watching him. Jacob could see her blue eyes even from across the room. She was sitting down, her harp on her lap, but she was sitting proudly, and her head was—as usual—uncovered. She still had that damned eagle feather, too.

He laughed suddenly. A sharp little girl, one who knew exactly when to nod and when to smile and how, at the same time, to keep her wits about her and her dignity intact. Simply by being herself, she had bested him. Already! Quite a woman!

He wished that Marjorie had been like that.

"Wool," he said aloud. "That's what I've got to offer. You want wool?"

Silence. He had frightened them. Well, he was going to frighten them some more.

He leaned forward, plunked his cup down on the table with enough force to make the boards rattle. "I said: *Do you want wool?* Speak up, dammit!"

From the merchants came a hushed flurry of stirring and breathing: a chorus of whispers. Yes, they wanted wool.

"You want *money*?"

Yes, they wanted money. Everyone in Furze wanted money.

"Show me." Jacob's voice was flat. "Let me hear you shout for it. *You want it*?"

The reply came in whispers: "Yes."

"Louder."

Hesitation. A collective breath. "Yes!"

"Louder!"

Face pale, eyes clenched as though he were being stretched upon an inquisitorial rack, Paul Drego led the reply, his voice all but sobbing. *"Yes!"*

Jacob was implacable. *"You goddam peasants, I've come to make you rich! You want that?"*

A chorus of voices, male and female, poor and poorer: *"Yes!"*

"LOUDER!"

"YES! YES! YES!"

Had he told them to bow down, Jacob knew, they would have bowed down. Had he told them to rise, they would have risen. Had he told them to fly, they would have made a valiant effort, and some were so desperate that they might have succeeded. He could have ordered them to dance, yelp like dogs, laugh, cry . . . anything. And they would have done exactly as they were told.

But Jacob had had his fill of toadying for the night. "All right then. We'll meet tomorrow morning and discuss details. You'll have your money." He paused, examined faces that were, at once, hopeful, despairing, and ashamed. "On my terms."

A sigh from the banqueters. Francis—red-faced, angry—would not look at him, but Jacob caught Natil's eye.

The harper looked sad. Well, he thought, that made two of them.

And, that night, at bed time, he did something that he had never done before. Instead of simply putting down a glass of wine and a crust of bread and crawling beneath the comforters, he asked Natil to play for him. She had not shouted, she had not crawled. She was proud, proud and sad both. Again, she had bested him, just like Marjorie had (he realized now) bested him, too . . . in her own way, on her own terms.

He could respect that; and for the sake of his sadness, and for the sake of the bitter gall that his money had become, he listened to the chime of harpstrings that night, trying to hear what Natil played.

"What do you think of the new girl?"

"She has the haunches of an ox."

Edvard and Norman, Francis's sons, had gotten into their father's study, pillaged his wine cabinet, broke open his small store of Spanish tobacco, and were enjoying themselves greatly. Smoke, wine, and women: the cardinal pleasures of two young men.

"But what haunches!"

Edvard was the blond. Norman had brown hair and a hint of a beard. In all other ways, though, they were more or less interchangeable, for they held the same opinions, shared the same desires and the willingness to satisfy them.

"Oh, I'll admit they're considerable." Edvard speaking here, sending his words up in a cloud of blue smoke to join the much larger cloud that had collected just beneath the ceiling beams. "Why, a man could get himself crushed between them."

Which made Norman fall abruptly silent and thoughtful. "What," he mused, "do you think it would be like to die that way?"

"What? Crushed?"

Norman was impatient. "Between a woman's thighs, dammit. Drat this pipe! Father spends a fortune on this New World weed and then he skimps on the equipment required to enjoy it."

"Just like Pierre, isn't it?" said Edvard. The young men always called their father Pierre. Sometimes they called him Pierre to his face. "A bit short of the mark, as usual. I'm surprised, actually, that you and I are here at all!"

They both howled at the joke, which called for a refilling of the wine glasses. As might be expected, this delay caused the pipes to go out, and it took a few minutes for them to get resettled.

"Now," said Edvard, "where were we? Oh, yes: the thighs."

"Her name's Omelda."

"Hmmm . . . not at all as exotic as . . . say . . . Dinah."

"Well, Dinah is one in a thousand. She can be exotic. If we pay her."

"Is she coming tonight?"

"Did we pay her?"

"Yes."

"Well then: yes."

"Good," said Edvard, sucking at his pipe. "I've a mind to be cultivating some Venus plots as soon as I can. I want to root down there in the good . . . moist . . . earth." He sucked again. "Dinah will do."

For a time, Edvard and Norman hummed in a toneless, two-part harmony as they propped their feet up on their father's desk, shoving aside the piles of curious old books that Francis had collected. Poisons. Drugs. Cabala. Edvard and Norman had not the slightest idea what their father was doing with such foolishness, but perhaps this was another area in which Francis fell a bit short of the mark.

More wine. Really, this was quite good. Father was gone. So was Grandfather. Aside from Claire—a source of amusement, no more—there was no one in the house to get in their way. They could do as they wished. If Francis found out about their depredations in his study, he might rage a little, of course, but he would do nothing more about it than he did about anything else . . . including being called Pierre.

A bit short of the mark there, also.

"I was thinking . . ." they both began at once. They stared at one another for a moment, startled, then laughed.

"After you," said Edvard.

"No, after you," said Norman.

"All right," said Edvard, "since you say so. I was thinking that Dinah is . . . sufficient. Wouldn't you say that, Norman? Sufficient?"

"Yes. Sufficient." Norman was getting an erection. "But only just sufficient."

"She is accommodating."

"Accommodating, indeed."

Edvard giggled like a schoolboy. "You can stick anything you want into her, and you can leave it there as long as you like. That's my Dinah!"

"*Your* Dinah!"

"Well, *our* Dinah."

"Much better." Norman squinted at a particularly large book bound in heavy leather. *Commentaries*, read the spine. *Elijah del Medigo. Aldine Press*. Whatever the commentaries in question were about, they were in the way, and so Norman kicked them to the floor. There was a small explosion of dust, a crack of bindings.

"Nuhhh," said Edward. "Pierre won't like that."

"Naaah," said Norman. "Ask me if I care."

Edvard smiled, relit his pipe, refilled his wine cup. "*Our* Dinah."

Norman smiled, too.

"Anyway," Edvard went on, "I do think Omelda's thighs are a little scary, but can you imagine what they would feel like wrapped about your neck?"

Norman tipped his head back and stared at the ceiling, completely lost in the magnificence of the thought. His erection, flagging as a result of its exposure to Elijah's *Commentaries*, was suddenly revitalized.

"Could she . . . be bought?" he wondered aloud.

"Dammit, Norman, she already *belongs* to us. We don't have to buy her!"

Norman lifted his head. "They're much better if they go along with it freely, Edvard. You know that. Dinah acquiesces because she is paid. Omelda . . ." He fell again into wonder. "Oh my . . ."

Edvard was warming to the idea. "She's already in the house, and I know the passages to the servants' quarters. I even marked the panels so that I know which lets you into what room. We can get in any time if we wish."

The young men fell back into considering Omelda and her tremendous thighs.

"Like an ox."

"Very like an ox."

"Have you . . ." Edvard raised his eyebrows at Norman. ". . . ever tried an ox?"

Norman spat a mouthful of wine at his brother. "How dare you!"

"Well . . ." Edvard fell to cleaning, reloading, and lighting his pipe with a great deal of unnecessary fuss. ". . . you seem fairly transported at the idea of fucking one!"

Norman stared, then snorted, then giggled, then laughed out loud. "Very good, Edvard. Very good. But what will Pierre say?"

"About an ox?"

"About Omelda." Norman swung his feet down, planted his elbows on his knees, regarded Edvard seriously. "She hasn't been in the house for more than a few days. Father might not like her being . . . used . . . right away."

"He didn't say anything about that kitchen girl." Edvard spat in the corner. "Stupid thing. A bit of blood, and she leaves: imagine that!" He shrugged. "We're better off without her. In any case, Pierre didn't bother to let Grandpa know that she'd left without leave because he didn't want to waste the money on hunting her down. He went down to Furze with Grandpa for the same reason."

"Wasting money?" Norman prodded at the books. "He doesn't seem worried about wasting money on *these*."

Edvard shook his head. "He's afraid that Grandpa will give away the whole family fortune. I've heard him mumbling to himself about it." He abruptly fell silent, frowned. "Don't you . . . don't you ever worry that . . ." He sucked on his pipe, discovered that it had gone out, shrugged. ". . . something like that might happen?"

Norman was incredulous. *"Grandpa?"*

"No, I'm serious." Edvard's eye fell on a slender volume about Arabian poisons. He puzzled over it, then shrugged it off. His father had some peculiar reading preferences, indeed. "Pierre doesn't like this Furze deal at all. His tobacco farm in Spain is foundering because of the Inquisition.'' Edvard pulled the pipe out of his mouth, examined it. ''There's an Inquisition in Furze, too.''

Norman preferred talking about Omelda and her thighs, but he shrugged philosophically: there would be time for Omelda later. ''Grandpa knows how to make money. He knows how to keep it, too.''

''I wonder. He's old.''

''Yes.''

''And old men . . .'' With an abrupt, savage kick, Edvard sent another stack of books to the floor. ''Old men ought to die and get out of the way.''

And, on the floor, now heaped in a pile as confused and meandering as the house that contained them, their leather bindings split and their pages torn, lay Francis's books. His books on drugs, poisons, and magic.

A bit short of the mark. But close. And, perhaps, getting closer.

CHAPTER 12

Hadden and Wheat awoke to a world as new as their names. The night receded like gray mist before the sun as though for the first time, and, out in the shabby parking lot below Wheat's apartment window, the potholed and littered asphalt seemed a wonderful thing, alive with the random sparkles of mica flecks, gritty with dust blown in from the life about it, undulating not with the carelessness of a penny-pinching contractor, but with the very shape of the enshrouded earth.

The sky took on color and clouds. The horizon appeared in a gray haze. The traffic on the interstate sounded, yes, like the faint gurgles of an infant. And Hadden and Wheat stood at the window—arms about one another, coffee growing cold in their untouched cups—staring and listening, just staring and listening.

Hadden had looked in the mirror in the bathroom and had found someone else looking back. Yes, the man resembled George, but he was not George: he was Hadden. His beard had abruptly vanished, his cheekbones had altered, and his build had begun turning from stocky to slender.

And Wheat's clumsiness had fallen from her like a heavy cloak dropped to the floor. She moved with grace and surety, her face was vaguely but distinctly different, and her hands, when she talked, gestured swiftly and economically, like birds performing an aerial dance.

The morning was well advanced when they finally pulled themselves away from the outside world, reheated the coffee, and sat down to think. They had no idea what had happened to them, no idea where it might take them, no idea what they were supposed to do about it.

Wheat held up a hand that shimmered softly, even in

the daylight. "I'm almost afraid to go outside. Do you think other people are going to see this?"

Hadden shook his head. "No." He was surprised at his certainty. "Only we can see it. If this . . . whatever . . . happens to someone else, then they'll see it, too, but . . ."

He fell silent, staring at his own too-slender hand, worrying. In the course of a night drive through the mountains, an earnest conversation in a diner, and a day made holy by friendship and sex, he had been able to accept sudden and unexpected transformation, new thoughts and speech and sensations, and, in fact, his own casual acceptance of such things. Now, though, with the coming of another morning, doubts were beginning to surface.

Wheat noticed his silence, his furrowed brow. "Talk, Hadden. But what?"

"I mean . . ." He flexed his shimmering fingers, almost startled that he could claim this hand as his own. "This is happening fast, and I don't know what it is. I'm getting worried. Shouldn't we see a doctor or something?"

Wheat regarded him silently, then shook her head. He was surprised: she seemed so calm. A new mind, a new body—and intimations of more newness yet to come—and yet she accepted it all, embraced it as she had embraced him when, in her bed, he had entered her and they had become lovers.

"I'll tell you something, Hadden," she said. "Men don't know this, or if they know, they don't pay any attention to it. But I think you'll understand now."

He looked at her.

She shrugged. "You're not . . . really a man anymore."

His look turned to a stare, and then the cold set in. She was right. He knew that she was right.

"It's something that women know," Wheat was saying. "About doctors. Women don't know in their minds, of course. They know it in their bellies and in their breasts. I'm just now putting it into so many words." She smiled, shook her head at such sudden and fast-coming realizations. "This is so strange: I feel like I'm just waking up."

And then it struck Hadden that she had referred to women as though she no longer numbered herself among them.

"Doctors are there to make you normal," she said. "If they can't make you normal, then they give you something to make other people think you're normal." She laughed again, softly, sadly. "It doesn't matter what *you* think."

No longer a man. He was still struggling with the knowledge.

"But I don't want to be normal," Wheat continued as though casually throwing off a burden. "I don't even care whether people think I'm normal. This . . ." She rose, stretched. She was slim, possibly slimmer than she had been the day before, but she looked capable, strong. ". . . this is too good. I feel too good about it."

Hadden did not know what he felt. Despite the wide-eyed and childlike wonder that had found him, that had turned this morning to sunshine and diamonds, there was a gripping in his belly. He was not a man. What did that mean? *What was he*?

"What . . . what should we do then?" he managed.

"Us?" said Wheat. "I think we should leave this place."

This place. Again the language of estrangement.

"I've got five hundred dollars saved up. It's in my moving account. It was going to take me back to Montana someday. What have you got?"

"About a grand." It was from the engagement ring. He had returned it to the store an hour after he had bought it. The jeweler had not even had time to take his cash to the bank.

Was that . . . was that why Tina had walked out on him? Because he was not a man? Had she intuited what Wheat was just now seeing?

Wheat was looking at him, her cornflower blue eyes gleaming with a light that had nothing to do with the spill of morning from the windows; and he suddenly realized why she had spoken of women with a sense of distance: she was no more really a woman than he was a man.

She was something else now.

But she was smiling, unconcerned about the change, pulling it, in fact, closer to herself as, with clumsy fin-

gers, a baby might drag a favorite blanket to its mouth.
"A grand?" she said. "What on earth are you doing
running around with that kind of money in your wallet?"

Shamed by his loss, he hung his head, shrugged.
"Where do you want to go?"

"I don't know. I don't care." She went to another
window, pulled open the curtains, jerked the blinds up.
Street, buildings, sunlight: they all rushed in, and the
light limned her in a radiance that mingled with the aura
of silver that lapped about her. "This is all so new, and
it's so wonderful, but I want more. I want out of this
town. I want the desert. I want trees. I want mountains."
She turned back to him, eyes wide, bright. "I can taste
them, Hadden. I want them like I want food. Don't you?"

He was still struggling. The mention of the money and
the reason he had it had taken him back to another morning that, though only forty-eight hours departed—dear
God, had it only been two days?—seemed so foreign and
stale, seemed such a thing of the past he could not but
marvel that it still had the power to sting.

But it did indeed sting. It stung deeply. It put the bitter
poison straight into his heart. Tina had left, and now
Wheat had said that he was not a man. And, worse, he
knew it to be true.

"Then . . . what am I?" he said.

And Wheat finally understood. Going to him, she sat
down on the worn fabric of the sofa and put her arms
about his neck. No, she was no longer a woman, but she
had been one once, as he had been a man, and the gesture was therefore appropriate and comforting. "You're
Hadden," she said.

"But what does that mean? Hadden isn't a man. What
is he?" He was gesturing wildly, the changes that had
come upon him now overtaking him in a wave of shame.
What the hell was he doing here? What was this? Skin
that glowed with lambent fire? Alterations of face, body,
gesture, language?

Wheat grabbed his hands. "Listen . . ."

"What the—"

She stared into his face, and there was a flicker of
starlight in her eyes. He knew it was starlight. He was
frightened that he knew. But his knowledge and fright
conspired together and silenced him.

"Women know this, too," Wheat began. "We—"

"But you're not a woman!"

"That's right." She shook him, her grip unnervingly strong for such a slender being. "Listen to me, Hadden. Please listen, and try to understand. Try to feel it in yourself. You can do it now. I know you can. When you're a woman, you're always changing into something else. You start out as a girl. You have your first period, and suddenly you're a woman. Then maybe you have a child, and then you're a mother. Your breasts get full, and then you don't belong just to yourself any more, but to that little mouth that's looking to you for food. Then you reach menopause, and you're something else again."

He was staring at her, no longer struggling, for, yes, he understood. He understood it, he felt it, he knew it.

Wheat let go of his hands, sat back. "I'm something else now. And so are you. It's time that we both knew that."

"But . . . what is it that we are?" said Hadden, and the altered inflections and vocabulary of his speech struck him again. And, yes, he was even thinking differently, for he comprehended and felt the import of Wheat's words. There was an openness within him, a sense of free passage that had abruptly cleared. Women felt it, and he felt it, too. But he was not a woman. Nor was he a man. He was . . .

Something else . . .

He could not fight it. He had to go with it, to apply to his own body the lessons of necessity and inevitability that women knew by instinct.

"What are we?" he said again.

Wheat looked out the window at the blue sky. A smile spread over her face like a sunrise. "I don't know exactly," she said. "But I think we'll find out. I don't think that it will be kept from us." She tipped her head to the side, and her starlit gaze found Hadden. "Come on," she said. "Let's load up your van."

"With what?"

"With my stuff," she said. "It's time for me to go home. It's time for *us* to go home. Wherever that is."

With the coming of morning, Furze struggled up out of sleep like a drunkard shaking off the effects of a night's excess: glad to be free of its vertiginous nightmares, it was nonetheless uneasy about the upcoming day. Muddy streets steamed with the stagnant warmth of shit, vomit, urine, and, occasionally, blood; the sky was the color of buttermilk; the House of God stood blackly, like a finger lifted to the sky: inauspicious omens all.

But though Furze awoke to face another day of struggle, Inquisition, and penury, the town was now faintly laced with a sense of wild hope, for Jacob Aldernacht had agreed, in person, to discuss terms. To be sure, the terms would be his own, but Furze was in the position of a thoroughly ruined woman who was willing to sell soul and body both in order to put a mouthful of meat into her child.

In his combination shop and house, Paul Drego rose, kissed his wife, and ate breakfast, hoping that the moribund cathedral framed by his window was not a completely fitting emblem for his city. Elsewhere, James, smiling his silly grin still, made love to his sweetheart, and afterwards fed her the last of the delicate pastries he had scrounged out of his most recent miserly commission from David a'Freux, putting bit after bit into her little red mouth despite her (admittedly feeble) protests. Simon the Jew said his prayers. The convicted heretics who had escaped Fredrick's fate by earnestly abjuring what they neither understood nor particularly believed appeared at mass, their crosses of yellow felt prominent on the fronts and backs of their jackets . . . as would be the case for the rest of their lives. Siegfried of Magdeburg prostrated himself before the cross of his Savior, waiting, hoping for a vision of the divine, a vision that remained elusive. Albrecht privately debated, for the hundredth time, the question of the Inquisition.

Natil, though, was looking for her shawm player. "Renaud, have you seen Harold?"

Renaud, like most drummers, kept his fingers and hands in constant, rhythmic motion. This morning, he was sitting with his nakers in the middle of the room shared by the male musicians, tapping out an intricate rhythm, his eyes closed.

"Renaud?"

"Haven't—" *Bonk!* "—seen—" *Bonk, bonk!* "—him." *Bonkita-bonk!*

She looked to the other man in the room. "Reimbold?"

Reimbold played the cornetto, and was as hot as Renaud was cool. "That son of a bitch! He threw up in my bed last night, pissed on my horn, and then fell into a stupor!"

Natil was patient. She was in charge of the musicians, and though she was rather disturbed by the constant supervision they required, she had promised the Aldernachts that she would supervise them, and Elves—no matter how human they had become—kept their word. "But where is he now?"

"I don't know and I don't care!"

Natil sighed, withdrew, closed the door.

Now, Harold, shawm player and would-be womanizer, was very much in keeping (at one, in fact) with the spirit of Furze this morning, for in the same tavern in which Paul Drego and James had talked, drunk, and been overheard, he was attempting to simultaneously collect his wits and fight off a raging headache.

Hair of the dog. He was drinking beer and eating cold herring and hot bread: not quite what had gotten him into this condition, but close enough; and he had learned from years of experience that the way to beat a stomach revolted by the mere thought of food was to take it firmly in hand, give it a shake and a severe talking to, and stuff some kind of breakfast into it . . . accompanied by some kind of alcohol.

He felt absolutely no resentment toward Natil for the beating she had given him. The harper was a spirited woman, obviously accustomed to the rough intentions of rougher men, and he should have remembered that. If anything was going to induce her to spread her legs, it was charm. Charm and sweet talk and gifts. Harold knew charm and sweet talk, and gifts could be bought. But, in order to further his plans, he had to rid himself of the effects of what he now fuzzily estimated was most of a barrel of wine.

He resolved to keep track of his drinking. Next time. He would keep track next time. One had to pace oneself, after all. Next time.

He was calling for more beer as Natil, dressed in the costume of an Aldernacht servant, her harp in her hand,

descended the stairs of the house that Jacob had bought—
Jacob never rented anything—in Furze. From the servants' floor just beneath the roof she made her way down
one flight, her steps silent, her skirts rustling. Manarel,
Jacob's road steward, was standing, thick as a tree
trunk, before his master's closed door. ''Morning, Mistress Natil.''

''Good morning, Master Manarel. Have you seen Harold?''

''Not since last night. Me and two of the boys carried
him upstairs and pitched him in with his fellows. What
happened after that, I don't know.'' He fixed her with a
dark eye. ''Has he been bothering you?''

Natil laughed, felt a pang. So human. ''Not at all. I
simply feel that I really ought to keep track of him.''

''Well,'' he nodded, ''Harold's one who warrants it.''

Jacob's voice from within the room: ''Is that my
harper?''

Manarel cracked the door open. ''It is, Mister Jacob.''

''Send her in,'' said Jacob. ''I want some music with
my breakfast.''

Natil entered her master's room Harold ordered more
beer. A spirited woman, indeed. Quite a woman. And
all that hair!

He considered that it was her hair that had first at-
tracted him. Though there was certainly more to a woman
than her hair. At least, he thought, more than the hair on
her head!

He laughed, choked, spat a mouthful of beer out into
the rushes on the floor. ''Tapster!'' he called, pointing
to his cup. ''Refill this thing!''

It was refilled. Several times. The tapster looked
pleased. Harold's head felt even better. His mind, though,
was racing about, flitting from music, to Natil, to travel,
to Natil, to sex, to Natil . . . and to Natil . . . and to
Natil.

Natil played for Jacob—wondering all the while why
the music-hating wool magnate had suddenly taken such
a fancy to bronze strings—and, afterwards, chatted for a
few minutes about the dinner the night before.

''Those boys that Paul found: did they do all right with
the music?''

"Very well," said Natil. "They were quite the accomplished performers."

"Good. I might hire them." Jacob pursed up his lips, put his hands behind his head, leaned back against the pillows. "I'm going to give you a raise, Natil."

"Me, sir?"

He glared at her. "You're the only Natil in the room, aren't you? Of course: you. I'm giving you a raise because I like you. I might throw you out tomorrow because I hate you. How do you like working for me?"

Natil smiled. She doubted that Jacob knew how much she would have liked to have been tossed out tomorrow . . . or even today. "Thank you, Mister Jacob."

"Go on: get out. I'll have music with my dinner, too. Paul will be there. Just Paul. We'll be talking."

Natil nodded. "As you wish, master."

But as she was rising to leave, Jacob suddenly told her to sit down again. He leaned forward confidentially. "You've done some traveling, haven't you, Natil?"

"I have, sir." Into Africa. Across Europe and Asia. Up into Siberia. Across the straight that separated the Old World from the New. Across what she now knew would eventually be called the Great Plains and into the forests of the Appalachians and the Catskills. Down into the jungles of Central America, the rain forest of the Amazon, and the broad pampas of the future Argentina. Up again, crossing tundra, crossing ocean, to Europe. Looking for Elves. Finding none but herself. And now she herself . . .

"I have traveled," she said.

"All over."

Natil nodded slowly. "All over."

Jacob scowled, but Natil sensed that the expression was meant to disguise another. "You ever meet any gypsies out there?"

"A few, sir."

"Did you ever see a woman with them . . . a thin woman? Blonde? Blue eyes?"

Natil blinked. The Romany were a dark people.

"Maybe . . . maybe her name was Marjorie." Jacob was leaning forward, his hands clutching the comforter. "I . . ."

"It's not important, mind you."

"Of course, sir. I . . . do not think that I ever met a gypsy named Marjorie. Or with blue eyes and blond hair."

"Oh." Jacob nodded, flopped back in the pillows. "All right then. It really . . ." He fell silent, musing.

Natil rose and went to the door, her footsteps silent.

"It really isn't important," Jacob said suddenly.

Knowing that any response on her part would, at best, only add to the old man's evident pain, Natil simply bowed. But when she turned and opened the door, she found Francis standing just outside the room, his ear pressed against what was now empty space.

"Good morning, Mister Francis," she said primly.

Francis straightened. "Ah . . . yes. Good morning, Natil. God bless you."

He did not see her wince.

While Natil had been talking with Jacob, though, Harold had been having a conversation of his own. Though most of the tavern's morning customers seemed inclined to keep to themselves, looking up with startled and even frightened faces when Harold shouted, or stamped his feet, or called for more drink, the shawm player had nonetheless found a friend among them: a common laborer who, apparently, liked the beer, because he bought it by the full measure. The man was listening patiently, even eagerly, as Harold drew out, one by one, his views on women, music, travel, politics, even religion, and expounded upon each with rising warmth.

"Yes," Harold was saying. "I'm drunk, but you've got to listen to me, because there's wisdom in wine. Wine makes men wise and amorous and bold. They knew about that years ago! Listen . . ." He suddenly broke out in song:

"Istud vinum, bonum vinum,
vinum generosum,
reddit virum curialem, probum animosum!"

"Do you know what that is?" he asked.

His appreciative audience of one admitted that, no, he did not know.

"That's Latin," said Harold. "That's a Latin hymn . . . to Bacchus! Bacchus, the god of wine. Wine and wisdom! And did you know that song is . . . over three hundred years old. Now that's immortality. Heaven is for priests. Immortality . . .'' He waved his arms about to give his audience the idea that he was talking about music, or maybe Bacchus, or maybe drink, or maybe something else. No matter. ''. . . is for musicians! I'll take immortality over heaven any day. Any day at all. That's what *I* think.''

His audience nodded.

''Why,'' said Harold, ''there's more wisdom in Bacchus than there is in the Church! Yes, that's true.''

His audience was listening: eagerly. So were a number of the others in the room: frightened.

''I mean, what does the Church promise? Heaven. *I* say that heaven lies between a woman's legs. I've lived for twenty-two years, and I can tell you for a fact that any visions of heaven that I've been granted have come to me . . .'' He choked, laughed. ''Come . . . that's it. Ha! *Come* to me when my trusty prick was good and deep in womanflesh. That's heaven.''

The audience spoke. ''That's heresy, in't it?''

Harold, fuzzy and dull from drink, stared at him. ''I suppose so.''

And Natil was now on the street, her soft shoes treading silently. She was looking for Harold. With her harp tucked under her arm, she poked into taverns, bakeries, eateries, examined the interiors of leather shops and shoe shops, knocked on the doors of impoverished instrument makers, her quick, elven eyes searching for that pouty face.

But Harold was in another part of the city, and though Natil would get there soon enough, she was not there yet. The shawm player was still talking, his audience still listening.

''Heresy . . . hmmm.''

''Dard sure it's heresy,'' said the audience. ''D'ye admit that?''

''Well . . .'' Harold considered, then turned defiant. A man could have his thoughts and ideas, could he not? It was his own mind, was it not? He could think whatever he wanted, could he not?

''Yes,'' he said, ''I admit it. Guilty as charged!'' He held up a hand as though to swear, laughed.

''But you've heard the teachings o' the Church,'' said the audience. ''Surely you dan disbelieve the Church!''

Harold fixed him with a glare. He was not Jacob Aldernacht's shawm player for nothing, and he wanted that
understood. "The Church," he said, "is run by men like
me. And I'll bet that they find their little bits of heaven
between women's legs, too."

Natil entered yet another shop. She was asking questions now. The woman behind the counter wore the double crosses of a convicted heretic, and there was a
haunted look about her eyes that was more than accounted for by the scars on her arms.

"Have you seen a man—" began the harper.

"Nay," said the woman quickly. "Nay, I han't seen
na'one!"

Natil stood for a moment, perplexed. Then: "Very
well, madam. Good day."

She turned and left. The woman ran after her as far as
the open door. "God bless you, mistress! God bless you!
God bless you!"

"You think the Church is wrong, then," said the audience.

Harold was already nodding. "Wrong and wrong
again. Why, if I were pope—"

"But you can't be pope."

"I could be pope . . . if I were pope." Harold had
given up on bread and herring and beer an hour ago and
had devoted himself exclusively to the worship of wine.
"If I were pope, I'd get rid of this celibacy. Everyone
could have his heaven right now." He stared down into
his cup. "No one's celibate anyway," he mumbled. "It
just gets in the way."

"But the priests are the ministers o' God."

"The priests are men. Little venal men. Like . . ."
Harold brightened, preened. ". . . like me."

Gritting her teeth, Natil tried the churches and chapels. Crucifixes stared back at her, crucifixes that depicted
the blood and torments of long ago—or last week—that
had nothing to do with the grassy plain, the endless stars,
and the vision of a Woman that Natil still remembered
. . . but could no longer attain.

No Harold.

Harold's audience stood up. "I'm going to have to
leave you, Harold."

"I understand perfectly," said the shawm player. "Do

what you must do. I have . . ." He sniffed with an air of importance. Jacob Aldernacht's musician. *That* kind of man! ". . . work of my own to attend to."

The audience nodded, paid his bill, and left. Harold tested his feet to determine whether they would support him. Next time: he would have to keep track next time.

But when he looked up, he saw soldiers entering the tavern, and in a few moments more he discovered that he did not have to worry about whether his feet would support him or not.

Natil, arriving a few minutes later, found not a trace of Harold. He had obviously never been there. No one remembered him, no one had seen anyone of the sort that morning.

God bless you, mistress! God bless you! God bless you!

CHAPTER 13

Alone in the Aldernacht kitchen, Omelda was washing again, washing the floor, sending gray water across the gray flagstones with large, sweeping strokes of her big brush while, in her mind, she heard plainchant.

Asperges me, Domine, hyssopo, et mundabor.

Shrouded in a fog of song, unwilling to lift her voice in unison with it ever again, Omelda stared with ox-like stubbornness at the wet flagstones as though by so fixating upon the mundane and material she could keep herself from being swept away by her obsession. She stared, she scraped bits of bread and meat out of the cracks, she scrubbed at tracked-in dung. It was stupid, human, messy work. It was her work: the work of a mental prisoner.

This morning, though, the plainchant was vying with other concerns, for in the pocket of Omelda's gown was a piece of paper with writing on it: a poem. It was the latest of several anonymous offerings, the first having appeared about a week after she had entered the Aldernacht household. Slipped under the door of her tiny room while she was away, scrawled in a labored imitation of the cursive writing used in Rome, it was (again like the others) penned in wretched Italian. A love sonnet. Birds, unrequited passion, the seasons, fashionable melancholy based in obscure meditations: all the Petrarchian motifs had been scrambled together and spilled out onto the page in a kind of rhyming stew that was painfully marked by an overwrought sense of its own deathless immortality.

O, graceful little sparrow, you so wing . . .

Omelda had winced at the new verses as she had winced at the old. A nun from an abbey in which learning was still prized, she knew Italian quite well, as well as French, German, Spanish, Latin, some Greek, and even a little Arabic and Hebrew. She was literate and well read, and she knew good imitations of Petrarch when she read them. This was, most assuredly, not a good imitation.

And sorrowing for times past I hear sing . . .

Lavabis me . . .

Combined with the plainchant, the poor Italian muddled her brain even more than usual this morning, and she was crying again. She did not want to be in the Aldernacht house, not with Natil gone, but if she left, she would be hunted and captured, and her true status and origins would most likely be discovered. Natil would then be beyond her forever. And so, her tears falling into the suds and the sludge, she continued to wash the floor.

A step behind her, a polite cough. Dully, she looked over her shoulder. Josef Aldernacht was standing in the doorway, his hair curled and topped with a wreath of flowers, his fine Italian clothes hanging limply on his thin frame. One of Jahn Witczen's boxy lutes was in his hands, and he was smiling at her with the air of a young lover contemplating the gift of a rose from his beloved.

She knew then the origin of the poems.

"Mistress Omelda," he said with what Omelda understood as an attempt at a courtly bow. In the midst of things, though, his lute clacked into a counter and set the strings ringing, and as he hurriedly silenced them, he bent too fast and his wreath fell off.

Omelda still stared dully. "Good morning, Mister Josef," she said.

He resettled his wreath, cleared his throat. "Please," he said, "call me Josef. I am a humanist. The lineage of my beliefs stretches back to sunny Italy, to Urbino, where Baldassare and Giuliano and their circle of dear and devoted friends knew each other by first name. There were no pretensions of nobility there, no titles, only humanists and lovers of humanity." He bowed again. "I expect the same in my household."

Omelda nodded slowly.

Unaware of her fog, he grinned, swung up a leg, and planted himself on the counter. "Much better, O woman." He set the lute on his lap. "You should know, Omelda, that I am a great admirer of womanhood. All that is pure and noble and graceful dwells by nature in the fair sex. And I will even go so far as to agree with my comrade in spirit, Giuliano de' Medici, that there are countless ways in which women equal or surpass their brothers in ability, wisdom, and virtue.'' He sighed at his own words, the wreath in his hair drooping of a sudden to cover one eye. ''Don't you agree?''

In her present condition, Omelda could neither agree or disagree with anything. She simply did not have the mental space in which to form an opinion. But she knew what her owners expected of her, and so she nodded, plodding ahead with her task. More water. Scrub. Scrape. ''Yes,'' she said, ''of course.''

''I see,'' he said, ''that we also are comrades.''

''Yes . . . of course.''

''Do you like my poetry?'' He leaned forward earnestly. Ever the pining lover looking for something to love! ''I wrote it for you. You have . . .'' He sighed. ''. . . inspired me . . .''

''Yes . . . of course.''

He fingered his lute. ''I have a song.''

She suffered it. She could not but suffer it. It made little difference in any case, though, because she hardly heard it. Nothing save Natil's harp could banish her affliction, and though Josef strummed and plucked and twanged his lute, his voice, a thin, reedy tenor, intoning his lurching verses in a nasal monotone, what Omelda heard was chant. Plainchant. The Office for terce, of the Wednesday of the forth week after Easter.

Josef sang, and then, after taking her cracked and soapy hand in his own, gazed searchingly into her face. ''Adieu,'' he said softly. ''O dear woman.''

Omelda nodded. ''Yes . . . of course.''

''I will come again.''

''Yes . . . of course.''

He left her with her soap and her water and her plainchant and—she guessed fuzzily among the intrusive voices—went off to write more poetry and more songs, to commission another crate of an instrument from Jahn Witczen, to pore over volumes of humanist and classical philosophy that he did not understand.

Omelda went back to her washing. And when she was done, the Office was over, and so was the chant. For the present. But the present was good enough for Omelda, and as she packed up her bucket and her brush and

sluiced the dirty water into the gutter, the clean floor
seemed to her an echo of her clean mind, for both were
scrubbed and scraped and free of past stains . . . for
now. The floor, to be sure, would be filthy again shortly—
Martha and the cooks were already tromping in to prepare the midday meal—and her mind would be cluttered
again sooner than that, but for now they were both clean.

Silence: silence and privacy and clear thought. Omelda
relished these times, so much so that today she even gave
up food, for the room in which the servants ate would be
full of talk and noise and useless conversation, and she
was unwilling to squander her inner quiet with such dis-
tractions. She made her way, therefore, to her room, there
to sit, just sit, to stare out the window at the stables and
the street, to enjoy the quiet of a free mind.

She closed the door, sat down. The stables smelled,
the street smelled, but her thoughts were her own. She
could think about the stables and the street, and about
Natil's eventual return. She could even dream that someday she might return to her convent, take her place once
more among her sisters, find in that quiet abbey an outward sign of an inner peace in which chant was chant
and no more, from out of which worship proceeded, worship and a love as natural and free flowing as song.

She did not hear the panel in the wall slip to the side
on well-tallowed grooves, for it had been designed to be
silent. But she did hear movement, and she suddenly felt
hands on her.

"We want you, Omelda," Edvard was whispering.
Norman's tongue was prodding at her already, slipping
in and out of her ear, leaving a trail of wetness wherever
it went, and Edvard joined him from the other side, their
hands gripping her hair to hold her steady, slipping down
to cup a breast, prodding at her groin, lifting her skirts
and insinuating fingers into her vulva. "My, you're a
clean little one, aren't you?"

She fought for her mind, fought for her privacy. Her
body . . . they could have her body. It was dung, and
they could have it. But her mind . . .

Clinging to her thoughts as desperately as she was, she
did not protest as they stripped her with practiced male
hands and carried her to her bed; and they expressed to
one another—they hardly talked to Omelda at all—their

surprise that they did not have to tie her up and gag her as was usually the case with a new girl. Omelda, they exclaimed back and forth with giggles and boyish enthusiasm, was surprisingly compliant, even eager.

But she was not compliant, and she was not eager. She was hardly paying any attention. As they prodded her with penises and fingers, as they squeezed sperm into her mouth and her rectum, as they licked her and bit her and scratched her and moved her about like a doll, Omelda was elsewhere, wrapped in the privacy of her inner world. She thought of Natil, of harpstrings, of the stables and the street. She dreamed, with all the clarity of a focused mind, of returning to the only home she had ever known.

They could abuse her body, but her mind was beyond their grasp. And when they finally left her—soiled, bruised, and bleeding—she was staring at the ceiling, her inward thoughts gripped with a mental steel that made the iron prods with which they had violated her seem but wax.

Privacy. They could not take her privacy away.

"We'll be back," said Norman.

"You'll have to meet Dinah," said Edvard. "She's a . . ." He giggled. "a friend of ours. Just like you. But she's a little minx . . . and you're a bit of a cow. I can hardly wait to see you together." And then the panel in the wall slid closed.

Omelda stared. Thinking.

The dining table in David a'Freux's mansion was a lengthy affair: well over sixty feet of carved and inlaid rosewood that stretched all the way from the elaborate pointed arches and tiered steps of the entryway of the hall to the tall, grisaille windows at the far end. The food was rich, varied, and demonstrated its provider's appetite for superfluity. In much the same way, it was also tasteless.

Jacob was unimpressed, but with Francis at his side and Natil harping quietly in the corner—he had grown rather fond of the musician and now kept her at hand as a matter of course—he ate, made conversation with David, even found ways of actually being polite to this paunchy ox of a man who obviously thought himself quite as worthy of flattery as, perhaps, under the circumstances, he was. David was the present baron of Furze, and as such he had a say in any bargain that might be struck with the wool cooperative.

So Jacob and Francis ate and listened to David speak in magnificent terms of his lands (small and poor) and his battles (few and insignificant) and his ambitions (great indeed). There was no one else in the room save for an occasional servant. The sixty-foot table held David, Jacob, and Francis; the corner held Natil . . . and that was all.

"This is an age of nations," David was saying. "Louis pulled France together, and Ferdinand did the same for Spain."

Jacob could have sworn that Isabella had something to do with Spain. The pope, after all, had named two Catholic Kings. David, though, was a man who donned the harness of his chosen subject and pulled it along with the indefatigable determination of a plow-ox: he was not one to be distracted by facts. "And Henry did the same over in England. The Empire's still wallowing, of course . . ."

"Of course," said Francis. He was about to continue with some observations of his own—possibly about Isabella and the tobacco ventures he had in Spain—when Jacob quietly kicked him into silence.

David plodded. ". . . but everywhere else . . ."

Except, thought Jacob, *for Italy, the Netherlands* . . .

". . . men, great men . . ."

. . . *Poland* . . .

". . . are pulling their states together . . ."

. . . *Austria, Hungary* . . .

". . . and making them something to reckon with. Now I ask you . . ."

. . . *Serbia, and, to be sure* . . .

". . . what about . . ."

. . . *Adria.*

". . . Adria?"

Jacob had been half expecting it. Here was David and his ambitions, and here was Jacob Aldernacht and his money. It was depressingly inevitable.

With an inward sigh, he picked up his wine cup, held it out. A servant with a decanter sprinted out of the doorway to the kitchen, refilled it, and then sprinted away.

"We have to be realists, now," David continued, still straining against the yoke, his eye on the end of the furrow. "This is an age for realists. This is an age for men with foresight, men with plans . . ."

"Men with money?" Jacob prompted.

"Men like Louis XI of France." David continued with the furrow, straight across the field. "Men like—" He turned his profile to Jacob. "I'm related to Louis, did you know? Can't you see the family resemblance?"

Years ago, Jacob had lent money to Louis: an instant loan on the king's good word when that Burgundian affair had finally come to a head. He had rather enjoyed the king's penchant for plain clothes and manners and had, at a royal wink, played along with the joke when the Venetian ambassador had mistaken the monarch for a gardener.

But Louis had also lived within his means and paid his debts on time. David was nothing like Louis, either in appearance or, Jacob knew, in finance.

"Ah," said David, "but there's the question of money."

Francis was looking uncomfortable again, and Jacob guessed that his son's feelings had nothing whatsoever to do with the condition of his shins.

"That's the thing," David continued. "Money. It takes money to pull a kingdom together."

Jacob's eye fell on his harper. Natil had never asked him for anything, had, in fact, appeared startled and almost unwilling when he had raised her salary. She seemed content with a plate of food, a place to sleep, and her harp; and Jacob even suspected at times that had the woman been left destitute save for her instrument, she would have had no complaint. Perhaps that was why he liked her.

"You want money, don't you?" he said to David.

The ox fetched up against a stone wall, stopped, eyed the impediment. "Well, as a matter of fact . . ."

Francis sat up suddenly, opened his mouth. Jacob kicked him again.

"Tell me about your plans, baron," Jacob said amiably.

It rapidly became obvious both that David's plans were many and that his planning was as wretched and meandering as one of Josef's sonnets. With Aldernacht money in his treasury, David intended to equip an army. With the army, he intended to slowly bring all of Adria under his control.

It had obviously not occurred to him that the train of burned and wasted cities he would leave behind in the course of executing his plans would be incapable of providing him with the financial base he would need for the continuation of those same plans. But this was nothing new for the a'Freux family: David's ancestors had demonstrated the same execrable judgment when they had lost the Free Towns.

David finished, looked expectant. Francis looked despairing.

"Loans." Jacob leaned back in his chair, steepled his fingers, pursed his lips. "Loans are . . . difficult things."

David's eyebrows lifted. "Difficult?"

Inwardly, Jacob snorted. No, loans were not particularly difficult for noblemen. They borrowed, and then, unlike good old Louis, forgot to repay. Or, if they did repay, it was the people of their estates who actually came up with the money.

"Loans," he said, "have a way of coming due."

David flushed. "Are you insinuating that I could not repay a loan?"

Jacob *knew* that David could not repay a loan. In fact, he suspected that David, despite his airs and flourishes— or maybe because of them—was living a hand-to-mouth existence. "Not at all," he lied. "I simply think that there are better ways for you to get what you want."

David leaned forward.

"I'm prepared to discuss them."

"Do."

Francis, Jacob thought, was looking a little too pleased. But: "Furze," said the old man, "is not a wealthy town."

"Not at all," David admitted with reluctance.

"Your revenues from it can't amount to very much."

David's mouth clamped down as though he had found a burr in his cud, but Jacob knew what he was doing. This man who enveloped a seat on the other side of the table was no craven burgher whom he could shout and bully into acquiescence. This was a nobleman. Worse, this was a nobleman with delusions. Very well, Jacob would make the delusions work for him.

He glanced at Francis, who, suddenly anticipating Jacob's plans, had turned sullen, glowering. Furze was going to get the money. Furze was going to get *his* money.

"What I mean, baron," he said, "is this: if your revenues from Furze increased, you might have the money you want without a loan."

David sat back, considering. "Raise the taxes? I suppose I could do that."

Jacob stifled an urge to shout. Raise taxes. Of course. The people are starving, so you raise their taxes. Why not burn the city down, too? Stupid oaf! "No, no: there are other ways."

David looked interested. Francis looked despairing.

"Suppose," Jacob said, dropping his voice, "I guarantee that in a year, your income from Furze will double. And that it will double again in another year after that. And that it will possibly double again in another two. What would you say?"

David looked more than interested. Someone had just offered a ripe apple to the ox. "I'd say . . . very good."

"What would that do for your plans?"

"Everything."

"And if it then doubled again . . . as it well could?"

"More than everything."

Jacob eyed the baron, felt nothing but contempt. And old Louis's successor had dangled a patent of nobility before him as an inducement for that Italian loan. Pah! Rat shit and bird farts! "You're a very fortunate man, Baron David."

"Me?"

"You. You've got some good men in this city. Men like Paul Drego and the others in the wool cooperative."

At the mention of the cooperative, Francis winced.

Jacob continued. "I want to help them. I want to give them money so that they can make money. And when they make money, then . . ."

David stared, not quite comprehending.

Jacob prompted. "Then you . . ."

David still stared.

Patiently now. "Then you make mon—"

David finally understood. "I make money, too!"

Jacob nodded, sat back. He had Furze in his pocket. Paul and his boys would have their loan, with David's blessing. Not that it would really do David any good in the long run, for if the wool cooperative succeeded—and Jacob was determined that it would—Furze would soon have enough money in its treasury to buy outright a charter and independence. The luxury loving baron would be perfectly willing to sell his birthright and future for something that was a little more than a mess of pottage, but no more lasting.

For now, though, Jacob had David's approval and his good will. This last, perhaps, was even more important at present than his approval, for now that the matter of wool was settled, Jacob wanted something else from David. The baron of Furze had been involved in the recent theft of some Aldernacht property: a serious affair indeed. Jacob had a private army, and he could well have forced the issue, but he did not want to jeopardize the cooperative. Therefore, he was content to continue his subtleties, to use David, his plans, approval, and good will, just as much as he could.

"But," he said before David could relish his future income too much, "I think we've left something out."

David's ox eyes flickered. "Left something out?"

"The Inquisition."

"What—?"

"The Inquisition seems to step in everywhere," said Jacob. "It seems to spoil . . . everything." He nodded to Francis. "My son here could tell you about his tobacco plantations in Spain, about what the Inquisition did there."

"Indeed," started Francis. "I—"

"But . . . ." Yet another kick. Francis fell silent. ". . . he won't."

Out of the corner of his eye, Jacob caught a glimpse of movement at the door of the kitchen. Just a flicker: a shoulder, or perhaps a face, withdrawing suddenly. He knew what that meant. Like many of the people of Furze, one of David's servants was earning a little extra money on the side . . . by spying for the Inquisition.

"You know the law about confiscation, my good baron," he went on. "No one is immune. And bigger men than either of us . . . ." This was an outright fabri-

cation, for Jacob arrogantly defied any celibate little
cockroach of the Church to best him. ". . . have been
implicated in heresy, and lost everything. Including their
lives."

"I don't see—"

"What happens if . . ." Jacob shrugged. ". . . if
something happens?"

David was unwilling to part with the money that Jacob
had dangled before him. Just as Jacob had planned. "Impossible."

"Not impossible at all. One of my own men, I believe,
was taken by the Inquisition two days ago."

David abruptly fell silent.

Jacob picked up his knife, cut an apple in two, stuck
the point in and flicked a seed to the floor. "I want him
back."

David squirmed, caught between money and the Inquisition. It was not a comfortable position in which to
be. "I have no say in the affairs of the Inquisition."

Jacob flicked another seed to the floor. "You're the
secular arm in Furze. It had to be your men who picked
him up and took him in."

"If he's been arrested, then he's in the House of God,"
said David. There was a touch of fear in his voice. "I
can't do anything for him."

Jacob frowned. "You're the Baron of Furze."

"I'm a Christian, as are you," said David. "The
Church has the power to bind and to loose, in heaven and
on earth. I carry out the orders of God. I don't ask questions: questions are what the Inquisition is for."

Much as the ox had stumbled against a wall, so Jacob
now found himself smacking into simple faith, and it
occurred to him that faith, like everything else, had
changed. Honor had been commuted to cash, nobility to
trappings, and faith had turned into mere outward orthodoxy . . . and fear. But having seen Furze, its toadying
burghers, its virulent Inquisition, its fool of a baron, he
could not but wonder whether the faith that he remembered—a real faith, a real belief rooted in the mutual
trust of God and His people—had ever really existed, or
whether it was simply the delusion of an old man perched
on the brink of senility and death.

Jacob regarded the ambitious, frightened, braggart,

tremulous figure of the baron, saw too much of his own reflection, and was disgusted.

"So you won't help," he said.

"I can't help," said David. "If your man is guilty of heresy, he'll be sentenced. If he's innocent, then he'll go free."

Jacob's disgust turned to anger. Damned, stupid ox.

He kept his conversation muted for the remainder of the meal, leaving David to wonder whether Furze would become wealthy or not. That was fine. Let him wonder. Jacob was examining his options. Despite his wealth, he had been thwarted by faith and fear. Strong thing, faith, and fear was stronger still. Siegfried of Magdeburg was going to suffer, one way or another.

"Well," he said over a last glass of wine, "I assure you, baron, that I'll take all this under careful consideration."

The baron heaved himself up. "I do hope you'll see it my way, Mister Jacob, and lend the cooperative what they need."

His way! A short time ago, he had been willing to tax his city into the ground!

"I think," said Jacob, "that it might be arranged." He could have been talking about Furze, he could have been talking about Siegfried's punishment. Both were related, to be sure, and the second depended upon the first.

David was beaming. *His* way!

Escorted by a'Freux attendants and guards in the very best debt-ridden style, Jacob returned to his house with his son and his harper. Natil, having played for five straight hours, was tired, and Jacob sent her to supper and bed without asking for further music. Francis, though, was still inwardly raging, and he hardly waited until they had climbed to their upstairs room before his anger put his studied pomposity to flight.

"You never let me say anything, dammit! You treat me like a child! Why do you even bother taking me anywhere? Do you simply want to humiliate me?"

Jacob stood in the middle of his bedroom, wanting nothing so much as to go to bed, and he even admitted to himself that he wanted to go to bed with someone. A girl. A woman. Someone who would make the mattress

reek more of scent than of gold, someone who would
make the coverlets and throws seem a little less lonely.

He found himself wishing again for Marjorie. But he
had driven her away. And constant humiliation was probably what had done it.

"I don't let you say anything," he said, "because you
wouldn't say anything I'd want anyone to hear."

"I can bargain as well as you can."

"Maybe." Jacob looked at his bed. He did not even
want sex anymore. The old withered thing between his
legs was too dried up to do anything more than put a
bullet of sperm through his heart. He just wanted company. He just wanted . . .

Tired, he passed a hand over his face. Everything was
gone. Money was all he had left. Money . . . and children like Francis.

"You can bargain," he said, "but you'd bargain your
way right out of Furze. And I want Furze. I want it
enough that I'm even willing to let Harold suffer for his
own idiocy and—" He broke off, suddenly wondering
about Harold. The shawm player's arrest, smack in the
middle of negotiations with the cooperative, had been too
perfectly timed to be a coincidence. And then there was
Fredrick: an Aldernacht man to the core. Disappeared.
Probably the Inquisition. Doubtlessly the Inquisition.
And then that servant at David's house. Listening.

Did Siegfried want to scuttle the wool cooperative
loan?

Jacob went to the window, leaned out, looked up the
street toward the House of God. His jaw clenched. Siegfried was in trouble. Siegfried had just run into Jacob
Aldernacht. "I want it," he said. "Now more than
ever."

CHAPTER 14

In Natil's dreams, Hadden and Wheat were going home, taking I-70 westward, crossing the beautiful, tortured plains that had so tried Brigham Young and his followers, then turning south toward Arizona. They meandered through the land, touching desert and lake and ridge as one might try the light switches in a new house, peering at sunrise and moonrise and even pieces of gravel as though into new cupboards: *Look at that! I've never seen anything like that! I never knew that was here!*

No, Hadden and Wheat were no longer man and woman. They were, distinctly, something else. Buying hamburgers at a roadside steakhouse, using public toilets along a lonely stretch of I-15, clambering along steep escarpments in the Four Corners area, marveling along with the camera-toting tourists at the kivas and ancient ruins of Mesa Verde—they did all these things, but they did them as though they were strangers who passed this way in disguise.

But though any semblance of humanity had become for them a mere mask, something presented only for the benefit of others, they did not feel alien or separate. Rather, they maintained an unshakable conviction that they belonged here, that hamburgers, toilets, escarpments, and, yes, even tourists were all part of this world into which they had, suddenly and totally, come. This was what they had hungered for. This was real. This was home.

And Natil envied them, for she herself no longer had any sense of home or of belonging. She moved through the world at arm's length, and the unity of soul and substance that had once made her deathlessness not a burden but instead a simple, joyful being was broken now. Natil was a woman who happened to play the harp, and her footsteps, increasingly audible, sounded alien and tres-passing on the packed dirt of the streets of Furze as she made her way towards the House of God.

The tower stood up above the rooftops of Furze like a stubby finger, but the surrounding building was broad and low. A complex of offices, archives, tribunal rooms, prison cells, and, below ground, torture chambers and dank holes for confirmed and recalcitrant heretics, it had grown up over the twenty years that Siegfried had been Inquisitor, and now took up as much ground as a good-sized manor house. Its facade was plain: an unadorned wall set with windows, a flight of steps leading up to a doorway beneath three pointed arches. Its message was plain, too.

Natil climbed the steps and was immediately accosted by a guard in the livery of the a'Freux household. "I am here to see Siegfried of Magdeburg," she explained.

"Are you here to accuse sa'one?"

His eyes were bright, grasping. How much money, Natil wondered, did he receive from the Inquisition? Enough to make him eager. Enough to make any inhabitant of this impoverished town eager. "What is that to you, sir?" she said politely.

But she was a woman, and the guard was dismissive. "He's a busy man. He wan't see you."

"I am from the house of Jacob Aldernacht," said the harper. "He will see me."

Inquisitors summoned others: they were not them-selves summoned. But the name of the rich man from Ypris was a charm that turned custom on its head. A quick message to Siegfried prompted a quick reply: the Inquisitor would be in his office presently.

The corridors of the House of God were like tunnels, oppressively barrel-vaulted and lighted by hanging lamps. A second guard conducted Natil down a long passage that led into distance and darkness. Open doors allowed her brief glimpses of side rooms, branching halls. Here two Dominicans with raised cowls discussed something in undertones. Here a man who looked to be a common laborer passed Natil, gave her a look of inquiry: Damned? Condemned? Arrested?

Natil bettered her grip on her harp, held her head high. Many of her race had been brought through corridors much like this one, some in chains, some half dead, some staggering along and strengthened only by the vision of immanent divinity that was the birthright of the Elves . . .

. . . or had been, once.

And now Natil was here, but as she had fallen away from her race, so she had come to the House of God as a mortal, as the head musician of a wealthy household who was looking for one of her charges. Human, frail, limited, she was shown to a small office with a window and a desk. A crucifix in the Spanish style stared down from the wall with hollow, pain-racked eyes.

Natil bent her head.

The man who entered a minute later was dark: dark eyes, dark hair, dark beard . . . and a sense of darkness that hung about him, as though he wore some inner doubt or sadness as closely as his black mantle. But his eyes, when they fixed upon Natil, turned narrow and examining.

"You wished to see me," he said. His voice was noncommittal, severe, as though a lifetime of self-denial touched even the air that passed through his throat.

"God bless you, Brother Inquisitor," said Natil politely. "My name is Natil. I am here to inquire about a man I fear is your prisoner."

Siegfried sat down. His eyes changed their look not in the slightest. "I will not discuss what prisoners we have," he said. "But no one has anything to fear from the Inquisitor save heretics. Why do you say, then, that you *fear* that he has been taken?"

"I do not fear for his soul," said Natil, "since I believe that is in the hands of those who wish only the best for it." Absolutely true, and unchallengeable even by old Bernard Gui. But Siegfried was canny, subtle, and—in that there were indications that he was attempting to destroy the wool cooperative—extremely hostile to anyone who wore the Aldernacht livery. Had the stars been with her, Natil would have faced him with perfect equanimity. But the stars were gone: she could only speak from her heart, and with caution.

She made herself look into Siegfried's eyes. She saw pain there, pain and self doubt. She tried to keep her mind on compassion. But she could not help but wonder whether compassion did any good any more.

"But he has a body," she continued, "and I fear for his body, as do his friends."

"The body is worthless." Siegfried's eyes turned calculating. "It is dung. But you say that he has friends . . ."

Siegfried, fishing, had revealed that he did indeed have Harold. That, at least, was something, and many would have considered themselves fortunate to escape with such a prize. But Natil had given her word to the Aldernachts: she was their head musician, and therefore she had responsibilities. To Harold.

The sudden pang caught her off guard. She had had responsibilities to Omelda, too, and she had failed in them, was failing even now.

"Friends," said Natil. "As do you, brother."

He was plainly annoyed. "Speak simply. I want to know about Harold's friends."

Natil folded her hands on her harp, which lay across her knees. "You know his name. So you do indeed have Harold in custody."

"I will not say whether I have anybody or not." He stood up, fixed Natil with a stare that would have chilled someone who had any hope of surviving the interview. But Natil was not chilled, for she had no such hope. Nor did she particularly expect to be taken: she existed in openness and neutrality. "My office," said Siegfried, "is free of all impediments, for before the Inquisition, all impediments are swept away. I have no impediment from my superiors, none from my inferiors, none from the officials or ministers through whose offices I act, none from any witnesses whom I hear. And certainly none from you. If you have come to tell me about heresy, I will listen. If you have come to ask foolish questions about foolish men, I have no time for you."

He pretended to turn away as though he were going to depart, then abruptly swung back and fixed her with his stare again. "Are you a good Christian, mistress?"

Natil knew that he expected her to answer in the affirmative, knew also that he would then return to his question about why she feared the Inquisition. But she would answer truthfully. "No, Brother Siegfried. I confess that I am a very poor Christian."

He blinked, sat down. "Ah . . . why is that?"

"I am assailed, brother, by doubts. I am tormented by fear." She saw Siegfried's personal doubts deepen. Feeling as though she had just seized a venomous serpent by the tail, she continued. "My soul feels empty. My heart is filled with dust."

Open, direct, true . . . and square on the mark. Siegfried gazed, suddenly, beyond her. His lips moved, the words came whispered. "And yet . . . and yet . . ." But he shook his head as though to clear it. "Why?"

"There is so much wrong in the world. And so little that I can do about it."

He leaned forward. "Do you believe that?"

"I do."

A flutter of his office and his determination, then: "Do you not believe that God has a hand in the workings of the world? That He has given us the Church and her holy teachings to guide us toward happiness?"

Natil did not blench. She had to try to save Harold, but first she had to extricate herself from the web of accusation that Siegfried was trying to weave about her. "I believe," she said, "that human beings are stubborn creatures who turn away from good and embrace that which wounds them."

Nodding, pensive again, Siegfried missed her equivocation. "So I believe also," he said, again looking past her. "It is sad. It is so terribly, terribly sad. And I so often wish that God would make His will a little more . . . manifest to us." He sighed, interlaced his fingers, stared up at the crucifix as though beseeching it. Suddenly: "Do you also wish that, mistress?"

"I wish that the favor of the divine would be poured out upon the earth," said the harper.

Siegfried seemed struck by the image. "It would be glorious," he agreed. But the shadow about him deepened. "I suppose that, in the end, we are all poor Christians."

"We are . . ." The word caught in Natil's throat, but she pried it out. The truth. ". . . human."

"Errors," murmured Siegfried. "Errors and lies. The truth is always concealed." His melancholy was suddenly pierced by his office, like a dark cloud by a flash of lightning. "Have you come to defend Harold?"

"I am not so foolish," said Natil softly. "I am come because I am his superior, and am therefore responsible for his well being. If he is indeed in your custody, I ask that he be treated fairly, that his moral weakness be considered—"

Siegfried pounced. "Moral weakness?"

Natil smiled softly, cleared her throat. "Brother Siegfried, he is a musician."

Siegfried colored, but was suddenly suspicious. "Where did you get that honeyed tongue, woman?"

Natil stood up, harp in hand, showing not the slightest shred of fear. In fact, she had nothing to fear. Death or fading: it would at least be an end. "From life, Brother Siegfried." She started for the door, halted a heartbeat (she knew) before Siegfried opened his mouth to call her back, turned. "Did you wish to accuse me formally?"

At the bald-faced, fearless question, Siegfried started. The Inquisitor was supposed to act, not react. "Of . . . of what?"

"Of heresy. I am a very poor Christian. This I admit freely."

His opportunity flitted by like a hummingbird . . . and was gone. "Are . . ." He stumbled. ". . . are you trying to be . . . ah . . . better?"

Natil's reply was calm. She was far from her sources of peace, but she remembered what peace had felt like, and she drew upon that memory. "Always. As are you."

Four and one half billion years had given Natil much time in which to try to be better, and Siegfried was unprepared for the emotion that buoyed up her words like a quiet sea. Again, the Dominican had been caught in a slender web of sympathy and compassion, and, for a moment, Natil saw a flicker in his dark eyes, a flicker that said that, yes, Siegfried was trying, too. Trying hard. But if Siegfried were a Michelangelo attempting to batter Pietà out of his stony soul, then he was a lame Michelangelo whose crippled arms and blunt chisels could do little against the adamantine hardness with which he was faced.

Natil watched the flicker kindle, swell, and die. She sighed.

"Get out," said Siegfried, falling from sorrow into anger. "Get out. I will see that Harold is treated fairly—"

He caught himself. "That is, if we have Harold. I do not know whether we have him here or not. And I might well call you in for questioning at a later date, Mistress . . . ah . . ."

"Natil," said the Elf, who now knew that there was nothing that she could do here, nothing that Jacob could do, nothing, in fact, that Siegfried could do either.

The Dominican's glare deepened. "Natil what?"

"Just Natil."

"Get out."

As she passed through the door, she glanced back over her shoulder. Siegfried's elbows were on the wooden desk before him, and his face was in his hands. His black, Dominican mantle blended seamlessly with the aura of sadness about him.

Natil watched him for only a moment. For only a moment was it safe to watch. The stars were gone, and with them the shelter of prescience. But the compassion remained, and her inward sigh was gentle:

I am sorry, Siegfried. May you find what blessings you can.

Natil returned to the Aldernacht house slowly, reflecting that she, the last Elf, was perhaps the first of her kind ever to leave an interview with an Inquisitor in freedom. But was she, in fact, still an Elf at all? Elves had the stars and the Lady and the certainty of the web of patterns—the Dance—that went on about them. Natil had none of these.

But what did that say then about Hadden and Wheat? They had the stars, but where were the patterns? Where was the Lady? Natil had dreamed at least twice more since they had discovered the firmament within them, but there was still no sign of *Elthia*. Not a word, not a whisper, not a flicker of a Hand.

"You know," said Wheat, *half a world and five hundred years away,* "the problem with most things like this is that they always end. You always have to go back to the grind. But I have the feeling that this isn't going to end. Even if we go back to the grind, it won't end. It'll be this way forever."

"But . . ." *Hadden was looking at the highway, his conflicts crumbling away in a wash of starlight. Not a*

man. What then? It was now more a question of wonder
than of fear. "But everything has to end. People get old.
People die. It has to end."

"I wonder," said Wheat.

And Natil, threading her way through the impoverished streets of Furze, passing hawkers with little to sell,
housewives with unfilled baskets, wagons empty save for
a barrel or two of the cheapest of wines, was crying. For
herself, mainly. But she was crying also for Hadden and
Wheat, for people who had not been born, for Elves who
did not yet exist.

Forever? Without the Lady? Drifting, abandoned and
immortal, through the eons? Drifting until the sun
swelled and turned its planets to incinerated husks?
Drifting until . . .

She shuddered, sat down on a bench in the bare plaza.
Here were no trees, no fountains. Trees and fountains
required money. Only the skeleton of Albrecht's aborted
cathedral provided a glimpse of something that did not
have to do with a desperate scramble for day-to-day
bread.

"You must find Her," she whispered to the unborn,
the nonexistent, the future, the possible. "You have to
find Her. To live . . . without . . . ."

The tears overwhelmed her then, for she had lost Her,
had lost everything. She could not even save a wencher
of a musician from the claws of the Church. But would
Hadden and Wheat be able to do anything more?

"I wonder," said Wheat.

Natil's eyes were clenched, but for a moment, the un-
starred darkness behind her lids was broken by a flicker,
an image. Clouds, rain. A dark hillside. A tree, forked
at just above ground level, and yellow light streaming
through the fork, shimmering amid the falling water like
sunlight through a curtain of glass.

Startled, she opened her eyes, sat up, blinked. A
woman was standing before her, peering at her anx-
iously. "Are you a' right?"

Natil recognized her as the convicted heretic with the
double crosses. She nodded, still wondering what she
had seen. First, a 747, and now . . .

"I am well," she said. "God bless you, madam."

The woman nodded. "God bless you." Another nod, more vigorous. "God bless you!"

Unsteadily, Natil rose, and made her way back to the Aldernacht house. A forked tree . . . and light. What . . . ?

Lost in thought, lost in wonder, she blundered through the door of the house and scuffed up the stairs to Jacob's room. Without noticing that there were a few more servants near the door—and a stranger among them—she knocked, and according to Jacob's standing orders, entered without waiting for an acknowledgment.

She came to her wits inside. Jacob had a visitor. Across the table from her master was a short man with a round face and gray hair. His soutane was piped in purple, and there was an amethyst ring on the middle finger of his right hand; but the soutane was threadbare, the ring was small, and there was a sense of shabbiness about him, as though he too were infected with the constant poverty that was Furze.

The two men looked up from laughing at some joke. Natil bowed, murmured an apology, and was about to withdraw when Jacob waved her in. "Bishop Albrecht, I'll have you meet my harper, Natil. A pretty little find, even for a man who hates music."

Albrecht smiled. "I like music, Mister Jacob."

"But I don't," said Jacob. "Natil, this is Bishop Albrecht."

Natil, flustered, set down her harp and bowed deeply in the manner of the Elves, touching her forehead and spreading her hands wide. "God bless you, Excellency."

She suddenly recalled that a curtsy would have been more appropriate for a woman—a human woman—but it was too late now. Albrecht, though, did not appear to notice the irregularity, and to Natil's relief, he did not offer his ring for her to kiss.

"And God bless you, too, Natil!" he said. His voice was dry but hearty, and despite the furrows in his brow, there were laugh lines around his eyes. "God bless you, indeed! We have very little money in Furze, but I always point out that Christ was poor, so perhaps we're that much closer to heaven!"

Natil wondered whether Albrecht realized that, in some circles, his words would put him into prison . . . or into flames.

"Well," said Jacob, "if that's the case, then I'm good and damned."

"Oh, dear!" said the bishop. "I pray not!"

But Jacob, though he laughed, sent a knowing look in Natil's direction. *Harold?*

The harper sighed, nodded. Her reply was obvious. *They have him. I could do no more.*

Jacob's hand clenched on the tabletop, the knuckles turning white, but, outwardly, he was still cheerful. "I was just telling His Excellency here about you, Natil. A world traveler, a talented harper, and a free woman . . . save that at present she happens to be owned by the Aldernachts."

Unsure of how to answer, still puzzling over the forked tree, Natil only smiled, nodded.

Albrecht was musing. "Natil. A curious name."

Natil still smiled. "It is my name, Excellency."

"Ah . . . just so," said the bishop. "It's still curious though. I was just struck by the fact that I know of another Natil."

Natil allowed herself to look inquiring.

"Blessed Wenceslas wrote about her in his diary, which the Benedictines of Furze Monastery kindly allowed me to read." Albrecht coughed, smiled wryly. "Making sure, of course, that I understood what a privilege they were granting me."

Jacob refilled the bishop's cup with raisin wine. "Haughty bunch, are they?"

"Well," admitted Albrecht, "they perhaps have some cause. They've had a monastery down south of here for as long as there has been an Adria. Proud, yes, but they're good men. Real men. They believe in what they do, and they hold to Benedict's rule." He lifted the cup of wine, sipped. "Really, I've utterly no quarrel with them. Poverty, chastity, obedience . . . perhaps a little pride . . ." He sipped again. "But who isn't proud?"

Jacob frowned. "Poverty? The Benedictines?"

"Oh, yes," said the bishop. "They have some good revenues. But they give most of it away to the poor." He leaned toward Jacob. "Just between the two of us—and your harper—they're the reason that Furze has survived as long as it has. The nuns up at Shrinerock try, but they're as poor as mice. It's the brothers who have been the real help, though you can be sure they'll never admit it." He sighed. "It must be nice out there in Furze Monastery, Mister Jacob. But God has called me to Furze itself . . . and to the world."

There was a wistful light in Jacob's eyes, but his mouth was crooked. "And do they help with the Inquisition, too, Excellency?"

Albrecht came out of his reverie. "Help? Who?"

"The brothers."

Albrecht's face fell. "Not at all." For a moment, he brooded on his cup. "The Inquisition doesn't need any help, I'm afraid."

There was more to his words than mere statement of fact. Standing near the door, still wondering about the vision that had been vouchsafed her, Natil decided that what she was hearing was deep concern and shaken belief.

"Do you not like the Inquisition, Excellency?" she said politely.

Albrecht plainly was torn between speech and silence. While Natil and Jacob looked on, he struggled, debated, and finally chose speech. "A year ago, Mistress Harper, perhaps even a month ago, I would have said that, in its place, the Inquisition was a godly institution. Now, though, I've been thinking about it a great deal . . ." His eyes turned shadowed. ". . . perhaps too much, and I fear I must say that the Inquisition has most assuredly gotten out of its place. It oversteps its proper bounds, makes liars out of the truthful, heretics out of loyal Christians . . ."

He brooded for a moment, obviously uncomfortable with his heat, but inspiration struck again, and his white eyebrows and his index finger all rose simultaneously. "Why, even Wenceslas himself would have been haled before a tribunal, since—returning to your name, Natil (I beg your pardon, but it's a good example)—since among the pages of his diaries he wrote about something that was neither good nor evil, but which, he claimed, existed outside of such categories. He called it . . . um . . . well . . . Elves. And Natil, he said, was an Elf." He shrugged. "He wrote of them as though they were people. I confess I don't understand why he did so."

Natil stifled her tears. "I believe that Brother William

of Occam and Brother John Duns Scotus thought much the same separatist way, although they used different metaphors and figures of speech. Distinctions of that sort are, after all, the very basis of the *via moderna*."

"Anti-Thomism. Just so." Albrecht brightened. "A learned woman! A jewel for your household, Mister Jacob."

Jacob sat back with a satisfied—and, to Natil's eye, somewhat bitter—smile. "A jewel among the clinkers. I only *buy* the best, Excellency."

"Of course, dear harper," Albrecht hastened to add, "none of these good and evil and Elf questions have anything to do with you. Wenceslas wrote a hundred years ago. You could have no possible connection with the Natil of his diary."

Natil remembered to curtsy, remembered not to cry. "Of course not, Excellency."

"But just think," said Albrecht, plainly distressed. "Even Wenceslas would be considered heretical. It's terrible. It's just . . . terrible."

Natil looked at Jacob. Jacob looked at Natil. Here, then, was an ally. "Have you . . ." Jacob considered his words carefully. "Have you brought this up, Excellency? With . . . perhaps . . . Rome?"

"With Rome?" Albrecht smiled tiredly, rubbed at a knot of furrows that had suddenly descended upon his brow like a flock of crows on a weathervane. "I am afraid that Rome is more interested in revenues than in religion. Rodrigo Borgia . . . ah . . ."

Natil thought it. Jacob said it. ". . . has to pay off the bribes that elected him."

Albrecht coughed. "Oh, dear, Mister Jacob! Really!"

"Well, it's true."

The bishop's coughing metamorphosed into barely suppressed laughter, which itself seemed in danger of mutating into tears. "Dear God, yes . . . it's true."

"And he's too busy playing politics with the Papal States to worry about his Church, isn't he?"

Albrecht calmed himself with a swallow of wine. "True, true. I am sorry—heartily sorry—to say that it's all true." He sighed. "I do my best with what has been given me, but there is so much wrong in the world, and so little that I can do about it."

Natil's eyes were on the floor. So little that could be done. By anyone.

"Play something for us, Natil," said Jacob suddenly. "We're two old men having a glass of wine together and remembering . . ." His voice caught, and there was a hint of tears in his eyes. ". . . the good old days." But his eyes, tears and all, turned miserly. "Play something. Show us what you're worth."

Natil curtsied again and took her place on a stool near the hearth, glad of the chance to lose herself in her music. While she played, Jacob and Albrecht chatted about Furze and the wool cooperative. Albrecht was wholeheartedly in favor of the entire affair, and he did not hesitate to express his feelings:

"God bless you, Mister Jacob, but I'm glad you've come to help."

"Hmmph," said the merchant. "I don't recall that the agreement has been signed yet."

Albrecht looked at Jacob with a patient expression that set the latter to laughing. "All right, then," said Jacob. "Thank you, Excellency. We'll have Furze running like a well-made loom in another year."

Albrecht sat back, beaming, genuinely happy.

But after the bishop left—on foot, as he had, apparently, come—in the company of his chief clerk (who had waited patiently in the corridor all this time), Jacob stood at the window, watching him hobble away down the street. "I don't understand it, Natil."

A creak at the closed door told Natil that, with the departure of the servants, Francis was listening again. "Understand what, master?"

"Albrecht. Shrinerock Abbey poor as a mouse, indeed! As if he himself wasn't reduced to darning his own stockings! And that pathetic cathedral!" Jacob shook his head, bewildered. "He shows up in the middle of the afternoon, just drops in on me to say hello and thank me for my interest in Furze. And that's all. And him with a cathedral to be built."

"You mean," said the harper, "that he did not ask for a donation?"

"Never even mentioned it. Never mentioned it at all." Jacob stared after Albrecht, shook his head in wonder.

''I admire that. I really do. Dear God, he might get me into a monastery yet!''

Another creak at the door. Natil felt Francis's fear even through two inches of solid oak.

CHAPTER 15

With the arrival of May, Adria began to green in earnest.
Trees leafed. Daffodils covered forest meadows. Hya-
cinths burst out in violet clouds. The pastures between
Furze and Belroi lost their last recalcitrant patches of
brown, and people began to travel with some assurance
that they would neither be soaked nor frozen in the middle of a long trek.

The gypsies were on the move again, too. A hundred
years ago, they had been a novelty in Adria, but now
their small wandering bands were a common sight, and
they joined the wayfarers and the traveling merchants and
tradesmen, the narrow wooden wheels of their caravans
churning up the roads and byways, sending dust into the
air like smoke from a plodding fire.

They never stayed. They only passed through. They
were always only passing through, with nowhere to go
save the next stop, the next horse fair, the next encamp-
ment. They kept to themselves and to their own ways,
picking up seasonal work sometimes, or trading, or, occasionally, stealing from the complacent *gadja* who certainly owed *someone* a living because it simply was not
right that anyone have so much and not share it.

At night, daring girls from nearby towns might sneak
into their camps so as to consult with a dark-skinned
seer—the matter of a future husband, perhaps, or perhaps
how best to be rid of the present one—but the Romany
took their money and listened to their problems with a
detachment born of chronic separateness. Who cared
about these silly white folks, anyway? Laboring, laboring, laboring . . . and for what? Hardly better than the
horses that pulled the caravans. Just gullible idiots, really. Why, they clung to their priests and churches like a

child to mama's skirts. And as for any sense of propor-
tion . . . well!

This year, a band came up from Italy, picked up the
north road near the ruins of a village that had once been
called Saint Brigid, and headed up toward the coast. They
called at villages and hamlets, sharpened a few knives,
told a few fortunes, made off with a few chickens, and
packed up in the morning. They paused at Furze only
long enough to water the horses—because those who had
nothing for themselves had nothing to give to anyone
else—spent a week at Belroi, and wound up camping near
Ypris on a Friday afternoon.

Ypris—independent, wealthy, and staunchly bour-
geois—had no time for gypsies. The dark-skinned
strangers who suddenly appeared, whether singing and
dancing for pennies in the town square or looking for
odd jobs among the shops and houses and sheepfolds,
were, in the opinion of the townsfolk, hardly better than
beggars. Just human trash, really. Why, they hardly gave
more than lip service to the Church. And as for any sense
of property . . . well!

And so, in a spirit of mutual exploitation and intoler-
ance, the gypsies and Ypris coexisted. Odd jobs turned
up. Missing chickens did not. The strange songs in an
even stranger language became an accepted part of Yp-
risian life . . . at least for now.

But there was an old woman among the Romany who
kept much to herself: an odd occurrence among such a
communal people. She wore the dress and jewelry of a
gypsy woman, and she covered her hair with a bright
kerchief like a gypsy woman, but though she moved deliberately, almost with a sense of defiance, she never
seemed to be all of a piece, never seemed to really know
quite how one should act when clad in such a kerchief,
such jewelry, such dress. There was the look of a stranger
among strangers in her blue (blue?) eyes, and the hair
that escaped its cloth confines was the dirty gray color
of a faded blonde.

Wandering apart from her fellow wanderers, she
walked alone through the streets of Ypris, slowly becoming a strange and barely tolerated part of this strange and
barely tolerated Romany visitation. "Oh, that's her," the

townsfolk would say. "The one they call Reinne. She's an odd one."

And some would turn away from her because they thought that she was a witch. And some would give her money and food because she was old and tired and had a cough that told of lungs worn threadbare with consumption. And others simply ignored her, getting on with their busy lives as Yprisians always did.

Reinne, though, wandered, and if she asked about Jacob Aldernacht, no one thought very much of it. Jacob Aldernacht was, after all, famous. Everyone knew about Jacob Aldernacht. The kings of France borrowed money from Jacob Aldernacht. Of *course* this old, consumptive gypsy woman would ask about him . . . and that meant that she was up to no good, you could be sure of it!

Her inquiries, though, never actually reached the Aldernachts themselves, for about their house were walls and gates with guards who were paid to keep people like Reinne outside in the street where they belonged. Old Eudes slammed and locked his wardrobe doors as soon as he heard about the gypsies, Claire did not want to even look at them (children of God though they might be), and Josef, unable to reconcile such gap-toothed, straggle-haired people with his ill-understood humanistic beliefs, and unwilling to allow something like Reinne any part in the ethereal womanhood he worshipped, personally made sure that the servants knew to keep intact the privacy of the Aldernacht household.

And so Reinne wandered, and chickens did not turn up, and May continued, the countryside greening, the sheep bleating . . . and the Aldernacht household even more introverted than usual.

By the end of the first week, most of the children of Ypris were singing gypsy songs.

Omelda was moving stiffly these days, a condition brought on by muscle strains, rope burns, bruises, bite marks, and frequent and violent encounters with the metal toys that Edvard and Norman utilized in their sexual play.

The two young men were clever, bright, and observant. In the course of only a few days, they had noted that when the church bells rang the Office Hours, Omelda

might resist their advances and their uses of her, but it
would be at most a vague, fuzzy, half-hearted resistance.
This they did not mind in the least. Much better, though,
was her complete, doll-like compliance with their every
wish *in between* the Hours.

And so they invariably came to her when she most
needed privacy, when she was relishing her freedom to
think, to consider, to float in the vast silence of clarity.
And this, despite the intrusions of Francis's sons, she
continued to do, ignoring with the studied practice of
twenty years of introversion the externals that were forced
upon her. The ropes. The blunt cylinders. The clubs.
The hot wax and putty.

She did her work—Eudes and Martha had no complaint—but she did her work in pain. Nor did any thought
of reporting her abuse ever occur to her, for Edvard and
Norman had made it very clear that, in the absence of
their father and their grandfather, they were the masters
of the house. And, in any case, what was the word of a
servant against that of the heirs of the Aldernacht estate?

So she complied, and she suffered. She salved her
wounds with herbs, washed shit and sperm out of herself
late at night with a cup of warm water and a cloth, and
tried hard come morning not to look at herself in the
mirror. She complied, and she suffered, and, as ox-like
as she had ever been, she plodded through the hours and
the days, her inner sight more often than not fixed upon
Natil's return as obsessively as a tired draft animal might
stare at the far side of a field.

At the end of the week, she met Dinah, a taut little
athletic whore who seemed forever to have the corners
of her mouth turned up and the corners of her eyes turned
down. Eager and cheerful, she did as she was told for
money, as Omelda did what she was told because she
was owned. Together, separately, in and out of costume,
the nun and the prostitute mingled their bodies with one
another and with those of Jacob's grandsons, submit-
ting—willingly or unwillingly, it did not matter—to whatever demand was made upon them.

Dinah appeared to almost relish her own debauchery.
"I'm paid, and I'm well paid," she declared defiantly to
Omelda one day. "Why shouldn't I enjoy it while I'm at
it?"

Strapped to one another, the two young women lay with their faces inches apart. Omelda's legs were spread, Dinah's lashed together from ankle to thigh: a travesty of heterosexual coitus. To make the fantasy complete—or perhaps more tawdry—Omelda's skirts had been pulled up to her chin, and the breeches into which Dinah had been ordered were down about her knees. A country rape: milkmaid and young gallant. Edvard and Norman would, as was their practice, enjoy the little charade and push and prod and masturbate before they would allow both Omelda and Dinah to be women again . . . and use them as such.

Today, though, the young men had been called away by a quick tap on the door and a whispered message from a servant. They had obviously been expecting something of the sort, and had fastened up their clothes and rushed out of the room without a word to their playthings. And so Omelda and Dinah were left alone, one to fight for the sanctity of her mind, the other to wait patiently for further orders . . . and for money.

"It's my body," Dinah continued, "and I can do as I please. And if I get a little shit in my crook, why, God gave me a crook . . . and He gave me shit, too! I'll tell that to the priests any day of the week!"

Omelda's wrists had been tied to her ankles. The pain, searing up her spine and through her shoulders, precluded any mental silence or oblivion. "But wouldn't . . . you rather do . . . something else?"

Dinah gave a crooked grin that Omelda was unable to decipher. "Not much for a girl to do, is there, Omelda?"

"Well . . ."

" 'Cept become a wife, or a nun." Clad in her breeches and shirt, Dinah laughed. "A whore, a house-wife, or a nun! How 'bout that?" She winked at Omelda. "Now, if I were a real man . . ." She gave two or three thrusts of her hips. ". . . then I could do other things. But I'm not. And God made me so."

Omelda was trying to look at something else besides the face with the little upturned mouth and the little downturned eyes. "I wish I were a nun."

"Aw, they don't take girls like you."

Omelda stared at her, beyond her. They did. They would. They had to.

Please, Natil, come home. I want to go back, but I want to stay sane.

Just then, the door opened, and the two young men returned. Norman closed and fastened the door. Edvard was already reading aloud from a letter in his hand:

"Francis Aldernacht to Claire Aldernacht, the second of May, 1500, Furze."

"What's the matter with those messengers?" said Norman, annoyed. "That was over a week ago."

"Never mind," said Edvard. "Let me read. *Wife, I recommend me to you,* as if anyone could recommend Pierre for anything." Edvard's eye fell on the two women, and he patted Dinah's bare buttocks with a friendly hand. "Oh, my little darlings! We'll get back to you in a minute. You just enjoy yourselves: don't let us interfere." He went back to the letter. "Let me see . . . oh, here: *letting you know that, blessed be God*—really Pierre!—*I am well, and enjoining you to keep the commandments of the Church and the teachings of Our Lord Jesus Christ in your thoughts, words, and deeds.*"

Norman smirked, cleared his throat. Omelda stared up at Dinah. Dinah's eyes—still downturned—were half closed, as though she were mentally counting coins.

"All right," said Edvard. "Here it is: *I am become increasingly distressed by Father's irrational ways with the family's money, more so now than ever, for he speaks of plans that truly endanger the integrity of the Aldernacht firm. Recently, he had speech with the local bishop, Albrecht (a godly man, though rather witless), and actually talked of entering a monastery. He has, of course, persisted in his determination to loan money to the wool cooperative, and nothing I have been able to say has swayed him from this ill-advised move.*"

"Nothing," said Norman.

"Well, would anything Pierre had to say sway you?"

"Not at all."

"Well, then."

Omelda was hearing their words as though through a layer of gauze and wool: the accumulated pain of a week's worth of abuse, culminating now in half-dislocated joints, was blurring the room, the brothers, even Dinah. She wanted to scream, but knew that if she did, the present torments would seem as nothing compared with what would follow.

Softly, though, from within her, filtering up through the pain, present even before she became consciously aware of it, came the whispering sound of plainchant. Nones.

Nunc Sancte nobis Spiritus, Unum Patri cum Filio . . .

"Listen," Edvard was saying. "This is even better: *I thank Jesus and all the saints that I am a source of sound advice for my father, though it grieves me that I am so ignored. But others value me highly, and Baron David a'Freux asked me many questions about my investments, in particular the tobacco plantation in Spain. I had the honor of advising him well in this matter.*"

Norman laughed loudly. "Tobacco again!"

"I'm not worried about tobacco," said Edvard. "I'm worried about our money."

Norman nodded. "Grandfather is going to . . ."

Deo Patri sit gloria . . .

". . . spoil everything. *I certainly have no intention of dying a pauper because—*"

"Hush," said Edvard. "Listen: *But Father persists, despite my best efforts.* Damn that old senile fool! Both of them! *I fear that other measures might have to be taken in order to restrain him. I pray you, therefore: consult with Bishop Etienne, and find out whether the reverend gentleman has come closer to our way of thinking.*"

Norman blinked. "Bishop Etienne?"

Edvard tossed the letter onto the table. Oh, I overheard that. They're trying to have Grandfather declared mad. Or incompetent. Or something like that. It won't work."

"Pierre might have Bishop Etienne," said Norman, "but Grandfather has Charles."

"Yes, that's it exactly. The Church binds and looses in heaven, and Charles binds and looses in Gold Hall." Edvard became aware once more of the women on the bed. "Oh, my goodness, we have been ignoring you, haven't we, sir?" He prodded Dinah's rump. "Having a good time with the wenches behind our backs?"

"Always, Mister Edvard," said Dinah.

Omelda closed her eyes. *Surrexit, ac Paraclito* went the voices, and despite her previous frantic efforts to suppress the intrusive music, she now allowed herself to drift with it. The chant was slow, steady, comforting.

"Should we give Mother the letter?"

"Of *course* we should give Mother the letter," said Edvard. "Otherwise, when Pierre asks about it, she won't have gotten it."

"Oh . . . that's right . . ."

"But since Bishop Etienne isn't going to be able to do a great deal about Grandfather, I suppose . . ." Edvard folded his arms, contemplated Dinah's bare behind. "Dear God," he mused. "I could die for a rump like that."

Norman chortled. "Some have."

"What a way to go!"

"Yes. Yes, indeed. You come in with a spurt, and you go out with a spurt."

"And any number of spurts in between!" Edvard was already slipping out of his clothes, his erection full and straight. But he was still thoughtful. "I suppose we'll have to do something about grandfather ourselves."

Norman looked intrigued. "Do you have something in mind?"

"I do." Edvard reached down, tweaked the rounded womanflesh before him and left a bruise behind. "In with a spurt, out with a spurt. I think we may have a little job for our . . ." He laughed, tweaked again, left another bruise. ". . . country buck here!"

Norman understood, joined in Edvard's laughter.

Eyes half closed, Omelda drifted. *In sempiterna saecula. Amen.*

The bargaining in Furze was lengthy, and, at times, loud: Jacob, for all his age and his beliefs about his heart, was perfectly willing to shout down even the lustiest young businessman of the city. In truth, though, Natil noticed that much of his bluster was feigned: an obvious attempt to find out what the men of Furze were really like, whether their toadying at that first banquet had been the product of desperation or a sympton of a general spinelessness.

But Paul and his friends passed Jacob's test, and they were therefore rewarded with a signed agreement and the certainty of Aldernacht money, advice, and support. The terms were neither parsimonious nor prodigal, the debt incurred neither too large nor too small. The cooperative would have to struggle to make their payments, but that was, as everyone knew, good: the fight would keep them active and alert.

Natil, though, saw that her master did not particularly savor his success. In fact, Jacob had grown more pessimistic as the bargaining had proceeded; and his off-handed comments and careless dismissals of certain subjects told the harper that he was brooding increasingly on his lost wife, upon his children, upon his grandchildren . . . upon his entire life. He stoutly maintained still that he hated music, but when he retired, he now customarily had Natil play for him until he slept. The harper played the harp . . . and played along with the charade, too, for, to her eye, Jacob needed music now as he needed air and water and food.

And, indeed, the music seemed to help; and whether Natil dredged up old elven melodies that brought tears to her eyes, or played bawdy songs she had heard in the square that afternoon, or even lapsed into plainchant or into Hildegard's rhapsodic hymns, the old man, with perhaps a mistiness that no one save Natil ever saw, would drift off into dreams that could not but be far more pleasant than his waking life.

Natil's own dreams were mixed: pleasure and pain mingled seamlessly. Hadden and Wheat saw the stars, and, in their wanderings, began to feel that union with their world and those who inhabited it that was the birthright of the Elves. They still did not know what was happening to them, knew only that they wanted more of it; but despite their unmistakable alteration, their transformation from human to elven, from limited consciousness to immanent perception, Hadden and Wheat were still ignorant of the existence of the Lady, had no sense of the all-encompassing patterns. In her dreams, Natil called, cried out, shouted to them, but dreams were but dreams: the two did not hear. The Lady . . . they had not a clue that She even existed.

And then there was the forked tree: she had seen it again. Light still streamed from its cleft, putting the shadows and the rain to flight, but its meaning and the existence were mysteries to her. Icon? Symbol? Reality?

Natil did not know. But she took it as a sign, a sign from the Lady. It meant *something,* and she, like Hadden and Wheat, was sure that it would not be kept from her.

But her waking hours had become a burden for her; and if Jacob was finding solace in her harp, it was more than likely because she herself had come to take her instrument for her sole, unalloyed comfort. She was no longer an Elf, the Lady was beyond her, the patterns were gone, but she at least had her harp and her music; and those who listened to her play—Jacob, Manarel and the servants, her fellow musicians, or she herself—could still derive from it something that was a little more than mere enjoyment.

Francis, though, obviously heard nothing more than plucked strings. As much as Natil had noticed the father's growing despondency, she had also become aware of the son's increasing tension. He was agitated, distracted, and had refused to add his signature and his approval—not that it mattered much to Jacob—to the agreement with the co-operative. Now he could often be heard muttering to himself, and he appeared to be spending a great deal of time writing letters and posting them by private Aldernacht courier.

"Francis?" said Jacob that night when she mentioned it to him one night. "Oh, him." He settled down in bed, folded his hands behind his head. "I imagine you're right, girl. He *is* up to something. He and Claire have been off sniffing Bishop Etienne's rump. They want to have me declared mad, and they want his help. They think that we're living fifty years ago, and that bishops still have something to say besides *Burn the fucking heretics!*"

Natil flinched.

Jacob noticed. "A few yellow crosses in your family, Natil?"

The harper smiled thinly. "They never bothered with crosses for my folk."

Jacob's eyes widened. He whistled. "What were they? Cathars? Spirituals? Or did they get caught up in that Waldensian stuff a few years back?"

Natil touched a harpstring. "If I told you *Elves,* you would not believe me, would you?"

A smile added more wrinkles to Jacob's face. ''You've got a sense of humor, girl!''

Feeling as though an abyss had opened within her, Natil smiled, nodded.

'All right, then, we'll leave it at Elves!'' Jacob laughed. ''Now *that* would give Siegfried a turn, wouldn't it? Elves . . .'' But in the middle of his laughter, his eyes grew hard, and he muttered an oath. ''Damn that meddling priest. I'll have him . . .'' He groped, spluttered. ''I don't know what I'll have him.''

Natil understood. Harold's absence—and what that absence signified, both for Harold and for the wool cooperative—had been the source of a palpable sense of unease in the household. No one talked about it, but everyone, including Jacob, was thinking about it.

But it was more than unease for Jacob: it was anger. Accustomed to having his own way in all things, he was enraged by what he saw as the insolent temerity of a man who could steal outright a piece of Aldernacht property . . . with complete impunity. A move against Siegfried, though, would jeopardize or even destroy the cooperative deal, giving the Inquisitor exactly what he apparently wanted. ''He got Harold,'' said Jacob, ''and I'm convinced he got Fredrick, and he's after . . .'' He shook his head. ''I swear he's after the wool cooperative.''

''Does Paul know?''

''Paul and his boys didn't know until I told them. Farthest thing from their minds. But now they're starting to notice things: people listening, people watching their houses.'' Jacob snorted. ''Of course, anybody in this whole damned city could notice the same thing. Everyone's watching everyone else. Everybody's getting paid to say something or to say nothing.'' He frowned. ''Maybe Francis is right.'' He suddenly looked at the door and picked up an earthenware cup from the bed table. ''I said, maybe Francis is right. Maybe . . . ah . . . um . . .''

He suddenly sat up and hurled the cup at the door as hard as he could. It hit squarely with a loud crack, shattering in a splash of crockery.

''I'll teach you to listen at your father's door!'' shouted Jacob. ''You young whelp!''

Natil sat, eyes wide, a little stunned. She had not foreseen it. Of course she had not foreseen it.

Manarel opened the door a crack. "Did you need me, Mister Jacob?"

"Was Francis listening again?"

"No, sir. He has not been here this evening."

Jacob gave a harrumph. "First time all week, then. All right, Manarel."

"Very good, Mister Jacob."

Manarel closed the door. Jacob lay back down. "Sometimes he's there, Natil, and sometimes he isn't. But he's there often enough." He turned despondent. "Maybe Francis is right about Furze. But I'm betting that he isn't. Men like Paul and his boys deserve a chance. Siegfried isn't going to give them any, and so it's up to me. But I just wish . . ."

He passed a hand over his face, rose, and went to the window. The days were lengthening, and the sky was still touched with sunset; but outside, the squalid clatter of the streets had died without a whimper. Furze. Impoverished Furze.

"I just wish that I'd started a little sooner," he said. "Old Fugger gave his retired employees free housing—well, practically free—and here I am still hammering out deals in gold and silver. I should have started sooner. Maybe . . . maybe things would have been different." Rambling now, staring out as though at a ship on the horizon, one that bore something precious, one that was passing him by. "But I didn't, and I drove her away, and now I've got . . ." He turned around. "What have I got, Natil? Money. Three sons I'd disown if I had any sense. Two grandsons who aren't worth picking up horse turds with. And a wife who . . . well, I suppose she's somewhere."

He went back to the bed, sat down. His knobby knees poked out from the hem of his nightshirt. "What have I got?" He shook his head. "Not much. And it's too late to do anything about it."

Natil was silent. Her harp was silent, too.

"Play something, Natil. I want to go to sleep." Jacob crawled under the covers. "I've heard that some of those Irishman can work magic with their harps. Can you work magic, Natil?"

She evaded the painful question. "I play the harp, master."

Jacob persisted. "Can you turn me into a better man? Can you make me happy? Can you make people like me for something besides my money?" He laughed bitterly, waved away her answer. "Play something. Please." He grinned at her. "Ever hear a *please* from an Aldernacht before? Please, then. And work some magic if you can."

Natil played, and after he had dropped off to sleep—snoring loudly, even smiling a little—she rose to leave. But Jacob's request made her harp heavy in her hand, and she paused at the door. "I have been trying, master," she whispered. "But it does not work any more."

CHAPTER 16

Hadden stared through the dust-frosted windshield of the van, waiting for a stoplight to change. It was hot, and there was little traffic, but the town was small and took its time with such things as stoplights. Hadden was not worried about the time, though, nor was Wheat. Time was meaningless: they both knew instinctively that there was plenty of time now, time for everything.

I have the feeling that this isn't going to end, Wheat had said, and the certainty had remained with them. *It'll be this way forever.*

Forever. Waiting at this stoplight in a town that was, like all towns, ripe with the odors of humans who knew themselves only as what they were, hot with sun-baked asphalt and concrete, polluted with auto exhaust and diesel fumes and pieces of paper and bent beer cans, they were both thinking of forever. Wheat was staring as though she were seeing such things as cars, people, and storefronts for the first time—as she would always see them—but Hadden's eyes were elsewhere.

"Look at that guy," he said softly. His voice was pitched economically: loud enough to carry over the engine and the air conditioner, but no more.

Wheat looked. An old man was stumbling along the street, carrying what looked like clothing in two plastic shopping bags. His face was seamed and dirty, his hair matted with the dust of the field in which he had slept, his shoes held together with lengths of rope and duct tape gleaned from some dumpster. He moved with the air of a man who was wandering with no goal save another field, another dumpster, another night spent alone by himself or alone in the crowded bunkroom of a mission: Salvation Army, Fellowship of Christ, Saint Vincent de Paul, it mattered little which.

The stoplight held at red. Hadden and Wheat watched. Out there, stumbling down the long length of the sidewalk, were all the mortality and frailty and broken dreams that they had, somehow, left behind . . . or of which, perhaps, by some unlooked-for grace, they had been absolved. The world was a wonderful place . . . and yet . . .

. . . and yet there were these: the broken, the homeless, the preterit. Whether here before them or half a world away, there were men trudging on a journey that had no end, children with the fat, hollow belly of malnutrition, mothers rooting through garbage for something with which to feed their families, soldiers standing out there just . . . just shooting at one another.

It struck them, then: the thing from which they had been kept because they had been too busy with the wonder. There was Hadden, and there was Wheat . . . and then there was the world. All of it. And it could no longer be the world *out there,* because for them the world had, over a week ago, ceased being *out there,* their rapidly widening hearts reaching out, enfolding everything, turning it all, abruptly, into *in here.*

There was no escaping it. Ensnared by their hearts, by their change, by their absolution, Hadden and Wheat stared, and then were suddenly weeping with all the blunt, shocky realization of children confronted with an axe murder.

The light changed. They drove out of town, pulled over by a patch of scrub oak, and held one another, shaking from pity, from fright, from the knowledge that, yes, it would be this way *forever.*

Wheat was the first to pry her face out of her hands. Her fingers shook, but she reached into the back and pulled a bottle of fruit juice out of the styrofoam cooler. She opened it, drank.

"I wasn't ready for that," she said.

"I don't think anyone who really sees it ever is."

"You think there are others besides us?"

"Dear God, Wheat, I don't even know what *us* is."

The air was so dry that the melt and ice that had beaded the juice bottle a minute before were already gone. Wheat was pale, and she took a long pull at it before she held it out and told Hadden to finish it up.

"Silly me," she whispered, "I thought it was going to be pink clouds and bunny rabbits for the rest of my life."

Hadden found himself looking at the road. It stretched off into the distance, linking with other roads, highways, freeways, city streets, turnpikes. Flowing. Flowing on forever. Wheat's words did not make sense. "The rest of your life, Wheat?" he said. "What does that mean?"

Wheat clenched her eyes, shook her head. "I don't know what it means."

"What did it mean a few minutes ago?"

She was plainly frightened. "I'm . . . I'm stupid, all right?"

He set down the empty bottle, turned to her. "You are not stupid," he said, realizing as he uttered the words that a softness that was almost womanly had slipped into his speech. "You spoke the truth. You thought we were immortal, didn't you?"

The truth. Whatever they were, whatever they had become, they had to speak the truth. "Yes . . . I did . . ."

"You still think so." It was not a question.

"I do."

"So do I." Hadden sighed. "We're going to see that again, and again, and again. We're going to see it for a long time, I guess." The thought of immortality, of wonder and pain bound so inextricably together for so long overcame him, and he passed his hands over his beardless face. "We can give money away until we're broke, and it won't make a shred of difference. We can volunteer, we can give time, energy, and strength until we have nothing left . . . and it won't help."

"Don't say that."

"It's true."

"Yes," said Wheat. "It's true. But . . . we've . . ." She trembled with the effort of her thoughts. Immortality. ". . . we've got to do something. We can feel, and so we can . . . we can do something. Even if it's not much. Even if it's just a smile, or a word. Even if it makes just a little bit of difference, the fact will remain that somebody did *something*." And the sun struck her in the face as she turned to him, kindling the starlight in her eyes until it blazed like a nebula. "Maybe that's why we can feel this way. Maybe that's why we're here. Maybe that's why we've changed.''

And Natil, dreaming five hundred years in the past, was crying out that she was right, that such as Hadden and Wheat were entrusted with the Great Work, with helping and healing and comforting the world and those in it until the stars burnt themselves black and the heavens whispered into final silence.

Hadden was looking at his hands. Changed. Changed utterly. And more changes, he was sure, to come. He and Wheat had wept like children, and, indeed, they were children. But they would grow.

"But . . . but what gets us through all of it?" he said softly. The delicacy of his voice was coming through strongly. Gentle. Just loud enough to carry. "We can't go on like this forever. What gets us through?"

Wheat shook her head.

But Natil, in her dreams, was screaming. "The Lady, the Lady gets you through. She holds you when you fall, She speaks with you face to face. There is no doubt, no separation, no uncertainty. You and She are One. Ai, ea sareni, Marithae Dia! Cirya ephana ilei i—!"

But she had screamed herself awake, and the morning was streaming in through her window. Belroi. Like Hadden and Wheat, Jacob and his people were going home.

There are all kinds of wandering, but there is only one return. The gypsies, maybe, knew about that, for their routes looped far, but, like the seasons that determined them, never really returned to any place in particular. They were fractal patterns, these, paths that paralleled the road of a decade ago with young hands holding the reins where old hands had once held them, paths that never repeated themselves, but rather precessed with elusive similarity, as though there were a Lorenz attractor sitting out there somewhere, always calling, always dictating a return that was really no return at all, only an illusion of belonging, only a dream of order.

Reinne, the consumptive, might have been tracing something of the sort along the streets of Ypris, for though her steps took her on apparently random courses, they were nonetheless influenced and determined by an attractor, a center point that turned her endless looping and circling and retracing into an enfoldment of purpose, put a pattern to it: a wavering butterfly, or a seahorse tail that curled around, pointed towards, the house of Jacob Aldernacht.

Once, she actually had the audacity to violate the equations of nonperiodicity that held her to her interweaving course, and on a warm afternoon, she braved the glare of the gate guards and insisted that she be allowed up to the door of the house. The guards did not notice the color of her eyes or of her hair. No, what struck them was her demeanor, her certainty that, yes, there was a reason she should be allowed up to the front door, there was an urgent reason. And so, bewildered, they let her go.

The servant who answered her knock was properly horrified to find himself confronted with a ragged crone who lisped out the name of the master of the house, punctuating her words with a consumptive hack that left a thread of blood at one corner of her mouth.

"Jacob," she said. "Is Jacob here?"

"Mister Aldernacht," he said with severity, "has returned from a business trip. Although that is none of your business. Be off."

"Is he well? Tell me. I want to know."

"Get out!"

"What about Francis?"

"Get out!" Steeling himself, the servant grabbed her by the arm and hustled her down the walk, through the gate, and out into the street. "Get out!"

Reinne fell down when he let go of her, and, lying on the cobbles in the warm sun, she hacked up another wad of bloody sputum from her disintegrating lungs. "Are they well?" she wheezed through the slime and froth. "Do they have money?"

But the servant had returned to the house. There was no one to hear her questions.

The guards were disciplined. Orders of Mister Josef.

Omelda was only a servant, and a lowly one at that: incarcerated in the kitchen when Edvard and Norman were not abusing her, she did not even hear that Natil was expected home until Jacob and his party had ridden in through the gate and dismounted in the courtyard. But though a little more than a week ago Omelda had been eager for the harper's return, now she stayed where she was: in the kitchen, on her knees.

This sudden lassitude surprised her little, for, given the circumstances under which she now labored, she was unconcerned about whether or not she found a cure for her inner plainchant. A cure certainly would not change the behavior of Edvard and Norman. In truth, though, Omelda was not entirely sure that she did not now welcome the internal music, since it provided a kind of buffer to the abuse, an opiate that made the hours of forced copulation and sexual torture almost bearable.

And so when Natil, clad in Aldernacht livery, hurried into the kitchen, Omelda greeted her listlessly. It really did not matter any more. Rapes had studded her existence since she had left Shrinerock Abbey, but persistent, ritualized abuse had finally broken her.

"Omelda? Beloved?"

Nor would Omelda mention anything of Edvard and Norman even to Natil. This was a family that hunted down escaped servants with an army of mercenaries, that was willing to besiege a town over a matter of legal indentureship. What would they do in response to a clear-cut case of treason? Or, rather, what would they not do? "Oh, hello, Natil." She stood up from her scrubbing stiffly. These days, she did everything stiffly. "Welcome home."

There was a touch of shame in the harper's eyes. "I am sorry that I had to leave."

"Oh . . . that's all right. Don't worry about it."

"I returned as soon as I could."

"Yes . . . of course . . ."

Natil watched her for a moment, brow furrowed. "You are angry."

"No . . . not at all . . ."

But Natil did not look convinced. "We have work to do, beloved. We have lost time."

Omelda shrugged. "I'm . . . not worried . . ." She shrugged again. "They keep me . . ." The thought of telling Natil about Edvard and Norman occurred to her again, but she let it die. Telling would do no good. Telling would make everything worse. Her body was dung: let it remain dung. ". . . busy."

"Oh."

"So I . . ." Omelda mustered a smile, but it was crooked. ". . . hardly have time to think about anything . . . especially plainchant. I'll be all right. Don't worry about me."

Natil stared, her harp dangling from her hand. Omelda saw the wound, knew that she herself had caused it, knew also that there was nothing that she could do about it. Remaining silent or telling all, she could only pain others, herself, or, more than likely, both. So she left it at the traditional obfuscation of the battered woman: *I'll be all right. Don't worry about me.*

With another attempt at a smile, Omelda turned and went back to the floor, her callused knees hardly feeling the rough stone, her cracked hands inured to soap and water. *I'll be all right.*

From somewhere within the maze that was the Aldernacht house came a call: distant, eager. "Natil! Mistress Harper! Oh, I'm so glad you're home! Now we can have our little talk about music! I've written a duet!"

Omelda hung her head, her dark hair hanging down in frowzy dribbles. Edvard and Norman sounded just as eager when they stripped her and explained what they had planned for the afternoon. Music, sex, wool cooperatives . . . it was all the same: whatever the Aldernachts wanted, whatever the Aldernachts could buy, whatever the Aldernachts could take.

"It's only got about a dozen accidentals for the harp," Josef continued. "I'm sure you'll find it quite easy! Mistress Harper?"

His voice faded as he wandered off in the wrong direction. Omelda kept her head down. For a moment more, Natil stood, staring, as though suddenly confronted with the abject powerlessness of everything she held sacred. And then, finally, she turned away. "I will be here for a time, Omelda," she said softly. "For a little while. If you need me, you have but to call."

For a little while. And then Natil would leave. But that was all right: she had already left once before, and, as a result, her comings and goings now made no difference at all.

At the door, Natil paused. "Do you . . . do you sing at all, Omelda?"

Omelda paused in her scrubbing, fought to keep her

voice from rising into a scream. "I don't sing at all, Natil. It's not important. I'll be all right. Don't worry."

Plainly worried, Natil left. Her footsteps, soft but distinct, receded down the corridor until they lost themselves in the convoluted silence of the house.

Omelda scrubbed, worked dung and food out of the cracks, felt nothing, whether in her fingers, her knees, or her heart.

Francis Aldernacht himself had designed the majority of the Aldernacht house—was, in fact, still designing and adding to it—and as though the mansion were a reflection of a mind lost in convoluted plots, its endless corridors, multitudinous bedrooms, and seemingly pointless salons, gardens, walks, stables, and outbuildings sprawled across the southern part of Ypris like some particularly invasive species of prostrate weed. But as hugely magnificent as the house had grown, it had taken no form, no final shape, and was, in the end, just a collection of wood, plaster, stone, and brick, no more conclusive or committed than the mind of its creator.

Edvard and Norman Aldernacht, though, were willing and more than willing to make up for their father's lacks, and the day after Francis (still fretting and muttering about Jacob's squandering of moneys that rightfully belonged to *him*) returned from Furze, they entered his private study, unannounced, uninvited.

In the big chair behind the desk, Francis was smoking a long, elaborately carved pipe, his nicotine-drenched concerns swirling aimlessly from money to tobacco plantations to magic to poison to the death of a certain family patriarch . . . without, however, making much headway toward concrete plans for any of them. But what occupied him was not important to his sons, for they had known for years that though their father's mind might twist and turn and spurt out an occasional blossom, it would never bear fruit.

So the hidden (so Francis thought) panel slid back in response to the secret (so Francis thought) combination of pushes and pulls, and Edvard and Norman strolled into the study, themselves puffing on pipes rammed full of tobacco that was (so Francis thought) locked away in a hidden cupboard.

''Good morning, Pierre,'' said Edvard.

Francis sighed. ''I came here to be alone.''

''Well, that's all right, Pierre,'' said Norman, ''because we've come for the same reason. To be alone. With you.''

There was a stack of books on the table. Occult. Cabala. Poisons. A treatise on the toxicity of various fungi. Plans. All plans. All meandering, convoluted, ultimately fruitless plans . . .

Edvard shoved them aside, plunked his rump down in their place. ''Yes, indeed,'' he said. ''We've come to talk with you.''

Francis surrendered to the inescapability of the interview. ''What do you want?''

''We want to help you, Pierre.''

Their persistent insolence irked Francis, but he did not say anything about it. He never said anything about it. He had given up saying anything about it years ago, when Edvard and Norman had informed him that they did not give a fig about his opinions, wants, desires, or rights, and that they considered him rather petty for insisting upon or even mentioning such matters in their presence.

Since then, Francis had ignored Edvard and Norman, and Edvard and Norman had ignored Francis. It seemed important to the brothers, though, that they periodically remind their father just how little they respected him, and therefore they took every opportunity to insult him, try him, invade his privacy, appropriate his belongings.

''You want to help me,'' said Francis. ''Of course.''

''Really, Pierre.'' Norman shoved aside another pile of books and occupied the vacancy. ''You're so distrustful. Why would we *not* want to help you? I mean, after all, you're our father.''

Francis snorted.

''And we have a common interest.''

''Common interest . . . ?''

Edvard grinned. ''Money.''

Francis looked up at that. Behind the haze of smoke, Edvard's eyes were hungry, and there was a light deep within them that was much like the light in Francis's own eyes that he (so he thought) kept carefully hidden. ''Money?''

''The family money.''

Respect or disrespect, rights or no rights, Francis was now interested. "What about it?"

"I think you know very well, Pierre," said Norman. "It's a vast sum, a vast sum . . . and vast sums can so easily turn into small sums, if one is not careful."

Francis, recognizing thoughts that paralleled his own, had now gone beyond interest and into fascination. "That's true."

Edvard finally said it bluntly. "Grandfather is squandering the estate."

Unwillingly, then, torn between rapt agreement and caution: "I think so."

"He needs to be . . . to be . . ." Arrogant as the young man was, he suddenly appeared to be afflicted with a touch of his father's indecision when it actually came to uttering the words.

Norman, a little slower, was not so shy. He leaned across the desk. "He needs to be gotten rid of."

Francis cleared his throat, falling into the old pomposity. "Well, you know, your mother and I are . . ." He cleared his throat again. ". . . taking steps."

"Oh, Pierre! Go fuck Bishop Etienne yourself! You'll never get him to say that Grandpa is mad! Grandpa can buy him off in a heartbeat!"

Francis sat, stunned. "How did you know about Etienne?"

"How did we know about Etienne?" Edvard singsonged back at him. "How did we know how to get in here? How do we know where to find your tobacco? How do we know anything, Pierre?" He leaned closer. "We *find out*."

Francis's jaw clamped down on his pipe.

Edvard's eyes were bright. "Grandpa has to go. He has to be disposed of—"

"There are laws . . ."

"—legally."

"Oh, to be sure. Well, you know—"

"We can do it."

Francis's remonstrations abruptly ceased. He did not look at his sons. A cloud of smoke from burning tobacco drifted toward the ceiling. "You can . . . ?"

"Legally."

Francis's eye fell on the stack of books. Occult. Poison. Nothing had given him the courage to make the assay. But his sons had . . . had . . .

Legally. That was the whole point. It had to be done legally. And Francis knew without a doubt that, as unscrupulous and selfish as they were, they could do what they said they could do.

He took a deep breath. "What did you have in mind?"

Edvard sat back, smiling. "That's better, Pierre. Much better. Because, you see, though we can do it, we'll need your help."

Francis frowned, suspicious.

"For one thing, we need your financial help."

Francis's frown deepened.

"Because, if Grandpa dies—legally, you see—we want more out of it than the dribblings you've planned to hand out to us."

Deeper still.

"We want control of the firm. We want the final say. Oh . . ." Edvard held up a hand to his father's outburst. ". . . we'll let you in on everything, we'll even draw up a contract. In fact . . ." Laughing now, glancing at Norman. ". . . we'll insist upon it. Nice and legal. Buying and selling. True Aldernachts."

Francis sat motionless. His books had done nothing for him. But to throw in with his sons—even assuming that they could actually accomplish their goal—involved a bargain of diabolical import.

The wool cooperative, though . . . and that damned Bishop Albrecht! Jacob was squandering the estate. And if there were any way to keep it intact . . .

Edvard reached for the tobacco pouch, but, after a moment's thought, he took the pipe from his father's mouth and shoved it into his own, tossed the inferior article at Francis. "We can do it. And we will. Providing, of course, that you cooperate."

Holding a burnt-out pipe, staggered by the insolence of his sons, the enormity of what they planned, and their willingness to laugh about it, Francis hesitated, his thoughts swirling even more impotently than usual.

Norman was smiling. Edvard beamed. "Ah, Pierre, God must love you very much to send you two sons like us!"

An estate consisting of nothing, or an estate consisting

of . . . well, as much as Edvard and Norman were willing to give. Francis considered the choices for a time, then took the unlit pipe from his mouth.

"All right," he said.

CHAPTER 17

Dinah's head made a hollow sound as it smacked into the dark paneling of the passageway. Edvard, who had flung her, now leaned close, his blue eyes gleaming, his hand twined in her hair. "Listen," he said, "and listen well. We're taking a risk with you. We're taking a very big risk. You will succeed."

Dinah, her head ringing, fought with a suddenly uncooperative mouth. "I'm . . . I'm . . ."

Francis, from behind: "Edvard, really . . ."

"Shut-up, Pierre. I know what I'm doing."

"For the love of God, keep it quiet," said Norman.

The atmosphere of the passage was close, stagnant, full of man smells and wood smells. Dinah blinked, tried once more for speech, but Edvard was leaning close again, his white teeth gnashing as he formed the words, his lips opening and closing, puckering and relaxing. "You'll fuck him," he said. "And you'll make sure he's dead when you're done."

Dinah's head still spun, but her thoughts were petulant:

'Course I'll do it, 'cause that's what they want. I know what I can do. He'll die with a smile on his yawp . . .

"Because if you don't . . ."

"Edvard, please . . ."

"Shut up."

"Keep quiet, we're near the servants' quarters."

"You shut up, too."

Surrounded by men and by their heavy odors (and, she fancied, by their erections, stiff pricks brought up by the proximity of a half-clad woman with her dark curling hair and her soft curves and the scent of female melt moistening her thighs), Dinah wavered. "I'll . . . do it."

"Because if you don't," continued Edvard, "you'll

suffer. You'll suffer with all the torments that we can devise.''

I said I'd do it, why . . . ?

"Every particle of the Aldernacht fortune will be bent upon destroying you, little slut. There will be no escape for you. Do you understand?''

"I . . .''

He shook her. Her head cracked once again against the paneling. *"Do you understand?''*

The fear started then, a cold knot in her heart that trickled down to her groin, chilling her, drying up her willed arousal. Suddenly she could not think of the round fullness of a stiff penis inside her, suddenly she could think only of pain and death, of Edvard's lips opening and closing, puckering and relaxing like a hungry, toothed thing inches from her eyes.

I don't understand. I said I'd do it. How am I supposed to get him up and dead when they're talkin' to me like this?

In another part of the house, Jacob was down and awake. Eudes had tucked him into bed, and Natil had played for him, and now he was left alone with himself . . . and with his thoughts.

Alone. It was night, and the cracks in the shutters admitted nothing more than additional darkness, darkness that made the room seem isolated, lost. And Jacob, too, felt isolated and lost.

Bed's narrow. After Marjorie left, didn't have the heart to keep the big one. Pumped her good and full a few times in it, though. But look what came of it. Francis, and Karl . . . and that Josef. Nitwit. What good's his music? He'll be out on the street with his damned lutes after his brother takes over.

And Edvard and Norman and Francis half escorted, half carried the scented, rounded flesh of their murder weapon through the twisting passages that wound secretly through the house like the divertricular guts of a wooden animal. But Dinah's own guts were clawing at themselves now, rebelling at the hire, salary, and threat of her sexual orders, turning her arousal to ashes.

Jacob stared up into the darkness. Dinah stared at the wrong side of a wooden panel. Suddenly, she wanted to run.

"Remember what I said," said Edvard. His hand pulled the lever that opened the panel.

She was thrust through the opening and into the darkness of Jacob's bedroom. Oh, yes, she remembered. Her mind remembered. Her body remembered.

I'm dry now. I'm too dry. It's going to hurt, him going in and all. But I've got to do it, 'cause they'll hurt me if I don't. But they'll hurt me if I do, too, 'cause I'll get hurt doing it.

I hurt Marjorie. Didn't I just do a good job there? But I want her. I haven't had a woman in thirty years. Faithful unto death. Nitwit. I know where Josef got it now.

The panel ejaculated its subtle poison and then slid shut. There was no way out for Dinah now. If she tried to escape, she would be considered an intruder, possibly a thief, and Edvard and Norman would do nothing to save her. Her only way out was through the death of Jacob Aldernacht.

Man smell. Old man smell, like dry leaves and dust. Dinah picked her way across the room. She heard breathing, wondered what Jacob looked like.

I'm a woman. I can do this. And there he is, over there in the bed (can hardly see it, so dark) but he'll know my voice, and he'll know what I am, and that'll be all it takes.

Marjorie. Haven't had a woman since Marjorie. Don't even know what to do now. Kill me, most likely, to do anything. That would be the way to do it, now, wouldn't it?

And tears streaked Jacob's old, dry face as he thought of the wife whose embrace he had shoved so brutally aside thirty years ago. She was gone. Gone like everything. Only Albrecht and his fool's errand of a cathedral harkened back at all to the days of fantasy and delusion that Jacob had forced himself to remember and believe. No, it had never been like that—money had been around for a long time, and people who liked money had been around even longer—but it was a pleasant dream, and, half dozing, he allowed himself to dream it.

Odor, suddenly. Musk . . . and female musk. Still half-dreaming, Jacob let the scents envelop him. Marjorie had worn musk like that, once. He had been a much younger man, once.

Dinah stood uncertainly and silently at the side of his bed, wondering what to do, how to start. A virile young buck would have appreciated a quick leap and a warm cunt pressed against his mouth, but Jacob was old and, more than likely, asleep.

Got to do something, though. Got to get him up, get him in, shake him until he drops. He's old: won't take long. And then I'm going to leave Ypris. Knives in their pants one of these days, slit me up to the chin 'cause they're done with me.

Oh, and she moved under me, and she had those soft arms and soft lips. Don't know what she saw in me (but then the womenfolk don't have much to say in the matter, do they?) but she knew how to put me on my back and come down on me. . . .

Even as it dried, or perhaps because it dried, the scent of Dinah's melt wafted stronger. With shaking fingers, she peeled down the coverlet, took Jacob's inert hand in hers, moved it carefully to the curving round of her breast.

They all like waking up with their hand on a tit. Have to keep him from asking questions 'till he's pumped himself to death. Shouldn't take long please it won't take long . . .

God, and we'd laugh, and then she'd open her legs when I got my hands onto her breasts and we'd laugh some more. And then it'd be over and I'd be the same . . .

She closed his thumb and forefinger on her nipple, tried to feel the stirring in her belly that the gesture usually produced, but her fear had smothered any urgings from her loins, and so all she felt was manflesh cupping womanflesh without any real passion . . .

. . . and thank God for that 'cause I wouldn't have the nerve to stay here, trying to kill him with that thing

. . . stupid selfish son of a bitch, telling her that she was stupid, that she should stick to her kitchen and her

inside me, waiting for it to go limp and his eyes get that funny look in them that you know means it's all over. . . .

whelps. Hurt her. Of course I hurt her. Been hurting everyone for years. Wouldn't know how to stop if my . . .

. . . save what she was trying to squeeze out of her womb like an aborted fetus. And despite her efforts, Jacob still drifted in his dreams, his sleeping hand on her passionless breast.

. . . but my God he's not coming around and what can I do? I could sit on his face—

. . . life depended on it. Doesn't, though. Good thing, too. I'd be dead by morning if I—

Jacob's hand suddenly came to life, his nostrils flared with a sharp intake of breath.

?   ?

And Dinah, thinking quickly, shrugged herself out of a gown that was now dripping with the sweat of fear and flung herself on the supine elder, shoving her hands down to grab his manhood in stubby but practiced fingers, milking him rhythmically as she knew from years of experience that men like being milked (little finger finding that perfect groove beneath the foreskin), holding him between her spread legs and waiting, hoping, for that sudden lift, engorgement . . .

Eyes glazed from the abruptness of the attentions forced upon him, Jacob at first lay motionless, his body, awash in a welter of conflicting thoughts and longings, awakening in spite of three decades of disuse. It might well have been Marjorie who now stroked him with the wiles of a woman's hot desire, pressed her lips to meet his, moistened his thighs with her slick runoff.

. . . but I've got to feel this, 'cause I won't know what to do unless I feel it, and isn't he skinny. Maybe

Marjorie wore scent, and her tongue flicking my lips just like that. Women don't have any say about who

he's dead already. Please he's dead already.

they bed, but she made the best of it. . . .

Jacob, struggling up from sleep, his dreams banished by the stiffness of his erection and the weight of a lost wife now, in dreamtime, suddenly returned, opened his eyes in the darkness, heard the harsh gasps of the woman struggling on top of him.

Old bird, damn you, come, come, COME! Get that spit of seed out, give that last little jerk that the men always do, and then die! But he's not coming and they're on the other side of the wall and I know they can hear that he's not coming and he's waking up . . .

What's she doing in here? Don't recognize the voice. But she's like Marjorie and . . . that feels like Marjorie but it's not Marjorie. What the hell? Didn't think I could still do that. Why would she want to come back to me anyway? Just be more of the same. And that feels . . .

Heaving herself up, straddling him, she pressed her damp labia against his mouth. "I want you," she whispered, trying to project in her voice a sense of something that was not fear, that did not echo the rising panic now crawling up her back, down into her womanhood. "I'll be anyone you want me to be. I want you to want me."

But Jacob was crying now, for himself, for his lost wife, for the desire that had suddenly, uselessly, awakened in him. This woman on his chest was speaking to him in the accents of fantasy and delusion that could not but remind him, ever more deeply and painfully, of the deceit of the imagined past, of the uselessness of the future.

This isn't working. Got to try something else. They're listening, and I've got to make this work. Here, they like this. They always like this.

Can't be her. Dead now. I'm dead, too. They can have it. Stupid money. Paul and his boys will have to fight with Francis. Poor Paul. I'm dead.

Dinah strove, now shoving her breasts in Jacob's face (the skin of age against her, like a crinkling of parchment), now fondling him with ever increasing desperation, her breath coming with a hoarseness born of no passion save fear.

One of them would die tonight. She knew it. It was going to happen.

Whimpering, she straddled, milked, sucked, pressed, grabbed the weeping Jacob and tossed him on his stomach, gnawed at his buttocks, rimmed his anus with a dry, shaking tongue while her stomach clenched and the nausea of fright sent acid and bile up the back of her throat.

*Got to . . . try this . . . no,   Damn it all. Just give it all
this . . .   away.*

At last, Dinah—shaking, numb, exhausted—sat back on her trembling ankles and bowed her head. Defiled, debauched, degraded, and now dead, she bent over the still-sobbing form of her failure, her hands to her face, trying to comprehend the horror and the magnitude of what would happen.

*What's wrong with me?   What's wrong with me?
Don't I know what I'm do-   Don't I know what I'm do-
ing? Can't I do anything?   ing? Can't I do anything?
Do I have to die?   Do I have to die?*

Dinah sobbed, and Jacob sobbed, and while the whore contemplated her failure and her doom, the old man did the same.

His eyes flickered open. His hand groped, came up against Dinah's breasts. She flinched away, but he did not pursue.

His old lips moved. "I . . ."

She stared into blind darkness.

". . . I'm not worthy of you."

And then she fled, flinging herself off the bed, scrambling to the door, bloodying her hands on the unfamiliar latch. The hallway was dark and empty, and she had no idea of the layout of the house, but she ran nonetheless without light and without knowledge, bumping into walls, slamming into chairs and tables, sending the household into alarm and uproar with her clattering and clashing and muffled sobs and screams. They would find her, she knew. They would find her and kill her.

And perhaps it was instinct that led her through the mazed corridors of the labyrinthine house to the remote wing that housed the servants, and maybe it was instinct—or pain—that had kept Omelda from sleep that night; but the apostate nun heard the apostate whore in the corridor. Omelda found herself opening her door even though she was still half asleep.

"I'm dead!" Dinah was sobbing. "They're going to kill me!"

And Omelda, awake now, dragged the naked, frightened, thoroughly demoralized woman into her room, held her while she whispered, in frantic snatches and disjointed phrases, enough of a story to frighten her in turn, and then she bundled Dinah up in her tattered old cloak and led her down the hall to Natil's room.

But Jacob had also left his room. Dazed and despairing, he had pulled on what clothes had come to hand, and he had wandered down the hallway, undisturbed and unquestioned by the frightened servants. He saw little of anything, not only because he carried no light, but also because his inner vision was filled with Marjorie, with the wraith that had come to him in the musk-scented night and then, like Marjorie, had run away. Like the Marjorie of his memories, she had been weeping. Like the Marjorie of his dreams, she had been frightened.

"No . . . no . . ." he murmured. "Marjorie didn't die. She's . . . she's somewhere." He fetched up against the front door and, still acting without benefit of light, he unbarred it and passed out into the courtyard.

Shouts in the house behind him. A clatter of weapons. Manarel was bellowing at Eudes. Eudes was bellowing— politely and dryly—back at Manarel. A woman screamed.

The guards at the gatehouse started at his approach. "Master?"

"Let me through."

That was all he said. That was all it took. The master of the house asked, and it was immediately given unto him. Aldernacht money. Anyone could be bought. But he had not been able to buy Marjorie. No, she had left. And she was . . .

Tears were running down his face as he stumbled through the moonlit streets of Ypris, one hand covering one eye, the other eye staring into the darkness as though it might contain either horror or miracle.

Miracle found him first. Staggering, half falling down in the square, he felt hands on him, and then heard a voice that filtered through the night as though through the dryness of infinite years and the wet sputum of tuberculosis:

"Jacob. I know you, Jacob."

The moonlight was silver and treacherous, but he looked up into the aging face of a woman he knew not as Reinne . . .

. . . but as Marjorie.

As abuse and despair had broken Omelda's spirit, so fear and failure had destroyed Dinah's. The little whore sat on Natil's bed, her hands to her face, her defiant dark curls now bedraggled with sweat and despondency, her mouth downturned as much as her eyes.

She refused to answer questions about what had happened, and though Omelda told Natil as much as she had been able to piece together from Dinah's fearful blurtings, nothing made sense to the harper. Something about Jacob, and something about Edvard and Norman. Natil had read the grandsons' obsessions in their eyes, and so was not surprised that they would be involved with a prostitute. But Jacob?

"Do you know anything else about this?" she asked Omelda. Outside her door, the house was awakening like a fever victim rising from a nightmare. Men shouted, doors slammed. Somewhere, in the distance, Edvard cursed furiously about being gotten out of bed in the middle of the night, but there was dissemblance in his voice.

"No," replied Omelda. "Nothing."

Dissemblance again, but much closer, and decidedly not from Edvard. Natil peered at her. "Are you sure?"

Omelda turned away.

Natil ran a hand back through her hair, and, discouraged, shook her head. Human . . . and among humans. There was no Lady, there were no stars. She was on her own.

We've got to do something, Wheat had said, or would say in another five hundred years. *Even if it's not much. Even if it makes just a little bit of difference.*

Natil wanted to weep, but she held to the fading vestiges of her calling and knelt before Dinah, who, with her arms about herself, was rocking back and forth to some frightened inner cadence. "Beloved."

The once-defiant whore spread two fingers. An eye peered out through the gap.

"What do you need?" said Natil.

"They're going to kill me."

Natil kept her voice patient. "What do you need?"

Omelda was standing behind her. "She needs to get out of this house," she said tonelessly. "She needs to leave, to go far away."

Natil kept her eyes on Dinah. "Beloved, what do you need?"

Dinah spoke finally, gasping the words out as though she had been too long submerged. "What . . . what Omelda said. I have to leave. Edvard and Norman . . ." The gap between her fingers closed up, and she shuddered.

Natil frowned. "Edvard and Norman will not hurt you."

"You can't say that."

Indeed, she could not. She had broken her promise to Omelda, failed Harold, and, since yesterday's conversation in the kitchen, was now contemplating forswearing her agreement with the Aldernacht family. By what right did she now make statements with such calm assurance of their ultimate veracity?

She rebelled against her thoughts. "I say it. It is true. I will get you out of the house."

Dinah laughed bitterly. "They'll find me."

Omelda spoke up. "No, they won't. Not where you're going." She pointed at the prostitute. "Stay here. I'll be back."

She went to the door and slipped out into the hall. Alone at last with Dinah, impelled by the urgency of the whore's need and by what she sensed was potential danger to Jacob, Natil took Dinah's hands, pulled them away from her face. "What happened?"

"It's none of—"

Natil seized her by the shoulders, allowing a very human anger and frustration to possess her. *"It has become my business, woman!"* She glared into Dinah's face, wishing that some of the power of the vanished starlight might, for an instant, rekindle in her eyes.

Whether it did or not, Dinah trembled, nodded, and, haltingly, told Natil about the plot against Jacob. And about what Edvard had said to her just before thrusting her into Jacob's bedroom.

Natil sighed. *Human ways,* Terrill had said, long ago, with grief in his voice. Indeed, this was the most human of ways. The sorrow in the world seemed endless, and Natil found herself thinking of Hadden and Wheat, who were—would be—facing the same immortal dilemma that she herself appeared to be on the verge of resolving . . . or, rather, rendering moot.

What gets us through?

What indeed? Apparently nothing.

"And I failed, so they're going to kill me," Dinah finished. "I know it."

Natil nodded. She also knew it.

The door opened softly, and Omelda entered with her tattered bundle. She kicked the door closed, dropped to her knees, and began to undo the wrappings. "It's still in here, Dinah. And you need to . . ." Her voice almost broke. ". . . to go where it'll take you. For a while. At least for a while."

When she rose, she held up the common clothes of a woman. They were cut severely, though, and their color was an unfigured black that many washings had turned muddy gray.

Dinah blinked. "Those are nun's clothes. That's a habit."

Omelda approached, shoved the garments into her hands. "Put them on. And when you get out of here, you go down to Shrinerock Abbey. You don't have to be a nun, you don't have to stay there. Just talk to Dame Agnes, and listen to what she has to say. And . . . tell her that . . . that I'm . . . all right . . ."

Again, just on the other side of Omelda's tears, Natil heard dissemblance.

". . . and that maybe someday I'll be back. Maybe . . ." Omelda turned away. "Maybe you'll want to stay there for a while. You can decide what you want to do while you're there. Dame Agnes is a good woman. She'll take care of you.''

Dazed, bewildered, Dinah donned the habit, pulling back her dark curls and covering them with the veil, wrapping herself in the sexless, somber black of the Benedictines. When she was done, she stood, wavering, in the middle of the room, her debauchery debauched.

But smuggling Dinah—habit or not—out of the compound would not be easy. The household had been thoroughly roused, and Natil, bereft of starlight, had not been in the house long enough to know anything of the grounds. Omelda had never gotten over her initial bewilderment. Dinah herself knew only a few rooms.

Footsteps outside, a heavy knock on the door. Omelda jumped. Dinah looked ready to fling herself out the window. Natil signed to them to be still and went to the door. ''Who, please?''

''Manarel. Just checking, Mistress Harper. Are you all right?''

Natil sagged slightly. ''We are . . . ah . . . fine, Master Manarel,'' she said, and then she opened the door and beckoned him into the room. The big man entered, stared at Omelda, stared harder at the impostor nun, and then turned to Natil for an explanation.

It was not forthcoming. ''We need to escort this good sister out of the house, Master Manarel,'' said Natil. ''Can you help us . . .''

''But what—?''

''. . . without any questions?'' Natil hoped that her smile did not look as insincere as it felt.

Manarel frowned, folded his thick arms. ''I'm a steward of this house, Mistress Natil.''

''I realize that, honored sir.''

''I've given my word to protect this family.''

''Gracious sir, I know.''

''You're being too polite.''

Natil sighed, bowed. ''I try.''

Manarel glowered down at her. ''The house is in an uproar, Mister Jacob's disappeared . . .''

Dinah turned away.

''. . . Eudes is going on about intruders or something like that, and you . . .'' Tall and thick, he loomed over

Natil like an oak tree over a willow sapling. ". . . want me to help smuggle an unidentified nun out of the grounds."

Natil cleared her throat politely. "And out of the city."

Manarel clapped his hand to his forehead. "Dear God!"

"I am sorry to inconvenience you, Master Manarel," said Natil, feeling the hopelessness of the situation. "But—"

"Shut up. I'll do it."

The harper stared.

Still with his hand to his forehead, Manarel chuckled: a low rumble that appeared to well up from inside his chest like a small earthquake. "Yes, I'll do it, Mistress Harper. You braved the Inquisition to try to help Harold, and idiot though he was, Harold was one of ours. And so I'll return the favor tonight. But where is the . . ." He examined Dinah as though he would sooner have believed his horse to have taken the veil. ". . . good sister going?"

Dinah answered before Omelda could dissemble or Natil could equivocate. "South," she said, her voice hoarse. "To Shrinerock Abbey."

Manarel did not waste time: he had given his word, and he would allow nothing to stop him from keeping it. With a nod (and a trace of a glower) at the harper, he offered his arm to the false nun, and after a quick inspection of the hallway he took her away.

Omelda sat down heavily on Natil's bed. "It's not a good world to be a woman in," she said darkly. "I hope she makes it to the abbey."

"She's dressed as a nun," said Natil.

"That never stopped anybody." Omelda, staring straight ahead, appeared to see nothing. "*I* was dressed like a nun that first week, and that didn't do anything to stop the thieves who found me."

Natil covered her face with her slender hands. Tomorrow, she would leave Ypris and head south. To Malvern. To an end. She hoped. "They . . ."

"Used me for a few weeks." Omelda was still staring. "Or a few months. I don't remember now. My hair had grown out by the time they let me go: that was . . ." There was an old horror to the tale, but Natil heard something else, too: an immediate pain that had nothing to do with memories. ". . . that was a good thing."

"I suppose that everything that happens, happens as it should." Natil sniffed, the hot tears stinging their way down her fair skin, pooling between her fingers. "Because that is the way it happens."

"A charming philosophy, Natil." Omelda's voice held all the warmth of a stone.

The harper dropped her hands, nodded. She felt empty, drained. "Quite strange, I know. I am . . . no longer sure . . . exactly where I got it."

She took Omelda by the hand, then, and led her back to her room; but the house had fallen silent. No slamming doors. No shouts. No running feet. The corridors appeared to be deserted.

And then they came upon old Eudes in the hall. He was wearing a dressing robe that was as gray and dusty and faded as himself. But the trusty old wardrobe looked decidedly run down tonight: his moldings dull and chipped, his doors sagging on their hinges.

"Master Eudes?" said Natil. "Good evening, sir. God bless you."

"What's that? Eh? Oh! Natil." Eudes nodded absently.

"Is something wrong?"

Eudes stared for a full minute before he replied. "I'm . . . not sure. Maybe. Maybe not. The master found his . . . wife."

"His wife? Marjorie? She is . . . ?"

"Dying," said Eudes with a creak of peeling veneer. "Consumption. The physician says she can't possibly live more than a . . . week."

CHAPTER 18

Adoro te devote, latens deitas . . .

It was a matter of money. God's money. Ever since the days of old John XXII, the Church had been weighing with excruciating logic—and, sometimes, with excruciating pain—its virtue and vices, profit and loss, use and ownership. The Spirituals had fought against it. John had fought for it. Who, exactly, had won was still somewhat in doubt for many.

Siegfried, though, had no doubts whatsoever. God had won. In one way or another, the Deity who hid Himself beneath a cloak of bread and wine had triumphed. That the mild little men who attempted to do His will had no understanding of exactly *how* He had triumphed was of little importance. Men had not been created to understand, but rather to *believe*. That was their duty, that was their salvation.

But money was nonetheless a palpable problem for Siegfried these days: Furze was poor, the Inquisition was large. Despite divine triumph or the demands of orthodoxy, people had to eat; and since the Inquisition was not in the business of multiplying bread and fishes (at least, not yet), its servants had to be paid for their work.

Many people, much money. But though the possessions of accused heretics were confiscated and donated to the furtherance of the will of Holy Church—after a reasonable portion was tendered to the local representative of secular power—there was, in truth, not a great deal of money to be had in Furze to begin with. The coffers of the House of God, in fact, were all but empty.

Fra Giovanni brought the news, adding it to his customary morning report. He was nervous, worried. There was nothing to be had from Shrinerock Abbey, the Benedictine monks held a charter directly from the Holy See and were therefore beyond reach, and even the slow but steady transfer of principal from the cathedral fabric fund, he informed the Inquisitor, had accomplished little. Furze had gone bankrupt long ago. The Inquisition was in danger of following it.

Siegfried leaned back in his chair, looked out the window that was streaming with morning light. Oh, for a glimpse of divine radiance that would blaze forth with the same uncompromising brilliance as this sunshine! *Then* Siegfried would know. Then he would be sure. *Latens deitas* no more!

But the sunlight remained sunlight, and the Deity remained hidden. Siegfried was looking at the morning, that was all, and the coffers remained empty. Perhaps this was a test.

"What about Paul Drego?" he said.

Giovanni nodded toward the thick book that occupied one corner of Siegfried's desk. "It is all there, Brother Siegfried."

Siegfried looked at the book, was silent. Empty coffers and God's will. A heretic forfeited both his property and his right to enter into contracts and bargains from the moment of his heresy, and, according to this book of gathered intelligence and rumor, Paul had fallen into heresy long ago, even before he had, in the tavern with James, refused to swear (thereby branding himself a Waldensian), or speculated on the question of the poverty of Christ (thereby allying himself with the Beghards and the ignorant but pernicious Spirituals). But at that time, Paul had possessed little more money than James, and considerably less than Simon; and even Simon, the wealthiest man in Furze—of course he was wealthy: he was a Jew—had difficulty putting sufficient bread on his table.

But now the situation had changed. Or, rather, was changing. Paul was still poor, but he had the promise of Aldernacht money. But if Paul were indeed already a heretic, then the Aldernacht contract was null and void, and the moneys would revert to Jacob's family. Furze would remain poor and foundering, and the Inquisition would remain poor and foundering right along with it.

Siegfried picked up the book, leafed through a few pages of the close written entries. The tavern. Visitors at the house. Remarks made in the square. Denunciations from neighbors who might or might not bear a grudge over the matter of a basket of Christmas figs . . .

But if Paul had been heretical before the contract had been signed, then there would be no money.

God's will, God's triumph. Siegfried weighed the book in his hand. It represented weeks of work, but what were weeks against eternity? A final consideration, then, a final decision . . .

. . . and he tossed the book into the trash bin.

Giovanni looked startled. "Brother—"

"The results so far are inconclusive," said Siegfried.

"But—"

"The Inquisition, Fra Giovanni, is not accustomed to punishing the innocent. The guilty we track down with all the vengeance of angels and the determination of hounds: not even death can come between us and the punishment of the confirmed heretic. But we must have proof. Conclusive proof. Therefore . . ." Siegfried felt unclean. He had uttered a lie. But he reminded himself that it was a good lie, that God was depending upon that lie. ". . . we will look further at Paul Drego and his friends. We will watch him carefully, for though he may not yet have fallen into heresy, it is quite possible that he is very close to it."

Giovanni stared. Siegfried saw his thoughts. The book . . . the evidence . . .

"Give the necessary orders, Fra Giovanni. Have Paul watched. And . . ." There was another side now to Furze . . . and to money. Jacob Aldernacht. Wealthy beyond belief. And his house musician had uttered heresy. What if . . . ? "I will question Harold this afternoon."

Giovanni stared a little more, mouth half open. Then, abruptly, he gathered his wits. "As you wish, Brother Siegfried," he said, and he left the room.

His lie an ache of nausea in his heart, Siegfried found himself looking at the book in the trash bin. Gingerly, he picked it up, leafed through it once again. Waldensians. Beghards. It was all clear.

But, no: it was not clear. Siegfried was the Inquisitor of Furze, and he should certainly know whether an individual's heresy was clear or not. And so, in this case, he had determined that it was not.

On his way out of the office, he tossed the book into the fire.

People who visited the Chapel of Our Lady of the Angels a short time later were a little disconcerted to find Siegfried of Magdeburg prostrate before the altar, his forehead pressed to the cold stone floor, his clenched hands extended toward the tabernacle. The people came and went, but Siegfried stayed throughout the morning. It was a disturbing sight, to be sure, but perhaps not a surprising one: Siegfried was known to be a holy man. Why, according to some, he had never told a lie in his life!

Was anything, Jacob wondered, ever as he expected it? Was the past at all as he remembered it? He had grown used to the suspicion that his memories of the virtue and purpose of the past were fantasies, delusions, the grapplings of an old man with the futility of goodness; and, as though he were donning a kind of spiritual armor both against the world and his own more tender yearnings, he had responded to that suspicion with growing cynicism and cruelty. But beneath the armor, he had still (he realized now) harbored a small, vibrant hope that his memories were not all delusions, that his fantasies held a small germ of truth.

Marjorie, perhaps, had been that hope, that small flicker of spiritual optimism that had guarded him from abject despair. He himself had grown evil, had, seemingly, taken delight in deliberately smearing himself with the dross and corruption of his time. Marjorie, though— the Marjorie he remembered—had been good, pure, an angel of love and delight that he had driven out of his house; and he had carried the memory of her within him like a talisman.

But here was Marjorie now, come back after three decades of wandering with the gypsies. And here was Jacob's last delusion, his last hope, his last memory . . .

. . . exploded.

"How much money do you have now, Jacob?" Propped up on feather pillows, wrapped up in linen sheets and swaddled in comforters, Marjorie peered out from beneath a cap of gray hair, her blue eyes as crafty as

Jacob's, her brow set and intent. "Are you going to give me any *now*?"

Jacob sat at her bedside, old hands clasped on old knees, feeling the emptiness that came with desolation. He had thought that the little whore had finished him. But he had gone on: out into the streets, down the alleyways, straight into the arms of this woman.

He could not deny her: she was his wife. He knew it. She knew it. But neither could he deny that she was a living refutation of everything that had kept him sane and alive.

"All . . . all that you want," he said, still longing after the fading form of a banished angel.

Marjorie spat: blood and pus. "I don't want anything that's not mine. And your money isn't mine. You keep it to yourself, don't you? You don't give any of it away, do you?"

Jacob stared blankly. Eudes, dusty and dry, stood by the door, ready to depart on any errand that might be assigned to an old wardrobe and obviously wishing that one might come soon.

"I've given some away," said Jacob slowly, wishing this his voice did not sound so tentative. In his more grandiose moods, he had thought of himself as a viper that, like the serpent depicted on that old Visconti crest, devoured its enemies. But this viper was, apparently, a seedy old worm, without teeth, without venom. Useless. One might skin it, perhaps, and make a belt of it, but that was all.

Marjorie laughed. "Oh, you've given some away, have you? Sure you have."

"Madam . . ." began Eudes tentatively, "Mister Jacob is—"

"Thank you, Eudes," Jacob interrupted quietly. "I don't need you to defend me."

The old wardrobe nodded stiffly.

"You may go."

Eudes bowed amid a creaking of rusty hinges. He withdrew, shut the door.

Marjorie spat again. "You're like the gypsies, Jacob. You give a little, and then you take everything. Everyone's a *gadja* to you. Even your family. Even your wife."

There was a cramping in Jacob's heart, and he wished

that the little whore had killed him. He no longer questioned her appearance in his bedroom, no longer even speculated about who might have introduced her into the house. He did not care. He simply wished that he had died between her legs with a stiff prick and a smile on his face.

But he had lived—had not even had a good orgasm for his trouble—and he had found Marjorie. And now it was all tumbling down into a heap: all his dreams, all his illusions, all his fantasies. His armor, cracked, exposed him as a simpleton of an old man, a crab without a shell, ready to be gutted and eaten.

"Everyone . . ." he mumbled.

Marjorie nodded with a jerk that set her to coughing. A trail of slime and blood had found its way out of the corner of her mouth by the time she was done, and, with a harsh crow, she swabbed it off with a handful of sheet. "I'm gone," she said. "I heard your doctor talking to you. He won't give me more than a week. But I don't care. I'm here, and you'll feed me and take care of me, and I'll go comfortable. That's why I came back: to get something out of you for a change."

Jacob nodded. *That's why I came back.* Money. That was it. And if Francis and Edvard and Norman had gotten greed and avarice from Jacob, a strain of contempt for anything that could not be plunked down on a table in gold and silver, then from Marjorie they had inherited a crassness that had confirmed them in their single-minded, covetous, exploitative pursuits.

Marjorie had turned to the tray of food that lay on the bed table. She crammed a mouthful of cake between her toothless jaws and washed it down—along with the blood and slime that she had coughed up—with a full cup of wine.

"Why . . ." Jacob stared at the empty cup she left.

She threw it to the floor. It bounced away, clattered against the far wall. "Why what?"

"Why did you go?"

"Because you were a mouse, Jacob."

A soft tap on the door. Jacob recognized the knock. "Come in, Natil."

The harper entered. Her dark hair, with the exception of the single small braid that held the defiant eagle feather, fell unconfined and uncovered to her waist, and her slender arm cradled her harp as though it was an infant. "Master, I have come to offer my music."

Jacob nodded. "Thank you, Natil. I think some music would be—"

He turned back to Marjorie, and his words were choked off by the look of fear on the old hag's face. But Marjorie was not looking at him: she was staring instead at Natil, who had approached the bed.

Natil?

". . . uh . . . good for us both," he finished lamely.

Marjorie was muttering something under her breath. It sounded like a prayer, or a charm.

Natil nodded serenely. "Madam," she said to Marjorie, "I have heard that you are ill."

"I'm . . ." Marjorie fought with her emotions, dredged up words. "I'm dead."

"You are ill," said Natil. There was compassion in her voice, but it was not the compassion that came of the human fear of dying, that expressed itself in false sentiments and the fakery of brave words. No, Natil was compassionate because Marjorie was dying, because it was important for people to be compassionate. "And so I have come to play for you. Music can sometimes heal. At the very least, music can soothe."

"I . . ." Marjorie was still staring at Natil, and Jacob fully expected her to curse the harper and send her back out into the hall. But to his surprise, she seemed to wilt into herself, and she nodded meekly. "Yes. Yes, I'd like that. Play."

Natil settled herself on a stool in the corner. Her hands moved to the strings of her instrument, and a soft chord rang out. A melody followed: stark, unadorned, but comforting.

Marjorie looked as though she were a rat that had found itself in the presence of a snake. "Who's that?" she hissed.

"Natil," said Jacob. "She's one of the house musicians."

Her eyes crinkled up into a semblance of mirth. "And you just found her out in the square, didn't you?"

"Actually, Josef found her."

She laughed without any feeling. "Josef. That nitwit. Didn't know anything, doesn't know anything."

Hearing his own sentiments from his wife's mouth, Jacob rose to his son's defense. "You don't know that. He was a baby when you . . . when you left. Actually, he's a fine musician. And a scholar."

"He's a nitwit." Marjorie snorted, dribbling blood from her lips. Natil's music floated through the room. "I could tell. That first day I held him in my arms, he looked up at me with those stupid eyes, and I knew."

Jacob was afraid to ask her opinion of Francis and Karl. "And so you left."

"You were a mouse, Jacob. But you were a greedy mouse. You . . ." Marjorie stole an almost fearful look at Natil, but the harper was lost in her music. ". . . you got in my way. Always. Told me what to do. Didn't give me a moment's peace. Tried to fuck me every chance you got. I got sick of you and your orders and your tantrums. And I got sick of those mewling little kids you forced on me. So I ran away. I figured that nothing was better than something with you around."

The cramp in Jacob's heart tightened. Yes, yes: she was right. Had he not prided himself on his greed? "And you . . . you came back to die," he said hollowly. There seemed to be nothing about him that was not hollow.

"I figured that I ought to get something out of you." With a quick glance at the harper, she grabbed his sleeve. "You *owe* it to me. *You owe it*!"

Jacob stared into eyes that mirrored his. Fear. Disappointment. A desire for material objects that bordered on lust. Oh, it was all there, and when Francis came to the door a few minutes later, sanctimoniously and publicly performing what he perceived as his filial obligation to call upon his beloved mother, Jacob saw the same thing in his eyes, too.

He found that he hated Francis. He found that he hated them all. He found that he hated himself. The house was a sepulcher, the motto *In the name of God and profit* a hideous jest and epitaph both, as though one might bite one's thumb in the face of the advancing skeletal presence of Death itself.

Money. It was all money. Even Marjorie had grounded her departure and her return on money.

Jacob felt an unclenching in his belly, a sense of release. But it was not the release of fulfillment. Rather, it
was a crumbling, a destruction, the same yielding up of
stress and tension that came of a bridge or a castle falling
into ruin. Perhaps, he thought, trees would take root in
what was left of his heart. Maybe birds would come and
nest in his hair.

That evening, he sat by what he knew would be his
wife's deathbed. And, in many ways, his own.

A week went by. Two weeks. June arrived, the weather
turned hot, summery . . . and Marjorie did not die.

But as Jacob, in self-inflicted penance, revolved about
the continually decaying physical presence of his wife,
so, increasingly, did everyone else. As though the servants were infected with his blundering preoccupation
and obsessive involution, they began to wander through
a semblance of their duties that had only the vaguest ef-
fectiveness. Meals were served sporadically, breakfast,
perhaps, showing up on the table at midday, and dinner
after everyone retired—to be eaten cold and without appetite in the morning. Cleaning duties were neglected,
inventories (even when conducted by the indefatigable
Claire) hasty and incomplete. The house, embodied in
its duties and routines, fragmented, as though, turning
in upon itself, it was unable to cope with what it saw in
its own dark heart.

Alone, Omelda labored in the kitchen, washing the
floor, scrubbing the pots, scraping grease off the wood-
work. She was not ordered to do any of this; rather, she
simply acted with the same plodding, ox-like docility that
had colored her entire life, that had come to dominate
her personality as a result of mounting abuse. For though
the household as a whole had become disordered and
forgetful, Edvard and Norman continued to be attentive
to her. They had lost their plaything, Dinah—and who
knew where she was now?—and deprived therefore of the
pleasure of costume and theater involving the two women,
they fell back upon simple sex, degradation, and torture.

She saw little of Natil, but that was to be expected:
the harper was busy with Marjorie, and Omelda had herself absolved her from any further obligation to her former charge. No, Omelda would not, did not sing. No,

the voices did not bother her. No, she did not need anything, thank you. *I'll be all right. Don't worry about me.*

And so, mornings, hardly able to walk, Omelda limped
about in the confines of her room, lurching from bed to
table to chair, forcing her recalcitrant feet and legs to
move and bend until they were at last obedient enough
to carry her out the door and down the hall to the kitchen,
where she would spend the day scrubbing and scraping,
the plainchant alternately abusing her and dropping her
as regularly as did Edvard and Norman. Occasionally,
Eudes would come out of his somnambulistic bewilderment long enough to send her on an errand, and occasionally she would find her way to and from her
destination without mishap. More often, though, she
wandered, lost, for, having folded in upon itself spiritually, the labyrinthine house seemed to have become even
more physically convoluted than before.

She was lost one afternoon when she blundered into
an unused room to find Josef Aldernacht sitting at a table, an idle lute in his lap. Paper and pens and ink were
laid out before him, but they were dusty, as though they
had been untouched for days, perhaps weeks. Sunlight
streamed down on him through a tall window that was
opalescent with dust and neglect.

He looked up, started, rose hastily. "My lady."

Omelda wavered, half expecting him to remove her
gown and put her on the floor. Or tie her up. Or . . .

But this was not Edvard or Norman: this was Josef.
For an instant, Omelda was relieved at the thought of Josef's gallant but pointless worship of anything feminine.
He would not hurt her. He would not call her slut or
whore. He would not force her. Instead, he would honor
her, spout what fragments of Italian humanism he thought
he understood, perhaps compose (badly) a poem for her.

But today he did none of these things. Instead, he
bowed, stammered a faint greeting, and then sank back
down on his stool, his boxy lute on his lap, his eyes on
the table top.

Omelda felt faintly betrayed. "Is there . . . is there
anything I can get you, Mister Josef?"

Josef looked up. "Will you . . . sit with me for a moment, my lady?"

My lady. He had spoken the words as a thirsty man

might speak of water. Omelda nodded and, when he had brought a chair for her, sat down . . . stiffly.

A long silence. Josef was staring at the table top again. Omelda fidgeted with both discomfort and pain. Finally, the would-be musician, poet, and philosopher spoke:

"I have always had the greatest admiration for women, Omelda."

There did not seem to be any appropriate reply, so she merely nodded.

He fingered the lute. "I mean, even before I discovered the wonders of the Italian mind, it always seemed to me that all that was good and noble and beautiful resided in the soul of . . . woman."

Again, there was nothing to say. As far as Josef appeared to be concerned, Omelda was someone to whom to talk. She might have been a dog, or a diary, or a wall.

"It seemed obvious to me that, given such beauty of form and such excellence of heart . . ." Josef looked at her for the first time since he had begun to speak. ". . . I . . . I mean women in general . . ." He went back to the table top. ". . . that a certain nobility—no, beauty—of soul that is invariably denied the male sex could not but reside in womanhood."

Omelda was staring at nothing.

"And it struck me . . ." Josef abruptly swung round to her, and his eyes were pale and bright. ". . . that I was a very fortunate man, as all men are fortunate, for . . . having come forth into the world out of that . . . goodness and nobility." He blinked, looked away nervously. "Do you see my point?"

Omelda suddenly wanted to run, to be away. But there was nothing for her to run to, save for Edvard and Norman and their games. "I . . . don't think so," she said.

Josef did not appear to hear her. She doubted that he was actually paying much attention to her. "And then . . . and now . . ." He twitched, fingered the lute, suddenly looked at it as though he wanted to smash it. "It seems to me . . ."

Omelda sat still, wishing that he would forget that she was there, wishing that Edvard and Norman, too, would forget.

Josef lifted his head. "It is all . . . dust," he said

solemnly. "All dust. Nobility, and excellence of heart
. . ."

He seemed to be casting about in his mind, looking
for some way out of a snare. "But there is . . . no nobility. And she . . ."

The lute clattered to the floor as he got up and began
pacing. Omelda hoped that his steps might take him out
of the room long enough for her to escape. But he turned
to her, his eyes bright, his mouth set. "She brought me
forth, and she cursed me by doing so. I . . . I . . ." He
shook his fists. "I have to . . . to live like this, knowing
that from . . . such as her . . ."

Omelda stared at him, shaking, her bruised and lacerated vulva burning with the pressure of the hard chair.

"Why didn't she stay away? Why didn't she die out
there? It would have been better!"

She said nothing. She was a dog, a book, a wall. Indeed, Edvard and Norman had forced her to be all those
things and more.

Josef went down on one knee before Omelda. She
shrank away, but he clasped suppliant hands before her.
"I want to tell you something, my lady. You must listen
to me, for you are all that gives me hope in womanhood
and virtue anymore."

Womanhood and virtue. And bondage. And abuse.
And rape.

"I cannot stay in this house," said Josef, "for it tells
me too much of my birth, too much of what I am. I am
going to leave. No one knows this save you now, and you
must keep it secret. I am going to leave . . ." He spread
his hands. ". . . forever!"

He increased the spread of his hands as though to indicate just how long he considered forever to be. Omelda,
wide-eyed and in pain, nodded.

"I am going to join the company of men," said Josef.
"I will know dirt, and disease, and a world in which
there is nothing gentle. I will find my brother Karl, and
become a . . . a soldier. I might die in a field in Italy,
but I will die nobly, and without . . ." He glanced off in
the direction of the master wing of the house, where
Marjorie was slowly succumbing to pulmonary rot.
". . . without her."

He bent toward her. "I will have no reminders of my

past," he whispered. "None. My mind is made up. Farewell . . . forever!" He kissed her polluted hands as though they were fresh roses from a morning garden, then stood up and turned to go.

At the door he turned back. "Forever! Forever! Farewell!"

And then he left. Omelda rose, shaking, and hobbled away through the house, her stiff legs propelling her in whatever direction came to hand. Edvard and Norman found her, then, took her away, and used her for an afternoon's amusement.

But that night, as Omelda lay awake and in pain, she heard a side door of the house open and close, heard a creak from the stable, heard a rattle of the postern gate and a clatter of hooves. Josef, the humanist, was gone.

CHAPTER 19

Natil wanted to leave. Natil did not leave.

It was the old dance once again, the stately and tragic pavane that had so indissolubly wedded Elf and human since the first primate had descended from the trees with a precious spark of sentience: Natil stayed because Marjorie—consumptive, avaricious Marjorie—needed her. The old woman was dying, and though instinct prodded Natil in the direction of the front door and bold departure (or the back door and furtive escape), she remained at the bedside to play the music of transition: liminal strains that might comfort one who was about to pass a threshold, a hand of sound to hold that of the dying woman until, at the doorway of the breathless realm, Marjorie would pull hers away and continue on . . . alone.

But music, like all things elven and immortal, was failing; and though Natil might comfort, she could no longer heal. Marjorie remained Marjorie, and even with an unceasing flow of melody laving her as though with the waters of rebirth, not the slightest glimmer of compassion or peace awakened within her.

"Play that one again, Natil." Even her request for a song of solace was tainted with her habitual peevishness. "I liked that. Play it just the same. Play it now."

Straining with long-pent and human anger against its chains of elven tolerance, Natil's heart urged her to spit and then leave, but: "I cannot play it as I did, Madam Marjorie," she said calmly, "for I made most of it up as I played it. Such is the way of my music."

Marjorie did not fall into the same immediate and virulent cursing that would have characterized her response to, say, a servant who had brought a dinner she deemed insufficiently hot, or an additional blanket of less than first-rate quality. There was, as Natil had realized, a streak of fear in Jacob's dying wife, one that stilled her curses and moderated her demands when she was speaking with the strange harper.

Fear. Natil had seen it before. Marjorie, it seemed, was afraid of no one and nothing . . . save the slender musician-maid of her husband's household. But now Marjorie, after a long look at the door as though wondering whether anyone were listening (a needless precaution: even the obsessively inquisitive Francis had given up on the frightful hag) and a glance at Jacob's chair (empty for now: Jacob had retired to his bed in order to recuperate from a day's worth of abuse from his former love) turned to her, her face holding a combination of terror and defiance. "You can play it the same way if you want," she whispered. "I know you can. Your kind can do anything."

And at the tacit accusation, Natil felt something wither inside of her. Her kind. What did that mean anymore? "I do not understand."

"You're one of . . . of *them*." Marjorie's eyes, detecting weakness on the part of one she had deemed essentially invulnerable, were bright. "I know."

Natil felt empty. The feeling had grown habitual, a constant reminder of loss and homelessness. "One of . . . them . . ."

"They call you Elves. Demons. I know. I recognized you that first day we met. I know from the way you play. The gypsies taught you to play like that, after you cheated them of their birthright."

First an Elf, and then a thief. Indeed, the world had changed! But Natil found herself shrugging off both accusations. The Elves were gone, faded; and this Natil who sat by the bed of a dying consumptive seemed to be in no way connected with their immortal lives. Natil lived in cities. Natil was a servant. Natil slept. Like her human sisters, Natil fought off the grasping hands of amorous males, stuffed her face with bread and meat, dreamed dreams of delusion and hope.

Elves awakening? She might as well dream of marrying a king, or of slipping five hundred years forward in time so as to join the impossible myth that had taken shape in her careworn brain.

"I am afraid . . . ." Natil fingered her harp. At times,

she wondered that she was still able to play it. Perhaps all the songs were delusions also, as were all the memories—joys and sorrows both. Would she fade? Probably not: she would die hacking up blood and bits of lung just like this old woman before her. "I am afraid that you are wrong, Madam Marjorie. I am only a harper. As human as you."

It was the truth. It hurt her that it was the truth, hurt her badly, and the pain in her heart obviously found in her voice enough of an egress to make even one such as Marjorie blink, stare, grimace with the expression of a woman who had been proven wrong by mere physical fact.

"As . . . as human as I . . ." Marjorie peered at the harper as though seeing her for the first time, blinked again. "And . . . you're right, aren't you? You're just a woman, aren't you?"

"It is so," said Natil. "Just . . . a woman . . ."

Fear vanished, to be replaced by contempt. Marjorie lifted a peremptory finger. "Play something more. Don't give me any more excuses."

"I am tired, Madam Marjorie," said the harper, rising. "I would like to go to bed."

Marjorie heaved herself up to protest, started coughing, threw up blood. The dark red stains spread out on the white linen sheets. "One more song," she managed between gouts.

Natil weighed her harp in her hand, then shrugged and sat down. Helping and healing. The old dance still held her. She could not leave this terrible house. She could not even leave this bedroom.

With the strings blurring and doubling to her eyes, then, she played one more song, one that, years ago, she had heard sung by a simple village priest who in turn had learned it from an old monk: a simple bit of plainchant from the Cluniac rite for the dead. But voices and hearts and needs had modified it both in melody and in words, and over the years it had mutated from the second ecclesiastical mode to a scale that was essentially alien to the corpus of Christian rite, and from a plea addressed to a transcendent Deity to the cry of a child for its mother:

A porta inferi
erue, Domina,

animam meam.

Natil played the loss she felt, the bitterness of the tears she could not seem to shed for a life she could hardly remember. With simple statements of the music and even simpler harmonies, she allowed a fifteen-second melody to build into an hour's improvisation as Marjorie, satisfied at having gotten what she wanted, settled back on her pillows with her gnarled hands folded and a half smile on her face.

Her eyes were closed, and so immersed was Natil in her music and in her deeply private grief that she did not notice when the old woman stopped breathing. But when the harper came out of her trance, wiped the webs of music from her sight, and looked up, she discovered that Marjorie had died, passing quietly out of life with a last benediction from a once-immortal hand.

She touched Marjorie's cold fingers. Once, Elves had helped people to live. Now they helped people to die. But, she reminded herself, she was not an Elf. She was just a woman.

She stood up, fatigued, sorrowing. It was very late, and the house was dark and quiet. Jacob, doubtless, had collapsed into his bed, or over dinner, or at his desk, his body simply refusing to endure yet another nocturnal vigil over his wife's slowly eroding body. Perhaps there were watchmen at the gate, and perhaps an accountant or two still labored by candlelight over columns of Aldernacht figures—profit and loss, credits and debits—but, here in the house, Natil was alone with the dead, the dead she had helped to die.

She wondered for a moment about Wheat and Hadden. Was that the reason that the Elves would come back? To help the world die? Was that old derelict on the street the emblem of the entire planet? Varden's vision had contained much more than the hope and promise of future rebirth. He had seen things . . . terrible things. Wars that wrapped the globe in destruction, and weapons that could incinerate millions in a heartbeat, and forests and lakes dying, and the earth itself poisoned.

Was that the reason? Or was it indeed all (the doubt coming back) just delusion? Natil no longer knew. Perhaps she had been harping too long, blending myth with song for too many years.

Marjorie's fingers had been cold even in life. Now they were more than cold. The eagle feather in Natil's braid fluttered in a stray draft, and she recalled what the friends who had given it to her had said to the dying.

She bent low, kissed the still face. "Good hunting, Marjorie," she whispered.

And then she picked up her harp, rose, left the room. Her tasks were done, her duties all ended. She could leave. She cared little about Aldernacht greed or the willingness of a bitter old man to besiege an entire town over a runaway serving girl. She was a harper. She could go anywhere. And if, as she had for so long deluded herself, she had once been an Elf, then where she would eventually go—where she now so fervently prayed that she could still go—not even Jacob Aldernacht with his money and his ships and his private army could follow.

Her soft shoes made dusty sounds on the bare floor of the hallway. Perhaps she could slip out the postern, and perhaps she could do so without detection. She hoped so. She wanted to sleep under the stars tonight.

But a pang of conscience made her hesitate at the juncture of two corridors and, after a moment, she turned in the direction of the servants' wing. She would not leave Marjorie lying dead and unattended throughout the night; she would not leave a corpse to be discovered in the morning like a piece of discarded furniture. She would tell someone. And only then would she leave.

She padded down corridors, through rooms, feeling her way with her hands because she had no light and only Elves could see in total darkness. The layout of the Aldernacht house was confusing, but if its maze of secret passages was still beyond her, she had at least mastered the visible and ordinary portions of it, knew the turnings that she would have to take. She would tell Eudes of the death, and then she would be gone.

As she approached the last flight of stairs, though, a noise made her stop and pause with her foot hovering above the first tread, her ears straining for a repetition of something that had sounded so out of place in a house tenanted by the dead and the would-be dead that it was almost blasphemous.

There it was again: a soft moan, half stifled, accompanied by deep laughter.

And the moan had been Omelda's.

But it had not yet come from the servants' quarters, and in only a minute or two (yes, there it was again, and again), Natil had determined that it did not emanate from any of the rooms customarily inhabited by the Aldernachts, but rather from somewhere *between,* from the secret corridors and chambers that interpenetrated the mundane living space of the mansion as a shaman's spirit world co-existed with mundane matter.

Another moan. Another whiff of laughter. Natil shuddered. It was Omelda. She knew that it was Omelda. And she knew also that the deep, mannish mirth came from the throats of Edvard and Norman.

She heard again the words of the betrayed and forsaken woman. *I'll be all right. Don't worry about me.*

I'll be all right. Natil put her free hand to her face. *"Ai, Elthia."*

Again, a moan, soft, but carrying with it an edge as of velvet-wrapped glass.

Steeling herself against the wrench that each cry put into her, Natil began examining the walls of the room in which she had stopped. Paneling, molding, tapestries. Her hands explored the walls section by section, her knuckles tapped cautiously, her ears listened.

Nothing. She moved on to the adjacent corridor, the next room. Foot by foot she probed the vertical surfaces, searching for a hollowness, a yielding, a shift in the sound of the moans and laughter, anything that might indicate that something lay beyond the visible surface of stone and plaster. With nothing but the most basic of human senses available to her, she continued. Slowly, methodically. Feel. Listen. Tap.

And then a supposedly solid panel felt less substantial than its fellows, and with an instinct born of desperation—or perhaps from an increasingly innate understanding of the habits of human thinking—she reached behind a hanging and found a catch. For a moment, her fingers felt its shape, learned its use. And then she pressed it.

A soft click. Her hand told her that the suspect panel had swung back a finger's breadth.

Silently, still in darkness, Natil pushed the panel open, entered the passage, heard the volume of the moans and laughter abruptly increase. Hesitating only briefly, she closed the door behind her and heard it click into place. She had no idea how to get out, but she did not particularly care. She would either find Omelda, and from there would take her escape wherever she could find it, or she would die within the walls of a house that, in her mind, had already become a tomb.

The passage branched, branched again. Natil listened at every turning and bifurcation, chose her direction accordingly. The moans grew louder. So did the laughter.

Her universe had become an impenetrable darkness bounded by walls, floor, ceiling: a stagnant night filled with the smells of men and tobacco, of wine and brandy and unwashed bodies. And though Natil tried, as she moved through it, to remain detached, she felt nonetheless connected, involved, bound. Here was her heritage of mortal ways and mortal smells, of bodies that decayed even as they lived, of petty fornications and even pettier lusts. She could not see in the dark, she could not find the stars, she no longer had any real conception of the Lady. She slept and dreamed like any human. Did she now stink like one, too?

She held up her hands before her eyes. Not a shred of luminescence delineated them. Darkness. Just darkness. And smells. And the moans of the apostate nun to whom Natil had pledged protection and help.

Protection and help! Such audacity this harper possessed!

Grimly, Natil wound her way through the guts of the Aldernacht house, treading carefully, feeling for turnings, doors, obstacles. The moans grew louder, and still louder, and yet they remained muffled, sobbing: cries of hopelessness and—Natil feared—habitual abuse. Ahead, somewhere, was a place where pain had become custom.

I'll be all right. Don't worry about me.

Shaking, the harper approached a solidity ahead that she sensed was a door. From just behind it came the moans . . . and a voice:

"Farther in, Norman. I want to feel it from here. No . . . go on. It feels good." Then, sharply, impatiently: "Dammit, go on, she's not complaining, is she? That's it. Yes, by God, yesyesyes . . ."

Feeling her face go cold, Natil set down her harp, felt the door, groped for a latch, found a knob . . .

"Oh, God, yes! Keep at it now. I can—"

A sudden click from the door stopped Edvard in mid-sentence, and, an instant later, Natil's dark-accustomed eyes were dazzled by the meager light of the two candles that illuminated the room beyond. She saw the glow of quiet flame on Omelda's smooth, white skin, the glistening of her dark hair. But she also saw her bent head, her bound and contorted arms and legs, the long prod protruding from her bloody anus, and the burns and lacerations and bites that studded her body like the rampant stigmata of plague.

Edvard, conjoined with her as she swung suspended in the center of the room, was staring at the opening door. But he could, Natil knew, see nothing. Her eyes were dazzled by light. His were confounded by darkness.

Norman, though, still half dressed and unencumbered, was heading for the door. "What on earth? I thought I gave orders that—"

Natil found that she did not need the stars. She did not need the Lady. She did not need elven instinct or magic. She had instead two hands and two feet. She had teeth. She had will and strength . . . and an anger that had abruptly burst the narrow and restricting confines of compassion and mercy and overflowed like molten lead. Norman had not even reached the door before he was seized by the throat and dragged into the dark corridor. He did not even have a chance to cry out before his skull struck the far wall and shattered on the thick oak paneling.

He fell in a heap, wheezed once, shuddered, and then lay still. Natil charged into the room, face pale, eyes wide, hands reaching.

Edvard had scrambled away from Omelda, but there was no escape from the room save by the single door. Pale, naked, his arms waving and his manhood limp with fright, he attempted to dodge past the harper, but Natil's long harper fingernails raked across his eyes and sent him staggering back as blood and aqueous humor sheeted down his face.

One scream, two screams shuddered through the air, threatening to awaken the house. But before Edvard could utter a third, Natil clubbed him to death with a stool, striking again and again long after the life and breath had left him, striking until the ribs collapsed and the flesh split like the skin of an overripe fruit, striking until Edvard was no more than a ruined heap of gristle and bone. And only then did she drop her weapon and stand, breathing harshly and loudly—silence was for Elves, silence was for the dead and the faded—listening for movement, for alarms, for shouts.

Nothing. The room was isolated, far from any ears that might be aroused by stray or suspicious sounds.

In the center of the room, Omelda still hung, prod inserted, blood seeping from bites and scrapes and anus and vulva. Tenderly, Natil freed the young woman, her hands shaking, her heart laboring with horror and with the utter frustration of a healer who had no more healing to give, of a wielder of magic who had found her powers all turned to dust. She was not an Elf. She wished that she was.

Omelda was only half conscious, and dull moans and other sounds that Natil could not place dribbled out of her mouth. Her eyes rolled back and only whiteness showed between her lids. She gave no sign that she recognized the woman who had come to her.

Edvard's body was a puddling blot of darkness in the corner as Natil sluiced Omelda's wounds with water from a pitcher that stood on a nearby table. She bathed her forehead, made her drink a mouthful or two. Slowly, the young woman's eyes rolled into sight, her lids parted, and her fingers, blue from the shackles that had held her, twitched and took on life.

"Na . . ." She struggled to get the name out. "Na . . . til . . ."

The harper bent her head. Protection. Help. It was all over. "You are safe now, beloved."

Safe? How dare she!

"Ed . . . vard—"

"They are dead."

Omelda nodded vaguely. Then: "I want . . . to go home."

Natil almost wept aloud. She, too, wanted to go home.

"I want . . . to go back . . . to Shrinerock."

Eyes closed, tears breaking free at last, Natil nodded slowly. "But what about the chant?"

"I don't . . . care. I'll go . . . mad out here."

"Omelda . . ."

"I want . . . to go home."

Natil put her hands to her face. "I . . . understand . . ."

"Home."

Dropping her hands, Natil looked at the room, shuddered at the thought of how many times Omelda must have been brought here. Madness lurked everywhere, but certainly its kingdom was the Aldernacht house, for here it roamed with impunity, and its worshipers were legion.

"Natil . . ."

"We will leave tonight," said the harper. "We will leave now. I will carry you if I must."

But—dogged, ox-like, with the dull determination that had seen her through two years of wandering and untold abuse—the apostate nun clenched her teeth . . . and staggered to her feet. "They've hurt me worse than this," she said softly, a breath more than a voice. "I'll walk."

And she did. Guiding Natil, still losing blood in thin streams that streaked her white legs and marked the floor with scarlet footprints, Omelda walked out of the room, down the hall. Her steps were definite, purposed, as though she had been carried or driven or dragged this way often enough that the turnings and the doors and the hidden panels had rooted themselves in her memory just as the intrusive and iterative plainchant had fleshed itself within her soul.

Natil followed her, no longer lithe and elven and silent, but staggering with the weight of horror that had fallen upon her. But what she had seen was inevitable: humans did not reserve their lusts and their hatreds only for the immortal and the compassionate, but spread them thickly everywhere. And not the Dance of interaction and life governed their deeds, but only the crazed causality of dull, stupid chance.

Grievous actions, grievous thoughts. But she followed Omelda to her room and, as though in a dream, stripped off her livery and donned her old clothes as the apostate nun compounded the old bloodstains of her rags and tatters with new spatters and drips. Then, down another corridor and down stairs, and at last there was a door that opened near the stables and sent the mingled odors of horse piss and rotten straw into the passage.

In the faint light of moon and stars, Omelda bent to

examine herself, grimaced at her wounds. But then, after binding her skirt up between her legs so that she would not drip blood and provide an uninterrupted trail for any pursuers, she shrugged and stepped outside.

And perhaps it was that final, utilitarian action so steeped in resignation that finally goaded Natil's thoughts and heart into rebellion, for the harper suddenly found herself gripping the door frame as though to rip it out of the wall and bring the whole house down along with all the hideous changes and transformations that circumstance had forced upon her. But her eyes were fastened upon the stars that shone above the rooftops of Ypris: bright, illimitable, emblematic of an inner firmament that had for countless millennia imbued her life with a vision of sacramental wholeness.

She remembered. She forced herself to remember. She was not human. She would not be human. Even if the core of her being had been so reshaped by a changing world that she had become, yes, human, mortal, redolent of the stinks of sentient monkeys, she would reject it. If will or determination counted for anything in this mire of venality, then will and determination would change her again, reshape her spirit, give her back her heritage.

Her dreams were not delusion and fraud. Wheat and Hadden would drive across the deserts and mountains of another land, would find the pain of human suffering leavened and transformed by a vision of the stars and—maybe—the touch of *Elthia Calasiuove*. Four and a half billion years of healing and helping, of loyalty and love, would not be proven to be the fever dream of a terrified soul. She would believe. She would be certain. She would make it true.

And much later, after passing streets and climbing walls, Natil stood watch while Omelda whimpered herself to sleep in a stand of trees far outside the city. But while she watched, her blood-spattered harp was in her hands, and her fingers were seeking among the bronze wires a strain of elven melody that might help to bring it all back, to make for herself a place she could call home, whether in this world, in a far distant future, or, if necessary, only in her mind.

"I am an Elf," she murmured. Will. Determination. "I am an Elf . . . forever."

CHAPTER 20

What gets us through?

The question remained, stark and uncompromising, as Hadden and Wheat drove toward Denver. They swung north at Albuquerque, passed through Las Vegas and Raton, climbed through the Sangre de Christo mountains, and descended into Trinidad to eat at the McDonald's just off the highway.

Here, surrounded by brick buildings a century old, by the rusting undersides of railroad trestles, by the dark faces of descendants and relatives of the migrant farm workers who picked and harvested their way across the Southwest—following the crops, following the seasons—the question came again, shouldering its way through the plastic and the gloss and the hamburgers. *What gets us through?*

But the wind from the east took the pollution from the air and left the mountains clear and focused. Even between the railroad trestles and the highway overpasses, the sky was blue; and just out beyond the parking lot, where the asphalt did not quite reach, was dirt, simple dirt, patched with spotted spurge and crabgrass and wild lettuce and all the weeds that owed their allegiance not to any human desire or will but only to the sun and the rain.

Hadden was looking out the window. Dirt. Weeds. Growing things. Yes, as was the case everywhere, there was poverty here, and the hands of human beings had sullied much; but the land was still beneath it all, and the mountains were lovely, and the sky . . .

"It's a nice day," he said softly, staring, his Big Mac forgotten for the moment.

Wheat—blue-eyed, slender, with the wide gaze of a

child who had seen, perhaps, a little too much—was nodding. "It is."

"Is that it, do you think?"

"What?"

"Is that what gets us through? Nice days?" He laughed quietly, self-consciously.

She smiled, dropped her eyes. "Hell of a thought, isn't it?"

Her lapse into her former manner of speech made them both laugh out loud, and there was something silvery in their voices that put a pause to twenty or so restaurant conversations, made eyes flick toward the man and the woman over in the corner booth.

Wheat glanced about, blushed. "Oops."

Hadden was still looking out at the mountains and the sky. A smile, faint but genuine. "We're here. They'll just have to adjust, I'm afraid."

"But what about us? We'll have to adjust, too. But to what? And what are we?"

"We'll figure it out."

But on the way out, they both saw the resignation in the eyes of the young women behind the counter, and there was a dull, plodding manner to the other customers. Faint expectations, frustrated hope. This was it. This was all that could be expected from life: work (maybe), and an occasional meal in the plastic and gloss of a fast-food restaurant. And Hadden and Wheat knew again that they themselves had been blessed. Oh, there would be work, to be sure, tedious and mind-numbing upon occasion; and there would, doubtless, be any number of impersonal meals in coffee shops. But they had seen the mountains and the sky, fields of stars and fields of wheat. And they would, they knew with certainty, continue to see more. Still . . .

. . . still there was pain in the world. And they saw it. They felt it. Deeply. Terribly.

What gets us through?

There was something. There *had* to be something. And when Hadden pulled out onto I-25 fifteen minutes later, he had already made up his mind that his destination would not be Denver. He would, instead, pass through that city, guiding the van toward that strange little turnoff from Highway 6, the one that, weeks ago, had caught his imagination and his spirit, lifted them, and begun the process of transformation that had led him first through the mountains, and then onward onto fields of mingled sorrow and praise.

He nodded to himself. Wheat looked at him inquiringly. "Denver?"

"I want to show you something first," said Hadden. "I want to show you where it started. For me. Maybe it'll finish there for both of us. Or maybe it'll start to finish. I don't know for sure. But I want to show you. And I want to show myself."

Eudes found Marjorie's body the next morning, her eyes decently closed, the covers tucked up beneath her chin, and—oddly enough—a look of quiet peace on her face. Pausing only long enough to cross himself, the trusty old wardrobe ran to fetch his master; and Jacob, who had fallen asleep over a plate of cold dinner and been left undisturbed throughout the night, came to kneel beside the corpse of his wife . . . and his dreams.

She was gone now. The little farce was finished. His fantasies had been shown to be fantasies, his avarice and spleen permanent constituents of his personality from which there was, and would be, no deliverance. The grave, perhaps, would save him, but that was all.

Jacob's heart was cold as he rose from the bed and told Eudes to inform Bishop Etienne of the death. "I want a big funeral," he rasped at the steward. "Big. Spare no expense. Make up some expenses if you can. Throw as much money away as possible."

Eudes blinked, arched a molding, bent his stiff and wooden frame, and departed. Jacob stood for another moment at the deathbed. Then:

"I hate you," he said. "I hate you all."

He turned and walked out of the room, only to meet Francis in the hallway.

"Father! I heard . . . I mean—"

"She's dead."

For a moment, Francis looked relieved, and then, properly and pompously, he put on grief as another man might have donned a cloak. "I'm . . . sorry . . ."

Quiet and dry as Jacob's voice was, it contained an ocean's depth of contempt. "The hell you are. You didn't want her any more than she wanted you. Neither did Josef. I saw the look on his face. Damn near threw up.'' He glared at his eldest son for a moment more. "Where is he, anyway?''

"Josef?''

"Who else? He should know that he's safe with his books now.''

"He's . . .'' Francis stared, flustered. "I mean, didn't you know?''

"Know? Know about what?''

"Josef is gone. He left the other night. He took some food, a sword, and a horse.''

Jacob stared, the chill in his heart deepening, bringing on, slowly, a sense of frost, then of ice. Frozen. Frozen and dead. "Did he say anything?''

"Nothing,'' said Francis. "Not even a note. No one heard him leave.''

Jacob passed a hand over his face, felt the sere dryness of aged skin, the graying bristles of an unshaven beard that stood stiffly, like the stubble of wheat in a reaped field. Josef. Gone. Small loss, really, but—

Small loss? But that was what Marjorie would have said. A nitwit, she had called him, even from his first breath, his first tentative suck at her teat. And had it been Marjorie, then, who had first named him so, who had first branded him with the unkind and hasty appellation that had clung to him, turned from mother's curse to destiny? Was that it? Had the lad never even had a *chance*?

Jacob pressed his fists to his temples. His heart was cold, but his brain seemed ready to take fire and burn down the house.

"Well, you know,'' said Francis, squaring his shoulders and clearing his throat, "I suspected he'd come to this. Gone down to join Karl, I guess. He won't last a season—''

His words were cut short by Jacob's fist. Francis lurched, gagged with the impact, fell against the wall. Jacob placed his foot against his son's forehead and shoved him all the way to the floor. "That's my son you're talking about, you insolent young pup!''

Francis was holding a cut jaw. Blood was seeping through his fingers. "I'll remind you . . .'' He gagged, coughed. ". . . that he's my brother.''

Jacob resisted the impulse to kick him. "Oh, really! For years, he's a nitwit. He's an idiot. He's a fool. He's not worth taking into any of the family confidences. You always used to beat the snot out of him when you were growing up together because you said he offended you. By living, no doubt! But a little blood on your chin, and he's suddenly your dearest brother!" He crowed with sarcasm. "Oh, such virtue! Such fraternal love!"

Francis's blood streaked a white, angry face. He crouched against the wall like something about to spring.

For another moment of contempt, Jacob stared down at him. And then he turned away. "Josef was worth ten of those dogs that you and Claire whelped."

Francis staggered to his feet as his father clumped down the corridor. "I . . ."

Jacob spun. "You *what*?"

"You're . . . insulting my wife and my sons." Francis's voice was venomous, as dark as the blood that covered his chin. "I demand an apology."

Jacob almost laughed. "You won't get one. Go feed your pigs. I'm surprised they're all not here to fight over the carcass."

Francis's eyes burned with impotent rage, but Jacob went off down the hall without another look at him. Marjorie was gone. Now Josef was gone, too; and Francis was probably right: the lad would not last a season. He might not even last a mile. Jacob's heart turned even colder, turned towards death, as he considered all the opportunities he had been given—opportunities missed or rejected—to make something of Josef. But, no: he had treated his sons just as he had treated Marjorie—

He stopped, clenching his jaw. There was the fantasy again. Just as he had treated Marjorie? But how had Marjorie treated him? She had abandoned him. She had ridiculed her sons. She had rejected everything because everything was not hers.

And so: Josef. And so: Francis. And so, more than likely: Karl. And so, the next generation down: Edvard and Norman. All fine specimens of the old Aldernacht sperm!

"Eudes!"

In a moment, the old servant creaked into sight. "Yes, Mister Jacob?"

"Those orders I gave about Marjorie. Cancel them."

"Cancel . . . ?"

"Bury her like a pauper. No ceremony. Find a plot somewhere, sew her into a shroud—canvas if you can find it—and have a priest put her in. That's all."

Eudes, blank as a varnished board, nodded faintly. "Yes, Mister Jacob."

He started to go off, but Jacob called him back. "One more thing. When I die, you bury me the same way."

"But—"

"Those are my orders. I'll have Charles draw up the papers this afternoon. Just shovel me under and leave it at that. Like a pauper. Because that's what I am. That's all I am. Understand?"

Eudes stared, awash in bewilderment.

Jacob took a step toward him. *"Understand?"*

"Y-yes . . ." Eudes looked ready to bolt. "Yes, Mister Jacob."

"Off with you, then."

The wardrobe left quickly. Jacob clenched his hands. A pauper. Yes, that was exactly what he was. He had once possessed dreams and fantasies, but no more. He had money, but money could not keep the cold from his heart. He had sons . . . once. He had a wife . . . once.

Now, nothing. All he had left was . . .

"Natil!" he called suddenly. "Natil! Come here! I need you!" He wanted music. He wanted song. He wanted the honesty he had always read in her face and eyes.

But Natil was gone, and, an hour later, after a search of the house and grounds and city had been unable to produce the harper, Jacob stood in her small room. The Aldernacht livery she had worn lay strewn on the floor, and her fantastic garb of cloth and beads and feathers was gone. A few scraps of rags, some bloody footprints, evidence of belongings gathered fearfully and in haste, but that was all.

And though there were signs aplenty of something more than a simple unauthorized departure, Jacob flared with the rage of the abandoned. He could understand that Marjorie had left him. He could reason out a meaning behind Josef's action. But this blatant and traitorous flight on the part of the harper was beyond any kind of for-

giveness or mercy, and his anger—already overflowing—
turned to violence.

"Manarel," he said to his road steward. "Call up the
guards. I want a troop of men saddled and armed by mid-
morning. I want Natil found."

Manarel, who had seen his employer's anger many
times before, asked no questions. He simply bowed.
"The men and I will leave immediately, master."

Jacob shook his head. "I'll be going with you."

Manarel stared.

"I want to kill the bitch myself," said Jacob, and he
was fully cognizant of the double meaning inherent in
his words.

"I want to hear everything. I want to hear the truth."

Harold was neither a hero nor a defiant representative
of free thought. He was a shawm player. And though he
was used to the many kinds of hardship intrinsic to a
musician's life—fleas, hunger, knife fights, an occasional
fist to the face—he was unprepared for the methodical
and surgically precise torments inflicted at Siegfried's
command. Needles in nerves, the touch of red hot irons,
a tongue dragged forward and seared white: all these were
well beyond both his cognizance and his endurance, and
they extracted from him, thickly interspersed with
screams and blubberings, a tale of pernicious and widespread heresy the monstrousness of which astonished
even Siegfried.

"And you confessed to this so-called priest how many
times."

"I . . . I . . . I . . . hundreds . . . hundreds . . ."

"Come now, Harold. Do not play with us."

His eyelids were bruised from clenching. They seemed
black holes in a skull. "Fifty. I confessed fifty t-times."

"Are you sure?"

Stiff with crusted burns, his tongue could hardly form
the words: "Th-th-th-thirty-five."

"All right then. And what did he tell you afterwards?
Who did you meet? You returned to your master, Jacob
Aldernacht, did you not?"

"I . . . I swear . . ."

"Do not speak to me of swearing. You and your kind
absolve one another regularly for swearing in an effort to

preserve your sect. This I know. Simply tell the truth.
Tell us about Jacob Aldernacht.''

But despite his torments, when it came to Jacob Aldernacht, Harold turned suddenly reticent. Siegfried had
expected this, though, for silence invariably meant guilt.
Yes, Jacob Aldernacht was a heretic, and his plans to
bring gold and prosperity to Furze were but a furtherance
of his efforts to establish a kingdom of Satan in the middle of Christian Europe.

''Tell me everything. Tell me the truth.''

Harold held out for two weeks. Admittedly, he was not
formally tortured during that time. But fourteen days and
fourteen nights of incarceration in waist deep sewage at
the bottommost level of the House of God, his only support the chains and shackles that held his nailless hands
above his head, his only food bits of black bread mixed
with the coarsest of beans, his only drink an occasional
mouthful of water, his universe bounded by darkness and
the screams of his fellow prisoners, his broken legs rotting away in the fetid water, his face bitten and gnawed
by rats . . .

Harold told them everything.

He told them the truth.

''If we arrest Paul Drego,'' Siegfried told Fra Giovanni over supper that night, ''Jacob will be warned of
the interest that Holy Church has taken in him.''

Fra Giovanni had never recovered from his puzzlement
over Siegfried's dismissal of the book of evidence about
Paul, and his superior's words now did not aid his recu-
peration in the slightest. ''But Paul Drego is guilty. Jacob
Aldernacht is . . . is in Ypris. He's out of our reach.''

Siegfried felt the rankness of a second lie building up
on his tongue, tainting the savor of his spiced quail. But
was it a lie? What was a lie when compared with the
deception and fraud that, every day, was perpetrated in
the name of Satan, that, every day, snared thousands of
otherwise innocent souls in the coils of heresy and
dragged them down into the eternity of hell?

Undeterred by logic or equivocation, the rankness persisted. Siegfried had not slept well since he had thrown
away the book of evidence. And, despite his increasingly
obsessive devotions to the Blessed Sacrament—*Adoro te*

devote—he wondered whether his longed-for vision of divinity was not now farther away than ever.

What do you want, dear Lord? What do you want from me? Devotion? You have it. My life? You have it. My duty? You have it. O my Lord and my God, I will give You everything that is mine to give.

But despite his internal pleas and offers, the heavens refused to open.

I will give You everything.

And he was beginning to fear that they would refuse forever.

I will give You the fortune of Jacob Aldernacht.

Giovanni was staring, waiting. Siegfried roused himself from the bargaining table, spoke slowly. "Paul is guilty. That is true. And Jacob is in Ypris . . . out of our reach. But he will not remain so forever: this my heart tells me. One day he will return to Furze, and then . . ."

Will that be enough then, O my God?

". . . and then he will find out what fate awaits heretics and enemies of the Church. Others, perhaps, have become lax in their prosecution of evil, but we have not."

Enough for me to see?

"No, we have not."

Please let it be enough.

Giovanni looked doubtful.

"Let us, though, at least make a start," said Siegfried. "Let us at least prepare." He looked meaningfully at Giovanni.

Giovanni understood . . . and was more bewildered than ever. "But that would be a grave irregularity before any formal examination of the accused."

"There might not be time for an examination," said Siegfried. "We already have a witness, though. Harold. And he is sufficient."

"But . . ."

"Now, Fra Giovanni."

And so, after the servant had soundlessly cleared away the remnants of dinner, Giovanni had parchment and pen brought in. He laid them out, dipped the quill.

In nomine Domini amen, he wrote. *Hec est quedam condemnatio corporalis et sententia condemnationis corporaalis lata, data et in hiis scriptis sententialiter pronumptiata et promulgata . . .*

Aside from names and dates, the form of such documents was unchanging. Even the list of crimes and the solemn declaration that torture had most certainly *not* been employed were customary, traditional, as fixed as the stars. It took Giovanni, therefore, but a few minutes to condemn Jacob Aldernacht. But when the friar started to write the date at the bottom of the page, Siegfried laid a hand on his arm.

"We will fill in the date later," he said. "God will provide it for us."

Still wondering, still worried, Giovanni rose, bowed, and departed. Siegfried, though, remained at the table. He read through the order twice to make sure that all was as it should be, and then be carefully rolled it up and slipped it into his sleeve. God would provide the date.

"Yes," he murmured softly. "God will provide for us. And then we will provide for God."

Albrecht sat with his feet dangling over the edge of the triforium gallery. The stars were clear in the night sky even though the moon was almost full, and darkness had engulfed the town, hiding it and all its affairs—venal and glorious—beneath a soft and comforting shroud of shadow.

Such, perhaps, were reasons enough for the bishop to feel particularly close to heaven tonight, but though the shroud could hide the affairs of Hypprux, it could not banish them, and therefore Albrecht was still fretting about Siegfried. In fact, since Paul Drego had made confession to him and received absolution for the few petty sins he had committed, he was fretting more than ever.

Paul was a good man. Paul was honest. In the privacy and sanctity of the confessional, Paul had professed his belief in and love for Christianity, and Albrecht had believed him. And Albrecht also believed the other matters of which Paul had spoken: of watchers and listeners, of a premonition that the Inquisition had already judged him guilty of heresy and was only staying its iron hand until it was satisfied that its case was beyond any challenge, sacred or secular.

So here was Albrecht, contemplating and clinging to the freedom of heavenly things because he was, on earth, inextricably caught. Caught between his Church and his conscience. Caught between the Inquisition and the wool cooperative. Caught between his suspicions and his trusts.

He bent his head. "Heavenly Father," he murmured. "I don't know what to do. Even if Siegfried would see me, what Paul told me falls under the seal of confession. And I fear that going to Siegfried would do nothing more than jeopardize Paul and the other cooperative members in any case."

He stared down between his fingers at the distant, moonlit floor. Siegfried was so . . . ambitious. Mattias thought so. And Albrecht, in his talk with Jacob Aldernacht, had all but admitted that he thought so, too. But what was one petty bishop against someone like Siegfried?

Vaguely, he recalled his clerk's words. The Wheel of Fortune. The Falling Tower. Just like that. Boom!

Pagan pictures. Heathen images. Albrecht shook his head. "I don't want anybody to go *boom,* Lord. I just want the people who deserve to be safe . . . to be safe."

He shook his head helplessly. Over the years, the Church had become a very strange thing, a thing with branches where roots should have been and roots dry and waving in the air: a topsy-turvy affair in which ambitious men ruled over holy men . . . and wanted them to be ambitious, too.

Albrecht, alone in the gallery of his cathedral, blushed at his thoughts. He had all but claimed that he was a holy man. "No, God," he said. "I didn't mean that. I meant . . . well, You know what I meant."

Yes, God knew. And Albrecht took some comfort in that. God knew. God would provide. Albrecht reminded himself to have faith, and when he rose, and when his wobbly knee gave way suddenly, it was, doubtless, faith that kept him from toppling straight off the edge of the gallery. The strength of his leg certainly had nothing to do with it.

Boom, he thought, crouched and sweating, his fingers still clawing for a hold on the slick marble. *It could all have been over. Boom. Such is the end that comes to ambitious men. Men who run Inquisitions. Men who want to build cathedrals. I'm no better than Siegfried. I'm no better than any of them. Dear God, forgive me.*

Shaking his head, trembling, he descended the stairs and went to bed.

CHAPTER 21

The road southwest from Ypris led across pastureland and fields of bracken that swept like a green wave from the Bergren River out towards the west. It threaded its way down towards Belroi among sheep and the men who tended sheep, and then continued on to Furze. But Natil did not take the road, for two women on foot could not hope to outpace pursuers on horseback. And she knew that there were pursuers.

She saw it in her dreams: Jacob's anger, the riding of horsemen from the Aldernacht courtyard, the glitter of weapons. But come morning, with the mists rising from the earth and the pre-dawn sky the color of a bowl of milk, she found rather comforting the fact that she saw it at all, for if her vision of the events in the Aldernacht household was true, then perhaps the same could be said of her dreams of the future awakening of the elven blood. There was hope in that, just as there was hope, albeit mysterious and incomprehensible, in her continuing dream of a forked tree from whose cleft came a golden light.

Maybe. It could be. There was, at least, hope. But for now she knew that she and Omelda were pursued, and so she led the young woman south toward the dark shadows that lay beneath the trees of Malvern Forest. It was only a few leagues, and by the afternoon of the first day, they had entered the wood.

Like everything else, Malvern had changed. The Elves were no more, and therefore something vital seemed to have passed out of the life of the forest. The hidden paths were gone, just like the Immortals who had once used them. The holy places—holy from use, holy from memory—were gone; and Natil feared that what had once been a living, thinking being like herself had dwindled, and was now just a forest.

She touched an oak in passing, drew her hand across the smooth gray bark of an ancient beech. Farther south, the trees were all new, hardly a century old: the legacy of the fire set by the free companies. But here in the northern marches were still the patriarchs and matriarchs of the forest, tall trees and thick trunks that, she was sure, surely preserved some remembrance of the old Malvern, the Elvenhome.

She called for a rest. Omelda flopped down on a bed of soft grass, covered her face with her hands, and moaned softly, but Natil took a moment to set her harp aside, put her arms about a trunk, and lay her forehead softly against the bark. *Are you there, my friend? Is anybody there? Is there hope? Does the world really work as the trees grow: summer into winter . . . and then back into summer once more?*

But where once she would have heard a faraway voice—grumpy but good-natured, perhaps, or laughing like a child—now she felt only a stirring. *Growth, it seemed to say, growth and being. Do not strive. The tree that strives fails and breaks. Only be.*

Her former life of healing and helping, of stellar potencies and comfort poured out upon the earth seemed so far away now. But it could come back. She told herself that it would come back, clenched the tree with the will and determination that it *must* come back.

Be an Elf.

A soft moan from Omelda made her turn. The young woman's hands were still pressed to her face, but now she was doubled over. It would take her body a long time simply to undo the physical damage accumulated over weeks of abuse and torture; but there was more to her pain than wounds and bites and bleeding, and when Natil knelt and examined her, the facts were obvious. Infection had set in. Faced with prods, filth, and neglect, Omelda's womb was beginning to suppurate. She was fevered, weak, disoriented.

"I can't go on," Omelda mumbled. Her face was flushed and hot, her hands cold; and when Natil, calling her name and shaking her repeatedly, managed to get her eyes open, she saw that they were glassy.

"You must go on," said the harper. She tried to keep her voice gentle, but it shook. "You must."

"Why?"

Natil passed a hand over her face. "Because . . ." It seemed hopeless. But her own words came back to her, her words and the words of the people she had, by act of will, reclaimed: *Nothing is impossible. There are merely differing levels of probability.* "Because," she stumbled, "if you do not, the Aldernachts will find us and take us back."

She did not state the obvious. She did not have to. What would Jacob do to the murderer of the Aldernacht heirs? But though her healer's hands still felt the unclean touch of death, she could find in her heart no objection to the killings. Indeed, had any arisen, she had only to look at Omelda's flushed face, examine, perhaps, the caked blood and pus on her thighs in order to lay them.

"Who cares?" murmured Omelda, sagging.

Gritting her teeth, wincing with the action, Natil shook her again. "*You* care, woman," said the harper. "I know you care."

The nun's eyelids fluttered. Fever.

Natil searched her memory, trying to recall the forest as it had been when she and her people had dwelt beneath its branches and leaves, sung in its meadows. "There is . . . there is a stream nearby," she said. "It comes down from the glaciers in the Aleser Mountains. It is cold. You will bathe in it."

Omelda moaned softly.

"It will bring your fever down," said the harper. "For a time. There will be other streams. And I know of herbs that will help. With the grace of the Lady, we will return you to your convent, and you can rest and heal there."

"No one can heal me," said Omelda, her tongue clumsy with sickness. "No one. They'll toss me on the dung heap at the abbey. They don't care. And I'll go mad anyway . . ."

"You do not know that."

Omelda pried her eyes open, and the glassiness of her stare fled for a moment before a flash of anger. "How the hell do *you* know any different, Natil? You haven't known anything since I found you up in Maris. What the hell makes you so sure they'll take me back?"

The harper sat back, wilted. "There is healing in the world." Her words tasted thick and sour, tasted like a lie. "I know."

Omelda glared at her. Natil saw it in her eyes: the child who had been abandoned, the intrusive plainchant that had threatened her with madness, the world that had exploited her and abused her, the promises that had been made to her only to be broken, the fever that would probably kill her. "Healing," she said. "Sure. Can *you* heal me?"

The words were a slap. Natil bent her head, pressed her fists to her temples. Her answer was truthful, but truth was perhaps the only particle of elvenhood she had left. "I cannot."

Omelda—dogged, deliberate, purposeful—dragged herself to her feet and went down to the river to bathe.

Manarel held the title of steward, but he was not precisely a steward. By training and disposition, he was a forester and a soldier, a quaintly honest man who had taken employment where he could find it. Jacob Aldernacht found him useful. At times like this he found him indispensable.

From Ypris, roads—wide and narrow, frequented and abandoned—led off toward many cities and towns and villages: Natil and Omelda could have gone in almost any direction. But Manarel knew what the passage of feet did to roads and fields, and perhaps he had also that most invaluable and extremely subtle sense of the world that, had it been dignified with terms like *prescience* or *clairvoyance*, would have landed him in the prisons of the Inquisition; and therefore, after he had studied the roads and the weather, and after he had looked over the pasturelands and ditches that surrounded Ypris, he pointed south. "That direction, Mister Jacob."

And Jacob, still raging, still finding in the truant harper an object upon which to vent his loss and his frustration, nodded. "Let's go, then," he said, his voice sounding old and raspy even to his own ears. "Let's find her."

Manarel looked uncomfortable. "What about the other, master?"

"The other?"

"Omelda. The serving girl."

"Oh . . . her . . ." Jacob shrugged. "She's not important. We'll bring her back. Whatever."

Manarel looked even more uncomfortable, and after he had swung up on his horse at the head of the troop of Aldernacht soldiers, he examined the horizon with his brown eyes, and bit at his lip in the manner of a man awakening to discover an adder on his chest. "Master . . . could I please say something—"

"Shut up," said Jacob. "Find her."

Manarel was respectful, and he knew who paid his wages. "Yes, master."

But as they rode, the day warming and the June sun beating down on metal hoods and felt hats alike, Jacob caught himself frowning. Despite his anger, despite years of unleashing whatever emotion happened to possess him—joy or sorrow, irritation or benevolence—on whoever happened to be about him, he found that a sense of injustice had wormed its way into his heart.

Natil's work? Maybe. Regardless, he was uneasy about his words to his steward.

He cleared his throat. "Manarel."

"Master?"

"What . . . what were you going to say?"

It was as near a thing to an apology as had ever come from the lips of Jacob Aldernacht, and the steward stared for a moment before he replied. "I was . . . going to remind my master . . . that Natil is a very brave woman. She even tried to gain Harold's release from the Inquisition."

She had indeed. At, Jacob recalled, great risk to herself. And now he could not but recall also the esteem in which he had once held her. A brave woman. And a thoughtful one. And an honest one. If she had left his service—without warning, without permission—she doubtless had possessed a good reason.

But his loss and disillusionment still gnawed at him, and his voice was sharp. "Is that all?"

Manarel hesitated. Then: "Yes, master."

Jacob fixed him with a look. "That's a lie, Manarel."

Manarel kept his eyes on the road. "Yes, master. It is."

Jacob chewed on his steward's words for some time, and was about to ask the obvious question when Manarel suddenly froze, reined in, and held up his hand to signal a stop. His face was set, his eyes narrow. Jacob knew his man well enough not to question the peremptory manner in which Manarel had halted the column.

"What?" the old man whispered.

"Something . . . something happened here," said Manarel, his deep voice rumbling softly. He pointed to a stain on the dirt that Jacob had not noticed. "That's blood."

"Natil's?" Jacob found that his voice was expectant, tense. Fear or gratification? He could not tell.

Manarel dismounted, examined the stain, raked his fingers through a pile of horse droppings that lay nearby. Jacob recalled with a strange sense of unease that Natil and Omelda had been traveling on foot.

"It couldn't be Natil," said the steward. "The signs aren't fresh enough. And look, over here: there are prints of boots. Men's boots. And nothing of the soft shoes that the harper wears."

"Well then . . ." But Jacob's voice trailed off, fading into an indistinct sense of worry. Men's boots. And blood.

But Manarel was looking elsewhere, examining other prints, other traces and scrapes, following the trail. There was more blood—old blood—and then a littler farther on, in the ditch at the side of the road, half covered with reeds and weeds, he found something else. He found the body of a man.

Josef's body.

Jacob, who had stayed at the steward's side, turned away, the world blurring to his eyes. His men, their mail and weapons, their horses . . . all turned into soft, indistinct smears.

"His sword is still sheathed," Manarel said softly.

"Of course," Jacob murmured distantly. "He didn't know how to use it."

"His purse is gone. So are his rings. He died of a cut to the throat."

Jacob did not look. "Yes . . . yes . . . he would have tried to talk his way out of it." Tears were moistening his dry, withered face. "He didn't last a season, did he? He didn't even last until the next town, did he?"

He heard Manarel straighten. "I'm deeply sorry, master. Mister Josef was a good man."

Jacob shook his head. "He was a nitwit. Just a nitwit. We'll carve it on . . ." His voice, gasping, broke into many pieces, but he continued. ". . . on his tomb. Josef Aldernacht. Would-be scholar. Inferior musician. Wretched poet. Family nitwit."

His words faded into the warm air. Silence. A snort from one of his horses. He sensed that Manarel was waiting for orders.

"Have . . . have two of the men take his body back to the house," said Jacob. "Have them tell Francis to bury him with all the customary flummery. Pauper's graves aren't for nitwits." He sniffed, smeared his tears with his sleeve, felt Manarel's stare. "They're not for nitwits. They're for idiots. And fools."

"As . . . as you wish, master."

Caving in. That was it. Everything inside of him was caving in. A crumbling, a shuddering, and then release . . . and descent. "Go on," he said. "Take care of it. And then we'll go on. We'll find Natil . . . wherever she is."

But his voice sounded faint, distant, as though he were not at all sure of what he would do with Natil when he actually found her.

Marjorie's body, in accordance with Jacob's orders, was sewed up in a canvas sack and tossed into the earth as though it were the corpse of a particularly troublesome dog. There were few mourners. Francis and Claire were present in all their funereal finery, making a very genuine show of their very genuine grief at such a very genuine loss. One or two servants appeared out of curiosity, the rest were there to attend Francis and Claire. Only Eudes demonstrated real tears: wardrobes could obviously become rather attached to the bitch of the kennel.

Edvard and Norman were not at the grave. Edvard and Norman did not appear to be anywhere. On the surface, this was nothing unusual: the young men often raided the chest in Gold Hall for a sack or two of florins and then went off to Hypprux or to Maris to squander the money. As often as not, they did so without notice.

This time, though, Francis sensed that there was something wrong. He was not a particularly imaginative man, but he had come to sense an oppression about the Alder-nacht house that persisted despite his attempts to deny it, that made the absence of Edvard and Norman hint at dark possibilities, frightening consequences. The summer was well along, and the rooms were, as usual, hot, some-times stifling; but certain parts of the house had acquired an abominable sense of closeness, as though walls were reaching to walls and ceilings to floors, as though rooms had shrunk to airless cubicles and corridors to the nar-rowest of shafts. He found himself staying away as much as possible, and when he actually had to go inside, he eschewed certain rooms, certain halls, avoided com-pletely the maze of hidden passages that wound through the house.

No, he spent his days in Gold Hall, fuming silently as Eudes and Charles readied and dispatched the hated ship-ment of wool cooperative gold, or in the gardens, look-ing with dull incomprehension at the fruit trees, or watching the industrious ants, whose winding trails—more numerous this year than he had ever seen before—snaked down the paths and even seemed to converge on the house. He examined the flights of robins and wrens, and noted with mild disbelief that a number of crows had apparently taken up residence in an unused room of the mansion, or had found some particularly plentiful store of summer insects within its walls.

There was another one, even now: his black head pok-ing out of a crevice, a long strip of red meat dangling from his ebony beak. A shrug, a flutter, and he was gone, but another was taking his place, plunging in where his brother had gone out.

And then the servants began complaining about an odor that was hanging about the west wing. It had started, they said, as a subtle presentiment, and had, in only a few days, become a stench. It was giving them headaches, making them gag, but no one had been able to determine its source.

And then a rat, scurrying away as Martha shooed and cursed it out of the kitchen, dropped something that, though slimy and partly decayed, was obviously the re-mains of a human finger.

* * *

The trail left by Natil and Omelda turned cold quickly, and, at camp that night, Manarel was shaking his head. "They must have left the road, Mister Jacob," he said. "Somewhere behind us. I can't understand how they could have done it without leaving some trace, but I think that's what happened."

A few feet away, supper was cooking over an open fire. There was no inn close by, and so even Jacob Aldernacht had to eat stew out of a bowl and sleep under the stars tonight. A soldier's lot. A mercenary's lot. The lot Josef had chosen, the lot that had killed him before he even had a chance to taste it.

Josef had been on Jacob's mind a great deal these last hours, occupying his father far more after his death than he ever had before it. And Jacob was also thinking about Francis and Karl. And Claire. And Edvard and Norman. His family. His nest of vipers. But then there was Natil, and he was no longer sure how he felt about Natil. And now Manarel was telling him that the trail, like everything else in his life, had gone cold, was lost.

"Do you want to backtrack, Manarel?" he said without enthusiasm, without taking his eyes off a fire which persisted in showing him Natil's sweet but serious face, her agile hands, the glint of her harpstrings. "Would that be best?"

Manarel fell silent. Again, Jacob remembered his steward's lie, the lie he had admitted but never corrected. No, Manarel had stopped short of saying everything about Natil and Omelda. Jacob had shushed him, and he had closed his mouth on the subject. Whatever his master wanted. Whatever his master ordered. Yes, Mister Jacob. No, Mister Jacob. As you wish, Mister Jacob.

"I think," said the steward slowly, "that it would be best to push on."

Jacob blinked. "Push on? Are you expecting them to come back to the road?"

"Maybe, Mister Jacob. But . . ." The steward obviously felt that he had drawn close to a forbidden subject. He cleared his throat, shook his head. "I . . . think we should go on."

Jacob interlaced his skinny, old-man fingers. The lie. "About the other day, Manarel . . ."

Manarel did not look up. "Yes, Mister Jacob?"

"What were you going to say the other day? When you said you had nothing to add, and I said you were lying."

Manarel seemed to consider his words as though they were so many bricks. Blunt living, a blunt man. "I think that if we go on, we will find Natil—and maybe Omelda—in Furze."

Jacob blinked for a second time. "Furze? What the hell are they going to do in Furze?"

Manarel looked cautiously about, but no: the other men were out of earshot. A whisper would not carry to them. "Something happened about two weeks ago. A little longer. It happened on the night you found Madam Marjorie."

Jacob winced. Would that night had never happened! First the strange little whore in his bed—and though he still had his suspicions, he had yet to find out for certain what she had actually been doing there—and then Marjorie. It had been the beginning of the end of everything.

"Go on," he said brusquely.

"The house had been roused by . . . well we're still not sure what. Someone was running about and crashing into things. I turned out the guards, and we all went looking. We didn't find anything, and so we settled down to making sure that everyone was safe and accounted for. That was when it . . ."

He fell silent, counting his bricks. After a time: "I knocked on Natil's door, Mister Jacob. She was there, but there were . . . others . . . with her."

Whores in his bed, Marjorie returning—Jacob was ready to believe anything. "What others?"

"Omelda was there. She didn't seem right at all. Natil was Natil, of course. She's always just Natil. But there was a nun there, too."

Jacob blinked, wrinkled his nose. "A nun?"

"Well, Mister Jacob, she was dressed like a nun. But I didn't think even at the time that she actually was. She didn't smell right."

"She didn't what?"

"She wore scent. Perfume. Nuns don't do that. At least not where anyone can notice them. But she was dressed up like a Benedictine. And Natil asked me to help her escape from the house."

Manarel's voice and manner told Jacob everything. "And you *did*?"

"Yes, Mister Jacob." Manarel looked as though he fully expected to be struck for his words, but he spoke them nonetheless. A brave man. Jacob liked that, just as—dear God!—he still liked Natil. "Natil is an honest woman. I'll never question that about her. She went to help Harold, and I fully believe that she'd jump into a bonfire to save a friend. She asked me to smuggle the nun out of the house and out of the town. And so I did."

"But you're sure she wasn't a nun."

Manarel smiled tiredly. "She propositioned me at the town gate. Said she needed money."

Jacob stifled a guffaw. "Did you take her up on the offer?"

Manarel selected a brick, dropped it on the ground with a thump. "No, master. She was frightened. Terrified. I didn't do anything. I just gave her my purse and told her to go."

Jacob nodded, admiring. Quite a man, Manarel. But a thought dawned on him. "Wait a moment. That nun. Round face? Little hands? Smelled like musk? Kind of a dumpling?"

"Yes, Mister Jacob. That describes her."

Jacob had never seen the woman who had come to his room: she had entered in darkness, had departed likewise. But he had known her touch, her hands, her lips. "The whore."

"Master?"

"Never mind, Manarel. I'm just clearing up a small mystery." But despite his words, the mystery had, if anything, grown more opaque. What did Natil have to do with the whore in his room? "What about Furze, though?"

Manarel bent his head. "It was such a strange thing, Mister Jacob, that I've thought a good deal about it. This is the way I reasoned it out. Most likely, only a nun would have a habit, especially a worn-out one. The nun was not a nun, though, and so the habit couldn't have been hers, but it fitted her tolerably, and therefore it couldn't have belonged to someone as tall and thin as Natil. That leaves only Omelda."

"But Furze, Manarel . . ."

The steward nodded. "It was a Benedictine habit. There's a Benedictine convent down by Furze, the only one in Adria. Natil never seems to do anything unless it helps someone else, and those bloody footprints in her room tell me that Omelda needed help, help she couldn't get from us. I think that Natil is helping Omelda return to her cloister. They started off heading south. Toward the convent. I think they've continued to head south. If so, they'll have to pass through Furze."

Jacob lifted his head, peered again into the fire. Yes, Natil helped everyone, whether they were important or not. Runaway nuns. Whores. Even stupid old men who had gotten away with more imbecility in their lives than they should ever have been allowed. But he had trusted Natil, and she, he was sure, had trusted him. She had even made allusions to a touch of heresy—Elves, indeed!—in her family, something that she would certainly have left unsaid had she not been confident that he would be discreet. Why then would she leave his service in the middle of the night without even a farewell?

Perhaps those bloody footprints had something to do with it. Perhaps the reason lay with Omelda. At present, though, it made no sense. But, now that he considered Natil's less than orthodox affiliations, Jacob suddenly realized how truly brave she had been to confront the Inquisition of Furze over Harold's welfare . . .

. . . and how utterly insane it was for her to go anywhere near that city.

His heart lurched. He willed it back to its task. Not yet. No, not yet. But as Manarel turned to him, startled and worried by his master's sudden pallor, Jacob gripped his arm. "We've got to hurry, Manarel. We'll break camp at first light. I won't even wait for the sun to rise. First light, mind you. And then to Furze, quick as we can."

CHAPTER 22

I-25 ran straight up through Colorado amid undulating foothills that, to the east, gave way to the Great Plains and, to the west, mounted into increasing heights and eventually touched the sky with the cold, white fingers of the Rocky Mountains. Suspended thus between landscapes—suspended between lives—Hadden and Wheat drove north. The sounds of engine and wind escorted them toward Denver . . . and towards the turnoff where the strange journey had begun.

The world was all before them, and despite the sudden shaking of their sympathies in a little Utah town, despite the constant question that now ate at both of them—*What gets us through?*—Hadden knew (and he knew that Wheat knew also) that the promise unveiled to him in a hidden valley of the Rocky Mountains and to her in the endless fields of Montana wheat would not be broken, that regardless of trial or sadness, *something* would get them through. Nice days, maybe. Or starlight. Or an immanent sense of home that enfolded them wherever they went.

Or . . . maybe something else.

Hadden found that he was smiling. Yes, something would get them through. The universe had taken them this far. It would, he knew, take them farther. Nor would it ever abandon them.

When he looked at Wheat, he found that she was smiling also.

"You, too?" he said.

She laughed. "Me, too. Do you want to try telepathy?"

He laughed. "I'd scare myself to death."

They both laughed.

He eased the seat back, wriggled his toes to loosen the stiffness, let the road rise to meet him. Pueblo came up like a sand castle. Colorado Springs was sprawling. For the last few weeks, still afraid that concrete and glass and asphalt might banish the spell that had ensnared them, they had intentionally avoided cities. But if the spell held now, if the starlight continued to gleam within them, if a faint radiance continued to suffuse their skin with something that went a little beyond mere health and youth, the urbanism they saw at least turned their thoughts to what lay ahead.

"Do you think that you'll go back to being a guard, Hadden?"

He was driving like a man with something on his mind, and he nearly laughed, because Wheat had, again, laid her finger upon his very thought. "I'm not sure," he said. "It paid the bills . . ."

Odd things, bills and jobs. He found himself regarding them as though they were spoiled children. *All right. If it will make you happy, I'll play your game. All right now, stop squalling. Here you go.*

". . . but that was about all. It wasn't going anywhere. I mean, minimum wage just doesn't ever go anywhere." But the thought occurred to him that it had been George Morrison who had not been going anywhere. In contrast, Hadden felt himself to be going everywhere. Suddenly, nothing seemed impossible: there were only differing degrees of probability.

"Promotions?" said Wheat.

He smiled. "Yeah. To a quarter more than minimum wage."

"Ummm. Sounds almost as good as waiting tables."

"I was going to ask you about that."

"I know."

They laughed again.

"I'm thinking of a fruit," said Hadden suddenly. "What is it?"

"Apple."

He stared at her for a moment, shifted his eyes back to the road with an uncomfortable squirm. "You're right."

Wheat shrugged. "It wasn't hard. What's the first fruit that anybody thinks of in this place?"

In this place. They were both using such phrases now. This place. As opposed to what?

But: "All right." Despite the flutter in his belly, Hadden went ahead with the experiment. "Try this one."

Wheat's answer came after only a few seconds. "Hazelnuts aren't a fruit."

He felt his eyebrows go up. "They most certainly are! They grow on trees: they're a fruit."

"Are not!" She hesitated, drumming her fingers on the window frame. "Well, maybe they are."

They both fell silent. He glanced at her. She was already looking at him, and he knew her thoughts just as, he was certain now, she knew his. *Let's . . . just not talk about this for now, huh?*

"Anyway," he said, "I'll probably wind up back in security, but I'm going to be looking for something else. Maybe I'll go to school. My father was a surveyor. I used to think I'd be a surveyor, and work outdoors." He mused. "That would be nice. Maybe I'll look into it."

Wheat was nodding. Colorado Springs dribbled into suburbs and then vanished. "And I'll be waiting tables for a while . . . but I think . . ." The scrub oak and wild clover rushed by, blurring with the speed of a homecoming that was always deepening, growing, as they plunged farther into what they were becoming. "I think I'll do something else, too. And you know, Hadden . . . for the first time . . . I really think that I can."

They were silent the rest of the way to Denver. Hadden guided the van through the afternoon traffic, took the tightly curving transition ramp onto Highway 6, and headed for the mountains. After forty minutes, he saw the small dirt road, but he had felt it long before that.

Burdened down now by Wheat's possessions, the van whined up the slope in low gear. Hadden kept the wheel steady, gripped it tightly through the patches of washboarding. Wheat was staring out the window, watching the passing trees, seemingly transfixed by the sky.

"You feel it, too," he said.

"Yes."

And that was it. They did not speak again. Not even when the road sloped down suddenly and brought the van to the same pancake of gravel and rock where George Morrison had, weeks before, shut off his engine and set the parking brake did they utter a sound.

Now, the man who was called Hadden parked,

switched off. He looked at Wheat, and she, as he expected, understood.

They got out of the van together and walked up the
slope, and there the birds were singing so loudly, the
sky was so unspeakably blue, and the trees and mountains were so absolutely perfect in their beauty and their
simple *being* that speech would have been either super-
fluous or outright sacrilege. And so they remained,
standing together, holding hands, silent as the afternoon
faded into evening, the slow changes of the hours and
the seasons mirroring and impelling the faster—much
faster—changes in their bodies and their souls.

Elves.

Natil was dreaming of them again, dreaming of the
reawakening. Evening turned to night in Colorado, the
stars blossomed, the moon flowered, and Hadden and
Wheat, changing, stood together, hand in hand, rooted
by their vision of a world made forever different by their
presence. It could happen. It *would* happen.

And then the vision shifted, and again she saw the
tree: forked, rain swept, streaming with preternatural
light, standing like an icon of absolute mystery.

Is it real?

The tree was a dream, and dreams were not real. But
Hadden and Wheat were a dream, too, and Natil was
unwilling to allow the slightest shred of doubt to cloud
her certainty of their future existence. And therefore . . .

It must be real.

And the Lady, she felt, was close, very close. To Hadden and Wheat. To Natil herself. And to that tree.

The tree must be real.

Still it stood proudly in the rain, its twin trunks leaning
outward from a central bole, the cleft streaming with
light as though a sun had kindled just on the other side
of . . .

. . . of whatever.

The sky was gray when Natil awoke: the day would be
damp and hot. Not good, not good at all, for Omelda
was still fevered, and though Natil shook her gently
awake, bathed her outward wounds, and fed her morsels
of bread and dried meat, it was obvious that she was
growing worse. She was weak, disoriented, and she now

lapsed continually in and out of awareness. She moaned and mumbled unintelligible syllables, her voice rising and falling as though in a sinister parody of melody, and Natil—despite herbs and attentions—could do nothing for her.

Listening to her curiously iterative babblings, then, the harper broke what meager camp she had made and, with difficulty, hoisted Omelda up from the ground and half carried, half dragged her along the overgrown path that led to the forest edge. Perhaps the young woman might find healing at Shrinerock Abbey, perhaps she might only find death. Regardless, Natil had promised to take her back to the only home she had ever known on earth, and that was one promise she refused to break as long as she had a will to call her own.

She was an Elf. Elves did not break promises.

When the trees thinned, Natil could see Furze. The Malvern River flowed coldly a short distance away, and though a long immersion in the river helped Omelda a little, her fever, aided and augmented by the stifling heat of the day, returned quickly, too quickly.

Beyond the water, the former pastureland was rank and unruly with weeds and neglect. It made travel difficult, and Omelda's condition deteriorated steadily. Natil knew what was happening, was powerless to prevent it: Omelda was dying from the inside out.

"Just two leagues, beloved," the harper whispered, though she did not know whether Omelda heard. "Just two. We will come to Furze, then, and maybe Paul Drego or James or one of the others will remember me and help."

Gripped in delirium, Omelda moaned and twitched, stared glassily at the distant town. "Unnh . . . unnh . . ."

"Just a little farther. Then you can rest, and after that I will take you home."

"Unnh . . . unnh . . ."

They reached the city in the late afternoon. The gate guards watched suspiciously as Natil paid the toll. "Look here, now," said one, "she dan't have plague, does she?"

"She does not, sir," said the harper. "She is ill with a fever. I must find help for her."

"Wha' do you intend to do in Furze?"

"I intend to find help for my friend, sir. Can you direct me to the house of Paul Drego? I do not know the way from here."

The guard suddenly looked interested. "Paul Drego? Of the wool cooperative? Wi' do you want to see him?"

"He is . . ." Natil wondered at the brightness of his eyes, the eagerness of his voice. ". . . a friend."

"Oh, surely." The guard cast a look at his companions. "A friend."

"Just so, sir. Can you tell me where he lives?"

Omelda stirred, flailed, mumbling frantically in a singsong voice that bore a faint resemblance to plainchant. But it was random, broken, fragmented, the Latin syllables slurring into one another and forming a melange of grunts and nonsense.

The guard backed away. "She's possessed."

"She is ill," said Natil firmly. "Will you deny her a chance to be healed?"

The blunt question slapped him into sense. "Nay . . . nay, nat at all." He pointed through the gate, gave her the directions quickly, shooed them both along. "On with you. On with you."

Omelda was still flailing as Natil took her into the narrow and squalid streets. The young woman's eyes rolled, her mumbled chant rose and fell. Natil heard the church bells tolling, though, and at last understood. It was time for vespers, and Omelda, pursued by her inner voices, was being spiritually compelled, sick though she was, delirious though she was, to stand alongside her fellow monastics.

The blatant failure made Natil bow her head. Helping and healing. What help or healing had she given Omelda? But she struggled on. The helping and healing would come again. She had so determined, she had so willed.

Abruptly, Omelda fell silent, her struggles ceased. Natil, startled and worried, eased her down to the ground near the waterless fountain in the middle of the town square.

Omelda was staring up at her, or perhaps beyond her, eyes wide and hectic. But her words were clear, distinct. "It's no use."

Hands to her face, Natil sagged to the pavement beside her.

"I'm dead."

The harper shook her head. "We can find help, Omelda. There are a few good men in Furze. Paul Drego will remember me. He will help us."

"They're all devils."

"Omelda, please—"

The apostate nun's voice suddenly rose, and her fists, pink and damp with the flush of fever that had possessed her utterly, clenched. "They're all devils! I'm telling you! I know! I know! From the beginning, I knew! They tossed me into the convent, then their damned religion tossed me out! And then they tied me up, and fucked me, and branded me with red hot brands!"

Natil turned to a passerby, a woman she recognized as the convicted heretic she had met before. "Some water, madam," she said. "Please."

The woman recoiled as though from a serpent, her hands pressed to the double crosses on her cloak. "God bless you!" she cried. "God bless you! Stay away from me! I'm no heretic! God bless you!"

"Please, sir," said Natil, trying another, a common laborer by the look of him, "some water for a sick woman."

But he gave her no water. He merely watched, watched and listened as Omelda continued to rave:

"You're not men. You're not priests. You're all devils. God looks down from the sky, and He sees you all. He knows what I am, and He knows what you are!"

Natil found that she and Omelda were alone in a tiny zone of quarantine in the middle of the square, a zone bounded by turned backs, averted faces . . . and, occasionally, bright eyes, open ears.

"We're all alone! I'm alone, and they tied me up. And look! Look! Look! There's His face! Leaning down out of the sky!"

More bright eyes. Natil took Omelda in her arms, tried to speak soothingly, tried to remember how it had felt to be an Elf, what it had been like to have a voice that could comfort, a touch that could heal. It had been so once. She was determined that it would be so again. She had been an Elf. She would be an Elf.

Omelda flailed once more and then collapsed, her strength spent. Natil bent over her, searched her face. She was still breathing.

But when the harper looked up, she saw soldiers in the livery of David a'Freux standing around her, pikes leveled. A gaunt Dominican was among them, and he nodded to their captain.

There was no escape.

Siegfried's forehead was pressed against his clenched fists, and he was unaware and heedless of the morning light that streamed in through the window like grace spilled from a bright chalice. He was looking within, trying to find in his darkness a glimpse of real light, a flicker of inbreaking divinity.

Adoro te devote, latens deitas . . .

Yes, he adored the hidden God who so shrouded himself within the shadowy manifestations of bread and wine. Bread and wine had, indeed, passed through the Savior's hands, and His benediction had forever infused those sacramental commonplaces with the deepest holiness. But Siegfried wanted more. He wanted to see. He wanted to be *sure*.

Tormented as he was by his recent descent into untruths, though, he now despaired of ever seeing, of ever being sure. God, far from drawing closer as a result of Siegfried's sacrifice of his own veracity, now appeared even more distant; and the Inquisitor's soul was dark with lies and obsessions about lies.

Surely his ambition could not be at fault: he had thrown away the evidence against Paul Drego only to further his pursuit of a greater quarry. Money and power and influence could draw many souls into the fiery embrace of hell, and if men like Paul Drego were bad, then men like Jacob Aldernacht were certainly worse. Infinitely worse. So much worse that they were worth whatever work, effort, self-denial or sleepless nights it took to arrest them, try them, and burn them.

But were they worth a lie?

Siegfried opened his eyes. On the table before him was the order for condemnation and confiscation. It was all according to form, all in order. It only wanted the date.

But it was founded upon a lie. Oh, Harold's testimony

was adequate, and more than adequate. But before Harold's testimony about Jacob there had been a book of evidence. A book about Paul Drego. A book that Siegfried had discarded . . . without cause.

He lifted his head. The sunlight still streamed in through the window, and from this high office in the House of God, the Inquisitor could see the tumbled and impoverished houses of Furze. Dusty streets. Poor people.

But he could see beyond the town, too. He could see green pastures and the sparkle of the Malvern River. He could see the distant forest, dark green with summer leaves, fertile as a fresh-turned field. And beyond the forest rose the Aleser Mountains, their lower slopes green with crops and steadings and stands of trees, their upper peaks white with snow that defied the best that the hot season could send against them.

It is summer, he thought. And for a moment, Siegfried began to grasp the real meaning of that statement. It was lovely. Green. Pliant with new growth. Everything that he saw was simple, contained, a truth unto itself.

Truth.

He bent his head again, his lies a weight within him, a hard knot of conscience just below his heart. Was even Jacob Aldernacht worth a lie? The season said no. The mountains and the forest said no. The pent innocence of his soul said no.

He lifted his head again, struck. His Master had given him ten talents, and he had, by his lie, simply buried them in a field, hoping that a flat return of the investment—without a shred of interest—would satisfy the Lender.

But Siegfried knew that it would not satisfy Him. And he knew now what he had to do. He had to give up the lie. He had to turn again to a life without sin, a life of innocence. He had to—

A tapping at the door. Giovanni entered, bowed. His movements were quick, almost furtive, and when he straightened, there was a deep crease between his eyebrows. "Brother Siegfried," he said, "we've taken a prisoner. Well . . . actually, we've taken two prisoners, but one is . . . extremely odd."

Still looking at the mountains, Siegfried nodded absently. Yes, he would give up the lie. And if that meant beginning the entire investigation over again, then that was what he would do. He had already restarted it once for the sake of a lie. He could certainly restart it again for the sake of the truth. "Odd?"

"Well," said Giovanni, "they're both strangers in town. And one is too sick to really bother with. I expect she'll die within a few days. The odd one, though . . . well, I can't make any sense out of the answers she's giving me."

Siegfried came out of his reverie. "Sense? Surely, Fra Giovanni, you have dealt with recalcitrant defendants before. Give her to David's men. Tell them what to do. You will get sense out of her, I assure you."

"It's not that . . ." Giovanni hesitated. The crease between his eyebrows deepened. "Could you talk to her? I'm afraid that this is beyond me."

"What is the problem?"

"Well, to begin with, she claims that she is not a Christian, and that therefore she cannot be a heretic. She also claims that she has talked to you before, and says that she wishes you . . . uh . . ." Giovanni shook his head. ". . . that she wishes you well. She simply doesn't make sense."

"Talked to me before? Who is this woman? What's her name?"

"She calls herself Natil. She's a harper."

Siegfried was on his feet in a moment. "Natil? Jacob Aldernacht's harper? Dear God, Giovanni! Grace has been bestowed upon us!"

Giovanni stared at him. "But I can't—"

"I will question her." Siegfried grabbed the order for Jacob's condemnation, rolled it up, shoved it into his sleeve. "I will question her immediately. This morning." The thought was hammering in his head: he had the key to Jacob's heresy in the House of God at this very moment. Perhaps, for the sake of truth, he would have to start over, but the path to his goal would be short and direct, for it would lead through the testimony—and, if necessary, the body—of Natil the harper.

They had taken her harp, taken most of her clothing, taken all of her freedom.

Natil was in chains, suspended by her wrists in darkness. The cell was dry, and she had not been tortured, but knee-deep water and deliberately inflicted pain, she was sure, would come later, as would, eventually, burning.

How many of her kindred, she wondered, had hung in chains like this, listened to distant screams and the drip of water, waited to see the steel instruments of torture and the scarlet rawness of compound fractures? Many. Thousands. Millions. The Elves had died hunted, and they had died broken, and they had died burned. And now Natil, the last, had followed her heritage not into the quiescent oblivion of fading but into the depths of the House of God.

She was in no pain. And, contrary to the intentions of those who had brought her to this place, she was not even afraid. Fear was applicable only to the unknown, and Natil knew without a doubt what lay ahead of her. If she felt anything at all, it was concern for Omelda, who was somewhere else in the prison, and sadness for herself, for all the Elves who would never again lift their hands to heal, for all those frail mortals who would never experience the grace of a sudden and unlooked-for resurgence of health or hear a voice of comfort.

She could do nothing about any of it, though. The Elves were gone, faded and killed, and Omelda was elsewhere, writhing in the delirium of a terminal fever. All Natil had was herself, and approaching death.

She sighed, rested her head against an arm, closed her eyes. Darkness confronted her, darkness as deep as that of this closed and lightless prison cell. Had she a single wish, she would have expended it upon that darkness: she would have wished for stars, wished that this last faltering Firstborn, so besmirched with humanity and the confusion of mortals, could once again see the illimitable light of that inner firmament. Let them rape her, torture her, burn her . . . just so long as she had the stars, just so long as she could—even in her last hour, even at her last moment—reforge that quintessential link with the people and the heritage she had, by act of will, reclaimed.

She felt a tear gather itself at the corner of her eye, run down her cheek.

Soon, she knew, they would come for her again. Fra Giovanni had met her answers to his elementary questions with disbelief and not a little confusion . . .

"Do you believe that the sacraments given by a priest in mortal sin are valid?"

"Sacraments, Fra Giovanni, come from within."

"You believe this?"

"Beloved, I do not work from belief. I know."

"You're a heretic, an enemy of Holy Church."

"I cannot be a heretic, Giovanni, for I am not a Christian."

. . . and, bewildered, had sent her back to her cell, there to be afraid until she was called forth once again for questioning.

Fear. Her head was heavy against her arm, her tears still falling. So much fear among humans. Fear of life. Fear of love. Fear of death.

She sighed, found what was left of her voice. "I will die," she whispered, "as I have lived. I will die an Elf. And I will answer these men as an Elf." Her tears fell faster. "They will know me, my Lady, and they will know You. And if they wish to kill me for that, then so be it."

And softly then, very softly, in the darkness behind her closed eyes, something flickered, grew: a sudden and almost subliminal luminescence that burgeoned just beyond sight, surged forward toward sense, toward knowledge, toward vision. And then, in a hundred sparkling hues, a thousand degrees of brightness, the stars suddenly appeared, gleaming softly within her mind.

Natil sagged in her bonds, but the starlight upheld her. And when she opened her eyes, she discovered that her cell, dark as it was, appeared to her in shades of blue and lavender. And once again there was a lambent gleam about her flesh, a silvery aura invisible to mere mortals.

She found her voice again, and it was not in any of the tongues of men that she offered thanks to the Woman who had made her, but in the ancient language of the Elves. She remembered it, knew it as she now, once again, knew herself, and though the words came to her as though limned in fire, they were as the touch of water upon her lips. *"Telete, Marithae."*

A clatter from the door answered her. Torchlight streamed in. She felt rough hands—the hands of men— on her. They unfastened her chains and dragged her into the corridor. Her foot caught on a stone step and she fell.

She felt the chains tighten. ''Hold,'' she said. There was an edge of immortality in her voice now, and the men obeyed instinctively. Slowly, unhindered, she got to her feet. ''I will walk, gentlemen,'' she said politely. ''You need not drag me.''

And so baffled were they by her tone and by her innate nobility that they fell back and allowed her to tread the corridors of the House of God on her own feet, by her own will. The Elf held her head high, and there was a gleam, as of starlight, in her eyes.

CHAPTER 23

The Aldernacht assault on Furze did not begin with cannon and siege machinery, with fireballs and heavy stones falling on the impoverished city. No, it began with small sacks of gold coins . . . falling into the hands of a few gate guards.

The men looked up at the band of Aldernacht soldiers, then down at the eloquently heavy sacks. Their leader cleared his throat. "Yes, your honor? Wha' can we do for you this morning?"

"I'm looking for a harper," rasped Jacob. "Calls herself Natil. Tall. Dark hair with silver in it. She has a dumpy girl with her."

The leader hefted his sack. Yes, eloquently heavy. His eyes, bright, seemed suspended between eagerness and suspicion.

"Go ahead, man," said Jacob. "Open it."

He did. The florins poured into his hand with a shiny clink.

"Where's Natil?"

The guard looked up at Jacob as though trying to think of an acceptable answer. "Uh . . . why . . . I . . ."

Jacob leaned down, spectacles glinting. "Just *tell* me, man."

"She cam this way two days ago," said the guard, his eyes turning avaricious and his hand shutting firmly on the gold. "We were just about to close up for the night. The girl was wi' her, and . . ." He hesitated.

Jacob caught the potential dissemblance. "And *what*?" said the rich man.

". . . uh . . . and then she went off into town. The girl looked sick. Crazy."

"Sick?"

"Fevered. They went off. Really."

"Sure they did," said Jacob, glaring. "And then you went off, too, didn't you?"

"I . . ."

"Come on, out with it. Who's paying you now?"

"I . . ." But he could not seem to get the words out. "I . . ."

Jacob grimaced. "Never mind, idiot. You've told me everything." Ignoring the toll basket—he had, after all, just given every one of the guards enough money for a house and a business of his own—he rode on into the city. Manarel and the Aldernacht soldiers followed.

The streets were narrow and pinched, and the faces Jacob saw were narrow and pinched, too. Most of the townsfolk went about their business as though their acts were dictated by the dust at their feet. A few, though, seemed to be watching everything in a way that reminded Jacob of the avarice that had so abruptly kindled in the gate guard's eyes.

Manarel trotted up beside Jacob. "Natil may well have left the city, master."

"Oh, she's here," said Jacob, glancing around. Furze suddenly looked as tawdry and sordid as his own house. What kind of vipers lived here? The same kind as lived under the motto *In the name of God and profit*. Furze was simply a little more honest in its display of poverty. "If that girl was sick, Natil was probably looking for help."

He glanced at Manarel. The steward was looking down the street, his eyes narrowed.

"Out with it. I *already* pay you, Manarel."

"I . . ." Manarel passed a hand across the stubble of his beard. "I didn't know Omelda very well. She worked in the kitchen, and I had other responsibilities. But I noticed that she was . . ." He hesitated, choosing his words. ". . . droopy. She never did look well. And then there was that other girl who went off without leave."

Jacob was startled. "What other girl?"

"Kitchen wench," said Manarel. "She'd been complaining about . . ." He flushed.

"Out with it, man."

"About Edvard and Norman," Manarel finished. "She'd been hurt, she said. She left about two months ago. The boys made sure that no one made anything of it.'' Manarel looked plainly uncomfortable. ''I suspect that something was happening.''

Jacob suddenly comprehended. Jacob had his money, Francis had his tobacco, and Edvard and Norman had something else. And now Jacob knew exactly what that little whore had been doing in his room, who had brought her there, and why she had been so utterly terrified, just as he understood the meaning of the bloody footprints in Natil's room, and her sudden flight with Omelda.

The frost in his heart turned to ice, spread. Such was the stuff that had oozed from his loins.

''I'll settle them,'' he said aloud. ''I'll settle them. One way or another. I'll settle them all.'' He looked up at Manarel. ''Let's find Natil.''

The steward nodded. ''Very good, master. But how? Furze is poor, but not small. Natil could be anywhere.''

''That's true, Manarel. But I've got money, and money can do anything. Particularly here.'' Jacob gestured at the people in the street. ''Look at them. Whoever buys their next meal, buys their souls. They'd sell their parents to the Turk slavers for a fraction of what I just gave away at the gate, and I've got plenty more with me. I'll find out where she is. But . . .''

He lifted his head. Not far up the street, the House of God lifted into the air a tower as stiff and hard, he thought, as a rapist's prick. *Elves,* Natil had said. But though it could not have had anything to do with Elves, her young face had been solemn, her blue eyes downcast.

The guard at the gate had said everything. Jacob shook his head. ''But I'm afraid I already know.''

Veni Creator Spiritus, mentes tuorum visita . . .
Prime. Prime in Furze, prime everywhere. In the monasteries and convents of Adria, as indeed in all of Europe, monks and nuns were filling their chapels and abbey churches with song. It was Whit Monday, only a day past Pentecost, and in countless naves and cells and cathedrals, hymns to the Holy Spirit, to reified divine love, floated up to heaven.
Imple superna gratia . . .
And Omelda heard the hymns as she had always heard them, whether sleeping in fields or in the beds of strange men, whether eating or working or being systematically

brutalized into sepsis by the attentions of Edvard and
Norman. She had heard them in Shrinerock Abbey. She
heard them now as she lay on a stone shelf in a dark cell
in the House of God.

Tu septiformis munere . . .

She had no idea where she was: that cognizance had
fled before the slow fire of her inwardly rotting flesh. But
though her knowledge was restricted to the fact that her
surroundings were dark and quiet, her awareness registered that Natil had, once again, deserted her. In the
swampy whirl of thoughts that was all that her fever had
left to her, Omelda knew that she was alone.

Tu rite promissum Patris, sermone ditans guttura.

She was now as she had begun, as she always had
been. Alone. Alone with her mind. Alone with the plainchant.

. . . infirma nostri corporis virtute firmans perpeti.

Nothing. Nothing and no one. Just herself and the
chant.

Hostem repellas longius . . .

Loneliness. Terrible loneliness. Cold loneliness. The
loneliness of a mind isolated, forsaken.

And so, as she had once before—prod in her anus and
teeth in her thigh—scraped out a little hollow of comfort
in the impersonal lines of chant, so she now turned once
again to the syllables and the tones, making of them a
kind of a chill and yet strangely accepting refuge from
present and past madness, crawling therein, surrendering
what was left of her consciousness to the chill embrace
of monody.

Deo Patri sit gloria . . . It was all she had. . . . *et
Filio, qui a mortuis . . .* It was all she had ever had. . . .
surrexit ac Paraclito . . . Music, chant: the deliberate
fusion of will and body and spirit into something that
rose beyond mortal concerns . . . and into the infinite.

. . . in saeculorum saecula. Amen.

Half-naked, in chains, Nakil walked unassisted and
unmolested from her cell to the door of the tribunal
chamber. And though one of her guards could not resist
a final shove and therefore put up his hands to thrust her
into the room, the starlight warned Natil, and she turned.

"Honored sir," she said politely, "pray do not disgrace yourself."

Her eyes met his, and, after a long moment, he lowered his gaze.

Natil passed through the door and into a large chamber that was lighted from the north by high windows. Behind the narrow tables that ran along the right and left walls were seated a scattering of secretaries and scribes and a few men whom she surmised were doctors of canon law. Before her, though, was a squat desk, and facing her across its three or four feet of dark wood was Siegfried of Magdeburg.

He remembered her. She was certain that he remembered her. His dark eyes fixed themselves upon her the moment she crossed the threshold, and in their depths she caught an eagerness and an expectancy that told her that he had much more interest in this morning's tribunal than might normally be warranted by the heretical remarks of a fevered woman.

She did not have to guess why. It was not Natil the harper who was on trial at present: it was Jacob Aldernacht. The wool cooperative had been the beginning, Harold had been the middle, and now Siegfried expected her to be the end.

But Siegfried was wrong.

Without prompting, she advanced to the center of the room. The position—central and surrounded—was supposed to put her in dread of the power wielded by her accusers, but she closed her eyes, breathed the starlight that filled her inner firmament . . . and there was no place left for fear.

And Natil felt the warmth of sunlight in her face as she smiled at Siegfried, wished him a good morning and a God bless.

Siegfried was unmoved. Natil recalled their first meeting, recalled the strange emotions that had gripped him, wondered at the touch of shame that was now shadowing his face.

"State your name, woman," he said.

"My name is Natil," she answered.

"Is that all?"

"It is."

Siegfried frowned. "Where are you from?"

"Most recently, I have come from Ypris."

"Is that where you were born?"

"It is not," she said.

"Don't equivocate, woman," he snapped. "I want to know where you were born."

"Then, Brother Siegfried," she said, "please ask me what you wish to know. I will . . ." She looked at the sunlight that puddled the brown floor. So lovely. She would not see it for very much longer. In fact, she would not see the world for very much longer. The thought made her sad, and she realized that, though she had seen pain and trouble, and though she was now facing a lingering and tormented death, it was nonetheless a lovely world. ". . . I will be happy to tell you."

A great calm, subtle but potent, had come back into her voice along with the starlight, and Siegfried blinked. But his office caught up with him in a moment. "Do you know why you have been brought before me?"

It was the old question, asked according to form, according to the advice of old Bernard Gui. Natil sighed. "I do."

She was, she knew, supposed to profess ignorance, and then she was supposed to protest her innocence when Siegfried advised her that she stood accused of heresy against Holy Church. But Natil was not interested in proper form or in the fanaticism of a long-dead Dominican: she was here to speak as an Elf.

The secretaries' pens scratched her answer onto white paper. A crow cried out harshly somewhere outside. Natil waited before the man who would kill her, reminded herself that everything that happened, happened as it should, happened when it should.

Difficult advice, she admitted. It took an Elf to believe it.

"You are accused of heresy," said Siegfried, continuing with his half of the formula. "You are accused of believing and teaching otherwise than Holy Church believes and teaches."

"I am not a heretic."

"But you would not be here were you not a heretic." Siegfried's gaze, boring out at her, met an impenetrable wall of starlight. "Are you saying that the Inquisition arrests the innocent?"

Natil sighed, shook her head. Sad. Sadness every-where. "Indeed," she said, looking into his face, "I am saying just that."

He was angry now. But it was a calculated anger. Ev-eryone knew that Inquisitors could do anything, everyone knew how dangerous and absolutely idiotic it was to make them angry: he was trying to frighten her. "Explain yourself," he said, thumping his fist on the table, ex-pecting her to quail.

She did not quail. "I am not a heretic against your Church, Brother Siegfried, because I am not now, nor have I ever been, a Christian."

"You are an idolater!"

The pens scratched on, the feathers of dead birds meeting the pulp of dead trees.

"And you yourself know," Natil continued, ignoring his derogation, "—or if you do not, you should—that countless scores of the innocent have met death at your hands."

Siegfried was momentarily speechless at her brazen statement, and the doctors of canon law were suddenly busy conferring in agitated whispers.

"Do you not know?" Natil went on. "Have you not seen it in their faces?"

Siegfried found his voice. "Are you questioning the authority and integrity of the Inquisition?"

"I am." No disrespect, no defiance tainted her voice. She was stating unequivocal fact, and Siegfried knew it.

His anger now genuine, he was on his feet, hands braced on the table, leaning toward her and about to shout when he appeared to come to himself. He looked around, then, his face pale, and Natil saw it: integrity. That was it. She suddenly understood his shame.

Siegfried sat down. "Where were you born, Natil?"

"I was not born, sir. I was made."

Dead silence in the room. Shock had stilled even the scratch of the pens. Siegfried tore himself away from his surprise, glared at the secretaries. "Write that!" he snapped. "Write that down!"

Haltingly, the pens resumed their work.

Siegfried could not meet her eyes. "Who . . . who made you?"

"In the tongue of my people She is called *Elthia Ca-*

lasiuove, which means, roughly, in your language, *Bright Lady Shining with Clear Radiance.*'' Natil's words were calm, even, and—as she knew Siegfried recognized because he had become obsessed with his own lack of inner veracity—the absolute truth. ''By Her hand was I called up out of nothingness, given form and name and consciousness, granted power and concomitant responsibility to all life.''

''What . . .'' Siegfried struggled with shock and words both. The pens scratched frantically, as though their holders were torn between duty and rapt listening. ''What are you telling me, woman?''

''I am telling you the truth, beloved. I told you when we first met that I was a very poor Christian. I am, in fact, no Christian at all. And therefore I cannot be a heretic. Torture me or burn me as you will, I have told you the truth, and therefore you know that you have no claim upon me.''

''You are—'' Siegfried cut himself short. No, not at all according to form. His hand, blotting his forehead, was shaking. ''You are an ignorant savage, harper,'' he said with an effort. ''You come before the Holy Inquisition with barnyard tales fabricated out of legends and myths. Doubtless, you will next seek to confound us with the old stories that baffled Aloysius Cranby years ago.'' Siegfried laughed, but Natil heard the hollowness. Integrity. His integrity was gone.

The doctors of law chuckled quietly. The scribes went on writing.

Natil regarded Siegfried in silence, and his tongue abruptly faltered. ''You know,'' she said quietly, ''that you are speaking an untruth.''

The statement struck him like a spear. He struggled with her intuition and her starlight . . . and with his own conscience. ''Vagabond!'' was all he could muster.

Sad. Growing even sadder. The last Elf—barely clinging to her status—condemned by a priest who was apparently torturing himself as much as he tortured his prisoners. ''Did you wish to try me for heresy, Brother Siegfried?'' she asked courteously, ''or for wandering?''

''Out of your own mouth are you condemned!''

''Condemned for what?''

''Heresy.''

"I cannot be a heretic, for I am not a Christian."

Siegfried lost patience. "Well, then what *are* you?"

"I am an Elf."

The pens fell silent again. A number of the scribes opened their mouths to laugh, then reconsidered and shut them. The doctors, who had again been conferring, stopped in mid-whisper.

Siegfried was speechless for a moment. Then: "You are saying that . . ." He could not find words, but Natil knew his thoughts. The prisoner was telling the truth. But the truth she was telling utterly eclipsed any picayune question of heterodoxy, was, in fact, so immense, so monstrous, that the churchmen present in the room could not, at first, even comprehend it.

"Inquisitor," said Natil, feeling a flicker of defiance, "you have before you the last of the Firstborn, the last Immortal. You have killed or saddened into non-existence all the rest of my people. When I am gone, the Earth will be yours, to do with as you wish." A small flash of wrath, which, after examining it carefully, she allowed. "I hope you are satisfied."

Siegfried stared. Then: "You are . . ." A long pause, because the truth in Natil's words was so compelling that he did not believe his own statement. ". . . mad."

She was fettered, but she stepped forward a pace, her bare feet noiseless on the wooden floor. Even the rattle of her chains was muffled and indistinct. "You know that I am most certainly not mad," she said. "You know— do not deny it, for I can see it plainly—that I am speaking the most truth that has been uttered in your presence in twenty years of Inquisition."

Rooted as the coachmen were by her voice and her words, no one moved, not even when she stepped forward another pace and confronted Siegfried across the polished surface of his desk. Natil felt a stirring within her, saw no reason not to yield to it. Her voice went up, liquid and hard-edged both.

"I will speak to you, then, as the last of my people. I will speak to you words that we perhaps should have uttered long before, but compassion stilled our tongues."

Silence. Stunned silence. Not a word. Not a movement.

"In the beginning, we saw your world coalesce out of

void, and as it solidified and cooled, we prayed for it and for its future. We saw life arise from pools of slime, and we encouraged it, fostered it, kept it from death. And when it took to the land, we sheltered it from storm and sun, fed it when it hungered, brought water when it thirsted . . .''

Siegfried's mouth moved silently. Natil read his lips. *My God.*

''. . . and when, after great eons, your race descended from the trees of Africa, hairy and bestial and knowing no more than food and sleep, we taught it the use of its hands and its voice, we showed it the use of tools.'' Grief welled up, threatened to make her weep, but she turned it to compassion and continued. ''We taught you stories and legends. We encouraged you to create others. And as we taught and healed and helped you, so we thought that you would, in turn, teach and heal and help one another.''

Siegfried's face was slack, his eyes stricken. What did he see? Hope? Revelation? Or a nightmare risen up from the past to threaten his kind and his Church?

Natil did not know. But she had to speak. It was her last chance to speak, the last chance of the Elves.

''And now,'' she said, ''the last of my race, I stand before you and ask you what we should have asked long ago.'' The wrath welled up in earnest then, welled up and carried her voice throughout the room as though a sudden storm had been loosed: *''With what audacity or excuse have you so turned upon me and my kind, and perverted the intelligence which we so carefully and compassionately fostered?''*

Silence. Lengthening, prolonged.

Natil bent her head, finished. And, as she had expected, she heard a step behind her. The blow came quickly: a shock, and a white light. She did not lose consciousness, but the floor came up like a fist, and though her stars quelled the pain in a moment, she discovered that, for the present, she could not move.

''Take . . .'' Siegfried's voice was hoarse, halting. He had seen. He had heard. He *knew.* And though he was trying to deny that he knew—trying to deny it to himself, trying to deny it to everyone in the room—he could not deny it. "Take her away. There is nothing more that we need . . ."

A long pause. Natil heard a voice: "Brother Siegfried?"

". . . that we need here. She has admitted everything. Let her be burned."

"Brother Siegfried, you don't suppose that she's—"

"I suppose nothing."

"But perhaps we should—"

"Burn her! *Burn her!*"

Hands were already seizing Natil's chains, and she was dragged out of the room, down the corridors. Her head bounced on the stairs leading to the dungeon, but the starlight was with her, and though she felt the blood start to flow from her nose and scalp, she did not cry out. She had already said everything. She had given to men the last words of the Elves.

They took her back to her cell and hung her up again. She sagged weakly: feeling was returning to her limbs much faster than any control.

The door clanged shut. She looked at the stars, breathed the light.

So much that was left undone, so little that she could do about any of it. Far in the future, Hadden and Wheat had themselves found out about the much and the little, but they had persevered in spite of that knowledge; and, drifting in an inner bath of starlight, drawing a sustenance and a hope from it that, she knew, could take her all the way through whatever fate—fading or burning— lay ahead of her, Natil saw them standing together beneath the stars of early summer.

And it suddenly struck the Elf that, for them, it was *Arae a Circa,* the Day of Renewal. Renewal for Hadden and Wheat. Renewal for the Elves. Renewal for the world.

Despite her condition and her future, Natil smiled, her tears mingling with her blood. It would happen. She knew now that it would happen. She had no more doubts, and if she regretted anything at all, it was only that the Elves, coming anew into the world, would have no knowledge of their Maker, no vision of the Lady, no touch of a starlit hand on their brows. *What gets us through?* they would ask, and the answer would be only hollow silence.

And with the rising of the sun, Hadden and Wheat blinked at a world remade. Shyly, like children, they turned to one another in the flood of new light, saw that the changes in their souls had been confirmed and complimented by changes in their bodies that went far beyond anything they had seen before: an utter purging of the last remnants of mortality . . .

. . . and humanity.

Knowing now what they were, they wandered hand in hand beneath the pines and the aspens, their steps soundless. They talked with birds, patted squirrels, wondered at the blueness of the sky, delighted in the breezes brought by this May morning. They climbed and explored the new Elvenhome, for it was a home, a home that had arisen within the Greater Home that Elves would always know.

"But . . ." Wheat was laughing, giddy and apprehensive both. A sparrow was nestled in her cupped hands, and it chirped gleefully before it took flight. ". . . how are we going to explain this to anyone?"

Hadden shrugged. "We don't. We find people who don't need explanations."

"Like who?"

He gave her a slow smile, a womanly smile. "People like us."

The wind caught her hair, whipped it in front of her face. She ran her hands back through it, blushed as they brushed past her ears. "Oh, my God . . . you think that there are others?"

Hadden nodded. "Yes," he said. "There'll be more." He looked up at the blue Colorado sky. "We're home."

Natil, hung like a piece of rotting meat in the House of God, awaiting the flames that would release her from life, watched as other lives unfurled. She saw Joan become Ash. She saw Lauri leave a broken-hearted past behind and embrace something so welcoming that she could neither understand it nor question it. She saw Amy flee from abuse, seize autonomy and starlight both, and take the name Bright for herself, her hope, and her determination.

And there were others. Raven. Web. Marsh. Heather. And their stories and their transformations all grew in Natil's mind as the hours passed and her death approached. Elvenhome of the Rockies. The land was bought, the cornerstone was laid. The walls—yes, there were walls now, but walls, like swords, had their place—went up, white and shining, and by elven hands and elven hearts they were all of a piece with the mountains and forests about them.

Once again, there were Elves in the world, but this time they did not keep to the forests and the wilds, but rather lived among their mortal brothers and sisters. They helped as they could, healed when they were able to make some vague sense out of the immanent starlight; but just as these actions were impelled by a dim, immortal instinct that was rooted in a past at which they could only guess, so also did a faint, racial memory urge them toward discretion: though they knew one another, acknowledged one another, and embraced one another, they said nothing of their existence to their human siblings.

And despite the confusion of such an immortal life of mixed love and caution, they had also to consider something else, for as their numbers had grown from two to several to a handful, so had the question:

What gets us through?

They did not know what would get them through. And Natil, five hundred years in the past, and imprisoned in the House of God, could not tell them.

For a moment, she saw the rainswept tree again, its cleft streaming with brilliance as though something divine were thrusting toward incarnation. It blazed at her, shimmering, aureate, and Natil found herself suddenly repeating, in common American English sparked with the lilt of an elven accent, the words she had heard from the lips of those who did not yet live.

"What gets us through?"

The language startled her, and she came to herself in the darkness of her cell. "What gets us through?" she whispered in English, savoring the taste of the words like the juice of some exotic fruit. "What gets us through? O my kindred, had I the power, I would tell you."

She hung her head, but a faint sound made her lift it again. With the exception of an occasional muffled scream or slamming door, the dungeon was silent. But now something had intruded into the terrible custom, something as strange as the English syllables that had, a moment before, echoed off the stone walls.

Faintly, in the distance, Omelda was singing—her voice high and clear, distinct and deliberate—intoning the Holy Office with an ethereal purity that brought to this place of darkness and pain something of brightness and divinity, set the very air vibrating with it, and then, slowly, faded away into illimitable peace.

CHAPTER 24

With difficulty, Siegfried kept his frantic steps from turning into a frightened run as he left the tribunal chamber; but his mind was less obedient than his feet, and it continued to leap ahead of him, looping relentlessly through Natil's testimony, dragging him toward panic.

Impossible though her story was, it was also absolute truth. Siegfried understood this instinctively, not only with a physical certainty that put a cold hand into his heart, but with the profound spiritual recognition with which the fallen confront what has been forever lost. And so he knew without doubt that the ancient legends so long dismissed as the maunderings of old crones and toothless widows were, impossibly, not legends at all, but fact.

Elves. Elves! Old Aloysius Cranby had not been a deluded fool, but had instead been setting his finger on the pulse of Adria!

But as for Natil's claim that she was the last, that with her death the threat would end, Siegfried would not allow himself to believe a word of it, for it was refuted by every instinct of the trained Inquisitor. Demons were sustained by the energies of hell, and therefore, far from being the last, Natil instead could not but be only one among countless others who were even now spreading their subtle poisons into Christian hearts. Perhaps it had been the Elves who had strengthened the Alpine Waldensians in their resistance. Perhaps they had also been responsible for the continuing outbreaks of Dolcianism and Lollardy in the passes of the Aleser Mountains. Perhaps . . .

. . . perhaps they even had a hand in the constant upwelling of heresy in Furze.

Siegfried's mind, racing, constructed with frightened speed a huge conspiracy, a network of infernal plots and snares that was, even now, reaching out to envelope all of Christendom. Of *course* Natil would claim to be the last, of *course* she would smile and treat him with devious compassion, of *course* she would speak with power and inhuman cunning: having been captured, her sole purpose was to lull him into a complacent acceptance of his victory . . . and so cause his downfall.

It was imperative that she be burnt immediately, and Siegfried was heading for his office with the intention of writing the necessary orders himself. But though he climbed the stairs with his thoughts hammering at him that Natil was a demon, that he had talked with her face to face not only in the tribunal chamber, but also in the comparative intimacy of his office, that such unmitigated cheek on the part of a demon was an ominous statement about the intentions of the Prince of Darkness, still Siegfried could not help but think, sadly, of what a sore trial it was to be a human being: to so readily see, touch, and speak with corporeal representatives of evil, and at the same time to be so distanced from the absolute goodness of God. God was hidden. Transcendent. Perceptible only through faith.

Adoro te devote, latens deitas.

Hidden. Hidden. But the demons—

"Lord Inquisitor!"

Siegfried nearly cried out. But no, this was no diabolical force come to carry him away, but only a servant of the Inquisition. "What do you want?"

"Some people ha' cam t' see you, Lord Inquisitor. There's a rich man down there."

Siegfried had no time for men, rich or not. With a continent-wide assault on Holy Church staring him in the face, he found himself with an armory full of feathers and milkweed pods, for the coffers of the Inquisition were all but empty.

He needed power, power and money. "Later," he said, preparing to brush past the servant.

"I told him you were busy, Lord Inquisitor," said the man, "but he wan't take no for an answer."

The wealthy were all alike: arrogant and demanding. But the thought of money made Siegfried pause. "You say he is rich?"

"Mor'n rich, brother. He's Jacob Aldernacht hi'self!"

Siegfried stood, struck. His hands clenched. Suddenly, he had no more doubts about God or Divine Providence. "O Lord," he said softly, "into mine hands hast Thou delivered him!"

"Brother Siegfried?"

Siegfried grabbed the servant by the shoulders. "Who is with him? Many?"

"He's got abou' a dozen soldiers wi' him, brother."

"Where are they?"

"Downstairs."

Siegfried tallied up the opposing sides in a moment. Jacob had a dozen. Well, that was all right, for the Lord had hundreds. And soon, very soon, the Lord would have thousands. The money of Jacob Aldernacht himself—servant of devils, co-conspirator with Elves—would see to that.

"Tell Jacob to come up to my office," he said. "I will speak with him. Alone. His men will wait down in the courtyard." He glanced at the servant. "Down in the courtyard," he repeated.

"Aye, Brother Siegfried."

"And then tell the captain of the guard that I want fifty armed men outside my office door as soon as possible. At my word are they to enter. Do you understand?"

"E'erything, master."

"Good man. God bless you."

The servant trotted off and, at a shout from Siegfried, increased his pace to a run.

The Inquisitor found that his heart was beating fast with the nearness of opportunity. Here it was. Minutes away. God had done His part, and now Siegfried would reciprocate. "Oh, my Lord and my God," he said softly, "give me strength."

But God had already given Siegfried strength, and it seemed that, with the sudden appearance of Jacob Aldernacht, He had given the Inquisitor something else, too: an assurance of His presence, an assurance that, yes, someday His humble and dutiful servant would look up to a sky split wide open by divine decree, and see, without the slightest trace of intervening shroud or veil, the face of his Creator.

Siegfried climbed the last flight of steps with a light heart.

* * *

"The Inquisitor wi' see you now."

Jacob nodded curtly to the servant. Generous handfuls of Aldernacht gold had quickly produced information about Natil, opening the lips of guard, informer, and citizen alike. Yes, she had entered the town. Yes, she had been looking for help for the girl who was with her. Yes, they had both been arrested by the Inquisition and led off to the House of God.

It had all been very simple: loyalties to Siegfried and fear of prosecution had crumbled before the promise of a few coins.

"The rest of your men must wait here," the servant continued. "The Inquisitor is a busy man."

"Yes, yes. Of course he is." Jacob did not bother to conceal his hostility. "He has to worry about burning harpers and shawm players, doesn't he?"

The servant stared. Insolence? Or a dull acceptance of the fact that, in Furze, the Inquisitor's word was law? "They must wait here."

Jacob wondered for a moment what a sack of gold would do for the servant's attitude, but he shrugged inwardly and started up the steps toward the doorway. He already knew what gold would do. He could buy the servant. He could buy anyone in Furze.

Manarel slid from his horse and laid a hand on his master's arm. "A moment, Mister Jacob."

The servant had paused at the door, waiting, but Manarel calmly conferred with one of his men, then took a coil of rope from one of the saddle packs. Slinging it over his shoulder, he bowed to Jacob. "I'll be coming with you, master."

Jacob gave Manarel a nod and started up toward the door again. Manarel was a big man, and could not but add to his master's words an air of intimidation that, alone, even gold could not convey. Siegfried had taken Harold, and now he had taken Natil: Jacob was going to make him understand that he was in a great deal of trouble.

But as the old man followed the servant along the interminable corridors and up the flight after flight of stairs that led to Siegfried's office, he could not help but wonder why the harper had become so idiotically important to him. She was, after all, only a musician, and Jacob, who had possessed no appreciation of music to begin with, had gained little during her tenure. For a corridor or two, then, he tried to put the whole affair down to revenge, to a determination to reclaim the harper because she had left him. But it was not that. And so, as he climbed another flight of stairs, he tried to consider it in terms of property: Siegfried, after all, had unjustly appropriated an Aldernacht servant. But it was not that either.

As he stepped out into the short corridor that led to Siegfried's office, then, he had to confront the truth. He was trying to save Natil because he *liked* her. Because he, in what was perhaps inexcusable vanity, believed that she, perhaps, liked him. Because she had played for him, advised him, listened to him, and had never—not once—given even the slightest indication that she was more interested in Jacob Aldernacht's money than in Jacob Aldernacht himself.

And that was it. He was trying to save her because she was good. Because his own family had turned out to be anything but good. Because, even in the flinty hardness of his avaricious and cynical heart, he yearned for that goodness.

Yes, that was it. And he would never tell anyone about it, either.

The servant, pausing at a door, caught sight of Manarel, who, silent as a shadow, had been following right behind Jacob. "The Inquisitor said that you were t' cam alone, Mister Jacob."

"I *am* alone," snapped the old man. "This is my steward. He's like a secretary: he's not here."

The servant was obviously about to repeat Siegfried's prohibition, but at the sound of sudden movement in some corridor far below—footsteps, shuffling, muffled voices—he nodded, opened the door, and bowed them both in.

Siegfried was waiting at his desk, looking very calm and composed. He did not rise, nor at first did he even acknowledge Jacob's presence. He shot a suspicious glance at Manarel, but the steward found a stool at the back of the room, sat down . . . and might not have been there any more. With a barely perceptible shrug, Siegfried proceeded to ignore him, too.

The door closed. Jacob stood across the desk from the

Inquisitor, folded his arms. He knew the game. He had played it often enough himself to know just how to put an end to it.

"All right, Brother Siegfried," he said, "and a very good morning to you. God bless and all that. Where's Natil?"

Siegfried tried hard not to flinch, but Jacob saw the flicker in his black eyes. Yes, he had Natil, and, moreover, he appeared—surprisingly—to be a little nervous about that fact.

Jacob suppressed a thin smile. Siegfried had good reason to be nervous!

"Who are you, sir?" The reply was measured, cool. If Siegfried had been shaken by Jacob's blunt approach, he was determined not to show it.

"I'm Jacob Aldernacht. But you knew that already, didn't you?"

"Aldernacht. Ah, yes. The wool cooperative . . ."

Jacob glanced back at Manarel. The steward was staring off into space.

" . . . Paul Drego, and the others." Siegfried spoke casually, disinterestedly, but Jacob knew that the Inquisitor could not have been more interested had there been a chest of florins on the desk before him. "Why are you here?"

"You now that, too," said Jacob. "You've taken my harper. I want her back."

He did not really expect Siegfried to comply instantly with his demand, but he nonetheless felt his anger rising when the Inquisitor merely examined him levelly and answered: "I believe I might have someone named Natil in custody. That, of course, is no affair of yours. Or perhaps it is: the Inquisition will decide."

"You know damn well it's my affair."

"Do you know why she is here?"

"I assume you've trumped up some charges of heresy against her."

Siegfried's eyebrows lifted innocently. "Trumped up?"

A sound, something between a scrape and a shuffle, came from the corridor. Jacob glanced at the door. So, he noticed, did Manarel. He noticed also that Siegfried did his best to ignore it.

"Trumped up," he repeated. "Natil's about as heretical as I am."

"Indeed," said Siegfried with another flicker in his eyes, "I know that."

"You know? Then why don't you—"

A bump from the corridor. Siegfried was staring at him with a curious sort of appraisal in his expression. The thought struck Jacob that there quite possibly was more going on in this room—and outside of it—than he knew.

All right, then. The direct approach. He dragged up a stool, sat down, leaned toward Siegfried. "I'll be frank with you, brother . . ."

"That would be in your best interest."

". . . how much do I have to pay you in order to secure Natil's release?"

"You say that you are as much of a heretic as she?"

The counter-question caught Jacob off guard, and he was about to reply to it when he realized the insidiousness of the trap that gaped before him. Obviously, in Siegfried's opinion, Natil was already guilty and condemned. And now, just as obviously, the Inquisitor was attempting to formulate an accusation against her master, too, thereby dragging the Aldernacht fortune straight into the Inquisitorial purse.

Jacob fixed him with a cold, gray look. "I'm not even going to dignify that with an answer, Siegfried," he said. "I'm not here to play games. You know the truth."

"Indeed." Siegfried looked pained and hopeful both. "Indeed I do."

"Shut up. You know that you've got about as much reason to hold Natil as you do to clap irons on this desk. In my entire life I've never met anyone as absolutely good as that harper."

"I believe you when you say that you believe she is good," said the Dominican.

There was an increasing sense of presence and movement on the other side of the door. Jacob glanced uneasily at Manarel, wishing that he would get up and . . . do something. But the steward continued to stare off into space.

"And I will tell you what I believe is good," Siegfried continued with great deliberateness. "I believe that what

Holy Church teaches is good. I believe that the law of God is good.''

''So I believe,'' said Jacob impatiently.

Siegfried smiled. ''You believe that I believe it. But while I believe some things, I know others. I know, for instance, that you are guilty of the most pernicious and evil heresy about which it has ever been my duty and trial to hear.''

''Oh, Christ!''

''Do not blaspheme. I know about you because I have heard it from Natil's lips.''

Jacob stared, startled by the Inquisitor's brazen lie.

''And you—trying now to bribe me in order to secure her release—give proof to her words.'' Siegfried eyed him. ''Do not attempt to deny it, Jacob Aldernacht. I *know*.''

Jacob rose up, heart laboring, fists clenched. But Siegfried did not move.

''God is merciful,'' said the Inquisitor. ''Confess.''

''The hell I will,'' said Jacob, and, throwing himself across the table, he seized Siegfried by his cowl, dragged him forward, and slammed his face down on the desk top. ''You sanctimonious son of a bitch, you got my shawm player, you got my harper, and now you're trying to get me, too!''

Siegfried, his nose broken and bleeding, struggled against the old man's outraged grip. ''You fool,'' he said. ''I already have you!'' He broke free, shoved Jacob away. ''Guards!''

The door flew open, and Jacob saw that the hallway was crowded with men. They wore the livery of David a'Freux, and their weapons were in their hands.

Blood was running from Siegfried's broken nose and dribbling down his chin. Shaking with emotion and eagerness, he pointed at Jacob. ''Arrest him in the name of God!''

But Manarel was suddenly in motion. He lunged at the Dominican, lifted him out from behind the desk as though he were a puppy, and hurled him straight into the mass of men and weapons that were just then pressing forward. The monastic projectile struck them squarely, toppled them back. In a moment, Manarel had slammed and barred the door.

Jacob was rather surprised: he felt little fear, only shock and surprise and incredulity. This was impossible. This was absurd. This simply could not be happening. And, damn it all, Siegfried was going to pay for it!

"We're . . . we're in trouble, Manarel," was all he could manage.

"Yes, master," said the steward. He was already uncoiling the rope he had brought. "But not so much as we'd be if we were now in chains."

The murmurings in the corridor were rendered unintelligible by the thick door, but Jacob heard Siegfried giving orders as Manarel shoved the Inquisitor's heavy desk flush against the wall beneath the window. The steward fastened one end of the rope to it, dropped the other outside.

"We must hurry," he said. "Climb on my back, Mister Jacob."

Jacob glanced at the door. "Manarel, Siegfried didn't accuse you. But if you help me . . ."

The steward waved away his master's concern. "I know about people like Siegfried," he said. "People like Siegfried never worry about whether people like me are guilty or innocent. I'm your man, Mister Jacob. That's all he needs to know."

A thud shook the door. The bar vibrated, but did not yield.

"Come, master: we need to be away before they realize what we've done."

Touched by Manarel's loyalty, Jacob did as he was told. Manarel bent over the sill for a moment, examined the one-hundred-foot drop, and then he swung a leg through the window and took hold of the rope. As though unaware of the weight of the old man on his back, he descended quickly to the ground, the rope slipping through his gloved hands with an audible whir.

The fast plunge made Jacob dizzy, but when his sight cleared, he found himself in an alley outside the walls of the House of God. The traffic in Furze was as light as the trade, and the alley was, in fact, deserted. Manarel's strategy had worked: if anyone had noticed the odd but fleeting sight of two men descending pick-a-back down the outside of the tower, they had not yet appeared to ask any questions.

"We'll have to hurry," said Manarel. "In a minute, they'll discover what we've done and have the city gates closed."

Jacob looked up and down the alley, then up at the tower from which they had escaped. He still could not believe it. "What . . . what about the rest of the men?"

Manarel's voice was matter-of-fact. "They'll cut their way out if they can. I gave them orders before we went into the tower. There's nothing more we can do for them." A horn blew within the House of God. Manarel looked up with a white face. "We'll have to run."

"We'll never make it through the gates."

"Master . . ."

Jacob was still shocky: he could speak of capture and death as though they were relevant only to someone else. "We'll never make it."

Another horn call. Shouting.

Jacob thought of Siegfried, wished that he had been able to smash his nose on the table once or twice more. "That son of a bitch."

"Master, please."

"All right, Manarel. Let's run. You'll have to carry me, and we'll have to find a place to hide."

The steward stooped, helped Jacob clamber onto his back. Hands cupped beneath his master's knees, he started off. "Shall we go to the house of Paul Drego, Mister Jacob?"

Jacob hung on, bouncing with each step. "That's the first place they'll look. And by now Paul's probably in trouble himself." Jacob was casting about in his mind for something that he could do, but all he could recall about Furze was the fact that its inhabitants—with a few marked exceptions—would do anything for a handful of gold.

Two guards appeared before them as they burst out of the alley. Manarel freed a fist, knocked them down, resumed his grip on Jacob, and took off around a corner. Zig-zagging through the maze of narrow, rubbish-choked streets, he wove among old and ill-kept carts, darted past startled housewives with empty baskets, cut between pairs of despondent horses. Always, though, no matter how he turned, he was moving away from the House of God.

Jacob jounced and bumped on Manarel's back. The fear was finally beginning to sink in now, and he felt the chill in his chest deepen. He had thought himself safe because of his money, but it was the odor of money that was drawing Siegfried and his hounds ever closer, just as it had drawn Francis, just as it had drawn Edvard and Norman, just as it had drawn Marjorie.

He could expect little from his family. Josef was dead, and with the entire estate in danger of confiscation, Francis and the rest would doubtless do anything in their power to preserve it, even if that meant denouncing the family patriarch.

As though denunciation would accomplish anything in the long run! Jacob knew about the Inquisition, and he was beginning to understand Siegfried, too. The Dominican had gotten a whiff of gold and now would not be satisfied until he had every last penny of the Aldernacht millions.

Manarel stumbled, almost fell. Jacob's heart throbbed, and a deep ache suddenly flowed like oil down his left arm. Siegfried, he reflected, would probably never have the chance to burn him, or, if he did, he would only be burning a corpse as dead as those he occasionally evicted from the churchyard so as to try and punish a heretic dead for fifty years or more.

Recovering, Manarel ran on. No pursuers. Yet.

But Jacob was not worried about death, for death could not worry someone who had come to find life a tedious affair of betrayal and disappointment. It was, rather, a raging sense of pride and anger that shoved his heart back to its duty and burned out the ache in his arm with outraged fire. His fortune, given over to the Inquisition? Never!

But there did not seem to be much that he could do about it, and without a generous supply of gold at hand, he was going to find that hiding places in Furze were going to be very hard to come by in a few hours.

Where did one find honesty and courage in a place as hungry as Furze?

And the answer suddenly came to him. Yes. Of course. It was obvious. The one place in Furze where Siegfried and his hounds would not think to look. The one place in Furze where Jacob could be assured of a fair hearing, a hand of friendship, and not a single question about money.

Oh, money would come up eventually. Jacob would make sure that it did. But certainly it would not come up in any way that Siegfried expected, and Francis and his little nest of snakes would certainly not approve. But that was all right. Jacob approved. In fact, as he thudded up and down on Manarel's back like a sack of rusty coins, he suddenly found it quite funny, and his old, cracked voice suddenly cut loose with a joyous guffaw.

"Master?" Manarel sounded worried.

"It's all right, man," said Jacob. "I haven't lost my senses." Though the air was rank with heat and ripe with the pollution of the city, he inhaled deeply and grinned. No dungeons for this old man, Siegfried! "No, not at all. In fact, I think I've just found them!"

CHAPTER 25

At the end of five hours, the church bells were ringing nones, Siegfried's broken and hugely swollen nose was swathed in a mass of white bandages, and, despite the powers of the Inquisition, which admitted no interference from any agency, earthly or spiritual, Jacob Aldernacht had not been found.

The complex network of informers that Siegfried had built up over twenty years could ensnare even the smallest and most insignificant heresy, but it could not catch Jacob. No matter that the gates of the city had been sealed within minutes after Manarel had slammed and barred the office door, no matter that it was physically impossible for the two men even to have reached the gates before the alarm had been sounded: Jacob and Manarel had, apparently, vanished.

"Look agaid," said Siegfried, his damaged nose precluding anything approximating his usually precise speech.

Fra Giovanni spread his hands. "Brother, they are gone."

"They caddot fly over the wall. They are dot debods." But by his own words, Siegfried was reminded uneasily of Natil, who still hung in chains in the dungeon. Perhaps some of them were not demons, but others had admitted to his face that they were indeed just that.

But Jacob himself was human. Of that Siegfried was certain. Human and heretical. "They are here," he said. "Id Furze. Fid theb. Search the streets, look in the basebedts, the cellars, whatever. Fid theb!"

And the searchers looked, hunted, questioned. And since they still could not find Jacob, Siegfried, panicked, ordered them to take others. Paul Drego and his family were arrested in the early evening. So was Simon the Jew. James the furrier and his sweetheart were surprised

in the middle of feeding early strawberries to one another. Singly and in groups, all the members of the cooperative were led off to the House of God to join the
Aldernacht men, who had been arrested after a bloody
fight in the courtyard that morning.

Siegfried questioned them himself, his bandaged nose
waving and bobbing as he alternately raged, pleaded, and
pounded on the wooden surface of the tribunal desk, setting the quills of his secretaries and scribes flying over
their pages in an attempt to keep pace both with the Inquisitor's furious flow of interrogation and his adenoidal
parody of nasal consonants.

"I dod't wadt to hear about your biserable bodey! I
wadt you to tell me about Elves!"

"Elves?" said James, who, still as naked as he had
been when dragged from his bed, terrified at the sudden-
ness of his arrest, and worried nearly to tears about his
beloved, appeared to be determined to cooperate if anyone would tell him what he was supposed to cooperate
with.

Siegfried flushed, pounded. "Elves! Dabbit! Do dot
pretedt to be stupid!"

Even Fra Giovanni was taken aback by the Inquisitor's
oath. Siegfried was a pious man. Siegfried never swore.

But Siegfried was swearing now with all the passionate
rage of a man who had just found himself within arm's
reach of his most bitter and deathless enemy. These
wretched idolaters and demon worshipers were not going
to get away with feigning ignorance in *his* tribunal. He
would torture all of them himself if he had to. He would
strip their skin and muscle down to the bone. He would
twist the needles into their joints until they wept for
mercy. Even now he could feel the mechanisms under
his thumbs: the knives, the oil smooth twist of the screws,
the quick scoop that would leave a man's eyeball dangling
on his cheek as he screamed . . .

"Dabbit!" he cried. *"Elves!"*

"Elves," seconded Giovanni, who was, himself, still
shaking from the interview with Natil. "You know." He
looked with uncertainty at Siegfried. "Elves."

"I . . . d-dan understand," said James, who now began to stammer with confusion and fright. "What about
Elves? I d-d-din't know they were heretical." Siegfried

glared at him, and he fell to his knees, lifted clasped hands. "I didn't e'en know they were real."

"They are real," said Siegfried, pounding once again. He remembered Natil's pale, lovely face, her long dark hair, the way her slender hands had clenched when she had spoken. A demon. A demon with all the pernicious beauty and eloquence of demons. And she had possessed the audacity to condemn the Inquisition itself! Well, her insolent words had done nothing for her, and since they had in fact alerted him to her plot, Siegfried decided that she could rot in her dark cell until all of her co-conspirators—including Jacob—joined her. They could all burn together, then, just like the Spirituals and the Dolcinians. "I know they are real. I heard it frob the lips of od of theb this bordig!"

"This morning," Giovanni translated.

"Shutup, Giovaddi!"

The friar cringed. The pens of the secretaries scratched frantically.

"Please, Brother Siegfried," said James, "I dan know anything about this! I really dan! I a'ways thought Elves were a fairy tale!"

"Take hib away! Brig id de dext od!"

Weeping, James was dragged away. But the next defendant to be brought before the tribunal was his sweetheart, and, with a cry, he reached out to her as they passed one another by the door . . . for which temerity he was cuffed senseless.

And Jacob was still missing.

"Bless me, Father, for I have sinned. Uh . . . should I say *Your Excellency*?"

"Father is fine, my son. How long has it been since your last confession?"

"Oh . . . Lord . . . I don't know. Years."

Albrecht looked aghast at the man who knelt before him in the quiet dimness of the curtained study. "Years?"

Jacob shrugged and, in order to satisfy the bishop, dredged up unpleasant memories. "I think Francis made his first Communion about then." Yes, Francis had made his first Communion, and then Marjorie had left. And

then Marjorie had returned. And how long had that been?
"Thirty years or so."

Albrecht crossed himself. "Go on, my son."

Jacob looked up, exasperated. "Excellency, I'm as old
as you are. Don't call me *my son*. Anyway, sons and
grandsons don't do anything except stick a whore in your
room and hope she fucks you to death."

Albrecht crossed himself again. "As . . . ah . . . as
you say. I'm sure you know more about that than I do,
Jacob." He brightened. "Jacob. Is that better?"

"Much."

"Go on, then. What have you to confess?"

Jacob almost laughed. Where did one start? "I've been
a wretch, Excellency. I've lied and cheated all my life.
And I've gotten money together just for the pleasure of
getting money . . . so I guess that makes me covetous,
too."

"We're all sinners, Jacob."

"Not like me, Excellency."

"But—"

"Leave it at that!" Jacob lifted his wizened face,
glared. "I took pride in my faults." He chortled. "So
there's another one."

"You're still proud."

"Of course I'm still proud! And I'm still covetous and
vengeful and devious and generally nasty." Jacob cleared
his throat, squared his shoulders. "I'm an Aldernacht."

Albrecht looked unnerved. "Ah . . . just so."

"But I want you to know, Excellency, that I've never,
never had anything to do with any heresy." Jacob considered for a moment, then added: "I've been too busy
making money to worry about anything like that."

"Indeed." Albrecht all but squirmed, and Jacob could
understand his discomfort. Two men, obviously on the
run, had knocked at his back door in the middle of the
afternoon and asked for shelter. No questions for now,
thank you. Explanations will be coming later.

And, yes, explanations were indeed coming, but Albrecht already looked as though he might well have preferred that they had been indefinitely postponed. "Well,
I believe you, Jacob."

"You do?" Jacob squinted at Albrecht through glinting spectacles. The bishop had been so matter-of-fact

about his opinion that Jacob could not help but wonder whether he were a little simple-minded. Or at least naive.

Albrecht examined Jacob, puzzled. "I said that I believe you. I ate with you and drank with you. We told impious stories together. I know you better than you think, Jacob. And I certainly know that you're no heretic."

"Does it bother you that Siegfried thinks otherwise?"

Understanding suddenly came to Albrecht. "Siegfried? What . . . what about Siegfried?"

"Do you remember Natil, my harper?"

"Ah, yes. Natil. Charming woman."

"Siegfried's taken her. He's going to burn her."

Albrecht clenched his hands and could not manage words for some time, but at last he shrugged helplessly. "He's burned many. And I've been able to do nothing about any of it."

Kneeling before the bishop, the picture of the repentant sinner, Jacob felt a gleam in his eye. A few minutes more, and Albrecht would be able to do a great deal about it. "You believe that Siegfried is wrong, Excellency?"

"I told you that I did. I've come to doubt the entire Inquisitorial process. After all . . ." The bishop looked glum. ". . . I've seen what it's done in Furze."

"All right. Well, now Siegfried's accused me of heresy, too."

"Oh . . . dear God, this is absurd!"

"I'm glad you think so."

Albrecht had grown agitated, and, rising from his chair, he began to pace up and down the study, wavering each time his bad knee threatened to fail him. It was a shabby little room, for what little money ever came into Albrecht's hands was inevitably funneled either into the purses of the poor or the fabric fund for the cathedral. Worn furniture, worn carpet, worn books. Only the curtains were fine and thick, as though the good bishop had decided that dark, muffling shields against the avarice and duplicity of the world were a wise and justifiable investment.

"Oh . . . dear God," he said again. "And there's nothing I can do. Even the popes haven't been able to stop the Inquisition. There was the whole thing over at

Carcassonne. And at Albi and Cordes. The Inquisitor simply ignored the papal order."

He caught himself. "But I was hearing your confession, Jacob. I'm sorry." He resumed his seat. "Heresy does not number among your sins. I believe that, but I am afraid that I can't protect you from Siegfried. Do you want absolution for your sins?"

"Absolution would be nice," said Jacob, still on his knees. "But I'm not sorry for what I've done."

Albrecht shrugged. "Most of us aren't, Jacob. We confess, and we have utterly no intention of changing anything at all about the way we behave. God, I think, understands." He made the sign of the cross over the impenitent. *"Ego te absolvo,"* he said formally.

"But I'm not sorry."

"Think of it as a second chance. We're human beings, after all. We need lots of second chances."

A second chance. Well, thought Jacob, why not? If he was indeed going to throw away a life of money and privilege and power, it was only fitting that his soul and heart should receive some kind of spiritual scrubbing. He feared, though, that the latter would more than likely burst under the unaccustomed strain, for a thick coating of sin was, doubtless, all that was holding it together. "All right," he said, nodding. He bent his head, wondered why his eyes felt damp.

Albrecht took his hand, raised him to his feet. "But I'm not sure what penance to give you, Jacob."

Jacob grinned, feeling again that wicked gleam in his eye. "That's all right, Excellency. I'll supply the penance. Or, rather, I'll supply the bargain."

Albrecht looked puzzled. "Bargain?"

"A bargain. In good old Aldernacht style." Jacob guided Albrecht to the table. Kneeling was for confession. Tables were for bargains. And he had a bargain indeed to strike with the bishop! "How would you like that cathedral of yours to be finished, Excellency?"

Albrecht stood, a little stunned. Jacob pushed him down into a chair, took a seat on the other side of the table. For the second time in a single day, he reflected wryly, he was sitting across from a church official. But this time the results were going to be considerably different.

"I . . . would like that very much," said the bishop. "Good."

"But I'd want to help the wool cooperative first."

Jacob stared. "You'd . . ."

Albrecht was unfazed. "They need it more than I. Furze needs it more than I. The cathedral is . . ." He shrugged sheepishly. ". . . my vanity, I'm afraid."

"Uh . . . yes . . . of course." Jacob felt almost dizzy in the presence of a man who was so undoubtedly good— or irredeemably mad. "Well, Paul and the others have probably been arrested by now. Siegfried wants the co-operative money as well as everything else."

Albrecht paled, then turned red. "That . . . that bastard of a Teuton! That barbarian! We try to pull ourselves out of the mire, and all he can see is another chance to further the Inquisition! I . . . I mean, I'll . . ."

Jacob held up a hand, but, inwardly, he was pleased. So Albrecht was not quite the perfect saint after all. Well, that was just fine, because a man worked better with a little smolder of ire in him. "Hear me out, Excellency," he said. "You'll be able to help the cooperative, take care of Furze . . ." He paused, smiled meaningfully. ". . . *and* get your cathedral."

"Oh, come now, Jacob—"

"Hear me out." Jacob shook off his last remaining doubts. Were he doing this out of piety, he would probably thereby ensure himself a place in Paradise. But piety had nothing to do with it, and so he was probably going to find himself in hell anyway. "I'm going to make you a wealthy man, Excellency. I'm going to make you the wealthiest man in Europe."

Comprehension suddenly came to Albrecht, but it was a comprehension tinged with horror. "You . . . you can't mean that—"

"Be quiet," Jacob snapped. "Listen. You'll be able to put Furze back on its feet—isn't that what you want?— and you'll be able to get your cathedral built, maybe even within your lifetime."

"But—"

"Hush." Jacob shoved his spectacles back up to the bridge of his nose. "This is what I'm going to do. I'm going to transfer ownership of my estate and my company—money, lands, factories, flocks, everything—to you.''

''But—''

''On two conditions.''

Albrecht stopped protesting, looked at Jacob carefully and (Jacob thought with a certain pleasure) shrewdly. ''What conditions . . . my son?''

Jacob almost laughed. ''You have to free Natil. And, I suppose, you have to clear me of heresy, otherwise Siegfried gets everything by confiscation.''

Unexpected as they were, the conditions left Albrecht reeling. ''Yes . . . yes . . . I suppose so,'' he said distantly. ''That would have to—'' But he suddenly came to himself. ''You're giving . . . everything?''

''Everything. You bring in Mattias, and I'll draw up the articles this afternoon.''

''But you can't do that, Jacob!''

Jacob was on his feet in an instant, feeling his frail heart laboring with excitement. His left arm ached again, but he fought down the pain. No, it was not time. He had things to do. He had to diddle his family, and then he had to diddle Siegfried of Magdeburg. And diddle them he would! ''I certainly can,'' he said. ''I'm Jacob Aldernacht, and I'll do anything I damned well please!''

Albrecht stared at him for a time, stunned and mute. Then reason reasserted itself. ''But I can't meet your conditions,'' he said as though relieved. ''I have no say in the workings of the Inquisition. Siegfried is beyond my control.''

Jacob smiled. ''He's beyond mine, Excellency. But he's not beyond yours.''

''How am I supposed to do something that the popes themselves can't do?''

Jacob felt the gleam in his eye again. This was business. This was his life. Good shoes, a shrewd head, and money in your purse! In the name of God and profit!

He turned, strolled to the window, pulled open the heavy curtains. Sunlight spilled into the room, and the faint and rather half-hearted cries of the despondent street vendors came with it.

Furze. Impoverished Furze. Here, the wool cooperative toadied for gold, the Inquisition confiscated it, the people argued and fought and betrayed for it, the informers and guards and secretaries and officials and judges and jailers and torturers who inhabited the House of God all worked for their tiny allotment of it. And whatever they got was never enough.

"I'll show you how, Albrecht," he said. "I'll show you how to do it. I'll draw up the papers, and Manarel and Mattias can witness them, and then I'll show you. All I ask after that is that you free Natil."

"Free Natil!" cried the bishop. "God bless you, Jacob, I'll free everyone!"

"Whatever." Jacob was looking down at the streets. In a few years, Furze would be a different city. Years? In an hour or two! "It's your money, after all."

Dame Agnes, abbess of Shrinerock, was both distressed and bewildered by the sudden appearance at her gate of a band of armed men and a heavy wagon. The men, for that matter, seemed just as distressed and bewildered as the abbess, and looked like nothing so much as a troop of boys who had been caught smearing someone's door knocker with red paint.

Their leader attempted to make the best of it by assuming a manner that was, at once, both official and apologetic. "Sorry to disturb you, Abbess," he said with a salute. "But we've got an order here to deliver this shipment to Shrinerock Abbey." He jerked a thumb at the wagon, then squinted at the high wall and the tower of the abbey church. "This *is* Shrinerock Abbey, isn't it?"

"Yes, my good man, it is." Agnes was breaking enclosure by talking to this burly soldier, but intuition told her that this was nothing that the old porter should handle, and in any case, breaking enclosure inevitably seemed to be a part of an abbess' job. Her nuns, however, every last one of them—with the exception of the new novice, Dinah—were leaning over the wall, gawking out of windows, peering through lattices and cracks . . . and this really would not do. What would she say to Bishop Albrecht when next he came?

"Well, then," said the man. "Here we are." He sat for a moment as though expecting instant comprehension on the part of the abbess. Comprehension, though, was not forthcoming. He sat a little longer, then fidgeted. "Aren't we?"

"What orders, sir? What shipment?"

"Well, Abbess, we were originally supposed to deliver it to Furze, but a messenger showed up on the road with a letter from our master, Jacob Aldernacht, saying to bring it here." He dug into his pouch, brought out a letter cylinder. Its cut cords dangled and swung.

"Jacob Aldernacht? Here?" Agnes took the cylinder, unrolled and examined its contents. The name of Jacob Aldernacht was familiar to her, and the order did indeed specify Shrinerock Abbey. But it did nothing to clear up the mystery. "Why don't you . . . ?"

She found herself staring up at the soldier. Having ridden up the mountain in the June sun, he was dusty and hot, but though his face was beaded with sweat, and though his mustache drooped, he was nonetheless a handsome fellow, and his arms were thick and strong and built, Agnes suddenly fancied, for encircling a maiden's waist.

She colored, swallowed, and . . .

Nichil est deterius tali vita,
Cum enim sim petulans et lasciva

. . . danced through her head. A handsome fellow indeed!

"Sir," she said, pulling her wits together and making sure that she looked anywhere but at the soldier. "I don't doubt that your master has given you these orders, but I'm obliged to inform you that you simply can't—"

"Dame Agnes!" called a cheery voice from some distance down the road. "A moment, please! Dame Agnes! Oh, do not send them away! A moment, please!"

Agnes caught herself looking at the soldier again. "Ah . . . Mattias?"

Albrecht's head clerk came galloping up, clerical robes flying. "Oh, dear!" he said. "I had hoped to get here first. Everything is perfectly all right, Dame Agnes. Bishop Albrecht sends his blessings and his permission."

"Permission?"

"To accept the shipment." Mattias beamed down at her. If the soldiers had been painting the door knocker, then the head clerk had obviously been pilfering melons . . . and felt not a bit guilty about it.

Agnes stood before the gate as though to stem the advancing tide of masculinity that lapped at the cloisters. "Mattias," she said, feeling not at all up to being a breakwater, "what exactly *is* this shipment."

Mattias shrugged. "Ah . . . I am afraid—"

"Mattias!"

"Gold," he said promptly.

Agnes was entirely awash. "Gold?"

The soldier spoke up. "One hundred thousand florins, ma'am." He colored. "I mean, Abbess."

"One hundred thou—"

"It is quite all right with the bishop," said Mattias. "Really. He sent this . . ." And he thrust a sealed parchment at Agnes.

Mechanically, she broke the seals, forced her eyes to read. "One hundred thousand . . ." Her voice trailed off.

"Florins, Dame Agnes."

But it was all there in the letter, written in a hand that she recognized as Albrecht's own, sealed with the episcopal signet. Agnes and her nuns were to assume temporary guardianship of one hundred thousand gold florins. A certain sum was to be released immediately to Mattias, and the rest was to be dispensed as called for by either Albrecht himself or a properly credentialed deputy.

"One . . ." Agnes, used to counting out abbey finances in pennies and coppers, stumbled over the sum. ". . . hundred thousand florins."

"In gold," said Mattias brightly.

"What . . ." Agnes was becoming increasingly annoyed with herself. Could she not put on a more competent face for these men? "I mean, why . . ." Were nuns of the rule of Holy Benedict such nitwits that the appearance of a bunch of soldiers and a few chests of gold turned them into babbling hens? "I mean . . . by Our Lady . . ."

The soldier nodded to her. Yes, a handsome man . . . and (oh, God!) there it was again. "It's all right, Abbess," he said. "The men will behave themselves. We'll just unload this wherever you want, and then we'll be off."

"But . . ." Agnes gestured, speechless.

Mattias turned pointedly official. "Dame Agnes, do

you have any particular objection to executing the orders of Bishop Albrecht?''

His tone and his words cleared Agnes's head in a moment. "Ah . . . thank you, Mattias. No, not at all.'' She pretended to read both parchments over again, though she did not really see a word of either. "Well, everything appears to be in order here, sir,'' she said without looking at the soldier. "I will, of course, accept the shipment. But I'm afraid that, despite your assurances, I'll have to ask you to unload the money outside. I'll have my nuns take it in. The abbey is not for men, and we are, after all . . .'' She glanced up at the faces that were crowding forward at the windows and the lattices and atop the walls, spoke a little louder. ". . . enclosed.''

The faces did not budge, but the sound of a footstep made Agnes turn. Dinah, the novice, pale and clad in a habit that was more a suit of tatters than a nun's proper garb, had come out of the gate. Her eyes were downcast and red. She had showed up at the abbey gate in that habit and with those eyes, and in almost two weeks neither had changed in the slightest.

Agnes held out her hand to her. Even had the small woman not brought news of Omelda, Agnes would still have taken her in, for she had seen heartbreak in the small woman, and deep shock, and what looked like a profound and unremitting desire to flee—preferably away from life, preferably into the echoing dimness of an abbey church—all of which Agnes had recognized in herself . . . and in a part of her own life now long dead and buried.

"Dinah?''

The little novice took Agnes's hand, looked up at the men. "Is Master Manarel there?''

"No, ma'am,'' said the soldier. "He's off with Mister Jacob.''

"Oh. All right.'' Dinah considered. Then: "You can let them in, Dame Agnes. Manarel was an Aldernacht man, and these are Aldernacht men. Aldernacht men are good men, not at all like the Aldernachts themselves. I . . .'' Her eyes clouded, and she shrugged. "I know.''

Agnes suspected that Dinah's evaluation of Aldernacht men was not at all accurate, but she was touched enough by the novice's words to give permission for the soldiers to enter the abbey. The men, in turn, were obviously so shamed and flattered by such imbecilic trust that, after carefully counting out Mattias's prescribed allotment, they took the gold into the treasury, set it down, bowed to the nuns, and departed without the slightest impropriety.

Arms folded, still guarding her gate, Agnes watched them go. Mattias was at her side, holding a hastily scrawled receipt. "The bishop thanks you, Dame Agnes, for all your help."

"I could use less thanks and more explanations, Mattias."

"Well, I suppose you could," he said. "But that will have to come later. For now, you have His Excellency's gratitude." He smiled, bowed, and swung up to the back of his horse. His hand went to the heavy sack that was now strapped to his saddle, but his eyes, Agnes noticed, were on Dinah, who was standing off by herself, watching the retreating soldiers as though they were taking a piece of her heart with them.

Agnes felt protective toward the girl. "Is something wrong, Mattias?"

"Ah, no, Abbess," said the clerk. "Dinah there . . . she is new, is she not?"

"She is." Agnes was not about to offer any further information. She knew, and Dinah knew, and Dinah's confessor knew, and that was the end of it.

"Her habit . . ."

"Is a hand-me-down," said Agnes. "We've little money here, Mattias. You know that. We can't afford new clothes for everyone."

"Ah, yes," said Mattias. "I see." But to Agnes's surprise, he grinned.

"Mattias?"

A chuckle. "That is about to change, Dame Agnes." He laughed, and then he slapped his horse on the rump and galloped off down the road as quickly as he had galloped up, his voice trailing behind him like a flag. "All that is about to change!"

CHAPTER 26

Whispers.

Whispers in Furze. Whispers in the streets, in the alleys, in the taverns. Where once had been the bright-eyed silence of listening, there were now whispers. Whispers everywhere.

Siegfried heard them, saw looks exchanged and the sudden stilling of lips that had, a moment before, been whispering, uttering something to which he was not privy. At first he tried to ignore it all, to proceed with his work, to give this order for confiscation or that order for arrest, but the whispers continued: pressing in, intruding everywhere. And whether he interrogated prisoners, said mass, read his Office, ate, meditated, or longed for a vision of the divine, the whispers were there, drifting out of anteroom and pantry and alleyway, rubbing up against his thoughts like hungry cats.

"What is it, Giovaddi?"

"I-I don't know, Brother Siegfried."

Someone was whispering in the hall outside the office. Siegfried rose quickly and jerked the door open, but no one was there, not even the usual guard.

The Inquisitor discovered that he was sweating, discovered also that he was now hearing whispers from the stairwell. Feeling dizzy—it was the pain, it had to be the pain—he closed the door, leaned against it. So much to do, and so little gold with which to do it. Even the money taken from the Aldernacht men was hardly enough to begin the work.

To be sure, he had Natil, but he knew without a doubt that there were others. Was that it? Was that what the whispers were about? Was Satan marshaling his forces? And just how many Elves were there in Furze? How many demons walked beside mortals right here under the nose of the Inquisition, spreading their lies and their heresy, massing for . . .

Massing for attack?

He wiped his palms on his habit. He needed money. And therefore he needed Jacob Aldernacht. But the wily old sinner had *still* not revealed himself.

More whispers. Down in the dark street. Coming, apparently, through the walls. Drifting through the air like smoke from the kitchens. ''We bust fidd out, Giovaddi. We bust fidd out.''

Giovanni shook his head. ''The only word I've been able to make out so far is *gold*.''

''Gold?''

''I hear it all the time. It's always gold they're talking about.''

''Gold.'' Siegfried pondered, feeling cold despite his persistent sweating. ''Why gold? Did Jacob's bodey show up?''

''There's been not a sign of it.''

Siegfried found himself staring at the bloodstained dent that his nose had left on the surface of the desk. He looked away quickly, feeling again the white hot pain.

''I've confiscated the houses and the possessions of the wool cooperative, as you ordered,'' said Giovanni. ''Perhaps that explains it.''

Siegfried fastened on the explanation hungrily. ''Yes, yes,'' he said. ''Doubtless.'' But the chill remained, and he knew that he was lying again . . . lying, this time, to himself. ''We will questiod the prisoders agaid id the bordig. If decessary, we will use force. They will see what playig stupid does for theb. We will fidd out for certaid what is goig od.''

But when Siegfried awakened in his bed the next morning, he did not hear whispers. His house was, in fact, very quiet, without the usual muted clatter that announced breakfast and the beginning of the day, without the sounds of footsteps or conversations.

He arose and dressed, making sure that the order for Jacob's condemnation was still safely tucked into his sleeve. The silence remained, clinging to the house like a funereal shroud. He opened the door and went down the hall. The silence followed. He called for his servants.

Still more silence. He opened doors, inspected a deserted kitchen, examined rooms. Silence.

There was no one in the house but himself.

Biting back an anger edged in cold fear, the silence pressing behind him like an unseen throng, Siegfried descended the stairs to the chapel. Fra Giovanni was waiting there for him.

"I don't understand," said Giovanni. "The House of God is deserted. I was waiting for a morning report, but no one came. The guards are gone, the servants are gone . . . the entire staff is gone."

A crow fluttered at the open window, landed, peered at the two men with a black eye. "It does dot bake ady sense," said Siegfried. "There is do od id the house. Do od at all."

And, as both men soon realized, there was no one coming to mass that morning, either.

"What's happened?" said Giovanni.

"I do dot know," said Siegfried. "But I ab goig to fidd out. I ab goig to fid theb, wherever they are, ad I ab goig to ask. Ad I had better hear a reasodable adswer!"

The morning was growing as Siegfried and Giovanni, after making a hasty confession to one another and rushing through morning prayers, went off into the streets of the city to look for the powers that had, apparently, deserted them.

What gets us through?

Natil wanted to know, not for herself, but for the future. Having reclaimed her heritage only to know the final and irrevocable failure of Omelda's death, she had nothing left but a guilt that would soon be forever terminated by the flames of the stake and—fragile, founded itself upon the ineffable workings of a Woman unperceived and unknown—a hope that would not find fulfillment for another half millennia.

What gets us through?

The Elves of the Rocky Mountains did not *know*. They had not a clue as to the existence of the Mystery that dwelt within a mind's reach. And, as far as Natil could tell, they would never know, would never have a clue as to the well of sustenance within them.

Dear friends, I would tell you . . . if I could. I would

*tell you how to search for Her. I would try to show you
how to find Her.*

In the distance, as though in reply, sounds. Clangings.
Chains falling on stone floors. Doors banging open and
slamming closed.

Natil lifted her head.

The sounds came closer, and now she heard men
shouting to one another. "Get that one open. My God!
Look at that!"

A crash . . . and a woman's sobbing cry.

Voices: yes. But here were no screams of pain, no
insinuating and accusing questions, no curt or sadistic
orders. Instead, Natil heard horror, urgency, and righ-
teous anger; and she stared in wonder, listening.

"Get that one outside, quickly. Give her some clothes
and some soup." A muffled response. "Then you *carry*
her, hobhead!"

Suspended between floor and ceiling as she was between grief and hope, Natil stared. *Manarel?*

Closer now: "Here they are, master. Ho! Aldernacht
men! On your feet!"

Even closer: the rattle—distinct, unmistakable—of an
iron door swinging open on rusted hinges.

"What the hell do you mean you can't find the goddam
key? I'll break down that door with your head if you
don't get it open right now!"

This last, from directly outside her cell, made Natil
start, for the voice—irascible, imperious, demanding—
could belong to none other than Jacob Aldernacht.

A jingle of keys, a clatter of metal—and a blaze of
torchlight invaded her cell. The Elf blinked, dazzled.
"Who comes . . . please?"

Jacob's voice was dry. "Your employer." She heard
him turn. "Come on: get her out of those chains. You
there, find her clothes."

"I've already got them here, Mister Jacob."

"Good. Where's her harp?"

"We're looking for it now."

"Well, find it! And bring something I can clean her
face with. She's better off than the others, but she's still
a mess."

Steps, hands. Natil's sight finally switched from lav-
enders and blues to torchlit reds and yellows, and she

found herself surrounded by men. Some were supporting her while others unfastened her chains. One stood nearby with a bundle of clothes. Off by the door, watching, was Jacob.

"Mister Jacob!" she cried. "Master!"

He scowled at her, his spectacles glinting. "What's this master crap? I distinctly recall that you ran out on me. Do you have any idea what the Aldernachts do with servants who go running off like that?"

"I . . ." The chains came off, and the Elf almost toppled, but the men—one of whom, she recalled, had dragged her down the steps of the House of God not twelve hours before—caught her and eased her down to the floor. Someone threw her old cloak about her shoulders to cover her nakedness, thrust her old eagle feather into her numb hands. "I can—"

"Shut up. I don't want to hear it. Damned musicians." Jacob turned to the men who were with him. "I'll handle Natil. Here, give me those clothes. Now go on and help the others. And *find that harp*." The men murmured, tugged at forelocks, and left.

In the light of a torch left burning in a socket by the door, Jacob knelt beside Natil. "How bad did they hurt you? Can you get up?"

"In a moment." Feeling was coming back to her arms now, sparkling through the flesh in welcome prickles as the blood flowed freely once more. As she rubbed them she examined Jacob through the starlight in her mind. Something had changed about him. Something had released, yielded. "I am not hurt badly," she said. "What is happening?"

"The House of God is out of business," said Jacob. His scowl wavered, cracked, and was abruptly replaced by a harsh laugh. "And you're an expensive woman!"

"I . . . I do not understand."

"Bishop Albrecht is the man in charge of Furze now." Jacob waggled his gray eyebrows. "Wealthy man. Fabulously wealthy."

Natil stared.

"And Albrecht just hired all of Siegfried's men right out from under him, at triple their former wages." Jacob cackled: nothing resembling humor seemed able to come out of the man unless it were edged in iron. "Quite a fellow, Albrecht." Another cackle. "He'll go far."

"But . . . but what about Siegfried?"

"Oh, he's off somewhere. Probably hiding. God knows, I'd certainly be hiding if I were him." A knock at the open door. Jacob looked up. "Ah, here's your harp. Give it here, Manarel."

Natil's hands were still weak and shaking, but when Manarel carefully set the instrument on her lap with a rough-hewn smile, her arms went about it instinctively. She laid her cheek against the wood, felt the scrape of tuning pins against dried blood.

After handing Jacob a basin of water and a cloth, Manarel left with a *God bless*, and Natil was once again alone with Jacob. "And you . . . you did this . . . for me?" she said, still almost unbelieving.

Jacob put a horny hand beneath her chin and lifted. With a damp cloth, he swabbed gently at the crusts of blood on her face, his scowl firmly in place. "I've never done anything for anybody except myself in my entire life," he said, "and don't you think that I'm going to be starting now. I did it for me." He released her chin, jerked a thumb at himself. "I'm a free man now. I've got no family waiting for me to die . . . and trying to help me to do it, I've got no debts, and I've got no regrets." He pointed at her. "And you're free, too. And so is everyone else in this hellhole."

Natil bent her head, the tears welling up. Some, indeed, might be free, but there was one she knew for whom freedom had come too late. "Omelda is dead."

"The serving girl?"

Natil nodded. "I was trying to take her home. She had been . . . hurt."

"Hurt . . ." Jacob looked away. "By Edvard and Norman, right?"

"It is so. They had . . ." The words failed. Natil forced herself to utter others. "I killed them. I—"

Jacob gripped her arm. "That's enough," he said. "That's enough." His mouth tightened, and his eyes clenched with something terrible, something dark. Then, slowly, painfully: "You saved me the trouble, girl."

Natil only looked at him, as pained by her guilts as by the bitterness that she heard in his voice.

"You saved me the trouble." And the bitterness came again, like a wave. But then he breathed, sighed. "And we'll leave it at that. Francis can shovel them in. And we'll put Omelda in the cathedral. And we'll just leave it at that."

Natil, though, could not just leave it at that. She feared, in fact, that she would never be able to just leave it at that. She had killed, and she had betrayed. So much she knew now about being human! "And what of the others?" she said softly.

Jacob's voice was a rasp. "They vary."

In two words, he had said it all, and when Natil was strong enough to don her clothes, pick up her harp, and walk, unassisted, out of the dungeon, she found that the courtyard of the House of God was littered with damaged human beings. Some, to be sure, like Paul and James and Simon and their loved ones, had not suffered much save from fear, and they stood together near the gate, Jew and Christian weeping freely and holding one another without hesitancy or qualm. Others, though . . .

Natil padded slowly and noiselessly among them, now and then pausing to touch, to speak a kind word. Here was a man who had not seen the sun in thirteen years, and he was now all but blind. Here was a man who had no legs because they had rotted off. Here was a woman who had gone a little mad, for she spoke to herself . . . and to others who were not there.

Men, women, even children: scarred and wounded and marked with hunger and torture and fear. And the men who had yesterday worked to make them that way now labored to tend their hurts, and asked solicitously and sincerely about their comfort. And all because of gold.

Manarel took Natil gently by the arm. "We're going to take the sick to the bishop's house," he said. "Albrecht has given it over for a hospital. He's sent for physicians from Belroi, even from Ypris and Hypprux."

And Natil finally saw, over near the wall, in the shadow of the high tower, the dead. They lay beneath plain muslin sheets. "Physicians?" she said, her voice catching. "That . . . that is good. There is much healing to be done here." She was still looking at the dead. A stray breeze fluttered one of the sheets optimistically, then let it fall.

"You need to rest, Natil. You need to have someone look at your face. I'll take you to the bishop's house."

But her fingers tightened on her harp, for she heard in his words a temptation to another betrayal. To yield, to depart? Never. She was an Elf, and there was helping and healing to be done. "I will go to the bishop's house," she said, "but I will not rest. I have work to do."

Manarel looked puzzled. "Work?"

She looked again at the dead. "I can harp," she said. "I can help . . . a little. I can heal . . . maybe. I must try."

"But, Natil—"

She shook her head, breathed the starlight, saw the shimmer of her hand bright against the brown wood of her harp. Elven. Forever. And that tree . . .

"It is why I am here," she said.

Albrecht stood in the triforium gallery.

It was the first time in years that he had come here in the daylight, but he thought it fitting that he now see his cathedral clearly, with no night or shadow to obscure it. He would, he knew, see it even more clearly as the years passed, when laborers would bring mortar and stone and pile them high, when artisans would come to make statues and colored glass, when carpenters would come to build forms and make roof beams.

There was nothing now to prevent it. Thanks to Jacob, the gold originally intended for the wool cooperative had been spread thickly among the informers and guards and secretaries and torturers of the House of God; and though for years they had worked for Siegfried and his plans, they now suddenly discovered that their sympathies lay anywhere but with the Inquisition.

And then the gold had spread further, glittering coins falling into palms that had previously been fortunate to know only dull copper and worn brass. Loyalties had abruptly altered, allegiances had been reforged. In the space of a night, the entire city had, either tacitly or outright, pledged its wholehearted support to Albrecht, bishop and benefactor of Furze. Even David a'Freux, who was always interested in money—whether in saving it through the monastic incarceration of an unwanted daughter, or in acquiring it through alliance with a silly old man with a gimpy leg—had fallen into line.

True, the loyalty had been bought outright (Albrecht had no illusions about that), and with gold now comparatively plentiful, other problems were surfacing: the price of a loaf of bread, for instance, had already doubled and redoubled twice over. But Albrecht was sure that things would eventually settle down, and that, when they did, he would have a chance to foster honest piety and unself-conscious charity . . . neither of which had been able to coexist very well with chronic hunger and poverty.

The future was full of hope—for the cathedral, for Furze—and Albrecht felt good about it. "I'll win them for You, God," he said softly. The afternoon breeze came in from the west, bringing the scent of a summertime forest and the deep green odor of pasturelands. "I'll win them. And I won't do it with prison or torture or tribunals, and I won't do it with money. I'll just do it by myself. With Your help."

He shook his head slowly, still almost unbelieving. It had all happened so quickly, and he could not help but remember, with a twinge of fear, Mattias's words: Boom! Just like that. Boom!

A sound behind him made him turn. Siegfried was stepping out of the shadow of the stairway. The Inquisitor's skin was the color of parchment, and his dark hair and beard were dusty and matted with dirt and blood. His grotesquely swollen nose was still bandaged, but there were fresh cuts on his cheek and a gash in his forehead. The fingers of one hand were bruised and scraped.

He looked rather like a madman, and Albrecht instinctively looked for a place to which to retreat. But there was none. The stairs were the only way up . . . or down.

"Brother Siegfried," he said politely.

Siegfried took a step away from the stairs and into the sunlight. Albrecht noticed that his mantle was dusty and torn.

"What . . . what happened to you?"

Siegfried stood like a splotch of night against the pale wall. "I udderstad dow what you did," he said slowly, his speech slurred as though with fatigue or perhaps injury. "Giovaddi and I asked questiods. We foudd out."

Albrecht said nothing.

"Do you realize what you have dod?"

Instinctively, Albrecht began to quail before the Inquisitor, but then, very deliberately, he checked himself.

He had seen what had been brought out of the House of God, had watched as Natil, herself injured, had bravely harped for people who had lost all hope, had listened to stories of torment. He had touched those who would never walk or see again. He had embraced those who did not have arms with which to return the gesture. He had kissed those whose lips were so swollen and scarred that they could not kiss back.

And as he returned Siegfried's gaze levelly, he realized suddenly that this was not a man to fear. This was a man for whom to feel only either blazing anger or the deepest compassion.

Albrecht stood up straight, braced his bad knee, took a step forward. "I let some people out of jail," he said. "That's what I did. I can't make the lame walk and the blind see, but I'm doing what I can."

Siegfried hardly seemed to hear him. "You have unleashed the forces of darkdess," he said. "You've allowed debods to escape. Satad hibself could be walkig the streets of Furze, ad you *would dot care*!"

Albrecht was incredulous. First heresy, and now demons! "Oh, come now, Siegfried!"

"Frob her owd lips I heard it!" cried the Inquisitor. "I had her before be, ad she codfessed everythig, ad dow you have furthered her plots." Siegfried clenched his fists. "Do you dot udderstadd? You have let all the plagues of the Apocalypse loose od the earth, and bed of God caddot eved walk the streets of Furze in safety!"

And then Albrecht understood how Siegfried had come to be so battered. The townsfolk, recognizing their former tormentor, had attempted to vent twenty years of fear and anger on him. Siegfried was very lucky to have escaped alive, and Albrecht suspected that he knew what had happened to Giovanni.

He breathed a silent prayer for the friar's soul. Then: "I'll make sure you get out of the city safely, Siegfried. But I'm afraid that there will be no more Inquisition in Furze. By my authority as bishop, I simply won't allow you to operate in my city."

Siegfried was suddenly raging, his white face turning red in an instant. "Your authority! *By* authority cobes frob the pope!"

"Yes," said Albrecht, who had seen firsthand how the Holy See operated. "I suppose it does."

"Do . . . do . . . that is dot right." Siegfried was shaking his head, clenching his fists, trembling all over. "It cobes frob God. That is it: frob God. God was the first Inquisitor. It was God who tried Adab and Eve id secret, who did dot call witdesses because He knew they were guilty, who foudd theb guilty by their codfessiods! I take by authority frob God!"

Albrecht felt his jaw tighten. From God!

But then, with an effort, Siegfried drew himself up and opened his arms as though to embrace Albrecht. The bishop, though, shrank back at his approach, again conscious that he was trapped against the edge of the gallery. There was no railing or balustrade, only a one hundred and twenty foot drop.

"Dear brother in Christ," said the Inquisitor, "you bust listed to be. There is a plot afoot that, if left udchecked, will sweep all of Christendob into Satad's hadds." His tone was almost pleading. "It cad be fought. It cad be checked. But you and I bust work together."

There was an unpleasant light in Siegfried's dark eyes. Albrecht neither liked it nor trusted it. "What plot is this?"

"Jacob Alderdacht," said Siegfried. "Jacob Alderdacht is working with debods. Elves. He is using his fortude to spread their idfluence. We bust use that fortude to cobbat the evil that is dwelling abonk us. Add we cad do it!"

Albrecht understood, then: it was money. That was it. Siegfried had gutted Furze, had stifled any hope of betterment for the city, and now he wanted to tamp down the last spadeful of earth on the corpse. "Jacob Aldernacht," he said flatly, "is one of the finest men I know."

Siegfried was undeterred. "He gave you his bodey. He gave it to you id ad attembt to thwart its codfiscatiod."

His words sounded to Albrecht like an accusation. "Yes, he gave it to me," said the bishop. "He gave it to me because he wanted to do some good with it. No layman can keep anything from you, Siegfried, and so Jacob put his money under episcopal authority."

Siegfried's hands clenched again, and what was left of his conciliatory tone evaporated in an instant. "You are in league with hib, thed! Adbit it! You do lonker believe id the teachings of Holy Church. In fact, you are dow actively working agaidst us. You are a heretic!''

Albrecht, though excruciatingly conscious of the drop behind him, stood his ground. "I believe in what Holy Church teaches," he said. "And Holy Church teaches that God became a common man, and walked the earth, and returned good for evil, and healed the sick, and . . ." To his shock, he discovered that he hated the Inquisitor and all that he stood for. ". . . and was finally tortured . . . and killed.''

"Heretic!" The word was half strangled, forced out through a throat constricted with rage.

Emotion made Albrecht's voice exceedingly calm. "You, Brother Siegfried, are a liar.''

Siegfried lunged. Before Albrecht could move, the Inquisitor had seized the front of his shabby soutane and was screaming: "Do you dot udderstand? I *had* to do it. We all had to do it! It was the odly way!''

"Brother Siegfried!" Albrecht struggled both to keep his balance and to pry himself loose, but the Inquisitor had the strength of a madman. Together, the two men tottered at the edge of the gallery. "Let go, brother! You need help!''

"I deed bodey!" Siegfried was shouting. "I deed bodey to fight Satad! You have to understand, Albrecht! I deed it! I had to lie, but dow I'b telling the truth! I deed your bodey! Give it to be!''

"Brother . . .''

"Give it to be!''

They spun, wavered, tottered. Siegfried clung to Albrecht and shrieked his demands in a voice that fragmented with emotion. Albrecht fought, pleaded, attempted to coax the Inquisitor into reason. And then the bishop's knee, always an unreliable servant, suddenly buckled. Albrecht collapsed, and his shoulder smacked directly into the middle of Siegfried's chest, sending him staggering back into empty space.

Albrecht made a desperate grab as Siegfried went over the edge of the gallery, and he managed to seize his sleeve; but in trying to check the Inquisitor's fall, he was pulled flat down on his chest, and the burst of broken ribs went through him like a bright light.

His vision blurry with pain, Albrecht looked down.

Held only by his sleeve, his feet kicking uselessly in the air, Siegfried was staring up at him.

"Please," said Siegfried. "Please."

"I'm holding you, Siegfried." Albrecht gasped as his shattered ribs ground against themselves, against his flesh. "I'll pull you up, but you need . . ." His hand was on fire with the strain. He could not hold Siegfried for long. ". . . to help me. Can you find anything to push against with your feet?"

But Siegfried did not appear to be hearing Albrecht. In fact, he did not even appear to be looking at him. He was, rather, staring past him, staring up at the blue sky, his eyes widening, deepening as though they had been confronted with the face of God.

Albrecht's hand burned. His arm felt ready to rip free at the shoulder. "Siegfried! Listen to me! Save yourself!"

But Siegfried, hanging only by a single torn sleeve, was still staring. "I . . . I see," he whispered. "I see."

"Siegfried!"

And then, suddenly, the sleeve gave way, and Siegfried was gone. His eyes shut tight, Albrecht put his head on the stone floor, heard the pounding of his heartbeats in the terrible silence: one, two, three . . . He counted up to ten before the silence was broken.

Shaking then, nearly sick, he crawled away from the drop, each breath a new stab of pain. He had put his hands to his face before he realized that he was still clutching Siegfried's sleeve.

He started to cast it aside, but something rustled in it, and, still in shock, he fumbled into the cloth and withdrew a rolled parchment. The black writing, dark as Siegfried's eyes, stared up at him in the bright sunlight.

In nomine Domini amen. Hec est quedam conedmnatio corporalis et sententia condemnationis . . .

His eyes flicked down to the bottom of the sheet.

Idcirco, dictum Jacobem vocatum Aldernactem hereticum et scismaticum quod ducator ad locum iustitie consuetum, et ibidem igne et flammis . . .

It was all in order. There was no date.

Albrecht bent his head, crumpled the parchment. "Boom," he murmured softly. "Boom." And then, ignoring the pain in his chest, he wept like a child who had been beaten.

CHAPTER 27

Albrecht was right: things eventually settled down.

Jacob stayed on in Furze as assistant and advisor, for not even the experienced and cosmopolitan Mattias knew much about managing such huge sums as were now controlled by the bishop. Then, too, someone had to contend with Jacob's family, for Francis and Claire, childless and grieving though they were, were nonetheless not at all inclined to let Jacob sign away the family fortune without a shred of protest.

But it was all numbers and words to Jacob, for as he had ceased to feel any connection, real or remembered, between himself and his money, so the complaints and threats of the nerveless couple in Ypris did not move him. Alternately laughing and snorting, he read Francis's letters aloud as Albrecht wrung his hands and paced the floor, but—perhaps fittingly—he replied to his son with the businesslike objectivity of a stranger. To be sure, Bishop Etienne was eventually trotted out with letters and documents attesting to Jacob's mental instability, but after Francis had thusly played his highest card, Albrecht put an end to the game with a solemn declaration that the Aldernacht patriarch was, and had always been, perfectly sane. And Albrecht's word was good and true: after all, Albrecht had money.

By far, though, the largest part of Jacob's efforts went into the Furze economy, which was by now reeling like a drunkard under the influence of an excess of gold. He made sure that the remainder of the hundred thousand florins was distributed equitably and reasonably among the men and women of the city, and his personal letters to northern merchants ensured that, within a week, there were goods to be bought in the marketplace—checking thereby the rapid rise in prices caused by too much money and not enough to spend it on. The people of Furze, for the most part, were a cautious lot—if poverty had not taught them prudence, the Inquisition certainly had—and after an initial burst of overindulgence, they resumed an appropriate degree of thrift.

Albrecht, was adamant: the wool cooperative would be taken care of before he would even think of starting any work on the cathedral. And so, with a sour sounding "It's your money" accompanied by a secret smile of approval, Jacob countersigned a draft on the Aldernacht accounts that quickly produced everything necessary to equip a nascent wool industry. Seed money, flocks, machinery: it was all there.

The cooperative being sound then, Albrecht gave his approval for laborers to begin construction, and by September, the bishop and the benefactor were watching from a safe distance as the big windlass took the first of the heavy roof beams up into the air. It lifted off, swung for a moment, then straightened; and at a shout from the master architect—a student of the great Alberti, no less!—it ascended without mishap and was pegged into place.

"They'll be working right up to the first snows," said Jacob. "But you'll have a roof on the apse for the winter."

Albrecht was nodding, obviously pleased. "We'll have Christmas mass in that part of the cathedral," he said. "It will be cold, but it will be wonderful. And the glassmakers showed me their designs yesterday. Beautiful." But as he looked up toward the triforium gallery, he frowned suddenly, and his eyes turned pained.

"Excellency?"

"It's nothing. Just . . ."

"Siegfried."

"Yes." The bishop passed a hand over his face. "I can't help but think that if I'd tried a little harder—just a little harder—I might have saved him."

Jacob still wished that he had been able to slam the Inquisitor's face into the desk once or twice more. "I think he got what he deserved."

Albrecht shook his head. "Nobody deserves that."

"You're right, Excellency." Jacob shoved his spectacles up with a scowl. "Nobody deserves that."

Albrecht did not reply.

The rope from the windlass came down. Another beam went up.

Albrecht shook his head bemusedly. "Alexander sent a message the other day. He's heard about Siegfried's death and wants to know if we need another Inquisitor."

"What are you going to tell him?"

"I'm going to tell him no."

Jacob scratched the stubble on his jaw. "Think that'll be the end of it?"

Albrecht smiled. "I've learned quite a lot from you, Jacob. I intend also to tell His Holiness that I'll be making a contribution to his building fund. He's thinking about restoring Rome, you know."

"Oh . . ." Jacob nodded, keeping his eyes on the ascending beam. "Yes, I'd heard about that. A large contribution?"

"Yes. Very."

"I think that'll be the end of it, then."

"I think so, too."

More beams. The nave was walled in nothing but daylight, but the apse was closing up nicely, as though to foretell the beauty of the completed structure. Like Furze, the cathedral was pulling itself together, taking shape. The future looked promising . . . because of money.

"It'll be a nice church," said Jacob.

"We have you to thank for that," said Albrecht.

Jacob waved the thanks away. "If you hadn't kept the idea of the cathedral alive, Excellency, it wouldn't be here to finish." He folded his arms. "What are you going to call it, anyway?"

"Well," said Albrecht, "I'd always thought it would be the Cathedral of Our Lady of Furze, but . . ." He fell silent. "But it's not just Furze anymore, is it? I mean . . . oh, dear God, I've been talking with David a'Freux too much. He's been going on about nations and all. Our Lady of Adria sounds good, I guess, but that still isn't right. After all, the money is coming in from all over Europe."

"All over the world, Excellency," said Jacob. "There's Turk gold and Tatar gold and African gold in your coffers along with everything else."

"Yes." Albrecht was still rather dazed by the strangeness of wealth. "Well, you see my point."

"Master!" came a clear voice. "Your Excellency!"

Jacob smiled broadly, for a slender woman was coming toward them along the length of what would someday be the nave. Her cloak was a strange patchwork of fabric adorned with beads and feathers, and an eagle feather fluttered from a single braid in her dark hair. She waved with her one free hand, for in the other she carried a small harp.

Like Jacob, Natil had stayed on in Furze. But where her former master had worked with money and words, the harper had labored among the casualties of the Inquisition, supplementing the efforts of the physicians with harp and song. And, true, she did indeed appear to have some uncanny abilities, for those who listened to her seemed to recover from their wounds more quickly than might be expected, and there was at least one instance of a completely useless limb suddenly regaining feeling after a particularly long immersion in her melodies.

She greeted the men as friends: with a hand and a smile. "It is a lovely day," she said, and Jacob heard, as always, music in her voice. A lovely day, and a lovely woman. That was Natil. That was just the way she was.

They had never again mentioned Edvard and Norman.

"A lovely day," said Albrecht. "It is indeed."

Jacob looked up. Autumn, he suspected, was going to be wet and cold, and there were dark clouds off to the west. "It won't be for long."

"How are the patients, child?" said Albrecht.

"By the grace of the Lady," she said, "they are well. The last is going home today. He still has no legs . . ." And a look crossed her face that told Jacob—and he had no idea why he was so sure of it—that she was absolutely convinced that she *should* have been able to do something about those legs, that the fact that she had not was a personal and all but unforgivable failing. ". . . but he has a family, and he has hands that can still work leather . . ." She smiled sadly. ". . . and he no longer dreams so much of the dungeon and the rats and the water."

Another beam was going up. The architect, standing on the ground, pointed. The supervisor, up in the gallery, shrugged. The architect shook his fist and ran for the stairs.

"That's the last of the Inquisition, then," said Jacob.

Natil nodded. But then she stood silently, holding her harp, fidgeting.

Jacob was suddenly uneasy. "You didn't just come to tell us about the patients, did you, Natil?"

"I did not." She dropped her eyes. "I have come to take my leave."

As he had feared. For an instant, Jacob felt deserted, and angry. But those emotions faded quickly, for they belonged to someone who had bought and sold people as though they were wool or houses or furniture. Nonetheless, as dismayed as any man by the imminent loss of someone he loved, he reached out to her. "Natil!"

"My work in Furze is finished." She took his hand. "There is nothing left for me to do here."

"But . . . we'd all assumed that you'd be staying, Natil. With as much gold as is going to be coming into town, you'll be paid well for your harping."

"But it is not to be paid well that I harp," she said simply.

Albrecht spoke, his voice grieved. "We would like you to stay, child. I think everyone in Furze would like you to stay."

Natil nodded. "I know. And a part of me shares their feelings. But . . . I have tasks . . ."

"What kind of tasks?"

She shook her head softly. The eagle feather fluttered. "I will know them when I find them."

Albrecht nodded slowly, unwillingly, and then he opened his arms and—a little stiffly, because his ribs still pained him—embraced her. "Well, if you must go, you must. I won't argue. But you have our thanks, Natil. Wherever you go, you have our deepest thanks."

Natil kissed his gray cheek. But: "I would have one other thing of you, Excellency," she said. And when she stepped back, she went down on one knee. "I would have your blessing."

Albrecht looked rather as though he thought it more fitting that Natil give blessings than receive them. "But—"

"Please, Excellency. After all that has happened . . ." And something about her tone told Jacob that she was

referring to much more than the Inquisition of Furze.
". . . it is important that our peoples be reconciled in
some way. For at least this hour, or even this moment."

"Our peoples?" The bishop was bewildered. "But I
don't understand."

"Please," said Natil. "I have given you my music.
Will you now . . ." She looked sad. "Please."

Still obviously puzzled, Albrecht lifted his hands. "May
the blessing of almighty God—the Father, the Son, and the
Holy Spirit—descend upon you, Natil, and remain with you
forever."

She bent her head. "My thanks."

But as though unwilling to really allow her to depart,
Albrecht dropped his hands to cradle her head while he
bent to kiss her crown . . .

. . . and then he froze, staring.

Natil looked up at him. "Be at peace, Albrecht."

The bishop's face had gone white. "Then . . ." He
could not seem to find words. ". . . what Wenceslas
said . . ."

"Was true, beloved. More true than you thought."

Pale, almost shaking, Albrecht released her and bowed
low. "Our thanks, Natil. Our deepest, deepest thanks."

"Blessings." She stood up in the sunlight. "I will
make a few good-byes to friends in the city, and then I
will leave. I will be gone by evening."

Jacob felt bereft. "Not even another night?"

"Not even that."

Albrecht was still, unaccountably, shaken. "We'll . . .
miss you. I'd hoped that you'd see the cathedral finished."

Natil was calm. "I do not know if I will see it," she
admitted. "But I have seen you." She smiled wistfully.
"And therefore am I satisfied."

Albrecht spoke quickly, then, as though afraid that she
would turn away and vanish. "Just one thing more, Natil. Just one thing more. I . . . I was wondering—that is,
Jacob and I were wondering—what to call the cathedral.
It was going to be Our Lady of Furze."

"A good name," said the harper.

"But it's not quite . . . right. What's your sugges-
tion?"

"Oh, my dear bishop, it is not my place to—"

"Natil, I ask one who may well know best. What would the old delMaris have called it? What would Blessed Wenceslas have called it?"

And to Jacob's surprise, Natil smiled without a trace of sadness. "I cannot say for certain," she said, "but if you called it Our Lady of the Stars, I do not think that the dead—or the living—would think it uncomely."

Albrecht looked at her for the better part of a minute. Finally: "A wise choice . . . harper." He nodded. "So it shall be."

Natil bowed, offered a hand to Jacob. He took it, but he shook his head. "You come back after you say your good-byes, girl," he said. "I want to escort you out of town." He peered at her in mock suspicion. "You ran off without permission once before: I'm giving you a chance to make up for it."

"Agreed," she said. "With all my heart."

And then she went off, eagle feather fluttering, harp tucked beneath her arm, beads and bells rattling and jingling gaily, and Albrecht watched her with a face that was at once much grayer and much more hopeful than Jacob had ever seen it before.

"Excellency? What's going on?"

Albrecht shook his head. "Oh, Jacob," he said softly. "There are wonders in the world." He stared after Natil. "There are wonders."

Rain would be coming soon, but Jacob felt a brightness growing within him, filling him with light, making all the world radiant, banishing the past as morning might dismiss a dark and evil dream.

He left Furze that afternoon with Natil on his arm, and as they walked out along the road that led south through the pasturelands, autumn was growing about them. The leaves were just beginning to turn—no colors yet, but a sense that color was somewhere just in the future—and the air was soft with the changing season.

"You were right, Natil," he said.

"Master?"

"Don't give me that master crap. I'm not your master. I'm just Jacob. I'm a pauper."

She laughed, and Jacob thought that he had never heard such a sweet sound. And, in fact, at his hearing of it, the brightness within him doubled and redoubled. "You were right, though," he said. "It *is* a lovely day."

She unlinked her arm from his and slid it about his waist. "Now you know how to see, Jacob."

"I have to add my thanks to Albrecht's." He squinted into the afternoon light, tried to use that as an excuse for the fact that his eyes were watering. He did not even convince himself. He did not care. "You've done everything for me."

She shook her head. "I was but your harper, Jacob."

"There you go again with that crap. Harper? You did everything. You even . . ."

He stopped suddenly, thinking of Edvard and Norman. Yes, she had done everything. Even the painful things.

As though she had guessed his thought, she changed the subject: "What will you do now?"

"Now?" He shrugged, wishing that he were young again—a man walking out into the fields with a maid—wishing that his memories of Natil might have more of a chance of displacing . . . others. "Well, there isn't much left for me to do in Furze. I've signed all the papers, I've convinced everyone who needed convincing that I'm not crazy, I've briefed Albrecht and Mattias on all the holdings and the idiocy that they might run into, and I hired Charles and all the accountants away from Francis. I can stay on as an advisor, maybe. But . . ." He felt, tasted, the brightness: it was good. And it seemed to him that Natil was right about something else, too: about moving on, about leaving when one's work was done. "But maybe I'll ask Albrecht to get me into that Benedictine monastery up across the way. I can use some peace and quiet." He grinned. "Maybe they'll take an old monk who used to be a rich man."

Natil shook her head. "If they take you," she said, "they will have a rich man indeed."

They reached a crossroads.

"It is time for me to go," said Natil.

"Where?"

"South." She weighed her harp, shrugged.

The regrets, the wishes, stayed with him. "You'll always be welcome in Furze, Natil."

"I know," she said. "Farewell, beloved." She kissed him, squeezed his hand, and went off down the road.

Jacob watched her for a long time, watched her through the shimmering veils of brightness that seemed to come up from the earth and down from the westering sun. It was autumn, autumn as sweet as a ripe plum, and it was time for an old man to think about retiring. But even retiring seemed to be bright, almost unbearably bright.

He found a tree off to the side of the road, climbed up into it, and sat down on a branch. Natil was a speck in the distance by now, and the light was still rising.

Brightness, falling through the air, welling up from within him, mingling with all that he could see. Yes, it was time; and when he thought he saw the harper turn once, wave, and then disappear over a rise, he lifted a hand into the brightness and waved farewell until he had not a scrap of strength left. But the brightness took over after that, and it waved and waved and waved . . .

. . . forever.

The rain came that evening, sluicing away the summer as the years had sluiced away the world of the Elves.

Natil had spoken to Jacob of making her good-byes, but in truth her leave-takings had lain not only within Furze, but across the world. For a hundred years, she had traveled, looking for Elves, and now that she had the certain knowledge that she was the last, she realized that she had also been saying good-bye to the last fragments of old belief and old recognitions. She had sung in a shaman's skin hut in Asia, had harped in tepees pitched on the plains of what would be called America, had played for nobles beneath a blue Italian sky, but it had all been a departure: the last soft kiss of mortal and immortal before the separation and the long darkness.

Now she was going to make her last good-byes, and as what lay ahead embodied perhaps the brightest of the latter-day memories that she possessed, she had saved it for the very end.

The rain continued. Traveling slowly, she worked her way around the big loop in the road that swung to the west. Saint Brigid had long been deserted, and only a tumble of stone and a ruin of rotting wood marked the place where once had stood a small, orderly village with tidy streets that meandered off as streets would; but she found what was left of Andrew's house, and the priest's house, and that pile over there—the rain was coming down even harder now, having not stopped for three days—must have once been the church. It was hard to tell. It had been a long time for humans, and humans were now all that counted.

She wandered among the ruins like a ghost for several days, without quite knowing why. What did she expect? Fading? Fading seemed all that was left for her. But she did not know how to fade.

A ghost herself, she wondered whether she saw other ghosts. Or perhaps these desolate heaps of rubble were so redolent of the past and its happiness that she could not but see them as they once had been, could not but see those she had loved. Andrew was there, working in his shop. And Elizabeth greeted Immortals at the door. And Kay smiled and snapped his fingers over a blissfully fragrant pot of stew. And there was Charity, who had once been old and ugly and unloved, but who had found grace and a new life through the power of the Elves. And a nasty little woman named Miriam was finding even more than that.

But Natil saw also—out of place here in Saint Brigid, but somehow appropriately present among these shades—Omelda. Dogged, determined as an ox, she stumped up and down the streets with a head full of plainchant and an indefatigable determination to win back the privacy of her mind. But for her the power of the Elves had failed, just as everything else that the Firstborn had touched had failed. With the passing of the centuries, everything had failed.

Just like the Firstborn themselves.

The rain came down, and, sitting on a tumbled wall, her oilcloth-wrapped harp resting on her lap beneath her sodden cloak, Natil saw Mirya and Terrill, hand in hand, passing into the forest just as they had on that last day, when they had given themselves and their existence to stop the fire that threatened all of Malvern. And Varden was waiting at the edge of the trees to welcome them, his young, maidenly face so full of the burden of pity that he had learned from his human cousins.

Together, they vanished.

Natil looked at her hands, half expecting them to have

grown transparent, ephemeral. But no: they were solid, even bright. They seemed to shun any thought of fading.

Did she, then, have more ahead of her? Was this a sign, a finger that pointed to more centuries of wandering and harping? Was she to continue, to live as she could, to perhaps wait for the rebirth and be present to witness it and to speak words of welcome that the world would not have heard for half a thousand years?

"Alanae a Elthia yai oulisi," she murmured, the rain drumming on her hood. But the Elves of the future would no more know the ancient tongue than they would know the Lady.

"I would teach you, if you would be taught," she said into the patter of falling water. She lifted her head. The rain came down like a cold hand, splashing her face. "And, O my Lady, if that is Your wish, then I will wait."

Thunder. Thunder in the distance.

But she had dreamed it all already, and she had not seen herself in her dreams. Hadden and Wheat and the others had awakened, had raised Elvenhome, had with self-conscious instinct set about their lives of helping and healing; but Natil had not been there. If her dreams had been true—and she knew now that they were—then she would not be waiting for the Elves of Colorado.

Death had been denied her. Fading would not claim her. Waiting was not an option. "What gets us through?" she murmured in English. "What will get them through?" She put her wet hands to her face. "Dear Lady, what will get *me* through?"

Night fell. The rain poured down from a sky that did not appear to know anything of moon or stars. But when Natil finally lifted her head, she saw, in the distance, a light in the forest.

Golden, shimmering up out of the falling drops, it shone like a star, at once evanescent and palpable, far away and within reach. And Natil knew it, knew what it was, knew where it came from. And she suspected that she knew what it meant.

It was a grace beyond belief, this sudden inbreaking of hope for one who had herself failed the hopes of others; but Natil was an Elf, and she knew about grace and hope, for in better times she had given both away freely. Like her people, she had loved without question. She had healed gladly and simply. She had offered a hand of friendship over and over again, despite rejection, despite pain, despite even death.

She had given without thought, and, if she had in these last days failed, then she had failed because she had tried to give. By what right, then, could she now question either love or grace? Here were both being offered to her, and she could only trust, open her hands, and accept.

She rose then, clutching her harp within its wrappings, and left Saint Brigid, left behind the good-byes and the regrets and the failings. She went into the forest, into the ancient home of the Elves. She went toward the light. And though the paths were overgrown, she found them. And though the ground was muddy, she crossed it. And though the streams were swollen with a week of constant rain, she forded them.

Wet birds huddled on wet branches and peered out at her from wet wings, damp foxes stared as though she were a stranger, deer started. Midnight came and she was still traveling, following the light that danced and beckoned. Quickening her steps, she skidded down slopes, slipped on paths that had grown treacherous with mud.

Up above her now, the light shone like a torch held aloft in summons, and Natil climbed, fighting for handholds, toeholds. She had almost reached it when she lost her footing and fell, tumbling back into a ravine. The stars spun and swam before her eyes, and when she came to herself, she was lying on her back in six inches of water, her harp sitting, wrapped up and unharmed, on her stomach. Still dizzy, she staggered upright, steadied herself against the bank of crumbling earth, and peered ahead.

A short distance away, rising out of the side of the hill, was a forked tree. Light streamed from its cleft, a golden brilliance that seemed somehow touched with the blue of sky and lake, the green of tree and herb, the brown of earth, as though the sun had taken all the colors of the planet into its arms and mingled them with itself.

Carefully, Natil climbed out onto the grass and approached. The Lady was there. Natil could not see Her, but she knew She was there.

"Elthia Calasiuove," she said, but there was no reply

save in the rain that fell, the wind that blew, and the light that streamed out of the cleft in the tree.

She freed a hand from her cloak, drew nearer. Her fingers slid into the radiance as though into a pool of water. She felt warmth, air. She pulled her hand away and looked at it. Not a mark, not a blemish.

"Elthia . . . " She was asking for reassurance, for confirmation, for certainty. But though in the past the Elves had worked only in knowledge, the world had changed, and the knowledge was gone. This, then, was a time for hope and for trust. This was a time for grace.

She set a hand on an outstretched limb, and, quickly, without hesitation, swung a leg through the cleft, through the light. It was a lesson, a reminder of what she had forgotten about giving and love, and when she felt—as she knew she would—solid ground on the far side, she planted her foot, closed her eyes, and shifted her weight to it.

And then she was standing in sunlight, standing in a grassy meadow that was alive with wildflowers. She knew their names—it did not seem at all remarkable to her that she knew their names, or that the language in which she knew them was American English. There was indian paintbrush. There was cinquefoil. There was columbine. And hollyhock and kinnickkinnick. And mariposa lily and starflower and wild hyacinth and yarrow. Prickly poppy waved on tall stalks, and morning glory twined up through thickets of scrub oak and chokecherry.

She looked up. Mountains surrounded her—tall mountains, taller than the Aleser, craggy and barechested with stone outcroppings—and on their slopes, aspens stood slender, fluttering with new leaves, and pines were dark and green with fresh needles. A hawk circled on a high thermal in the very, very blue sky, and when it saw her, it dipped its wings in greeting.

And far up beyond the hawk, almost lost in the ocean of air, were the parallel contrails and bright sparkle of a westbound 747.

You are invited to preview
an excerpt from
STRANDS OF SUNLIGHT,
Gael Baudino's magical sequel
to SHROUD OF SHADOW.

Sun.

It glared off the narrow band of asphalt that was Interstate 15, sending up heat shimmers that turned the distant mountains into the reflections of a troubled pond. But there was no water here in the Mojave Desert, only sun . . . and sand . . . and Joshua trees . . . and the ovenlike heat of a Toyota Celica that had possessed no air conditioning to speak of for the last ten years.

Sandy Joy shoved her sunglasses back on her head, rubbed at her good eye, wiped sweat out of her bad eye, and shifted her sweat-soaked back against the vinyl seat. The wind that blasted in through the open windows brought not a trace of coolness, and though she dropped her sunglasses into place and sucked at a can of cola grown warm with the unremitting heat, the liquid neither quenched her thirst nor eased the ache in her stomach. In fact, prompted by the reality of this journey—the sand, the scrub and trees, the road stretching off toward the mountains and then beyond into who-knew-what—the ache had redoubled, and the soft drink only gave her gut something about which to clench more tightly.

"I'll tell you, Little Sandy," she said to the doll that was seatbelted beside her, "you don't want to worry too much about what happens in Denver, because it sure as hell can't be any worse than what we left in LA."

She glanced at the doll. Little Sandy's cloth face wore, as usual, an expression that lay midway between the winsome and the pathetic, but it seemed today to be touched with something akin to absurd confidence.

Sandy put her good eye back on the road. Little Sandy was confident. Well, that was to be expected: Little Sandy had Big Sandy to look out for her, and that was the way it was supposed to be. But Big Sandy had no one. That was, she supposed, the way it was supposed to be, too; but how did one parent oneself when one's only role models were a mother who had committed suicide and a father who had—?

"That's enough," she said quickly. "In the name of the Goddess, that's enough."

But though she spoke the words solemnly, trying yet again to erect between herself and the past a barrier of the sacred and the numinous, her voice was tight, and another swig of warm cola did nothing to loosen it.

The Celica continued on, the road continued to rise to meet it. Joshua trees and scrub flicked by at half a hundred miles an hour, but the distances were such that, in the larger view, nothing changed. The same stretches of sand and waste unrolled to left and to right, and the same mountains—bleached and gray—shimmered in the distance. Sandy seemed to be getting nowhere.

As usual.

She frowned, grappled with the thought, tried to shove it away. But there it was, right outside her windshield: an emblem, symbolic as all hell, of her life.

Ladies and gentlemen, presented for your entertainment and delectation, an iconographic reification of symbological excellence, a summation, in short, of the puerile existence of one Sandy Joy, refugee from the lye-buckets and semen-stained cribs of the City of the Angels, dupe of her own hidden and unacknowledged optimism. Step right this way! Come inside, come inside!

And, indeed, the phantom barker (who, fittingly, spoke with the voice of her dead father) might well have been right. Twenty-five years old, and she had nothing to show for her life save blindness, a scarred face, and a personality that hobbled about like an amputee. This journey to Denver, she admitted, was quite possibly a grasping at a very thin straw . . . and a waterlogged one at that.

See the drowning girl in action. See her struggle. See her writhe and wriggle as she swims like a . . .

She drained the last of the cola, tossed the can onto the back seat. "Shaddup," she said aloud. "I'm over it."

The voice faded, and as though seeking a talisman to ward off its return, she reached back to a canvas instrument case that lay on the floor behind her seat. For a moment, she felt through layers of nylon and padding to the slender contours of a small harp, then, still looking for the charm, unzipped the side pocket and withdrew a bundle of papers.

With her good eye flicking back and forth between the road and the topmost letter, she sought the words that could hold back the barker. She had read them often. She had them memorized.

"*. . . pleased to inform you of your acceptance into the Hands of Grace program. We at Kingsley College are proud to be the facilitator of Professor Angel's innovative work, and consider it to be an invaluable asset to the academic, religious, and medical communities. We look forward to your arrival . . .*"

The letter was signed by the dean, Maxwell Delmari, and two pages down was the letter from the financial aid department about her fellowship. Then came the rudely typed article by Terry Angel himself and the correspondence she had received from him over the last two years. Futility? No: she had been accepted at Kingsley, had been given a fellowship, actually had the personal interest of Terry Angel.

She put the papers away with a sense of satisfaction, and she gave the harp a comradely squeeze. There was a place for her at Kingsley. There was a place for her in the Hands of Grace program. Terry Angel was going to teach her the ancient secrets of the harp so that she could help people. She might even be able to help herself.

She thought of the encouragement that Terry had given her, of his cautions and stern warnings about making a full commitment to his program. *Commitment and authenticity,* he had written, *are our armor against those in the academic world who will try to discredit what we do. Our byword, therefore, is research. Research, research, research!*

Yes, she was ready to commit. After twenty-five years, she was ready to commit herself to anybody who showed her the slightest consideration, ready to pledge herself to anything that offered an end to the futility and the pain. Terry had been willing to accept her, to make her a part of the Hands of Grace, and at the thought of his unlooked-for generosity, her eyes—blind and sighted both—were suddenly too full of tears for her to continue to drive.

She pulled off the highway, stopped, leaned her head against the steering wheel. She tried to forget about the past, to think instead about the letters and the encouragement, but the barker began to natter again, a needless and redundant reminder that the past was still with her, that the past was always with her, that no amount of wishing, fantasizing, therapy, or even the spells and ritual of modern Witchcraft would keep it away. It was just there: the irrefutable artifact of an incarnation gone wrong, an incarnation that had, so far, stubbornly refused any effort to alter its course in the slightest.

She pulled Little Sandy into her lap and held her, trying to find in the doll's soft body a sense of her own childhood self, trying to instill into it some feeling of safety and comfort.

"Oh, Goddess," she whispered. "I wish you could hold me like this."

But the arms of the Goddess lay in the future, at the end of a wretched life; and so, after a time, Sandy put the doll back into its seat, restarted the car, and continued across the desert. If she kept moving, she could make Saint George by nightfall, check into a motel, and find, in sleep, at least the end of this particular wretched day.

"Marsh? TK."

"Hey, dude." Marsh Blues covered the phone receiver with his free hand and smiled at the middle-aged woman who was sitting on the other side of his desk. "Hang on," he said. "This'll just take a minute."

He noticed her short nod, the slump to her shoulders. She was used to waiting. With an instinct that he still at times found unsettling, he had known from the moment she had shuffled into Buckland Employment that she had, in the course of her life, waited for everything. For a man. For marriage. For children. For children to grow up.

Now, both the man and the children were gone, as was the insurance money. And she was still waiting.

Marsh felt the pang; but TK was talking, his chocolate voice turned metallic and compressed by the phone line. "Man, the guy in Operations has done it to me again. I got to work tonight. I got to leave now."

Marsh made a small, impatient noise. "Again?"

A dark chuckle, darker than the voice. "Got me a southern boy here, Marsh. Tells darky jokes by the coffee machine, but oh! how he is the open-minded one when it comes to working them."

"Sixth night this week, isn't it, TK?"

"You got it, man. Sixth day, too. Been working double shifts. The money's good, but who cares when you're too tired to enjoy it?"

The woman across the desk had sunk down into her chair like a bag of flour, and Marsh examined her as he talked. Resigned. Resigned to waiting. Resigned to failure. TK was resigned, too. It was that way with most people. *Things happen,* they said, *it's just that way,* and the utter tragedy of it all was that the sentiment was accepted as valid currency everywhere. And here was Marsh Blues sitting in an employment agency thinking that he was going to change everything . . . why, he ought to have his head examined.

Forever was a long time to see things happen . . . just that way. Marsh tried not to think about forever. He failed. "OK," he said, thinking longingly of the long, slow, sexy notes that TK could draw out of a tenor sax, "I'll call the guys and cancel. They won't like it."

"Come on, man. I feel lousy enough. I got a cracker who wants me to quit, I been up all night, and my leg's hurting."

"That leg of yours again! Have you gone to the VA?"

"Yeah. They want me to pose for Desert Storm promo pix."

"Is that all?"

"Nothing much else they can do. Called *phantom limb syndrome.* Hurts like hell some days, but they'd have to start cutting my brain to get rid of it."

There were better ways. There *had* to be better ways. Ash had, after all, once cured leukemia, and had actually managed to heal Hadden of a gunshot wound. Self-conscious, rather shaken by the enormity of the experiences, she had never been able to do anything of the sort again, but, well, there had to be more of that somewhere. Maybe Natil knew something.

"Marsh?"

Maybe. But if she did, she was not talking about it. Marsh suddenly wondered—

"Marsh? You there?"

"Huh?" Coming out of his thoughts too quickly to keep them. "Uh, yeah." No music tonight. "Shit."

"No, man. Sheeee-it. Get it right. You want to play blues guitar, you got to get some color in you."

Marsh laughed. "OK. I admit it. I'm vanilla. But let us know how your schedule turns out. Maybe we can get together next week. We all miss the sax."

And, for a moment, from behind TK's habitual mask, a real face peeped out. "You don't think I do?"

"TK?" But TK had hung up. Marsh set the handset back in its cradle. It was just that way. It was just going to be that way. Forever.

It would not be so bad, he thought, had he some place he could go. It was not a question of a vacation, or an easy chair, or a warm bed in which he and Heather could hide in one another's arms. It was not a question even of the gatherings up at the Home, when they all, in one way or another, hid in one another's arms. It was . . .

He was not sure what it was, save that it seemed to be a longing both unspecified and unfulfilled, one that possessed him frequently, that, he guessed, possessed all the others who thought, with involuntary dismay, of forever.

He glanced across the big room. Two desks away, Wheat was talking to a shabby young man in overalls, her cornflower blue eyes big and sympathetic and filled with starlight. *It has to do with love*, she had said at a staff meeting long ago, and everyone, Marsh included, had fallen into stunned silence. *You have to look at the clients that come to you and love them, because they're people and they deserve it. You have to feel them, what they've been through, why they've come to you.*

No one had understood then. No one at the agency save Marsh, Ash, and Wheat herself understood now.

Love. That was it. And if it had to be forever, then it was going to be forever. And so Marsh turned back to the middle-aged woman—still waiting without a word of complaint, without a flicker of annoyance—and picked up her application form. "All right, ma'am," he said. "Sorry about the delay. There's an occasional wetware problem on this side of the desk."

She did not understand the joke. " 'S okay," she said. Her voice was barely a whisper.

"You've . . ." Marsh ran his eyes down the application. *It has to do with love.* "You've been with a few other agencies, I see." *Forever.*

"Yeah," she said. "They said they couldn't help me."

Marsh looked at her, held her image in his thoughts the way he might have held an apple in his hand, allowed the starlight in his mind to wash over it. Yes, he loved her. He could not but love her. "We'll help you, ma'am. We've got this attitude problem around here: you see, at Buckland Employment, we do things right or we don't do them at all."

She nodded, looked unconvinced. Marsh knew that she had only heard the second half of the Buckland aphorism.

He grinned. "So we'll do it," he said, holding the woman, the starlight, and the love in balance. But words and balancings were easy. Trying to find an adequate job for someone who had no work history, no skills, and an abysmal attitude promised to be considerably more difficult.

"Can you?" The woman looked almost eager.

That was good. Eagerness was good. Marsh nodded. It would be difficult, but not impossible. And as for the work history and the skills . . . well, Elves, as he had heard Natil say, were known for being ingenious.

But, ingenious or not, it was always going to be like this. Despite the love, the work—and the sorrow—would go on and on. Forever. Elves were immortal: what would get them through?

Heather knew that Kelly was upset even before she walked into the day care center, and when she stepped through the door, she found her blond, blue-eyed daughter reading a book over by the west window, her face mirroring a sadness that seemed terribly out of place on features that had known but five summers.

And Kelly's teacher was beckoning.

Heather ignored the woman, went directly to Kelly, bent down and put her arms about her. "Hi, sweetheart," she said. "Ready to go home?"

Kelly looked up with large eyes—large, sad eyes—and nodded solemnly.

In the glance that passed between them were wordless thoughts that flitted through Heather's mind with the softness of dove wings. "Bad day?"

Kelly shook her head. "Not bad," she said slowly. Her voice was quiet, steady, even without a trace of childish lisp. "Just . . . sad I guess."

Kelly's teacher was still beckoning. "Hang on, love," said Heather, giving her daughter a hug. "I have to talk to Susie."

"She's very sad."

"I know," said Heather. "They're all sad. You're sad, too."

Kelly nodded, went back to her book. Heather glanced at it. *The Jungle Book?* At five years old? Well, that was Kelly.

Susie took Heather into the corridor. "Kelly is a wonderful child, Ms. Blues," she said. There was a veneer in her voice, though Heather doubted that a human being would have noticed it. "It's so wonderful to have her with us."

"But . . ." said Heather.

Susie blinked. "But what?"

"My question exactly. Kelly is a wonderful child, *but . . .*" Heather tipped her head to one side inquiringly. It was an infantile habit she thought she had broken years ago, one that had, for some reason, returned with the awakening of the ancient blood in her veins.

Oh, well: Wheat always cried when she listened to old Judy Collins records, and Tristan doted on his wild birds and animals, and Dell and Fox hugged trees. They all had their excesses. Were they supposed to be perfect as well as immortal?

Heather winced inwardly. She was still not sure why the thought hurt so much.

"Uh," said Susie, "well, now that you mention it . . . she's been . . . uh . . . disruptive."

Heather stared at her. "Disruptive? *Kelly?*"

Susie waved her hands. "Not exactly disruptive, Ms.

Blues. I mean, not in an acting-up way . . ." Smiling a little crookedly, she fell silent and nodded to a mother who was just then racing up the hallway. High heels clicking on the linoleum, the woman dived into the classroom and came up with a child like a heron pulling a fish out of a lake.

"See you tomorrow, Ms. Walters," said Susie.

"Right." And the high heels clicked away.

Through the open door, Heather could see Kelly. Still reading. Still sad. "You were saying."

"Well, you see . . ." Sally had caught a loose strand of her red hair and was twirling it around and around her finger as though it were a weed she were about to uproot. ". . . like the kids were all supposed to bring in poems today to read."

Heather nodded. "Kelly had a very nice poem. It was by Dylan Thomas."

"Yeah. Well, Dylan Thomas—whoever he is—isn't someone I'd recite to five- and six-year-olds."

Heather could not suppress a look of annoyance. "It certainly isn't as though Kelly brought in *Do Not Go Gentle Into That Good Night* or something like that. She learned *Poem in October*. It's lovely. Did you actually listen to it?"

Susie was still twisting the hair. "Yes, yes, it was very nice . . . but . . ."

Yes, yes, thought Heather, *but she's sad. It's all sad. And she didn't understand a word of the poem, and she doesn't understand a thing about Kelly . . . which isn't surprising.*

Susie, she supposed, was doing her best. Day care at minimum wage was probably all that she had been able to find, and, in these days of recession, she was probably fortunate to have it. But Heather could not help but sense (her instincts reaching out to examine Kelly's teacher with a compassion that was, nonetheless, impotent) that Susie had hoped for more out of life than day care at minimum wage. With the fleeting awareness of old powers long faded, Heather saw wings, blue skies. Susie had wanted to fly. She had wanted to be a pilot. But the money (it was the old story) was not there, and there had been a child, and the father was not paying any support.

". . . but the other kids didn't know what to make of it . . ."

But Susie, Heather reflected, at least had a job. There were dozens of men up at the shelter who had none, who would have given much for a chance at what Susie had.

She passed a hand across her forehead. And dozens more who would have given much for a ham sandwich and a place to sleep that was more secure than a cardboard box.

". . . and it made a lot of them feel bad."

Caught between anger, pity, and sorrow for all that she could not do, Heather looked up, met Susie's eyes. Wings. Blue skies. And here she was. "Bad?"

"Well, you know, like . . . stupid."

A human mother, perhaps, might have thrown the stupidity back into Susie's face. But Heather was not a human mother. "Susie," she said slowly, softly, "Kelly brought that poem in as an act of love, and I'm sure that the other children appreciated it as such . . . as much as they could. Someday, they might remember that poem, and someday, one of them might become a poet, or . . . or maybe a holy person or something like that . . . because they heard Kelly recite *Poem in October* today."

Susie's expression had turned perplexed. Love? Holy person? What did that have to do with it? Her finger twisted the lock of hair all the faster. "Well," she said, "I understand . . ."

Futility. Impotence. *You don't understand at all.*

". . . but . . . well . . . like . . . could you make sure that Kelly acts just a little bit more normal?"

Heather transfixed her with a look, wondering whether Susie might be one of those few humans who could see the flash of starlight in an elven eye. But no, Susie only stared back without comprehension.

"I'm sorry," said Heather. "I don't know what normal is."

And, wearing the uniform of normalcy—heels, skirt, silk blouse, conservative jacket—Heather turned and re-entered the classroom. It was a quarter to six: the sun was westering, but the sky had clouded over, and rain was coming down. Kelly had put her book aside and was watching the falling drops, but she looked up at Heather's approach and smiled as her mother scooped her up in her arms.

"She's sad, isn't she?" said Kelly. Her smile turned shadowed, and there was a glistening of something more than starlight in her eyes.

"Yes." Heather's whisper was fierce with both a mother's love for her child and an elven love—no matter how senseless—for all. "Yes, honey. She's sad."

But she was thinking about day care, and about the future. This was not the first time that Kelly's differences had discomfited her teachers, nor would it be the last. She could, she supposed, quit her job with the state, stay home, and shield her daughter from such things. But next year there would be school, and then the years ahead stretched off beyond that, through school and into . . .

. . . into forever.

She could not shield Kelly forever. And, in any case, Elves were not supposed to hide from the world: they were supposed to work within it, to help and heal.

"Why?" A huskiness had crept into Kelly's voice.

Heather bent her head until their foreheads touched. "That's just the way it is in this place, Elfling," she whispered.

"Can we go see Natil?"

"We'll be going up to the Home tomorrow night. Everyone will be there."

Kelly nodded. "I want to hear Natil play the harp."

"I'm sure she'll play the harp tomorrow night. And sing, too."

"I want to play the harp like that someday."

Heather nodded as she carried Kelly out to the car. "It takes time," she said. "There is time."

Yes, there was time. Time for everything. But what would get them through all that time?

She buckled Kelly into her seat, slid behind the wheel. The streets of Denver suddenly looked alien, strange. *Dear God,* she thought, *this will go on* forever! *What will get us through?*

But as she pulled out of the lot, she could not but wonder whether the God she had known all her life heard the prayers of Elves . . . or cared.